a sister

Story & Art
Bastien Vivès

FOR ABLAZE

MANAGING EDITOR
RICH YOUNG

DESIGNER
RODOLFO MURAGUCHI

Publisher's Cataloging-in-Publication Data

Names: Vivès, Bastien, author.
Title: A sister / Bastien Vivès.
Description: Portland, OR: Ablaze Publishing, 2021.
Identifiers: ISBN 978-1-950912-26-1
LCSH Bildungsroman. | Graphic novels. | BISAC COMICS & GRAPHIC NOVELS / General
Classification: LCC PN6747.V58 S57 2021 | DDC 741.5—dc23

For advertising and licensing email: info@ablazepublishing.com

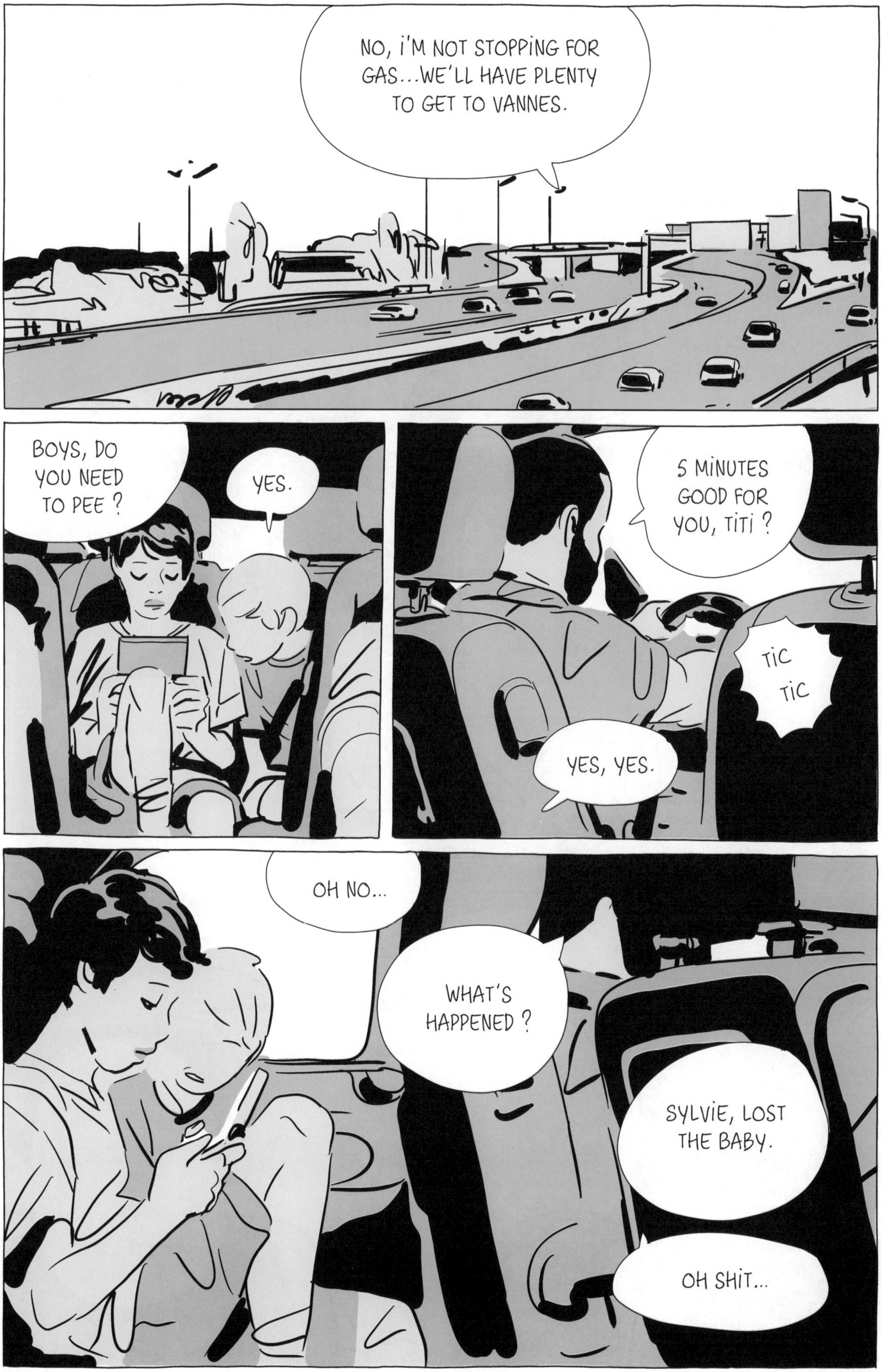
NO, I'M NOT STOPPING FOR GAS...WE'LL HAVE PLENTY TO GET TO VANNES.
BOYS, DO YOU NEED TO PEE ?
YES.
5 MINUTES GOOD FOR YOU, TITI ?
TIC TIC
YES, YES.
OH NO...
WHAT'S HAPPENED ?
SYLVIE, LOST THE BABY.
OH SHIT...

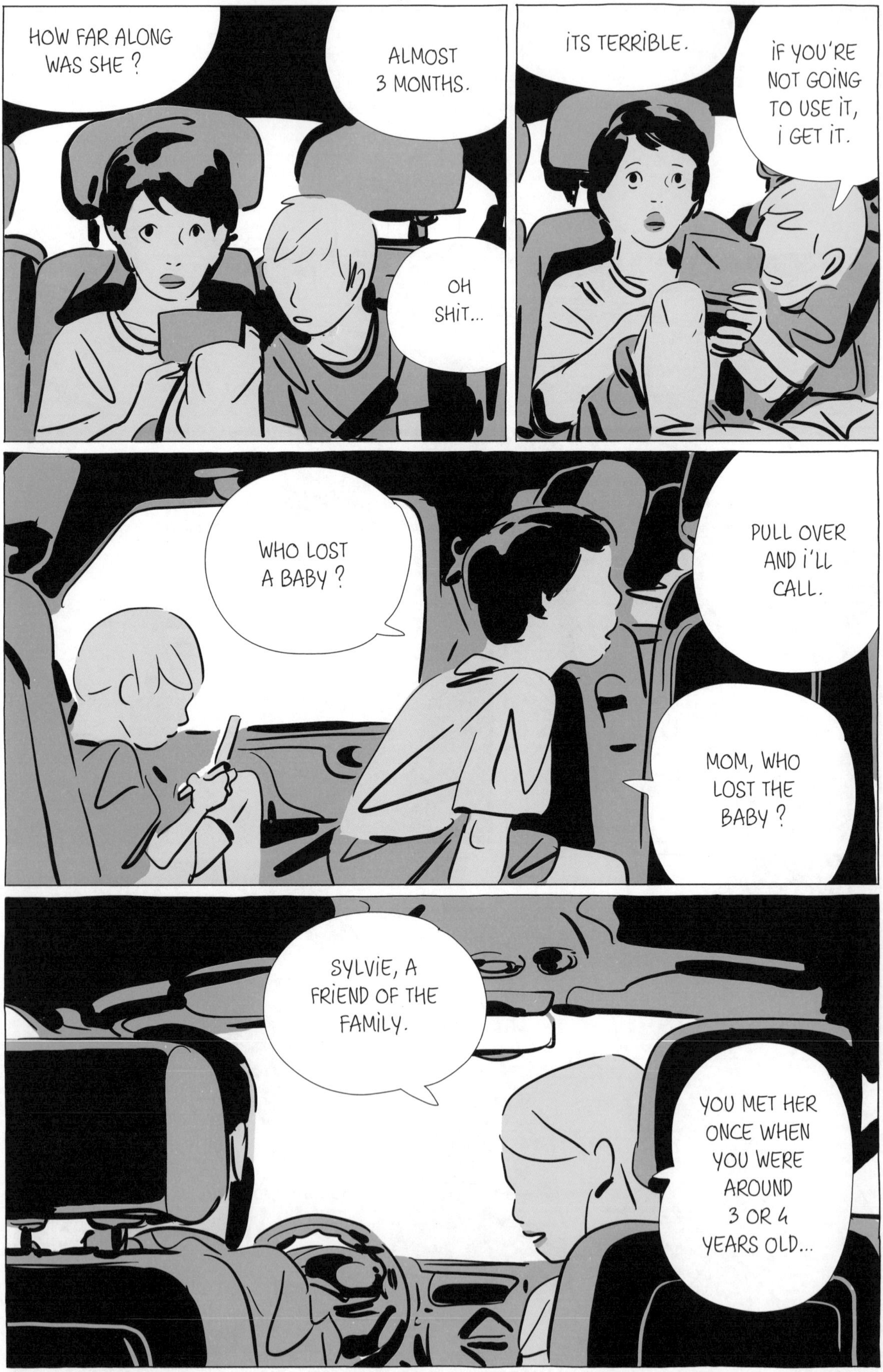
HOW FAR ALONG WAS SHE ?
ALMOST 3 MONTHS.
OH SHIT...
ITS TERRIBLE.
IF YOU'RE NOT GOING TO USE IT, I GET IT.
WHO LOST A BABY ?
PULL OVER AND I'LL CALL.
MOM, WHO LOST THE BABY ?
SYLVIE, A FRIEND OF THE FAMILY.
YOU MET HER ONCE WHEN YOU WERE AROUND 3 OR 4 YEARS OLD...

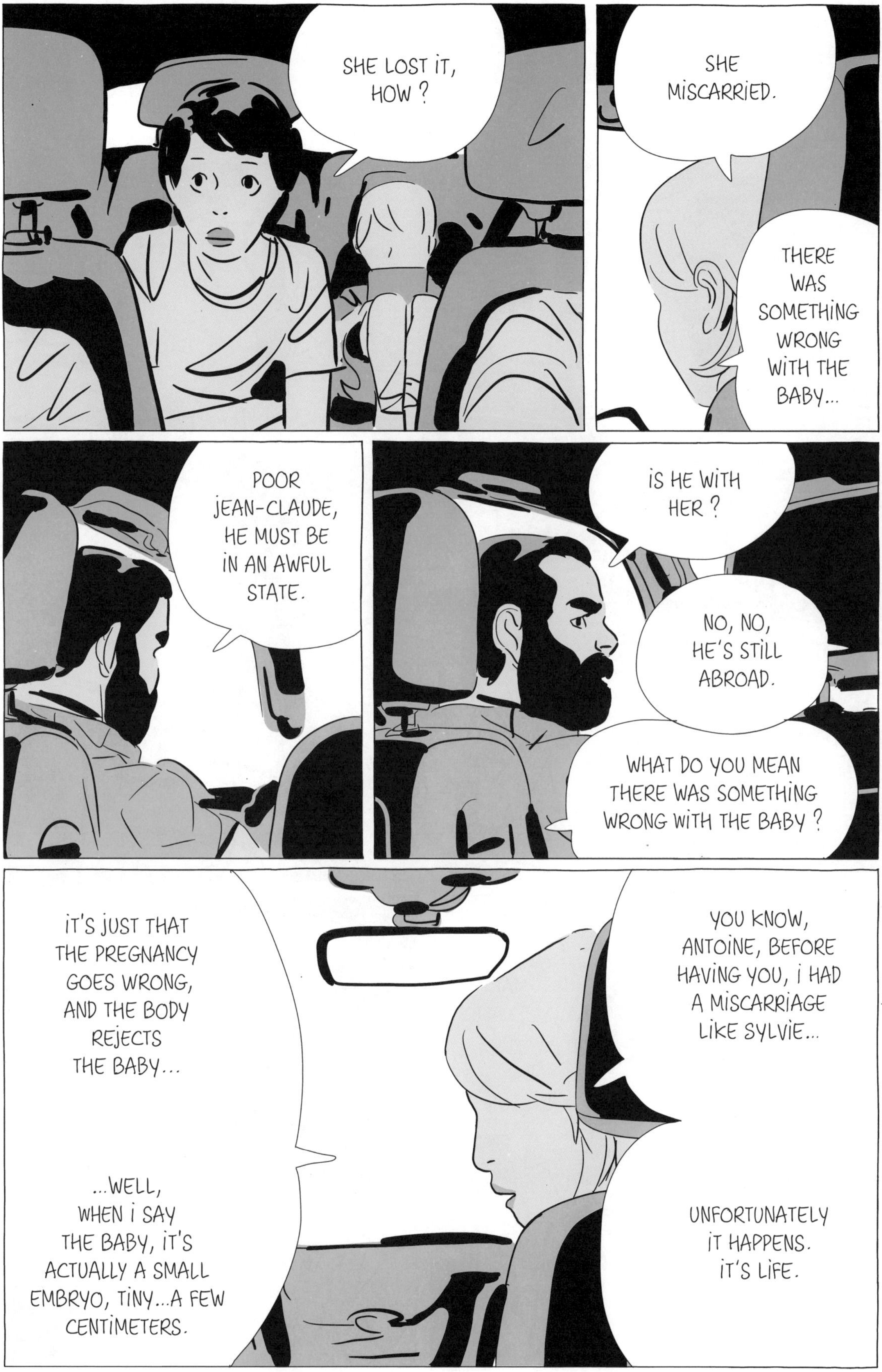
SHE LOST IT, HOW ?
SHE MISCARRIED.
THERE WAS SOMETHING WRONG WITH THE BABY...
POOR JEAN-CLAUDE, HE MUST BE IN AN AWFUL STATE.
IS HE WITH HER ?
NO, NO, HE'S STILL ABROAD.
WHAT DO YOU MEAN THERE WAS SOMETHING WRONG WITH THE BABY ?
IT'S JUST THAT THE PREGNANCY GOES WRONG, AND THE BODY REJECTS THE BABY...
...WELL, WHEN I SAY THE BABY, IT'S ACTUALLY A SMALL EMBRYO, TINY...A FEW CENTIMETERS.
YOU KNOW, ANTOINE, BEFORE HAVING YOU, I HAD A MISCARRIAGE LIKE SYLVIE...
UNFORTUNATELY IT HAPPENS. IT'S LIFE.

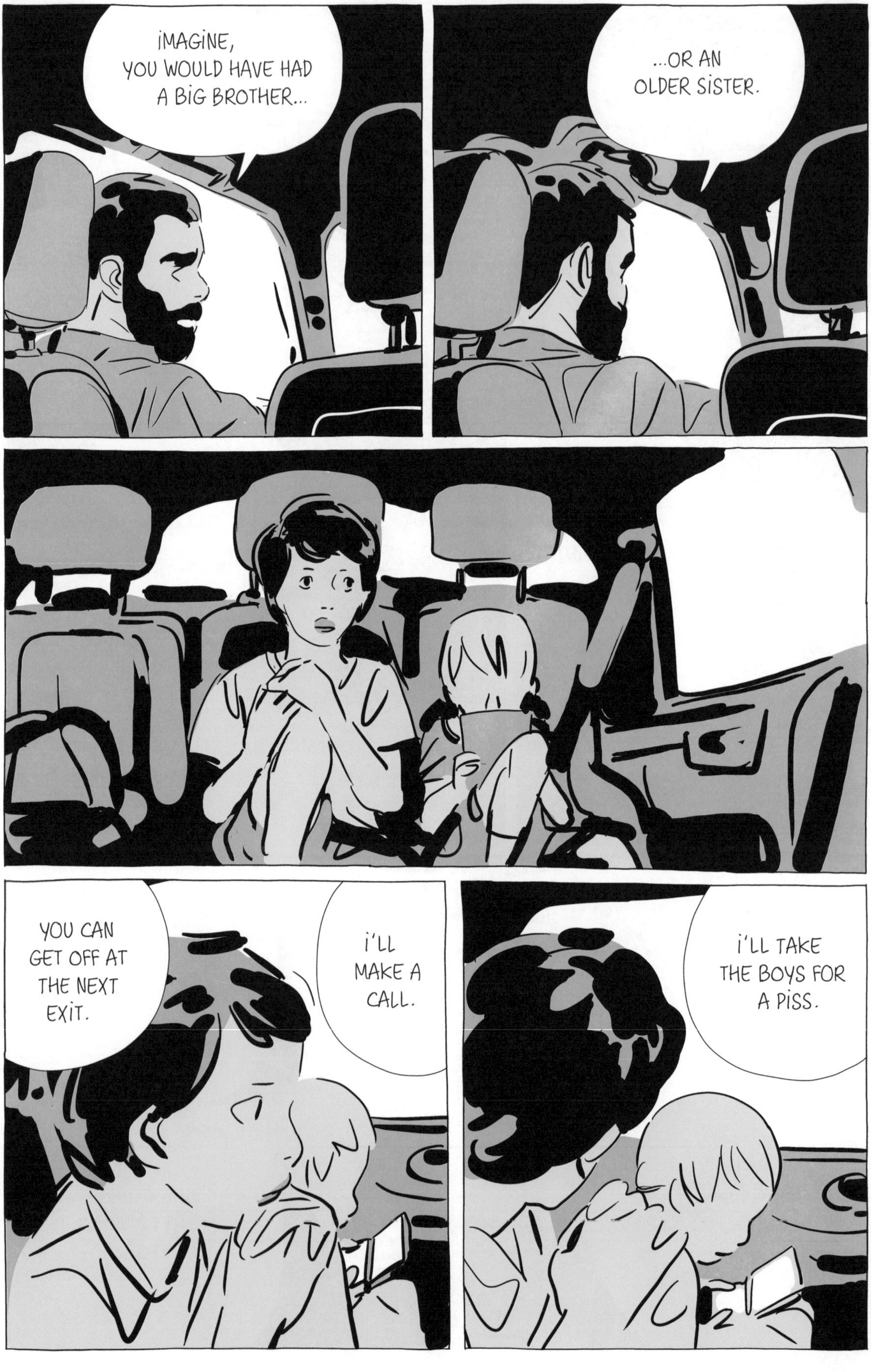
IMAGINE, YOU WOULD HAVE HAD A BIG BROTHER...
...OR AN OLDER SISTER.
YOU CAN GET OFF AT THE NEXT EXIT.
I'LL MAKE A CALL.
I'LL TAKE THE BOYS FOR A PISS.

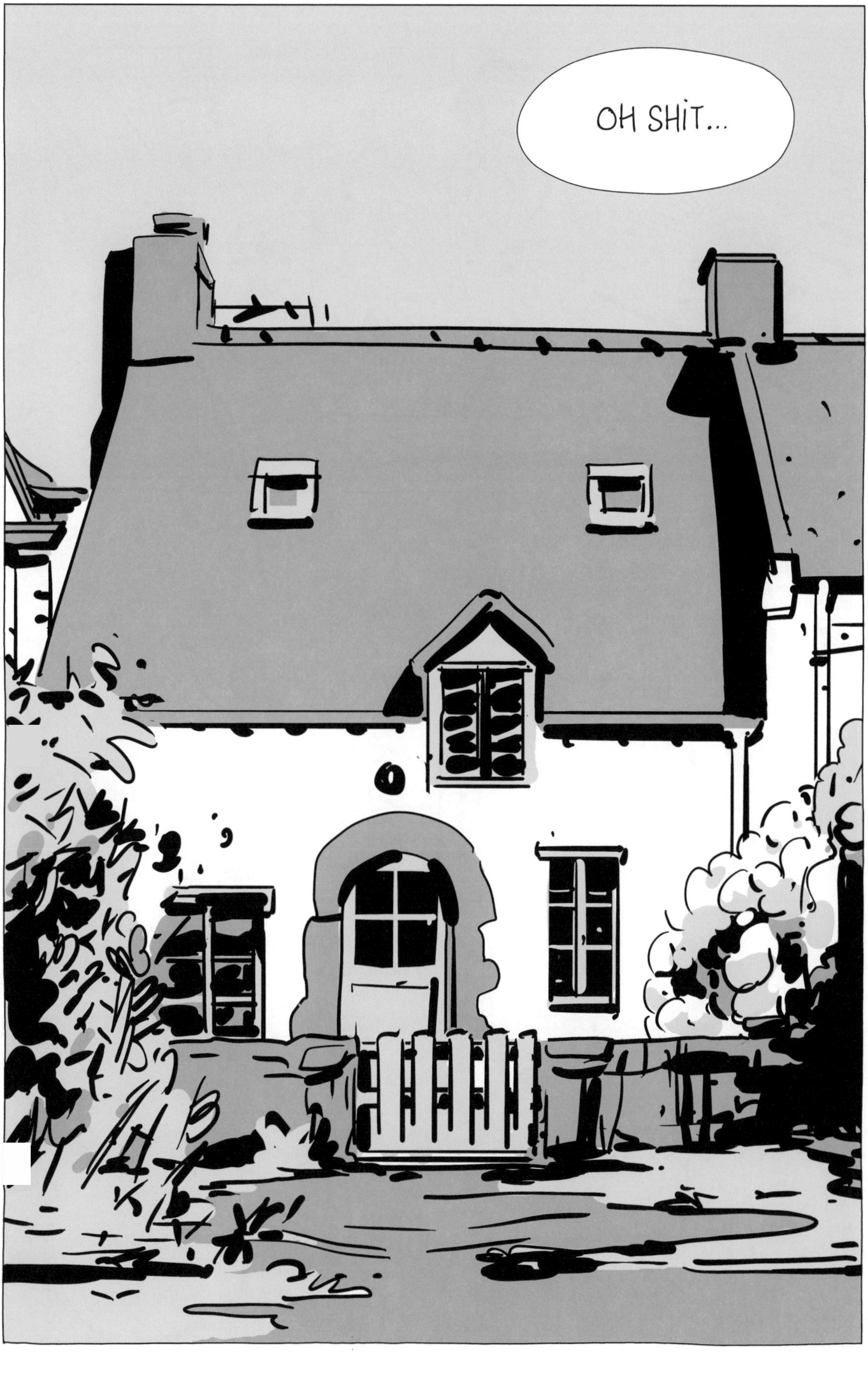
OH SHIT...

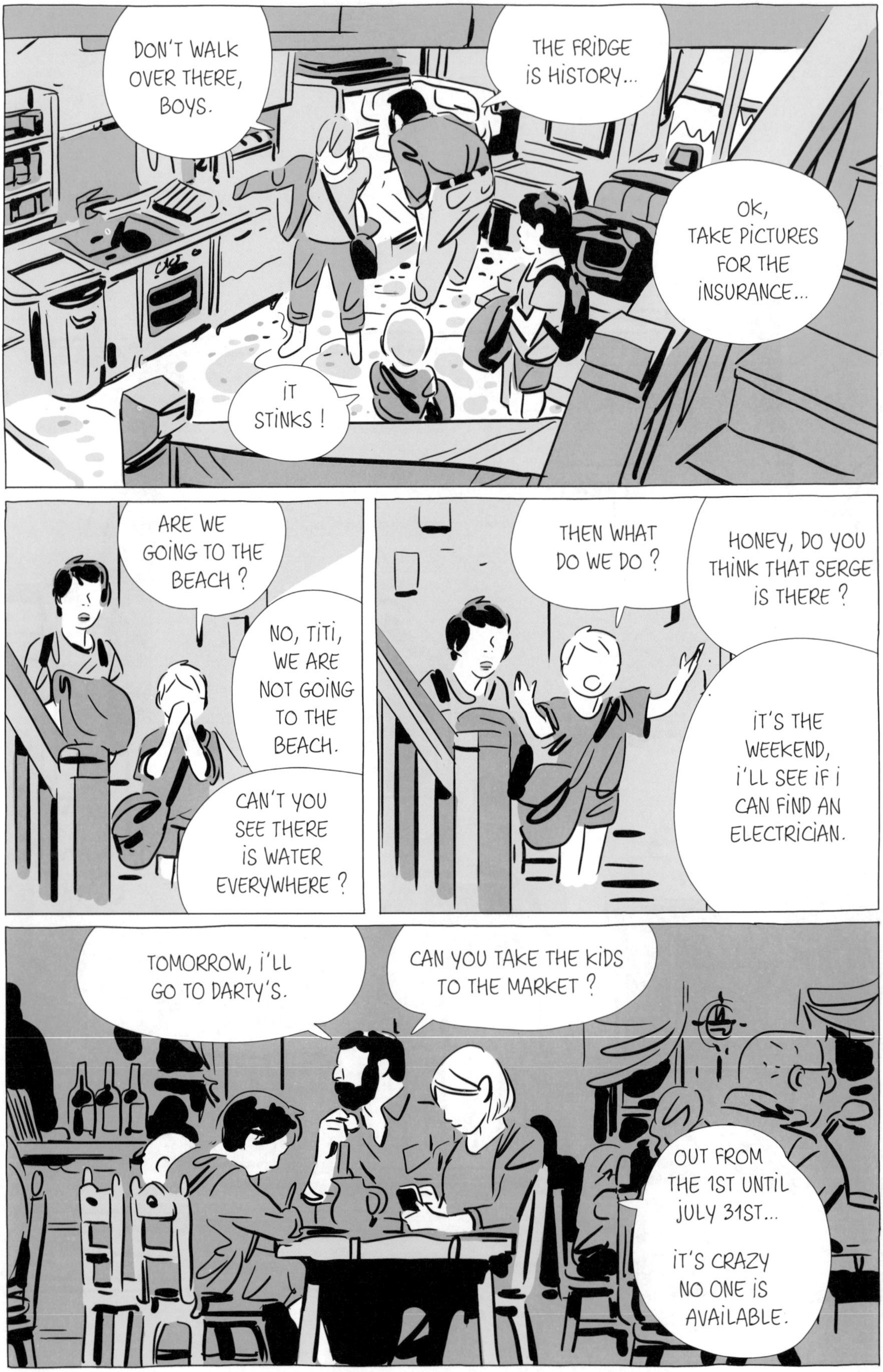
DON'T WALK OVER THERE, BOYS.
THE FRIDGE IS HISTORY...
OK, TAKE PICTURES FOR THE INSURANCE...
IT STINKS !
ARE WE GOING TO THE BEACH ?
NO, TITI, WE ARE NOT GOING TO THE BEACH.
CAN'T YOU SEE THERE IS WATER EVERYWHERE ?
THEN WHAT DO WE DO ?
HONEY, DO YOU THINK THAT SERGE IS THERE ?
IT'S THE WEEKEND, I'LL SEE IF I CAN FIND AN ELECTRICIAN.
TOMORROW, I'LL GO TO DARTY'S.
CAN YOU TAKE THE KIDS TO THE MARKET ?
OUT FROM THE 1ST UNTIL JULY 31ST...
IT'S CRAZY NO ONE IS AVAILABLE.

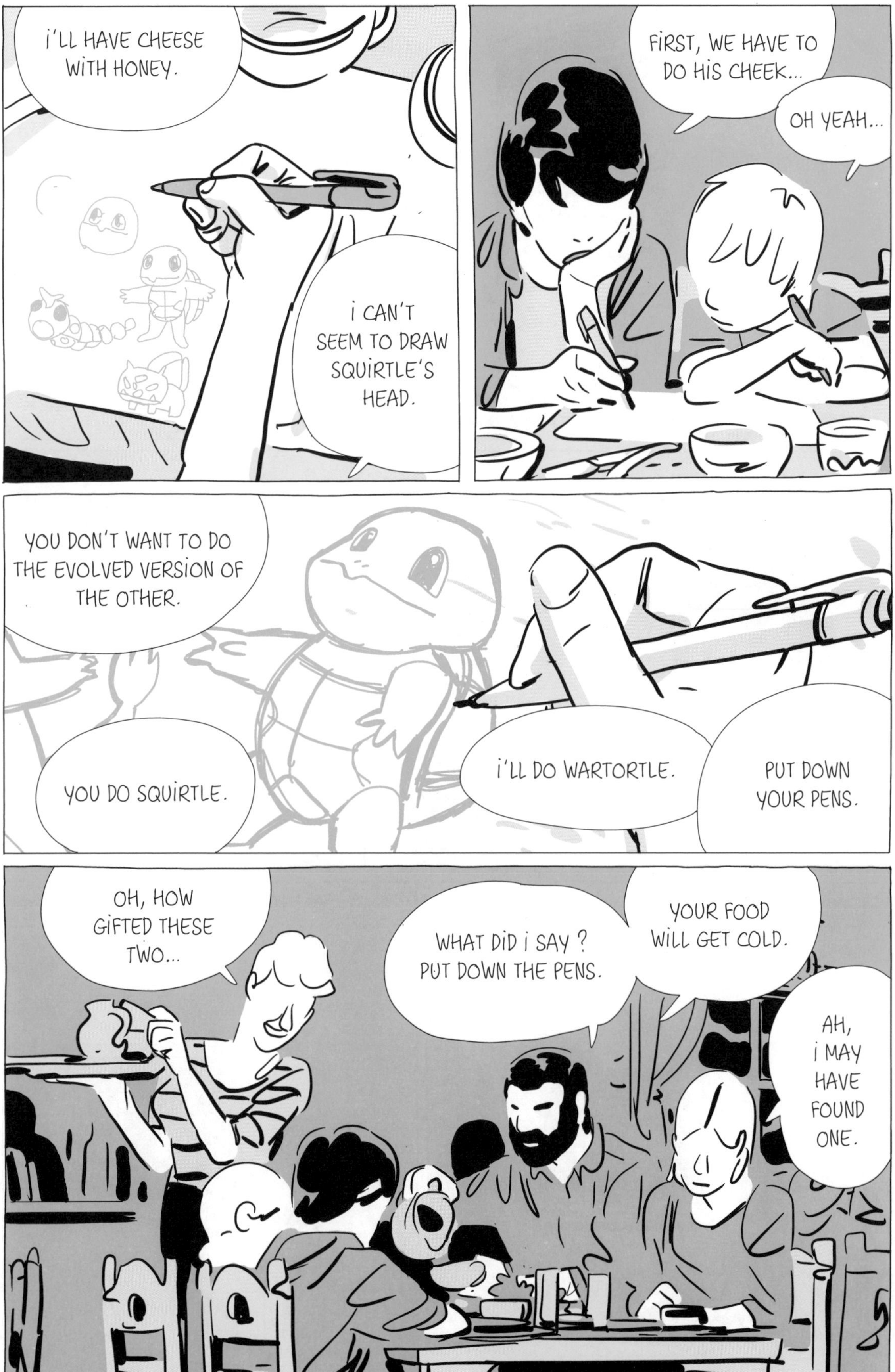
i'LL HAVE CHEESE WiTH HONEY.
i CAN'T SEEM TO DRAW SQUiRTLE'S HEAD.
FiRST, WE HAVE TO DO HiS CHEEK...
OH YEAH...
YOU DON'T WANT TO DO THE EVOLVED VERSiON OF THE OTHER.
YOU DO SQUiRTLE.
i'LL DO WARTORTLE.
PUT DOWN YOUR PENS.
OH, HOW GiFTED THESE TWO...
WHAT DiD i SAY ? PUT DOWN THE PENS.
YOUR FOOD WiLL GET COLD.
AH, i MAY HAVE FOUND ONE.

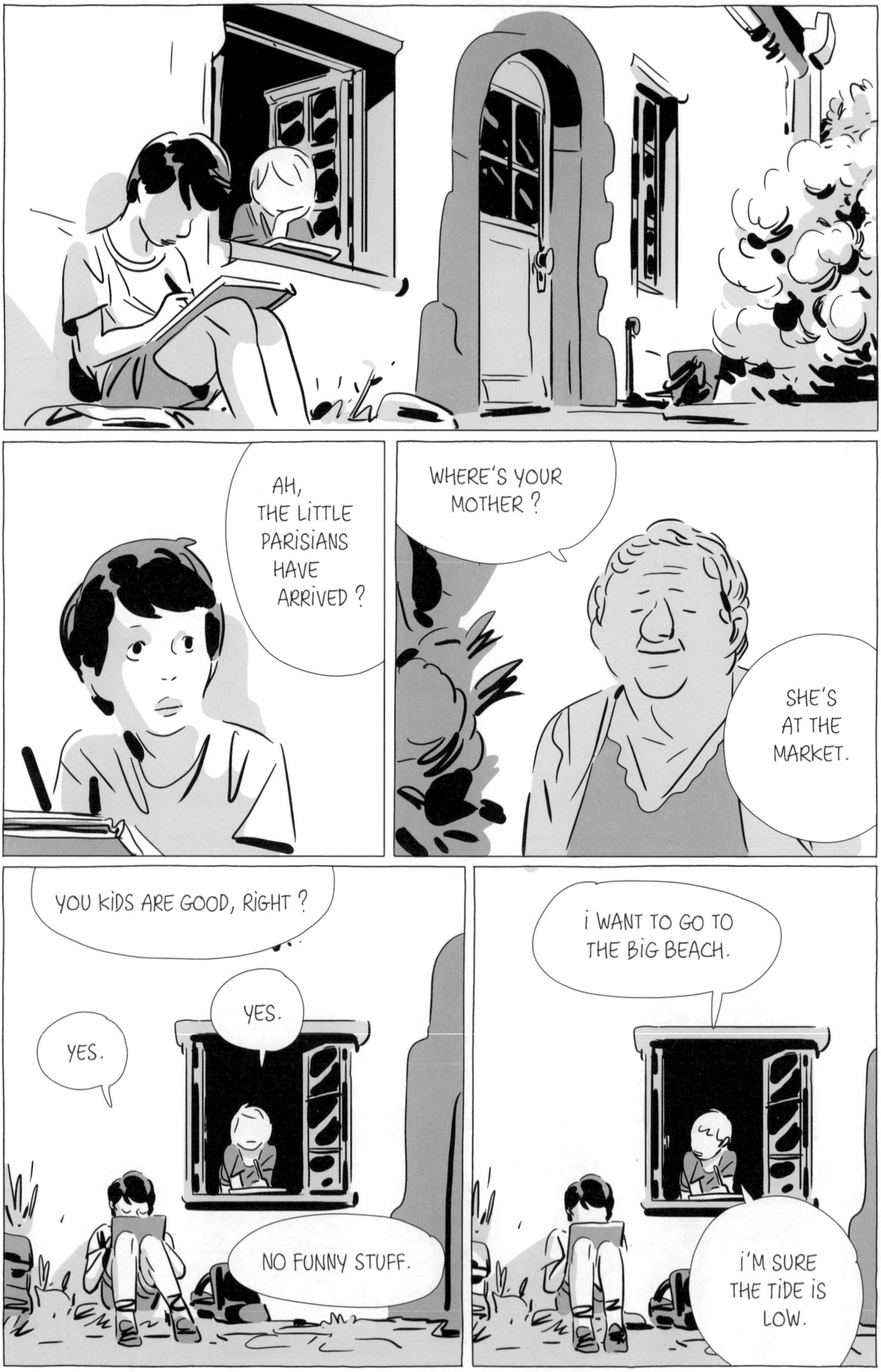
AH, THE LiTTLE PARiSiANS HAVE ARRiVED ?
WHERE'S YOUR MOTHER ?
SHE'S AT THE MARKET.
YOU KiDS ARE GOOD, RiGHT ?
YES.
YES.
NO FUNNY STUFF.
i WANT TO GO TO THE BiG BEACH.
i'M SURE THE TiDE iS LOW.

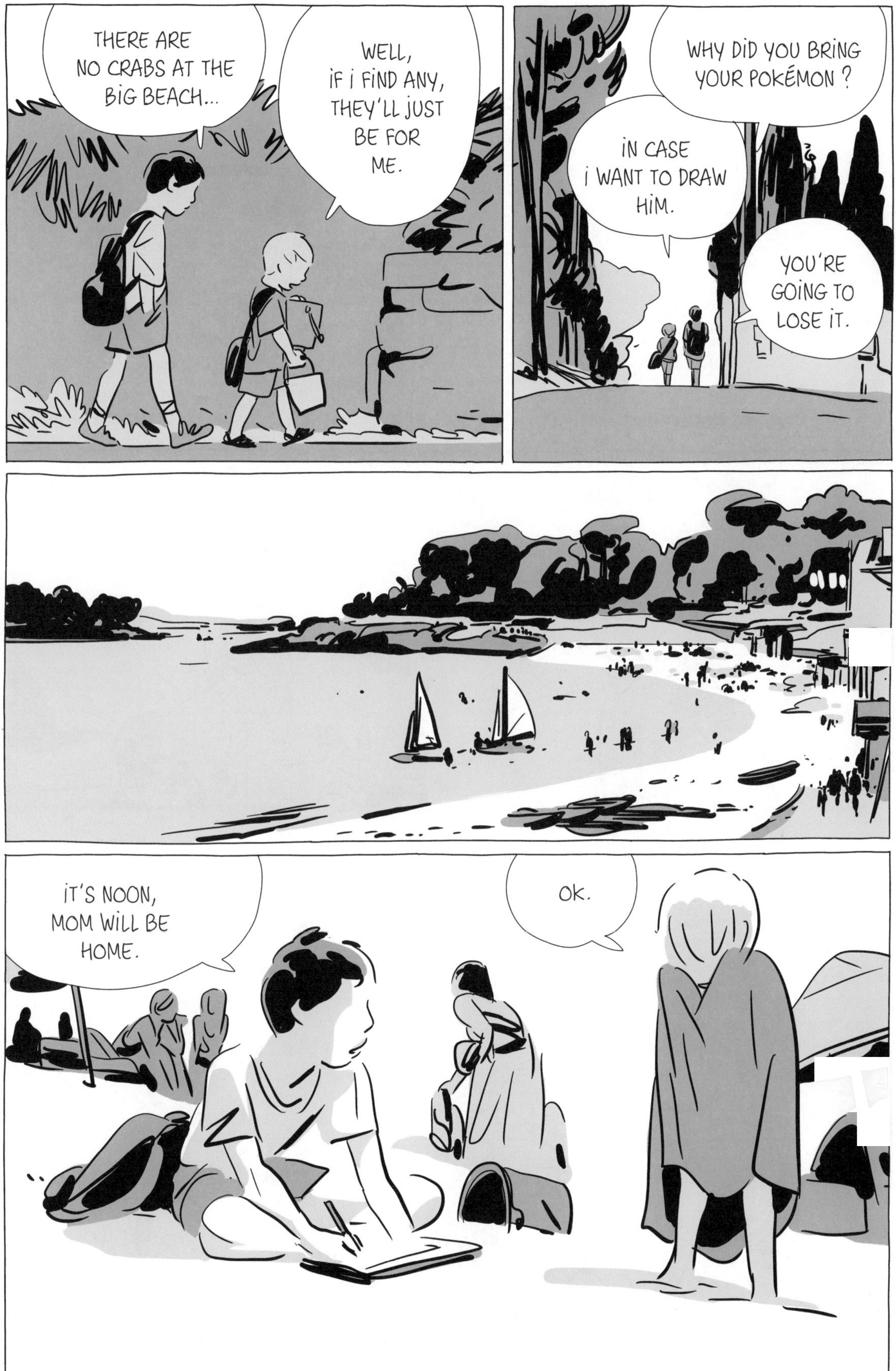
THERE ARE NO CRABS AT THE BIG BEACH...
WELL, IF I FIND ANY, THEY'LL JUST BE FOR ME.
WHY DID YOU BRING YOUR POKÉMON ?
IN CASE I WANT TO DRAW HIM.
YOU'RE GOING TO LOSE IT.
IT'S NOON, MOM WILL BE HOME.
OK.

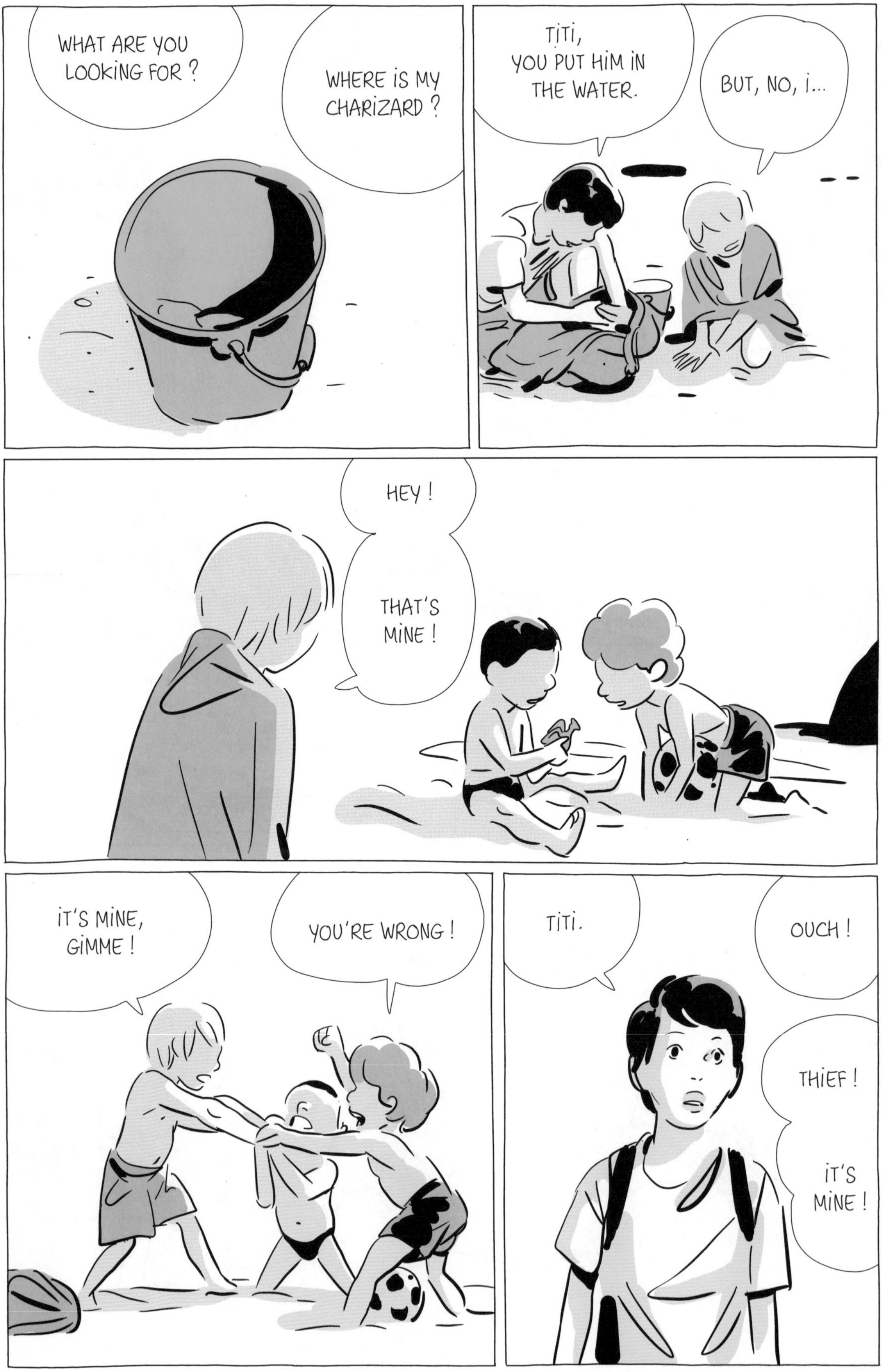
WHAT ARE YOU LOOKING FOR ?
WHERE IS MY CHARIZARD ?
TITI, YOU PUT HIM IN THE WATER.
BUT, NO, I...
HEY !
THAT'S MINE !
IT'S MINE, GIMME !
YOU'RE WRONG !
TITI.
OUCH !
THIEF !
IT'S MINE !

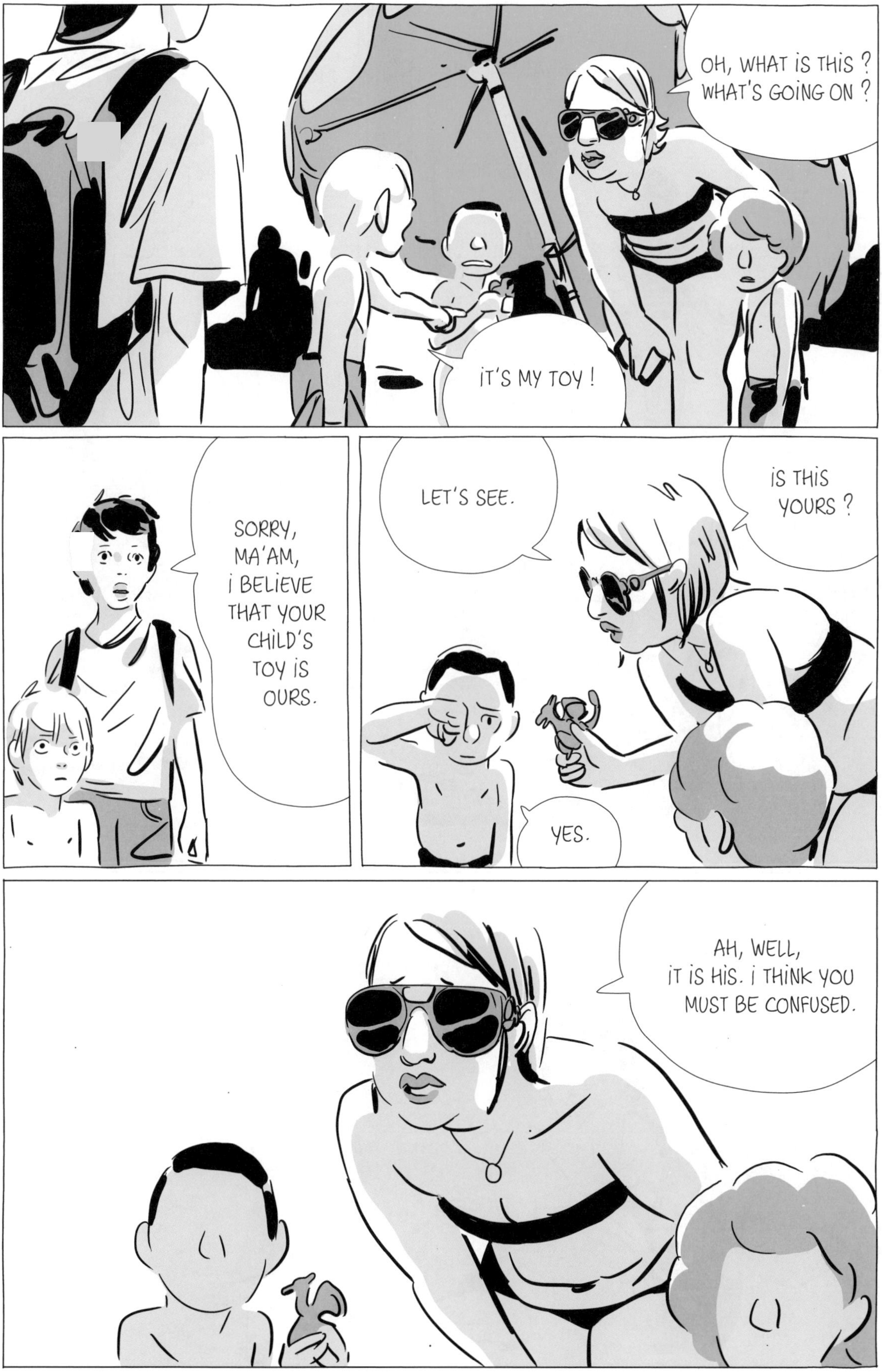
OH, WHAT IS THIS ?
WHAT'S GOING ON ?
IT'S MY TOY !
SORRY, MA'AM, I BELIEVE THAT YOUR CHILD'S TOY IS OURS.
LET'S SEE.
IS THIS YOURS ?
YES.
AH, WELL, IT IS HIS. I THINK YOU MUST BE CONFUSED.

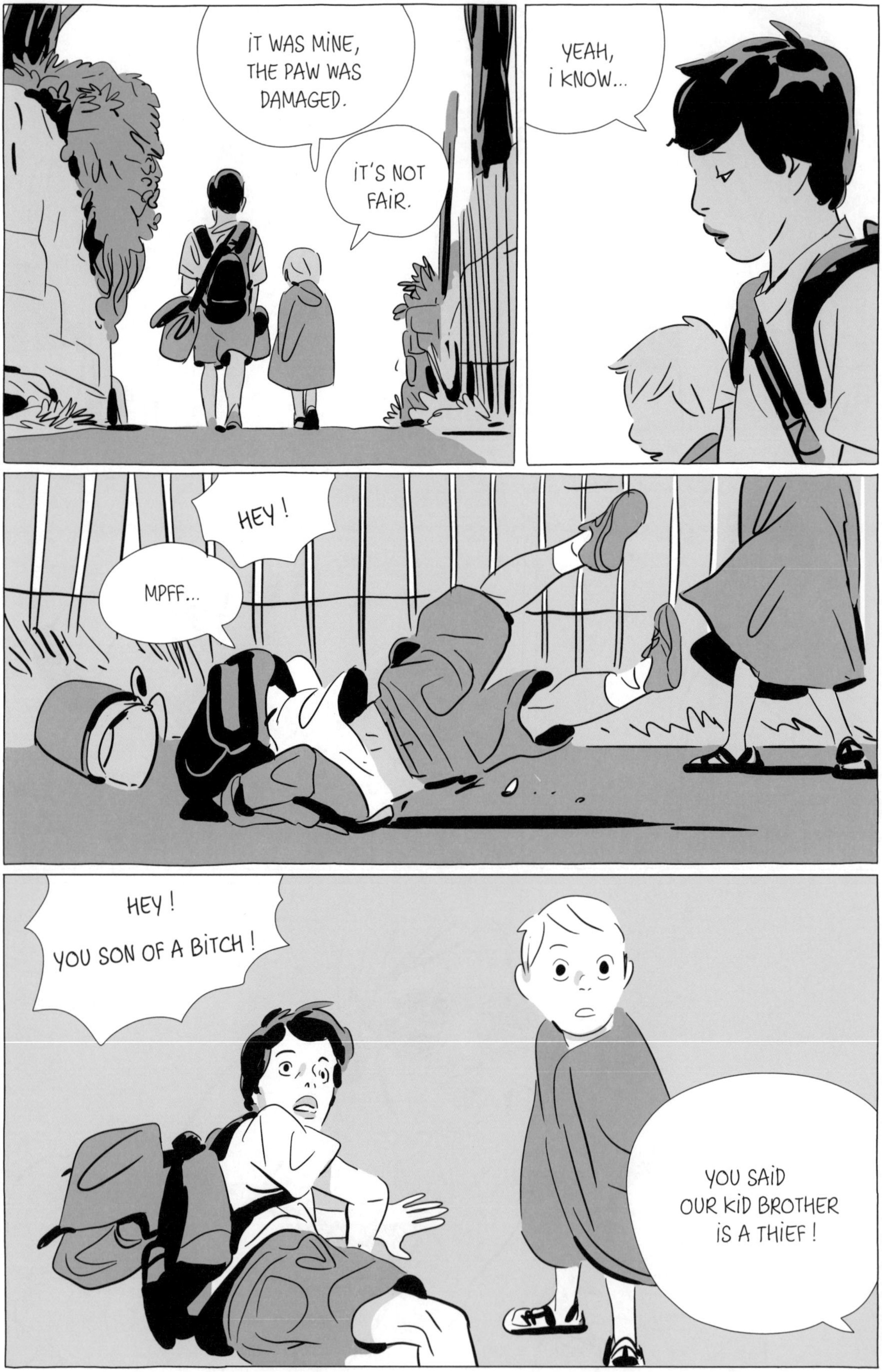
iT WAS MiNE, THE PAW WAS DAMAGED.
iT'S NOT FAiR.
YEAH, i KNOW...
HEY !
MPFF...
HEY ! YOU SON OF A BiTCH !
YOU SAiD OUR KiD BROTHER iS A THiEF !

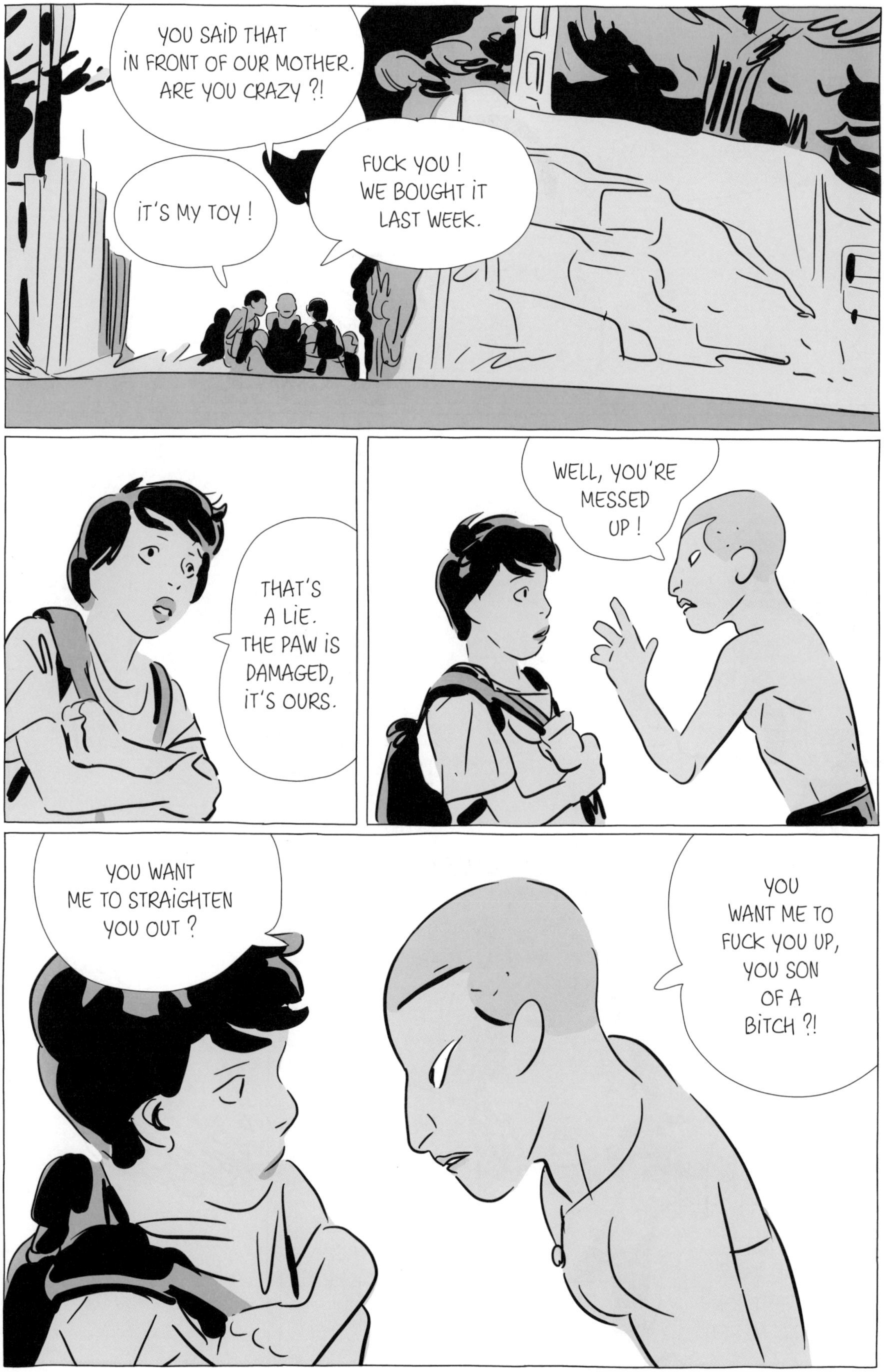
YOU SAID THAT IN FRONT OF OUR MOTHER. ARE YOU CRAZY ?!
IT'S MY TOY !
FUCK YOU ! WE BOUGHT IT LAST WEEK.
THAT'S A LIE. THE PAW IS DAMAGED, IT'S OURS.
WELL, YOU'RE MESSED UP !
YOU WANT ME TO STRAIGHTEN YOU OUT ?
YOU WANT ME TO FUCK YOU UP, YOU SON OF A BITCH ?!

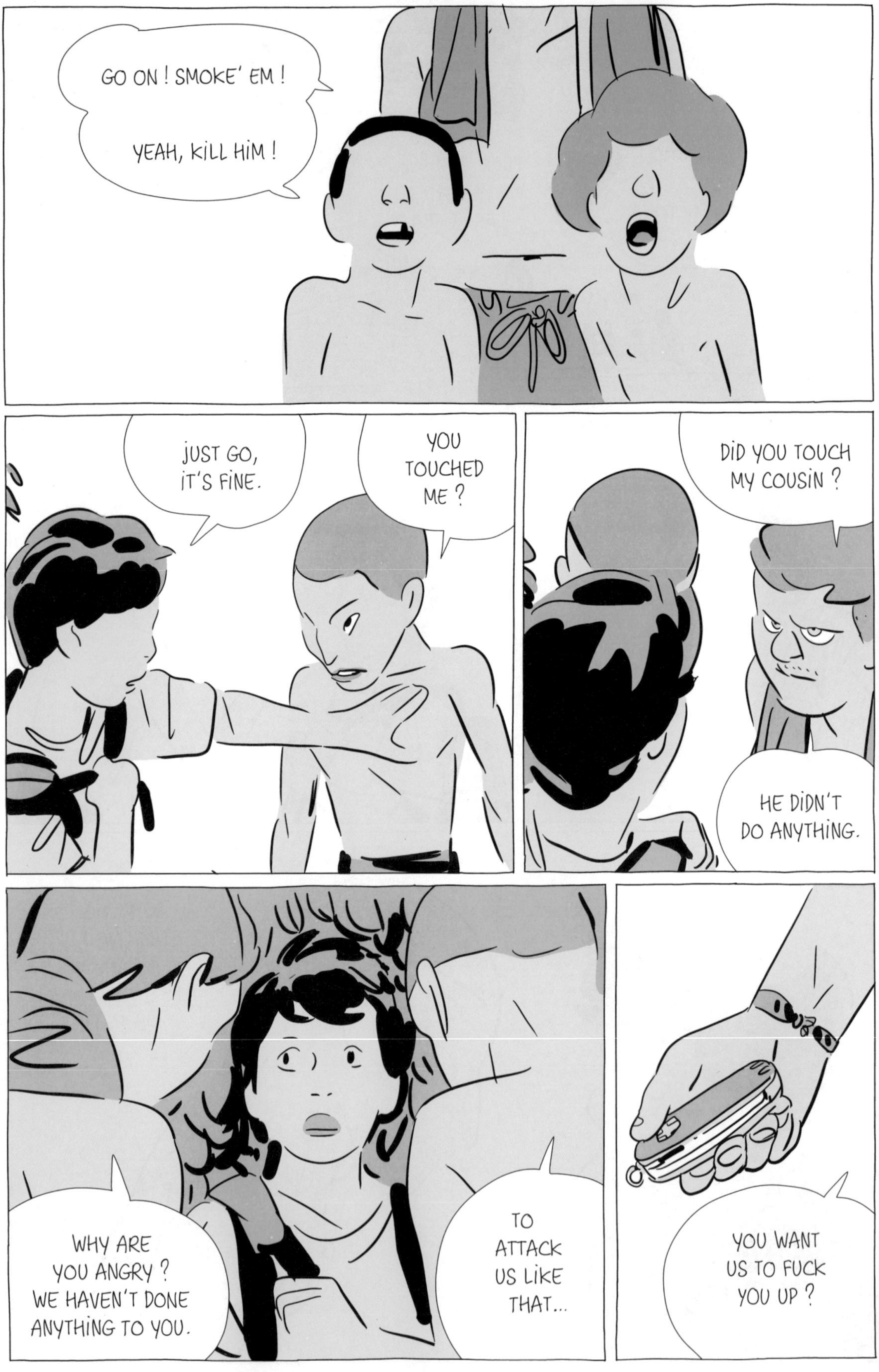
GO ON ! SMOKE' EM !
YEAH, KILL HIM !
JUST GO, IT'S FINE.
YOU TOUCHED ME ?
DID YOU TOUCH MY COUSIN ?
HE DIDN'T DO ANYTHING.
WHY ARE YOU ANGRY ? WE HAVEN'T DONE ANYTHING TO YOU.
TO ATTACK US LIKE THAT...
YOU WANT US TO FUCK YOU UP ?

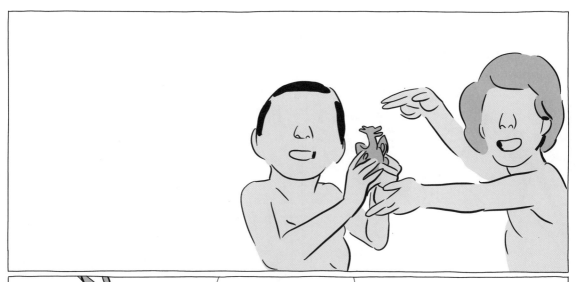

STOP, WE'RE GOOD...

ARE YOU SHITTING YOURSELF?

ARE YOU A MAN, OR WHAT?

GO ON, SHOW US YOUR BALLS.

DO YOU WANT SOME OF THIS?

LET GO OF MY BROTHER!

AAAAAAAAAHH!!!!

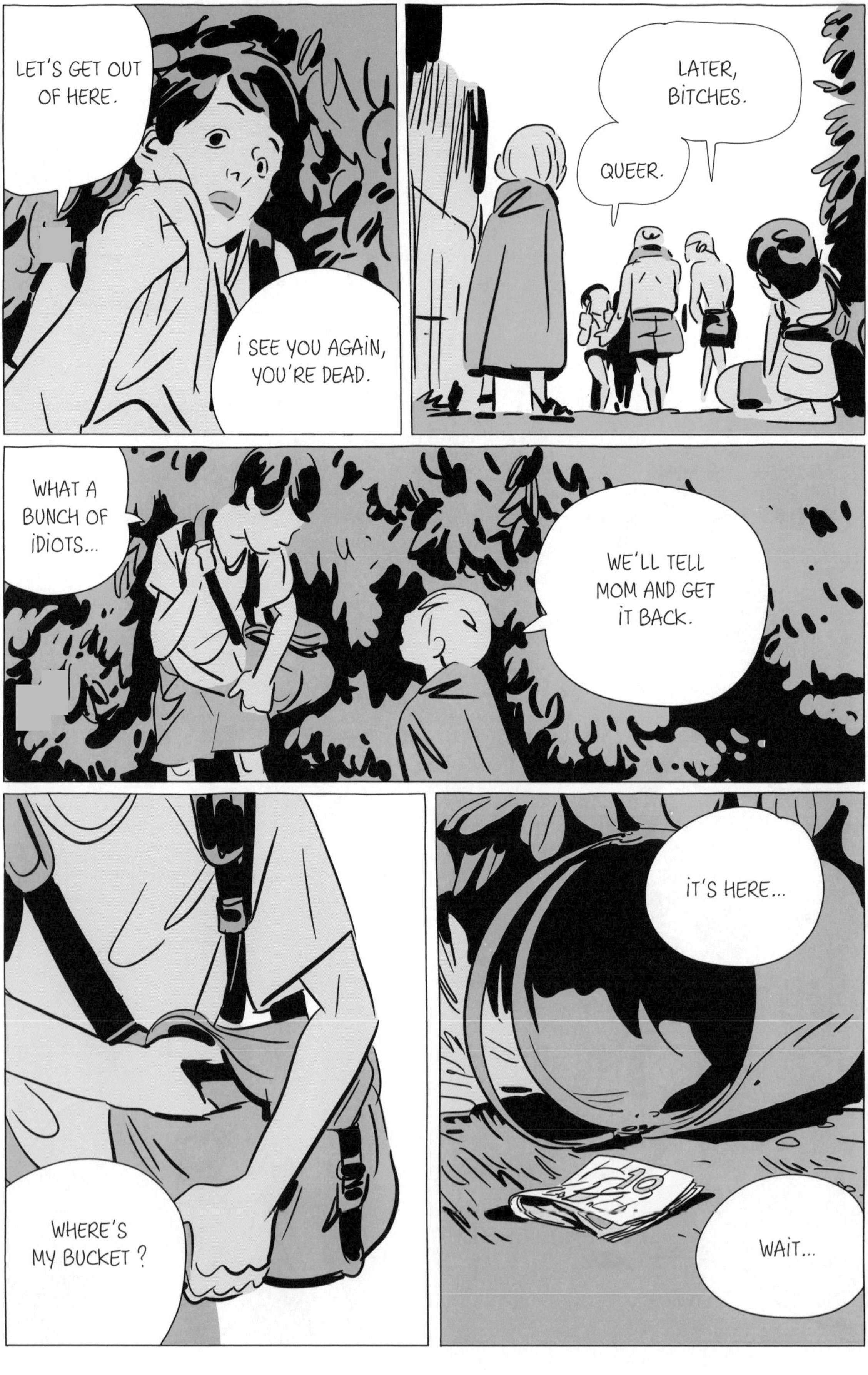
LET'S GET OUT OF HERE.
i SEE YOU AGAIN, YOU'RE DEAD.
LATER, BiTCHES.
QUEER.
WHAT A BUNCH OF iDIOTS...
WE'LL TELL MOM AND GET iT BACK.
WHERE'S MY BUCKET ?
iT'S HERE...
WAiT...

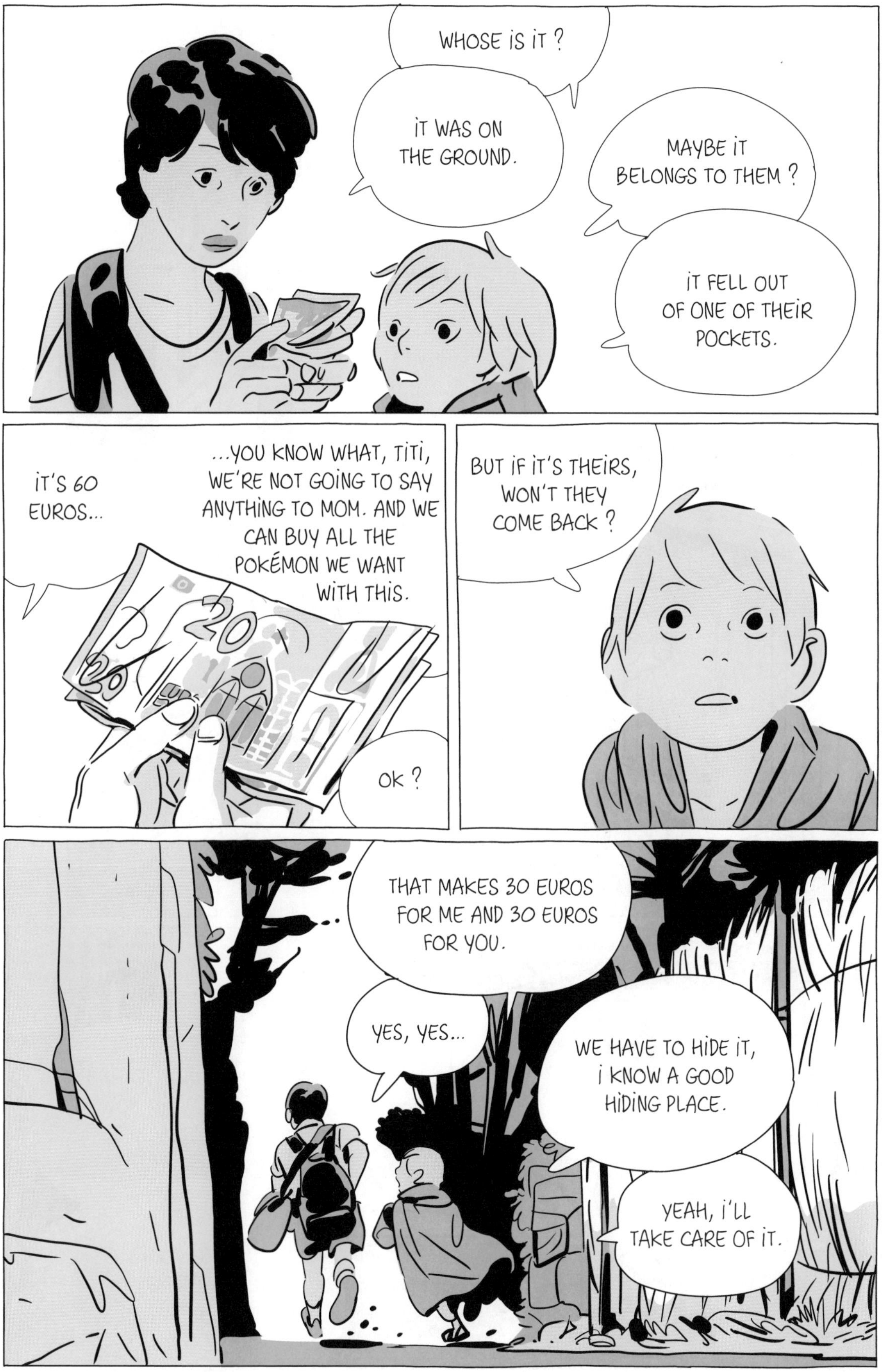
WHOSE IS IT ?
IT WAS ON THE GROUND.
MAYBE IT BELONGS TO THEM ?
IT FELL OUT OF ONE OF THEIR POCKETS.
IT'S 60 EUROS...
...YOU KNOW WHAT, TITI, WE'RE NOT GOING TO SAY ANYTHING TO MOM. AND WE CAN BUY ALL THE POKÉMON WE WANT WITH THIS.
OK ?
BUT IF IT'S THEIRS, WON'T THEY COME BACK ?
THAT MAKES 30 EUROS FOR ME AND 30 EUROS FOR YOU.
YES, YES...
WE HAVE TO HIDE IT, I KNOW A GOOD HIDING PLACE.
YEAH, I'LL TAKE CARE OF IT.

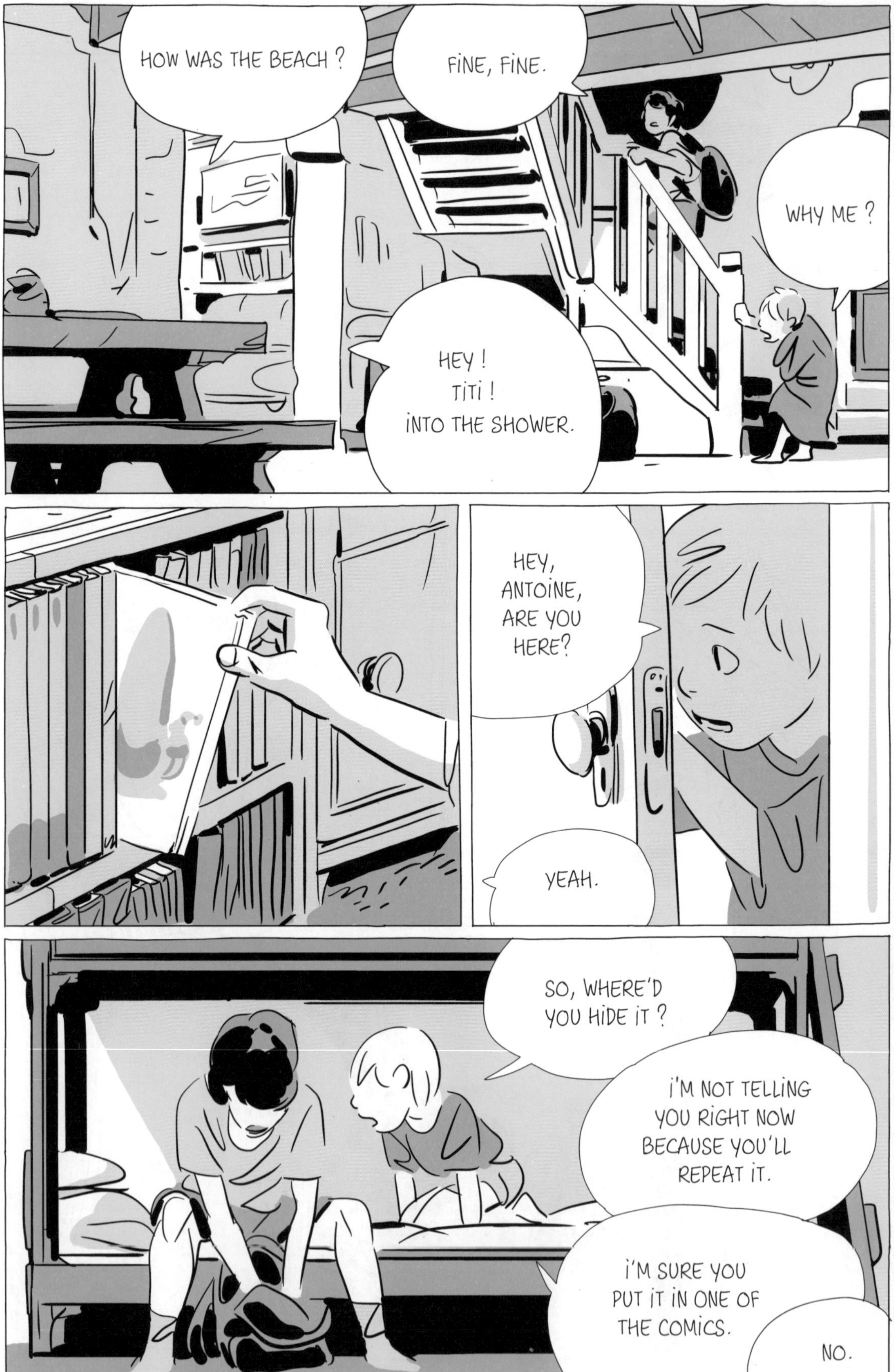
HOW WAS THE BEACH ?
FINE, FINE.
WHY ME ?
HEY ! TITI ! INTO THE SHOWER.
HEY, ANTOINE, ARE YOU HERE?
YEAH.
SO, WHERE'D YOU HIDE IT ?
I'M NOT TELLING YOU RIGHT NOW BECAUSE YOU'LL REPEAT IT.
I'M SURE YOU PUT IT IN ONE OF THE COMICS.
NO.

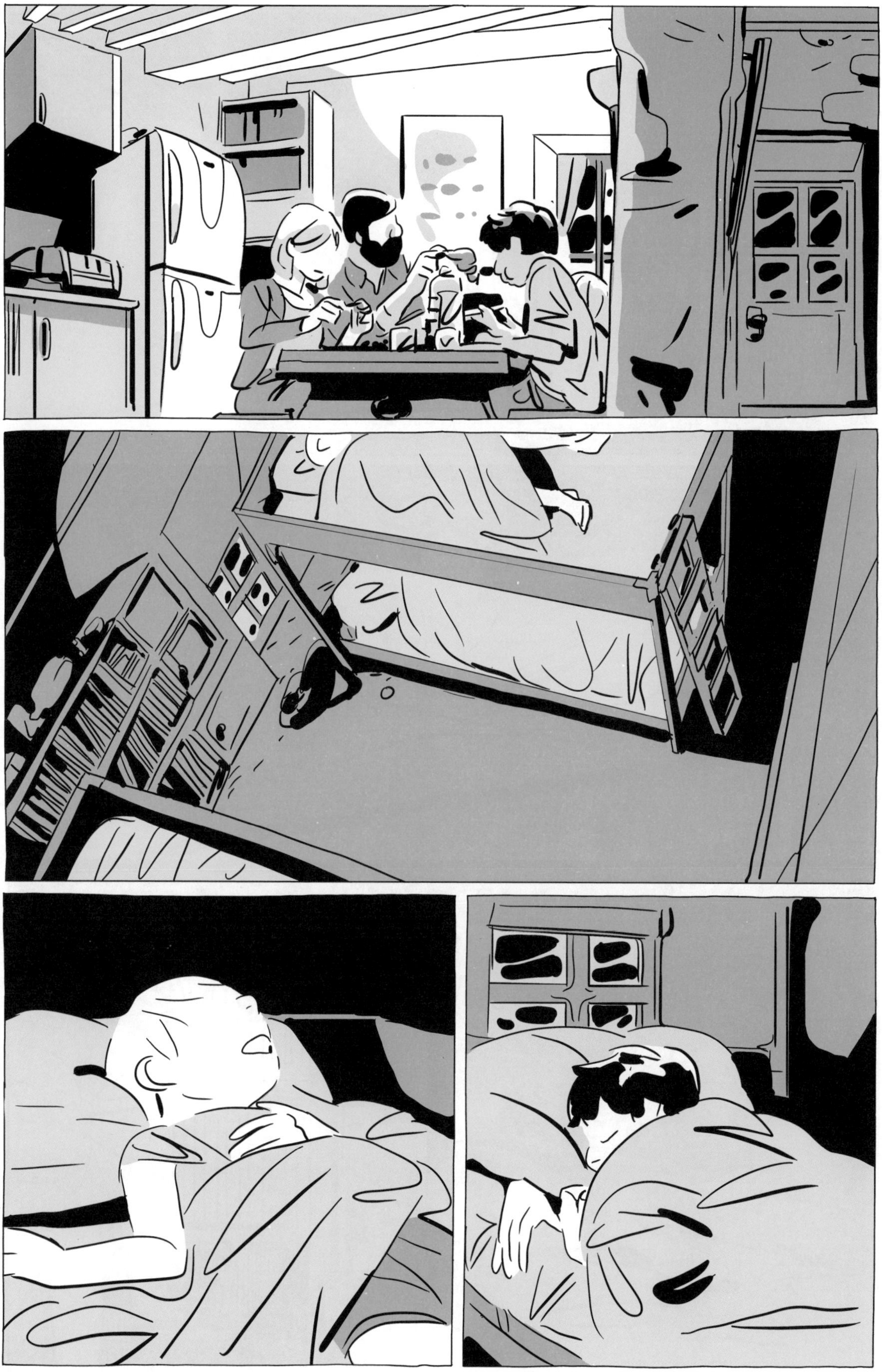

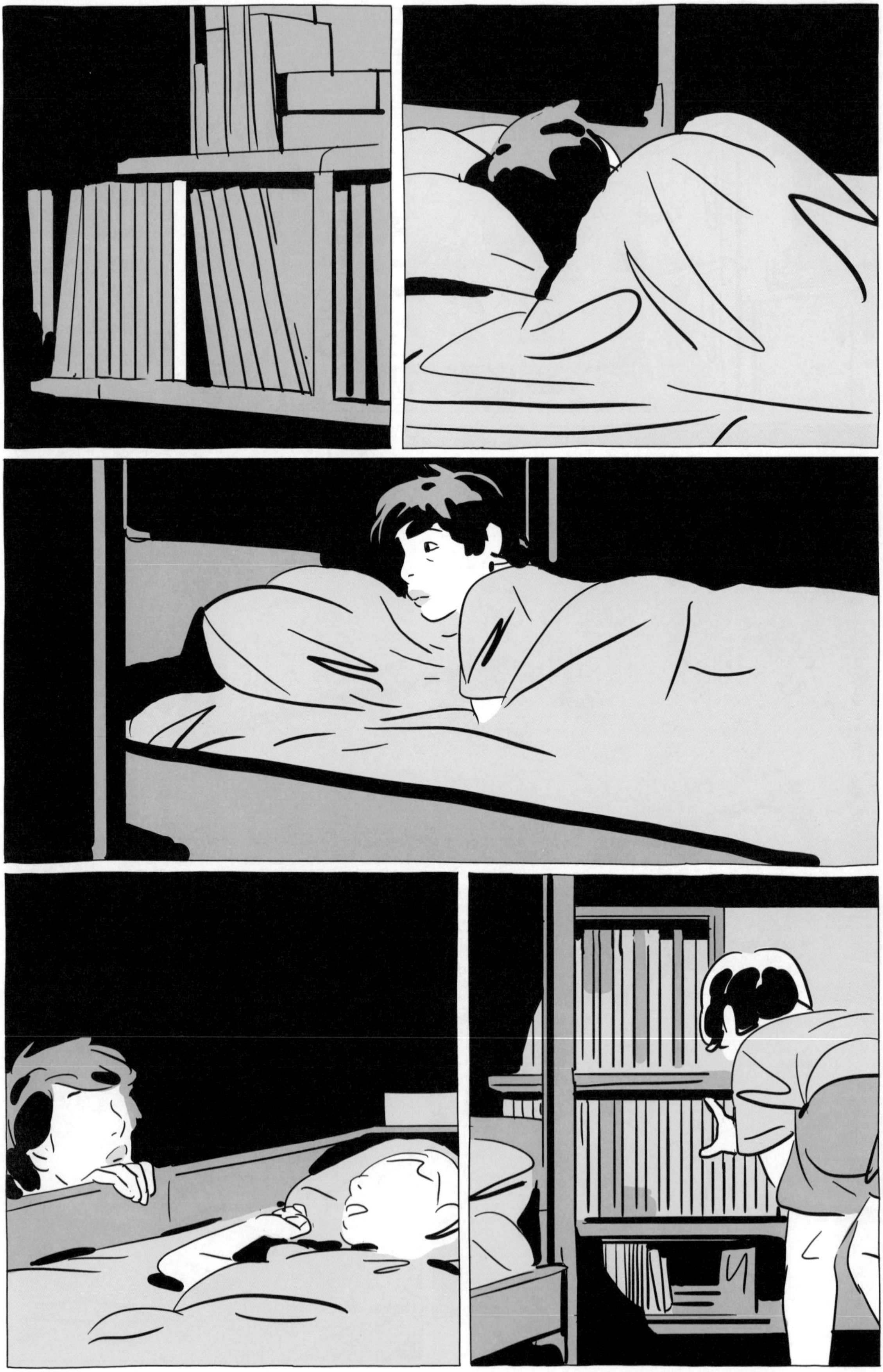

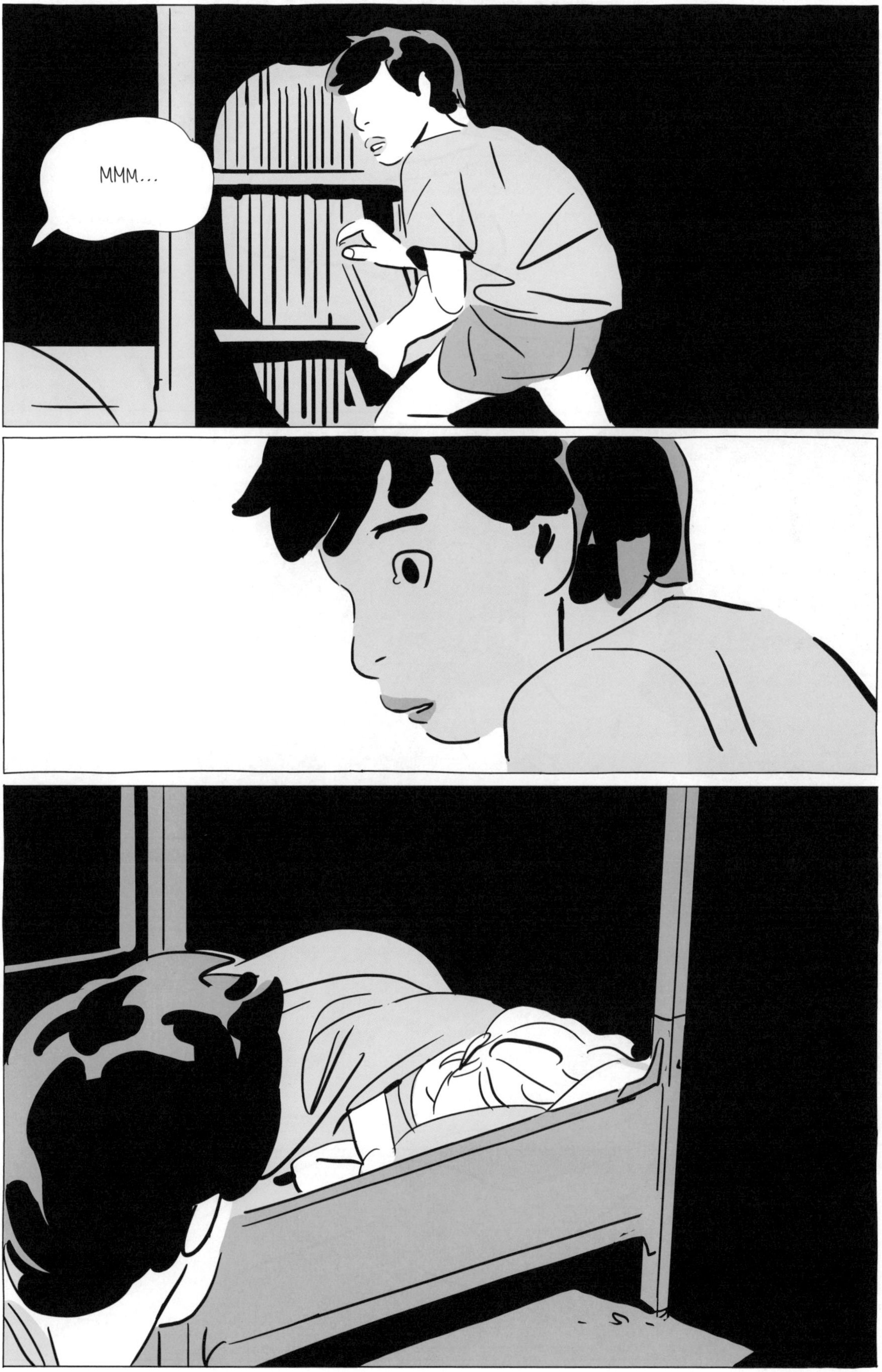
MMM...

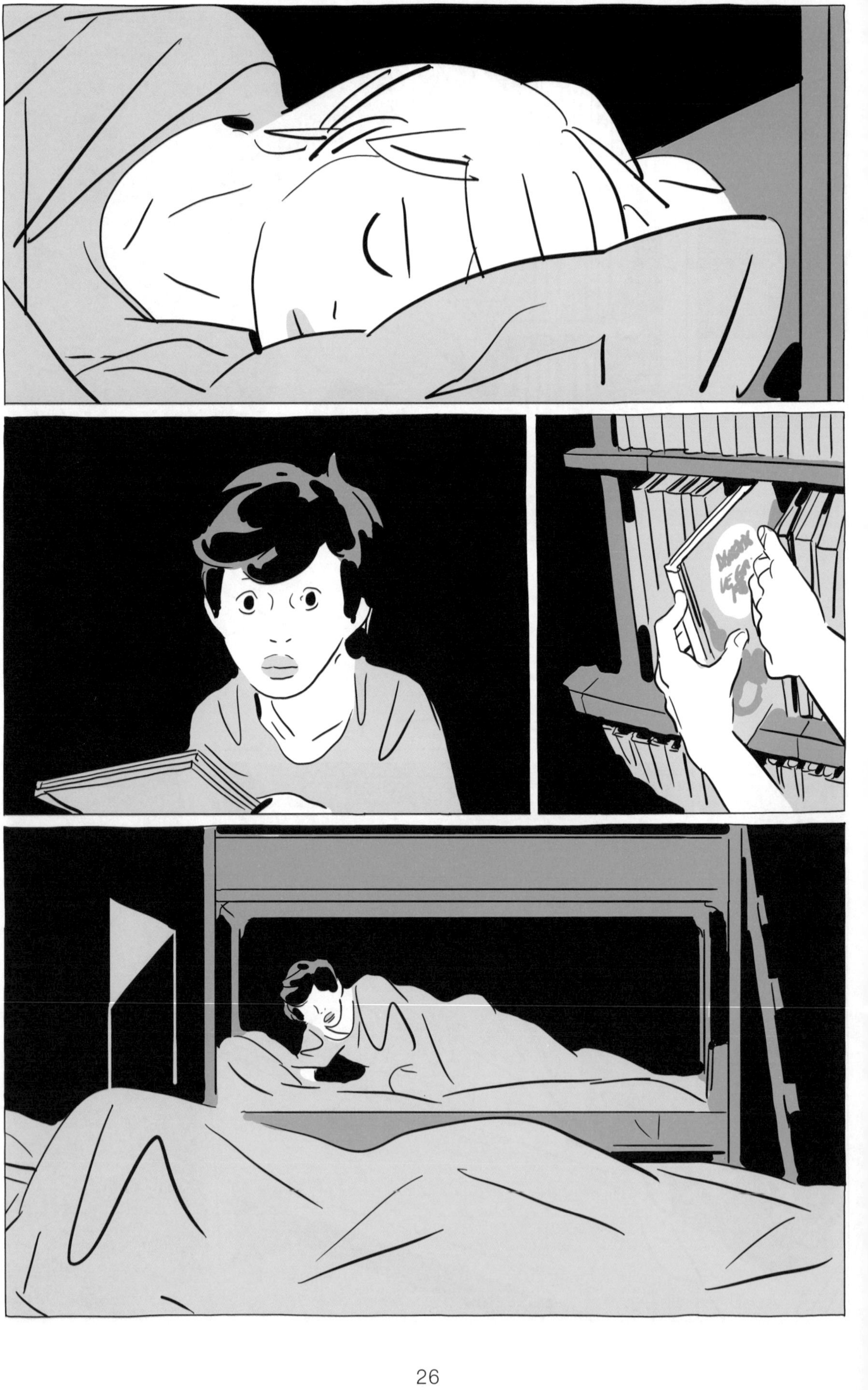

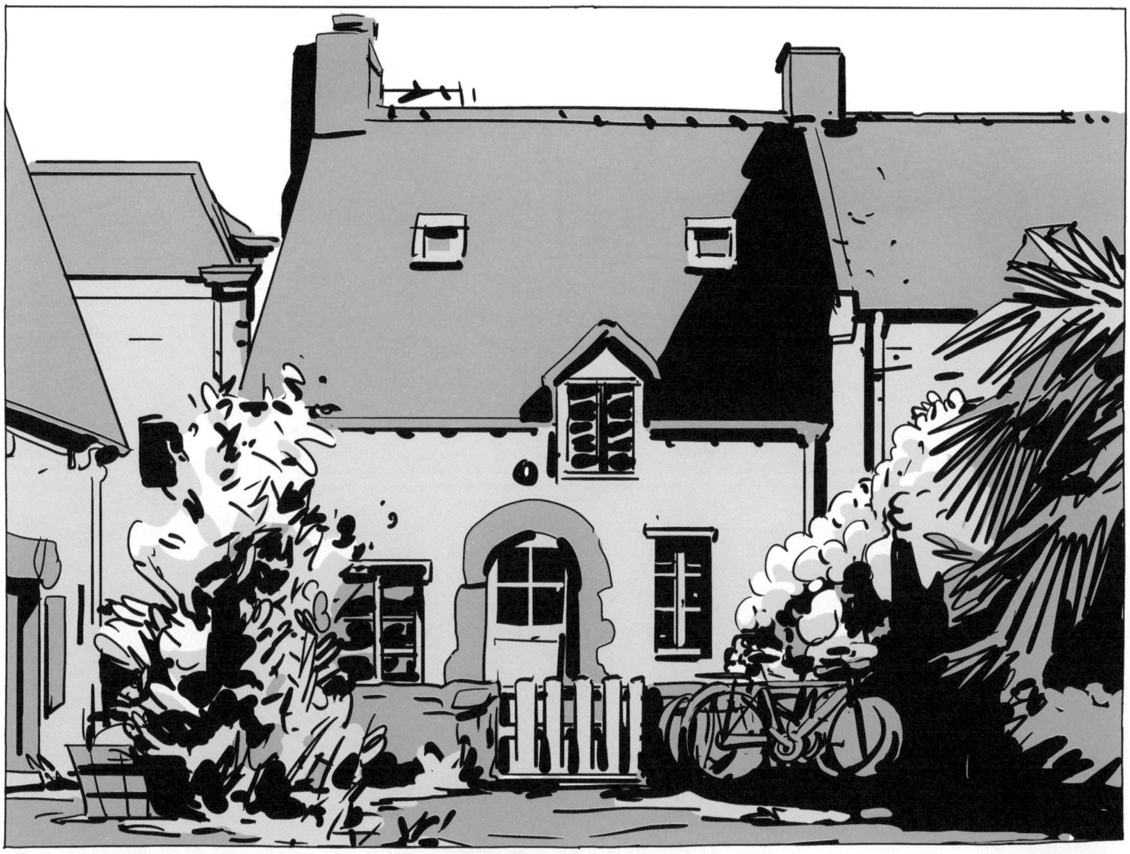

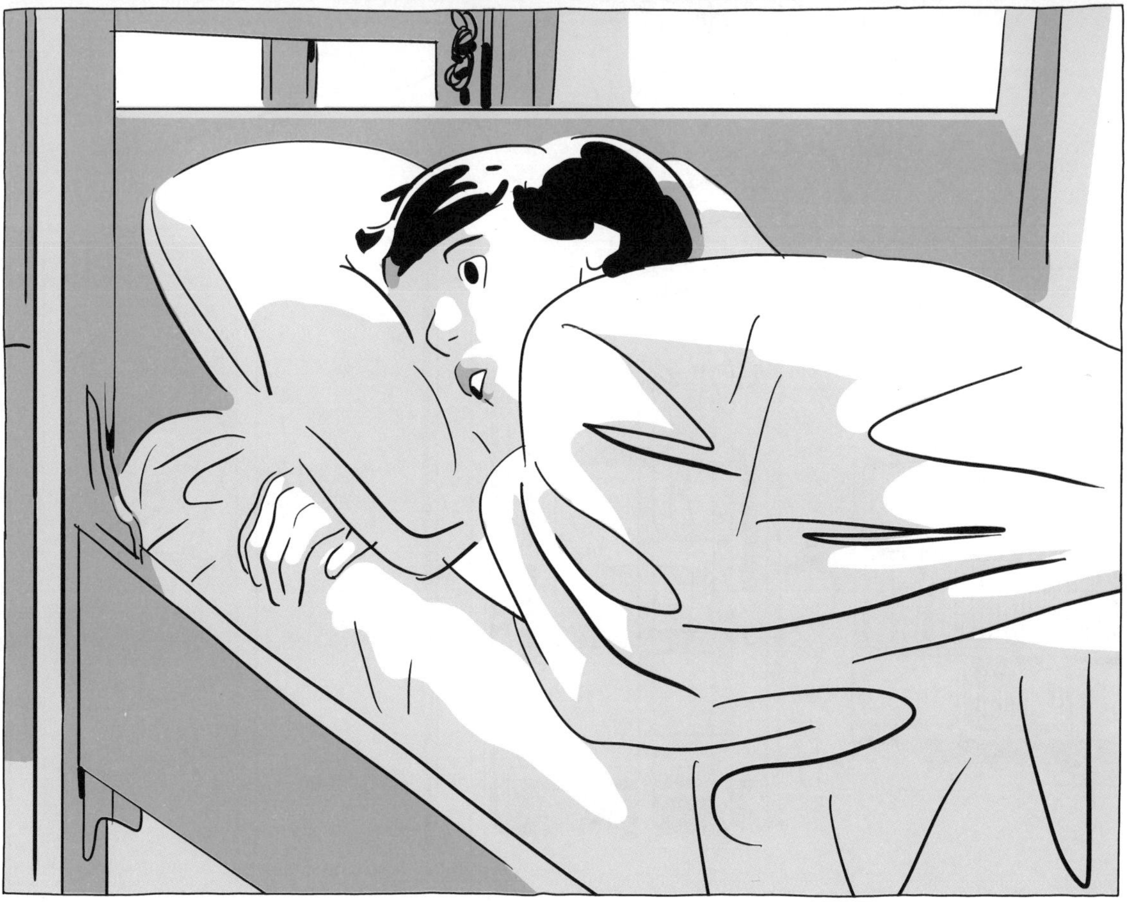

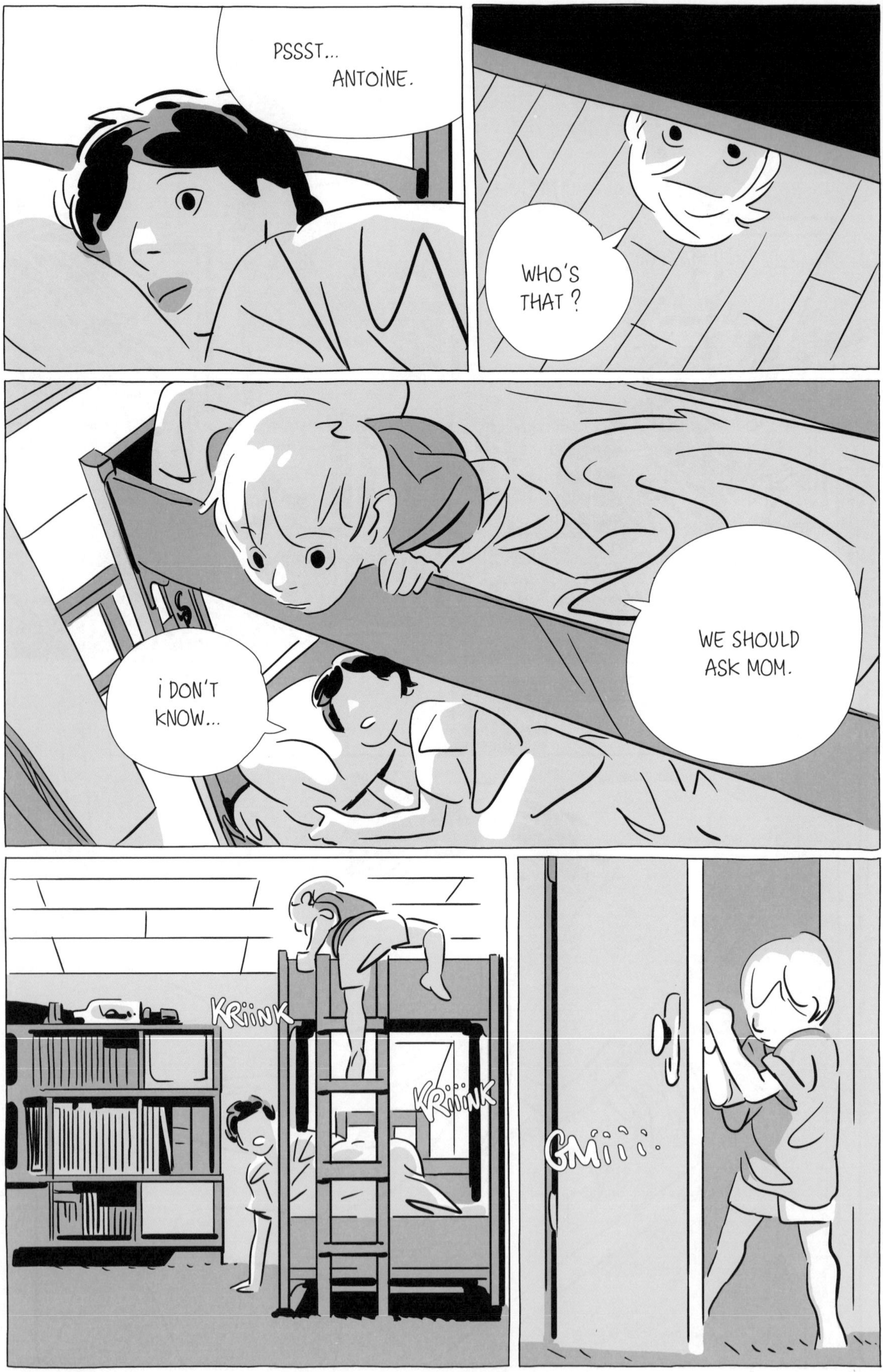
PSSST...
ANTOINE.
WHO'S THAT?
WE SHOULD ASK MOM.
I DON'T KNOW...
KRIINK
KRIIINK
GMIIII

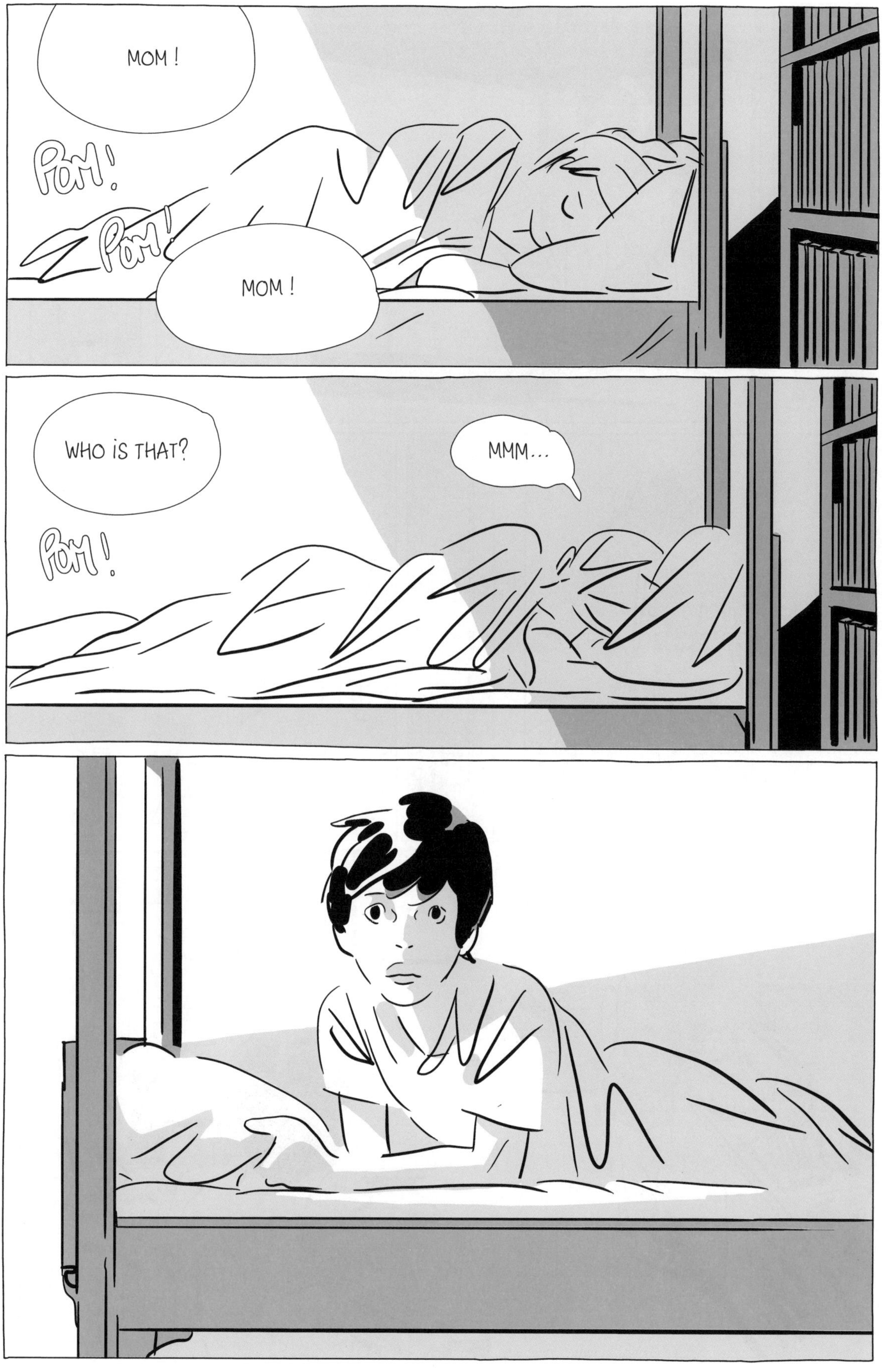
MOM !
POM !
POM !
MOM !
WHO IS THAT?
MMM...
POM !

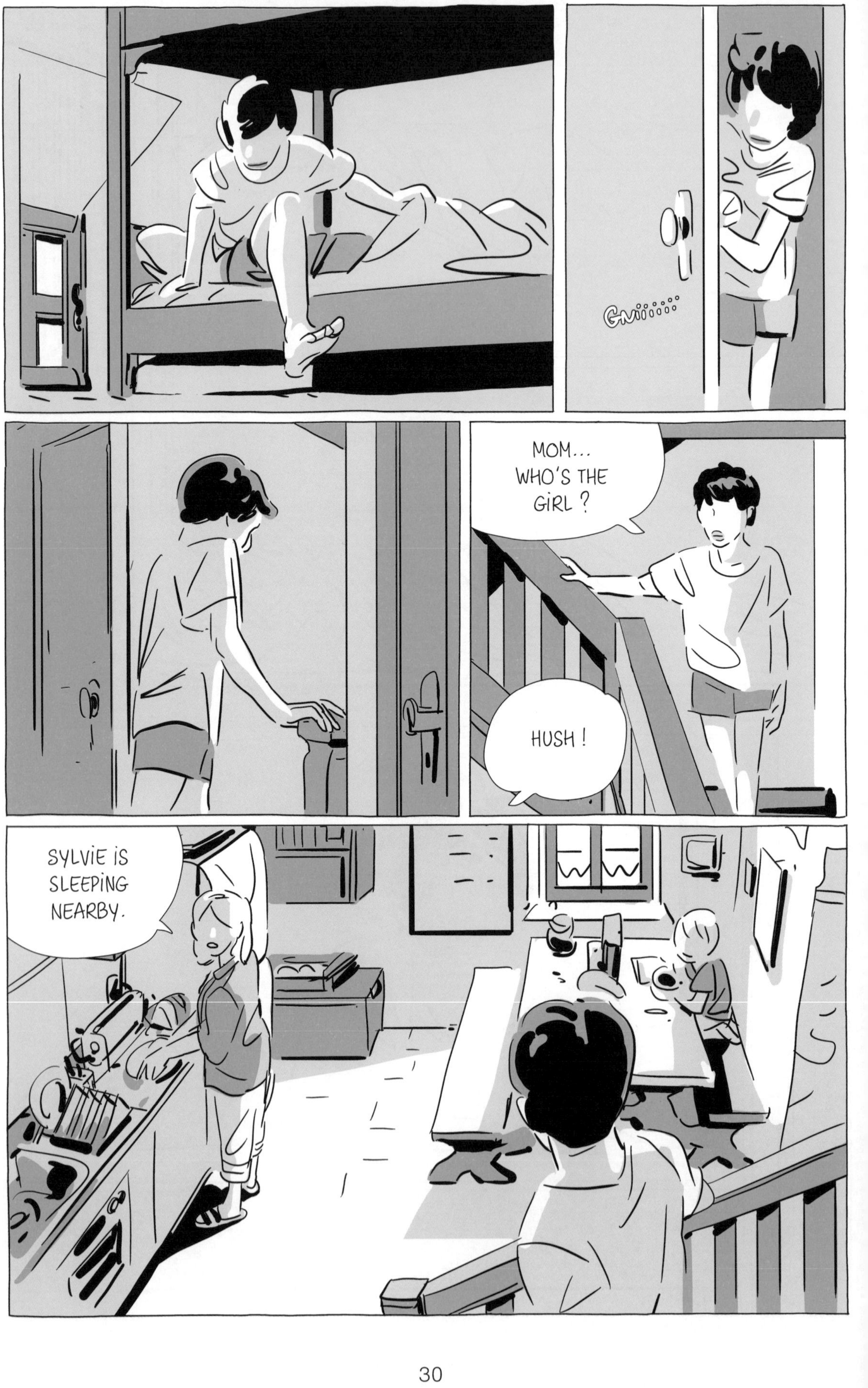
Gniiiiiii
MOM... WHO'S THE GIRL ?
HUSH !
SYLVIE IS SLEEPING NEARBY.

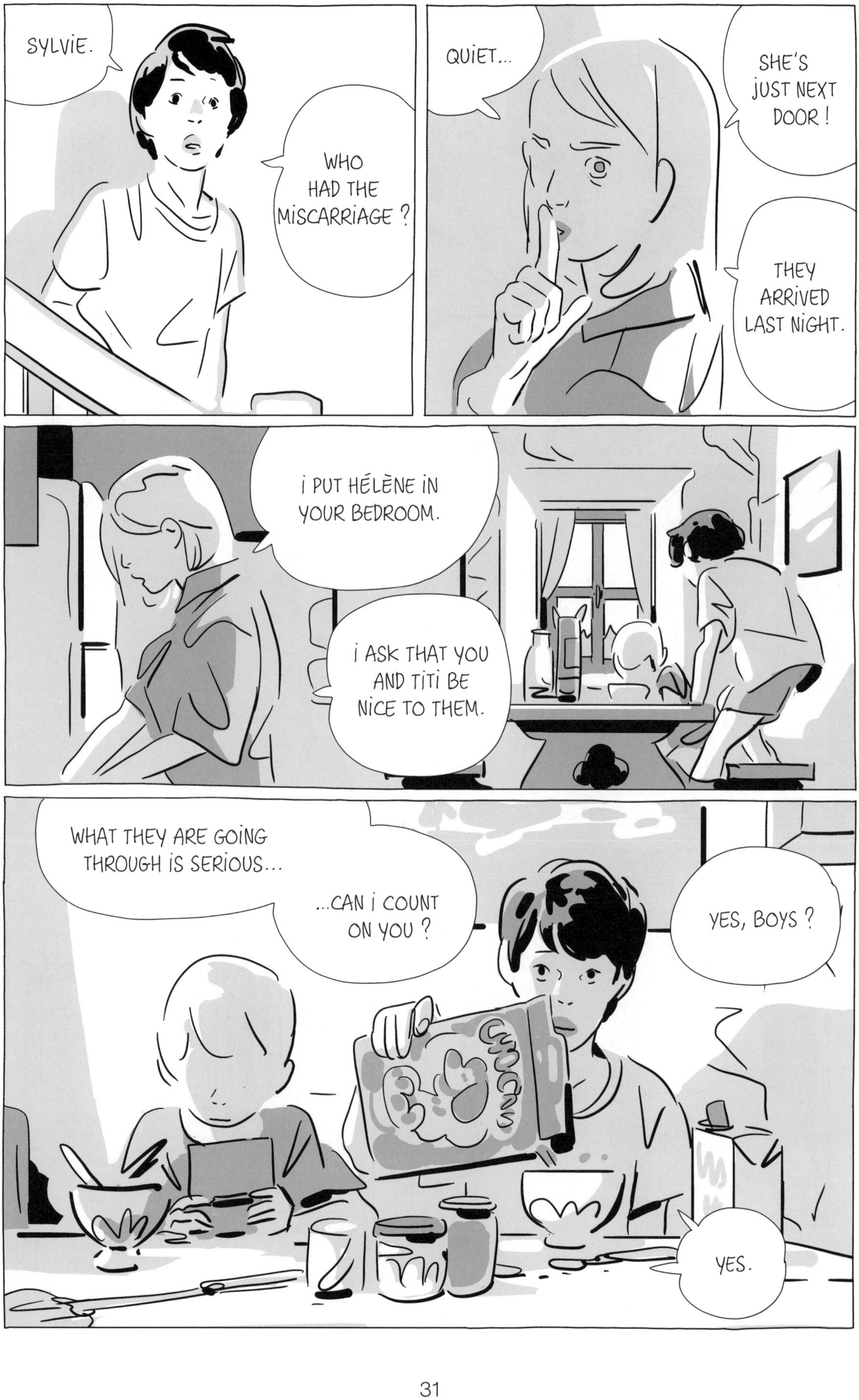
SYLVIE.
WHO HAD THE MISCARRIAGE ?
QUIET...
SHE'S JUST NEXT DOOR !
THEY ARRIVED LAST NIGHT.
I PUT HÉLÈNE IN YOUR BEDROOM.
I ASK THAT YOU AND TITI BE NICE TO THEM.
WHAT THEY ARE GOING THROUGH IS SERIOUS...
...CAN I COUNT ON YOU ?
YES, BOYS ?
YES.

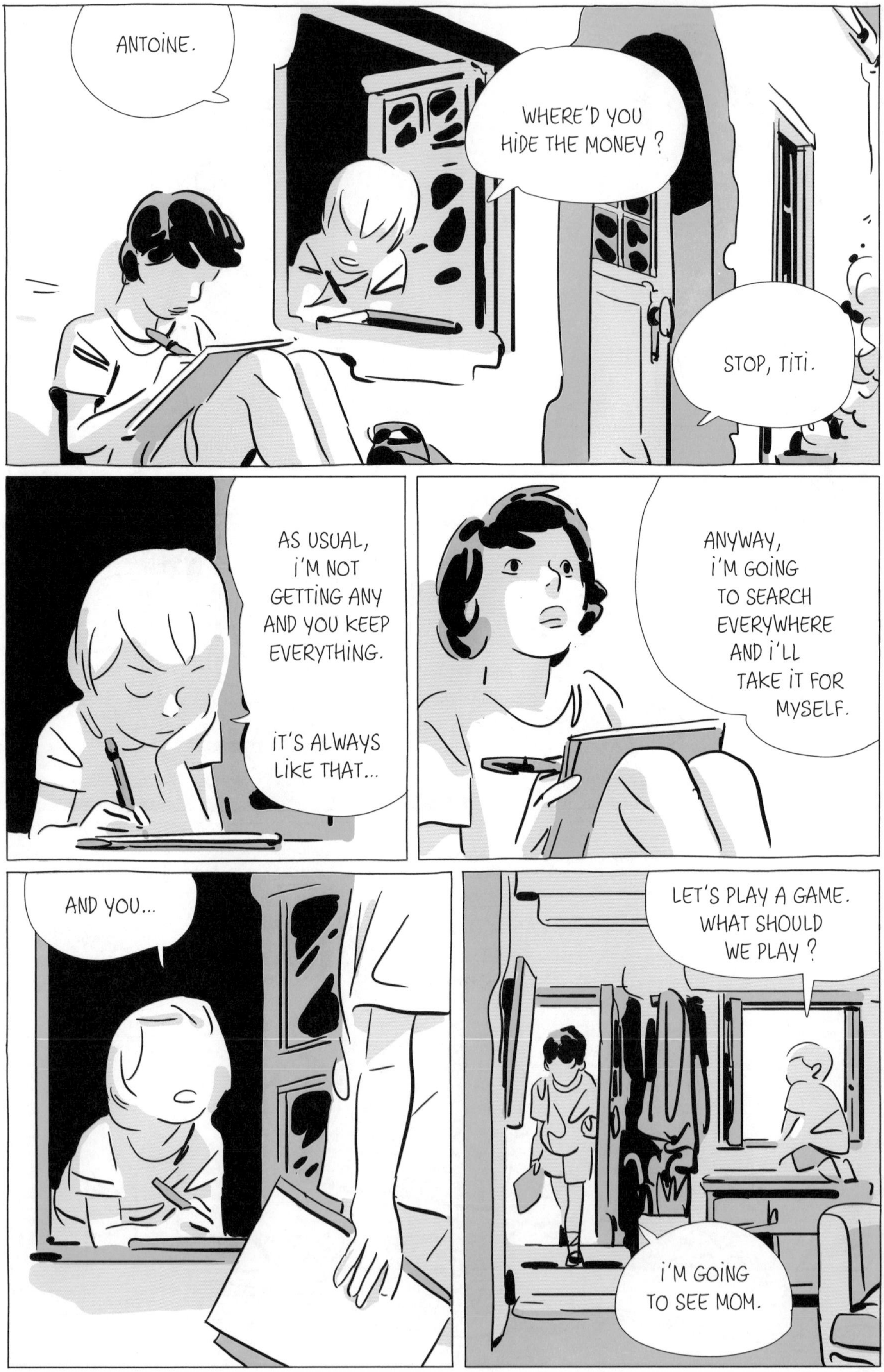
ANTOINE.
WHERE'D YOU HIDE THE MONEY ?
STOP, TITI.
AS USUAL, I'M NOT GETTING ANY AND YOU KEEP EVERYTHING.
IT'S ALWAYS LIKE THAT...
ANYWAY, I'M GOING TO SEARCH EVERYWHERE AND I'LL TAKE IT FOR MYSELF.
AND YOU...
LET'S PLAY A GAME. WHAT SHOULD WE PLAY ?
I'M GOING TO SEE MOM.

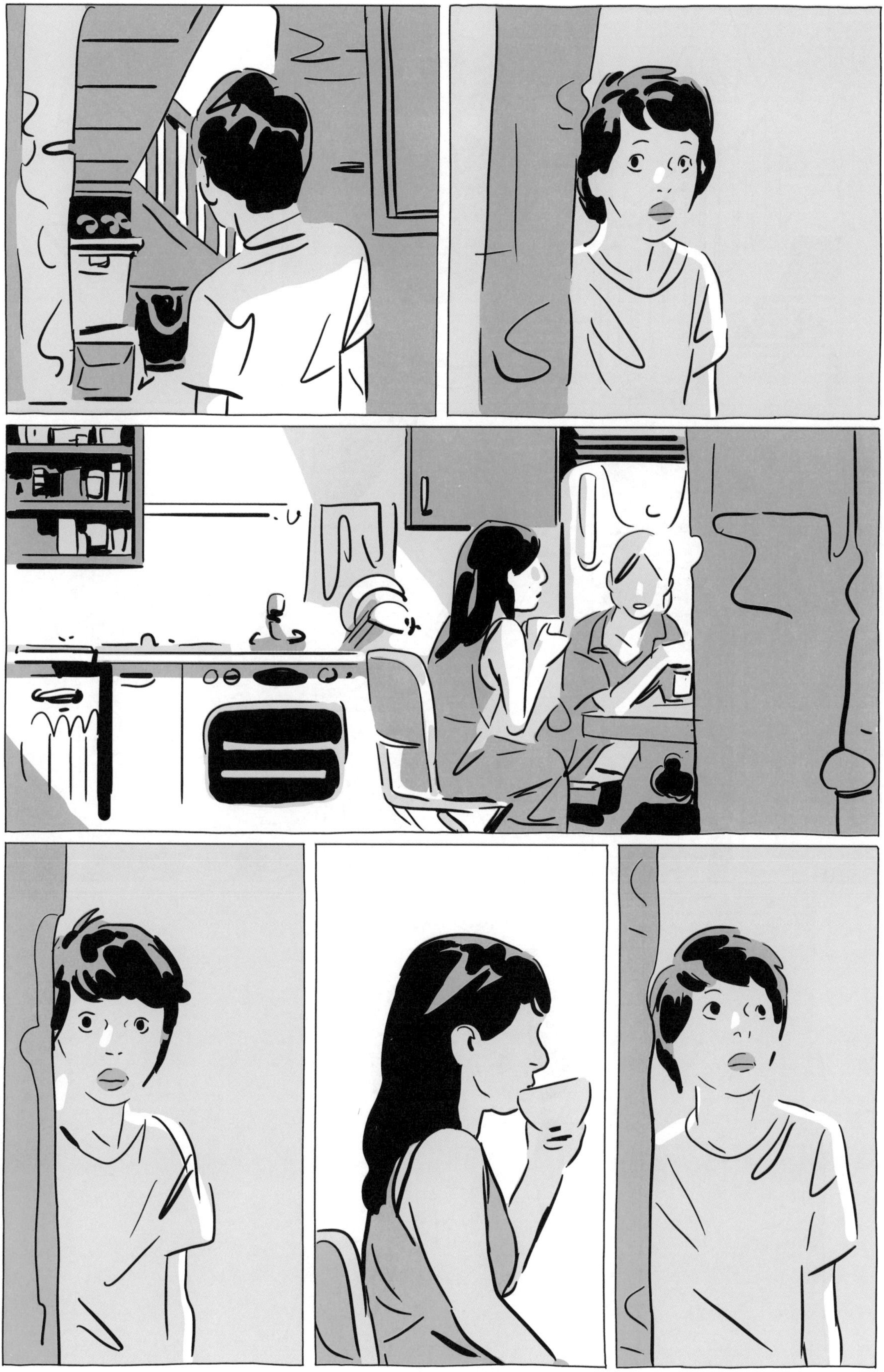

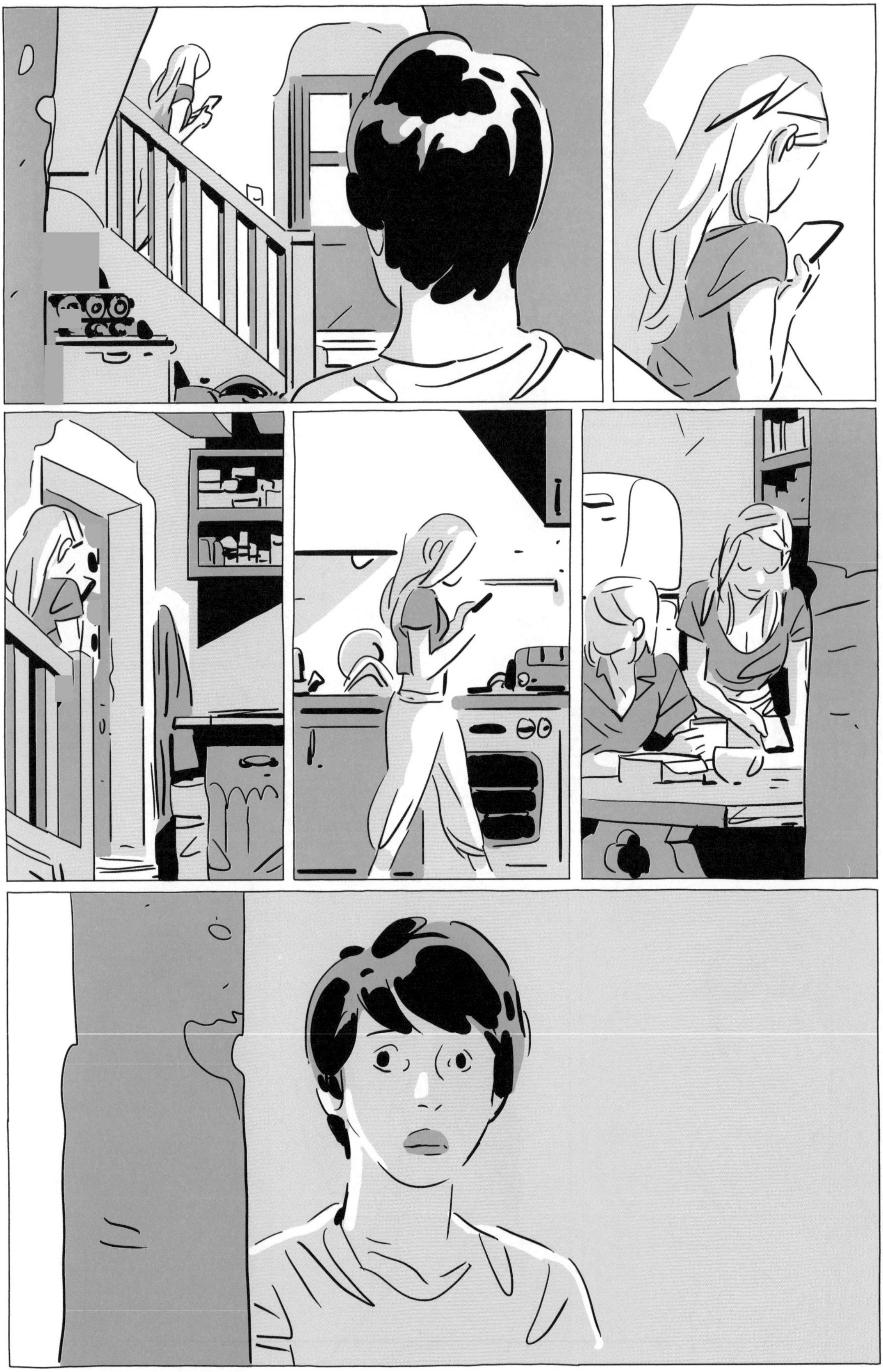

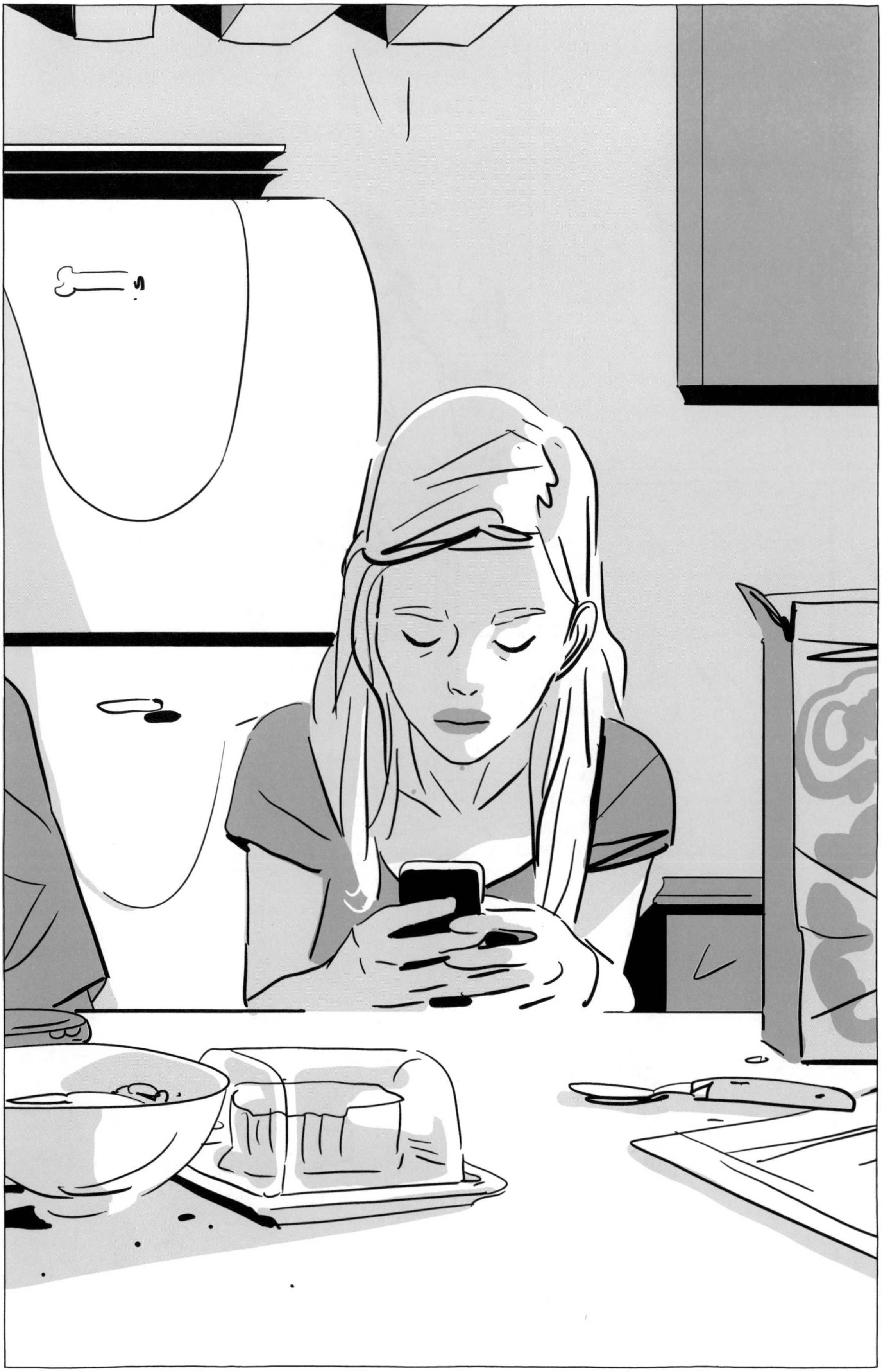

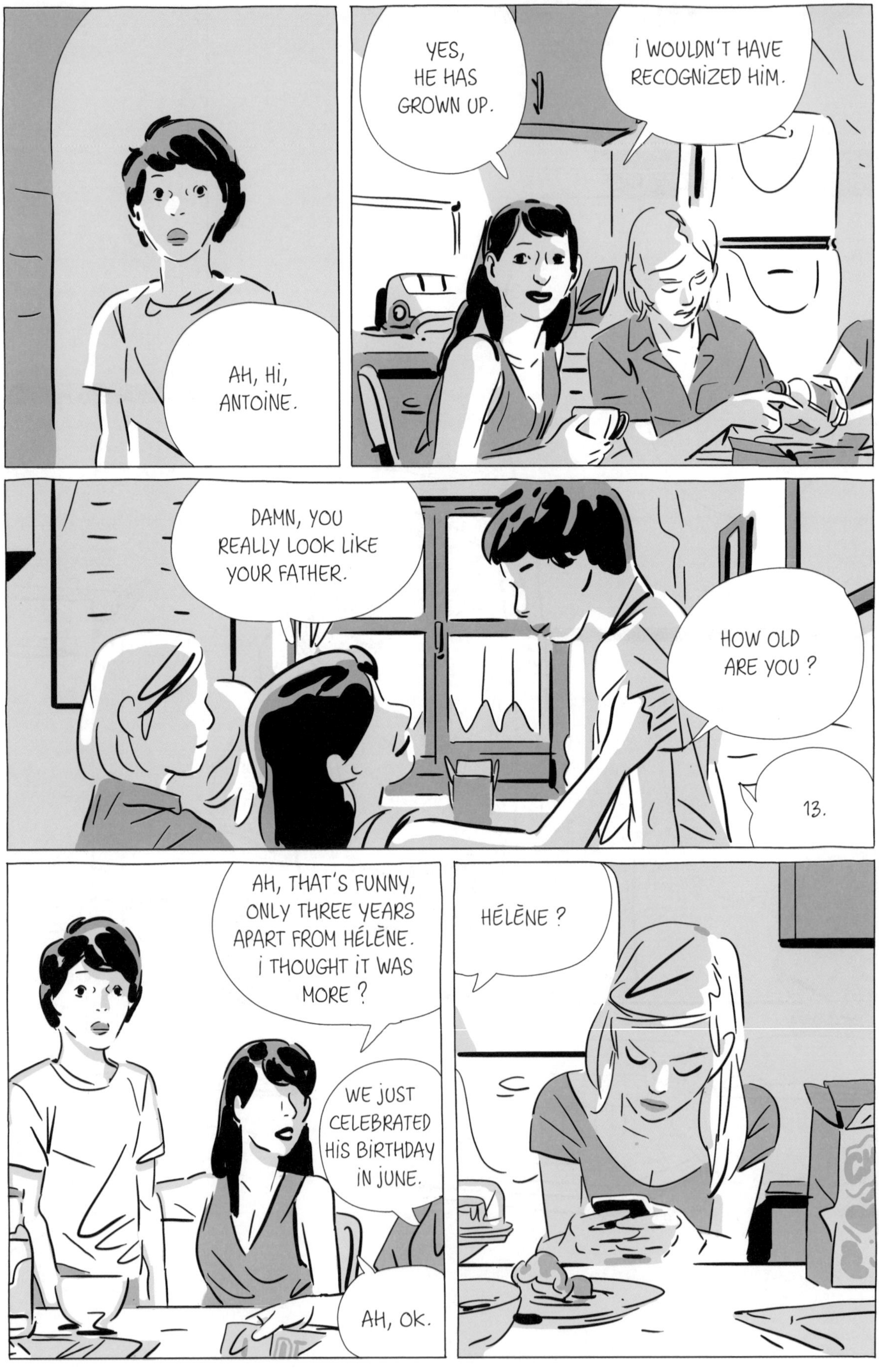
YES, HE HAS GROWN UP.
I WOULDN'T HAVE RECOGNIZED HIM.
AH, HI, ANTOINE.
DAMN, YOU REALLY LOOK LIKE YOUR FATHER.
HOW OLD ARE YOU ?
13.
AH, THAT'S FUNNY, ONLY THREE YEARS APART FROM HÉLÈNE. I THOUGHT IT WAS MORE ?
WE JUST CELEBRATED HIS BIRTHDAY IN JUNE.
AH, OK.
HÉLÈNE ?

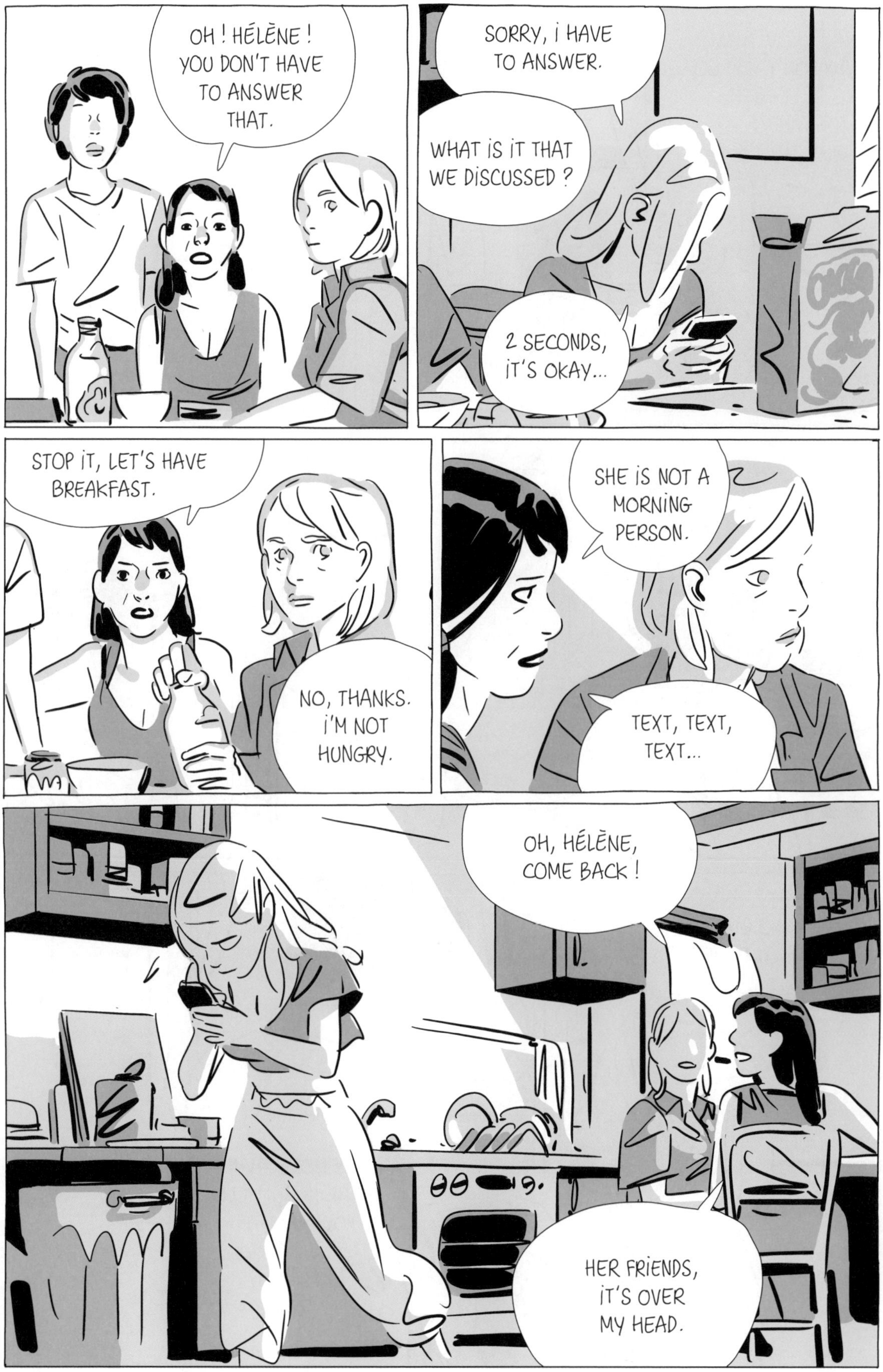
OH ! HÉLÈNE ! YOU DON'T HAVE TO ANSWER THAT.
SORRY, I HAVE TO ANSWER.
WHAT IS IT THAT WE DISCUSSED ?
2 SECONDS, IT'S OKAY...
STOP IT, LET'S HAVE BREAKFAST.
NO, THANKS. I'M NOT HUNGRY.
SHE IS NOT A MORNING PERSON.
TEXT, TEXT, TEXT...
OH, HÉLÈNE, COME BACK !
HER FRIENDS, IT'S OVER MY HEAD.

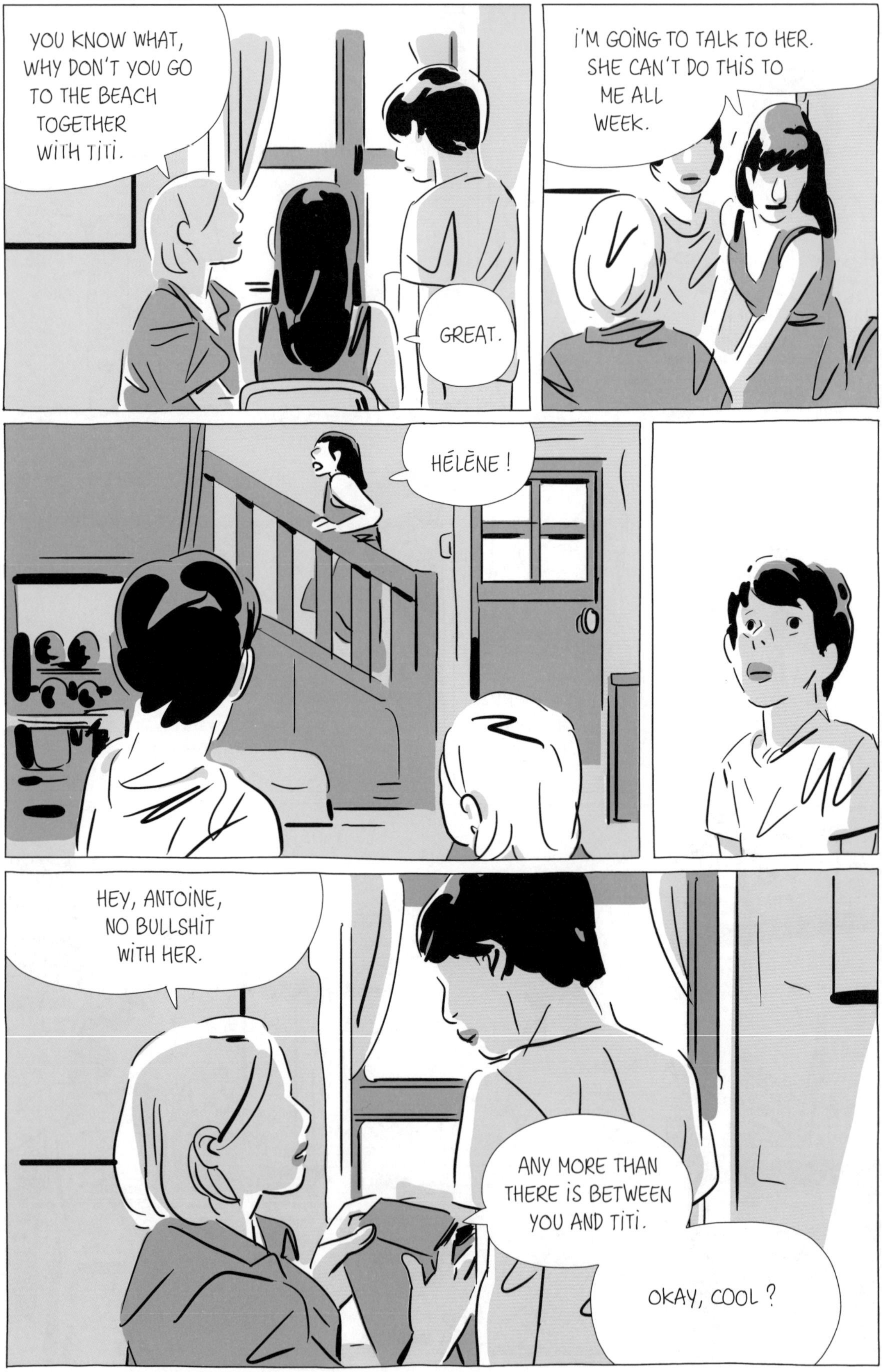
YOU KNOW WHAT, WHY DON'T YOU GO TO THE BEACH TOGETHER WITH TiTi.
GREAT.
i'M GOiNG TO TALK TO HER. SHE CAN'T DO THiS TO ME ALL WEEK.
HÉLÈNE !
HEY, ANTOiNE, NO BULLSHiT WiTH HER.
ANY MORE THAN THERE iS BETWEEN YOU AND TiTi.
OKAY, COOL ?

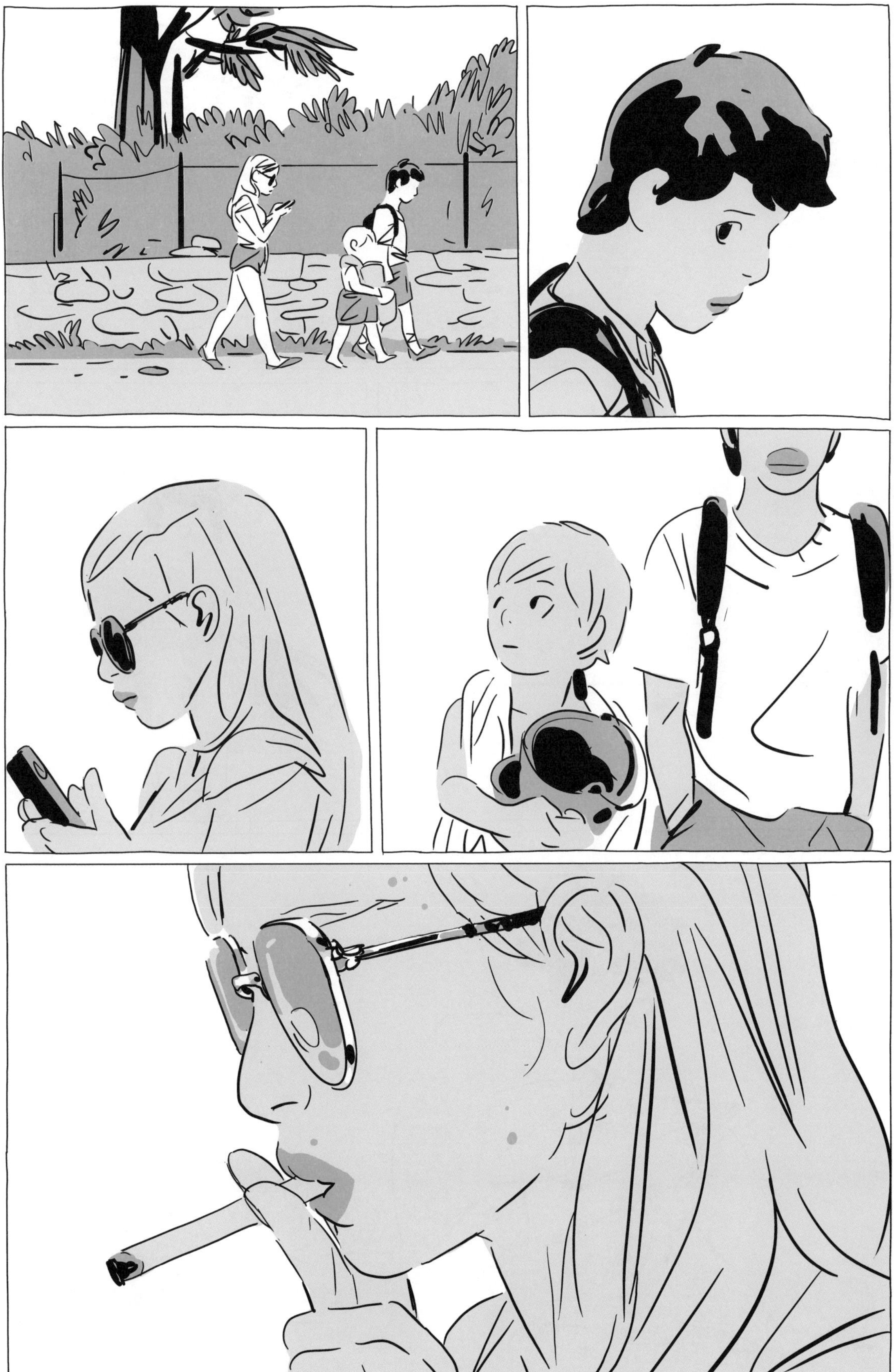

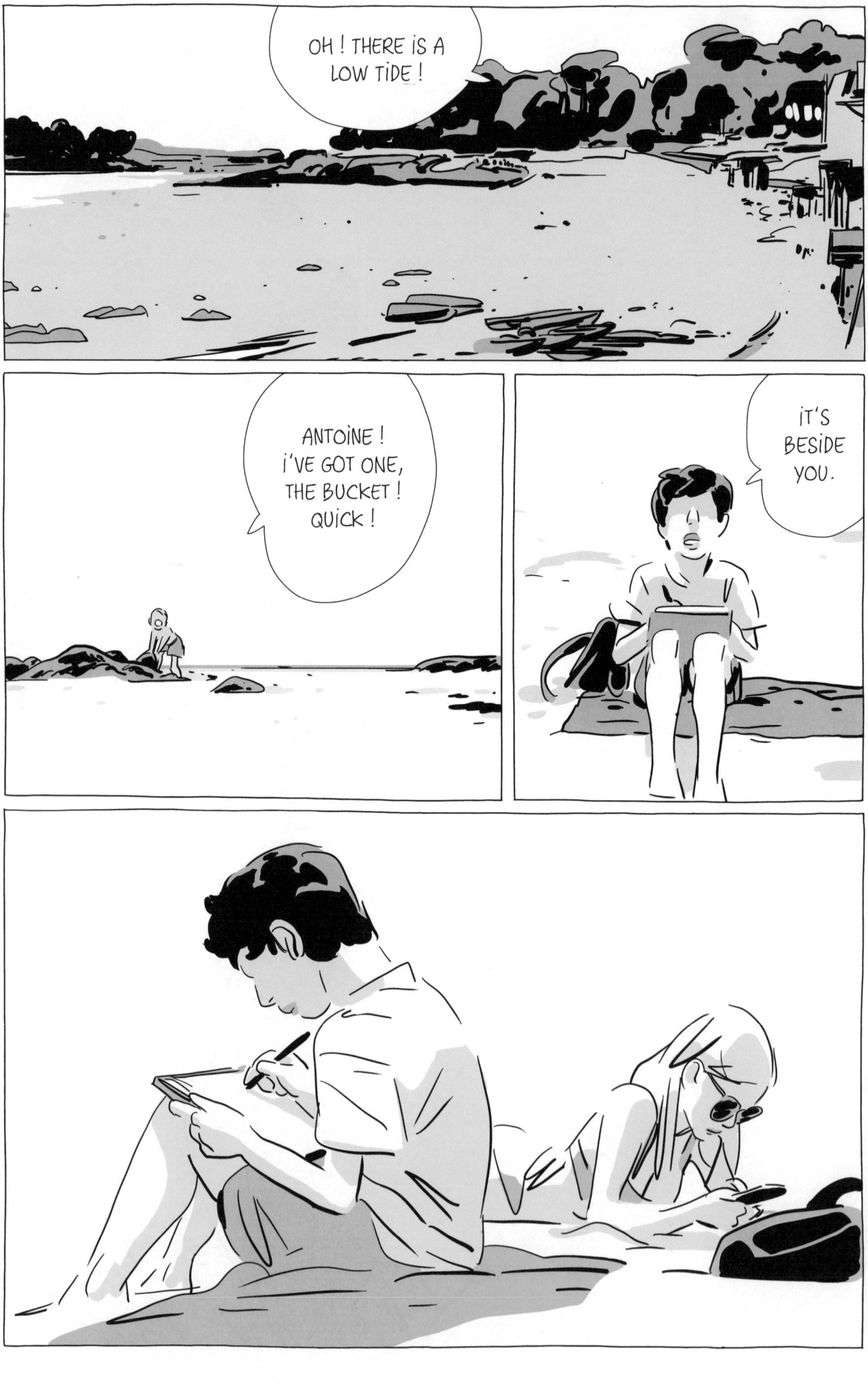
OH ! THERE iS A LOW TiDE !
ANTOiNE ! i'VE GOT ONE, THE BUCKET ! QUiCK !
iT'S BESiDE YOU.

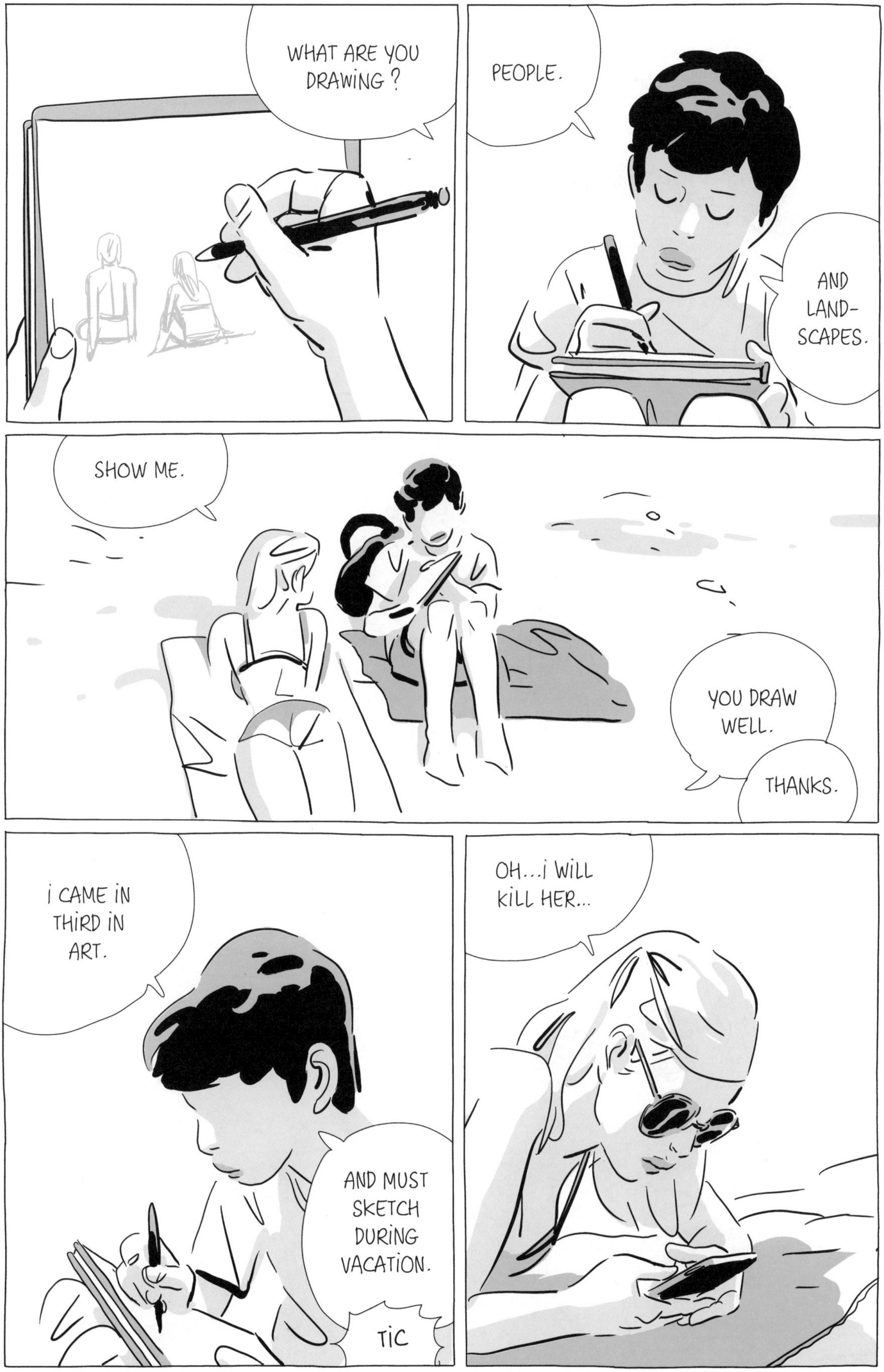
WHAT ARE YOU DRAWING ?
PEOPLE.
AND LAND-SCAPES.
SHOW ME.
YOU DRAW WELL.
THANKS.
i CAME iN THIRD iN ART.
AND MUST SKETCH DURiNG VACATiON.
TiC
OH...i WiLL KiLL HER...

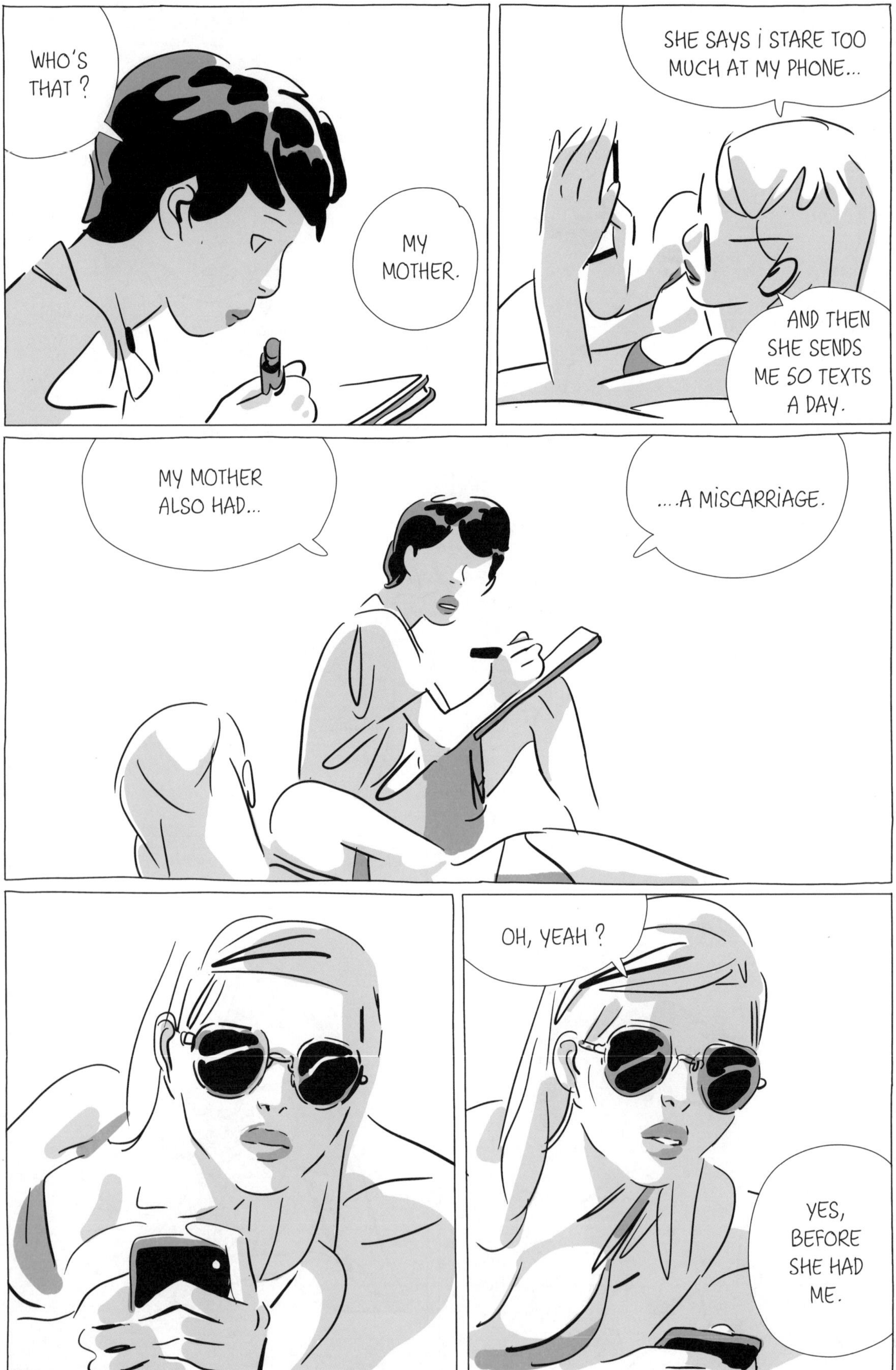
WHO'S THAT ?
MY MOTHER.
SHE SAYS i STARE TOO MUCH AT MY PHONE...
AND THEN SHE SENDS ME 50 TEXTS A DAY.
MY MOTHER ALSO HAD...
....A MiSCARRiAGE.
OH, YEAH ?
YES, BEFORE SHE HAD ME.

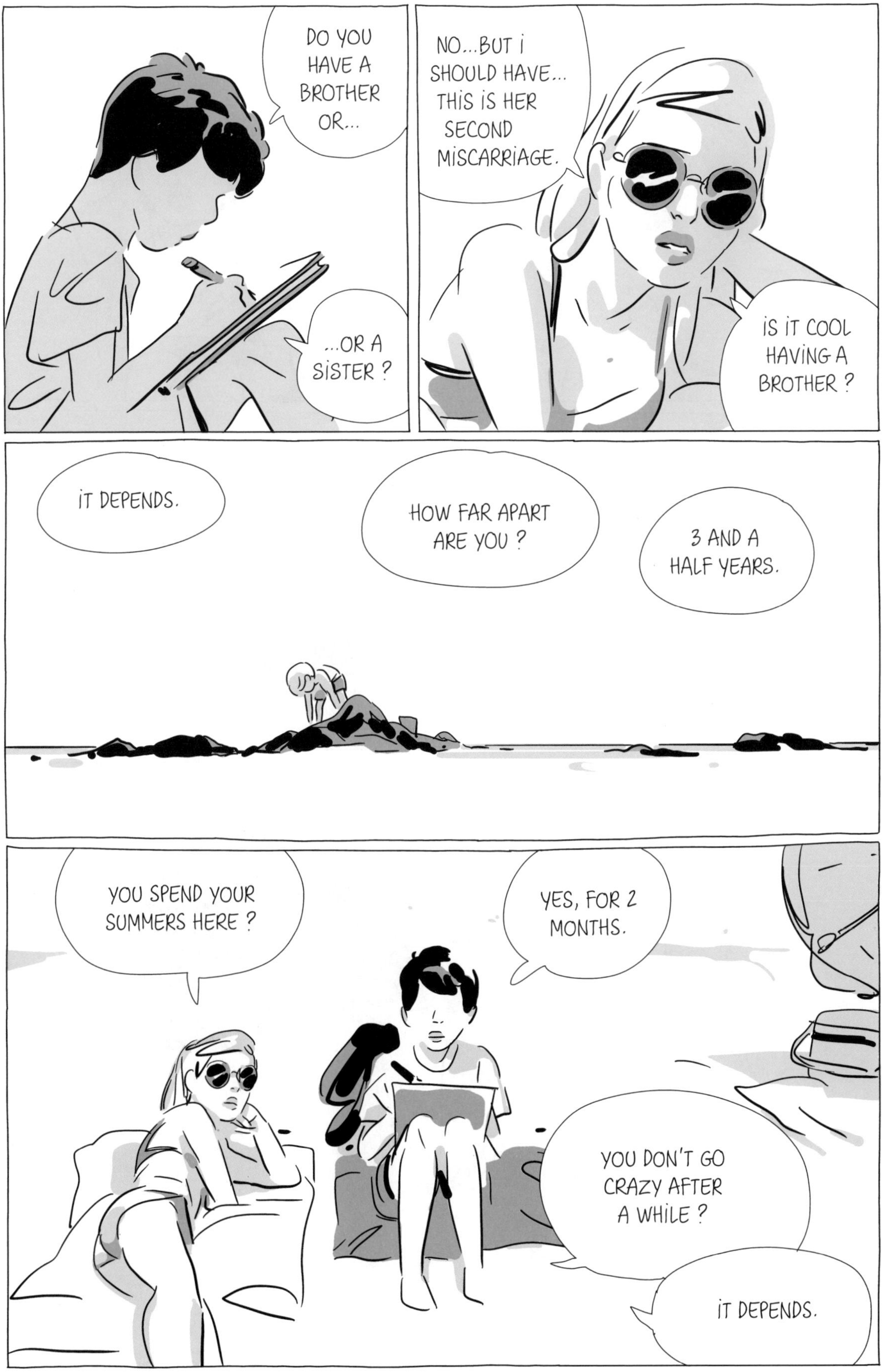
DO YOU HAVE A BROTHER OR...
...OR A SISTER ?
NO...BUT I SHOULD HAVE... THIS IS HER SECOND MISCARRIAGE.
IS IT COOL HAVING A BROTHER ?
IT DEPENDS.
HOW FAR APART ARE YOU ?
3 AND A HALF YEARS.
YOU SPEND YOUR SUMMERS HERE ?
YES, FOR 2 MONTHS.
YOU DON'T GO CRAZY AFTER A WHILE ?
IT DEPENDS.

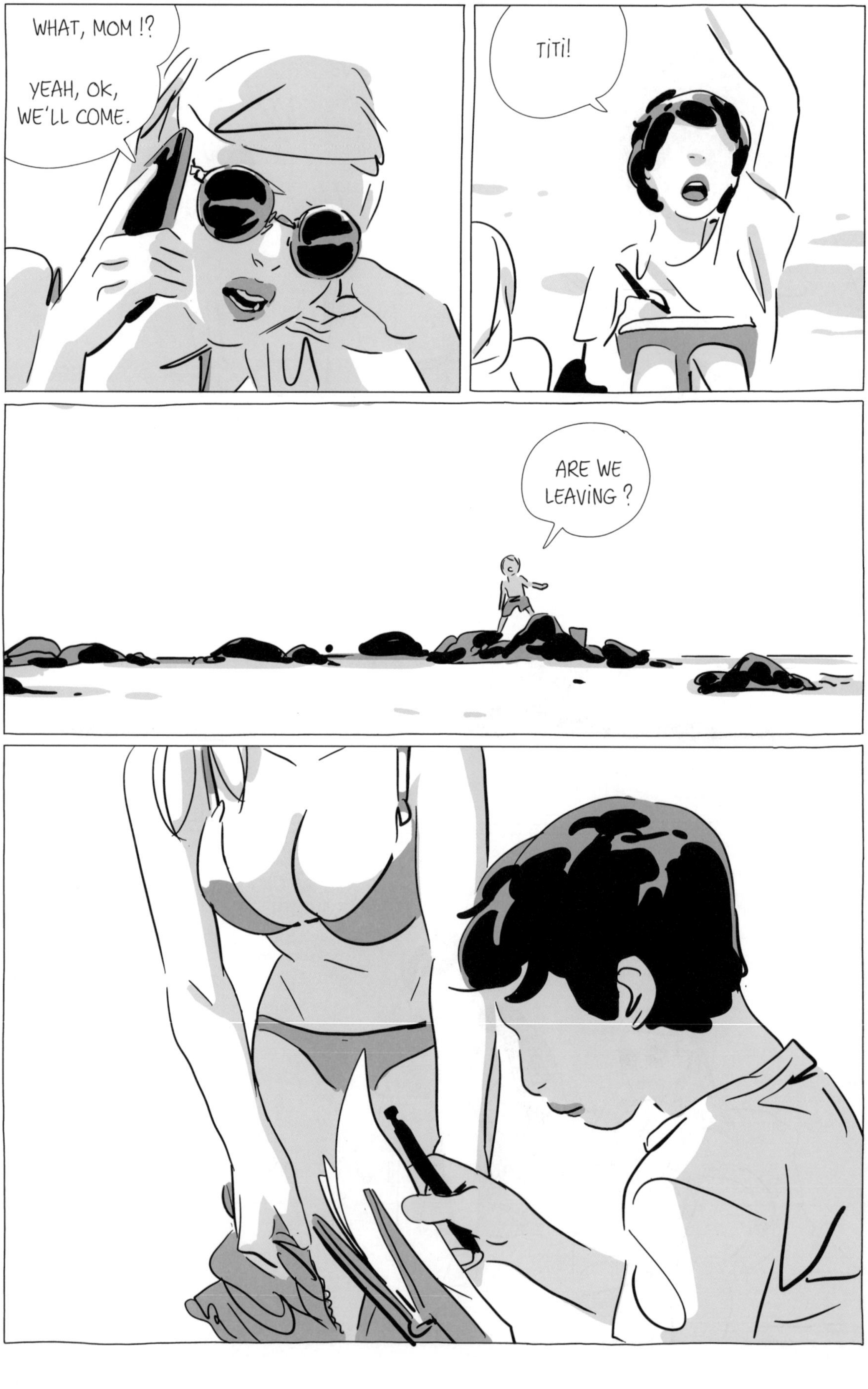
WHAT, MOM !?
YEAH, OK, WE'LL COME.
TITI!
ARE WE LEAVING ?

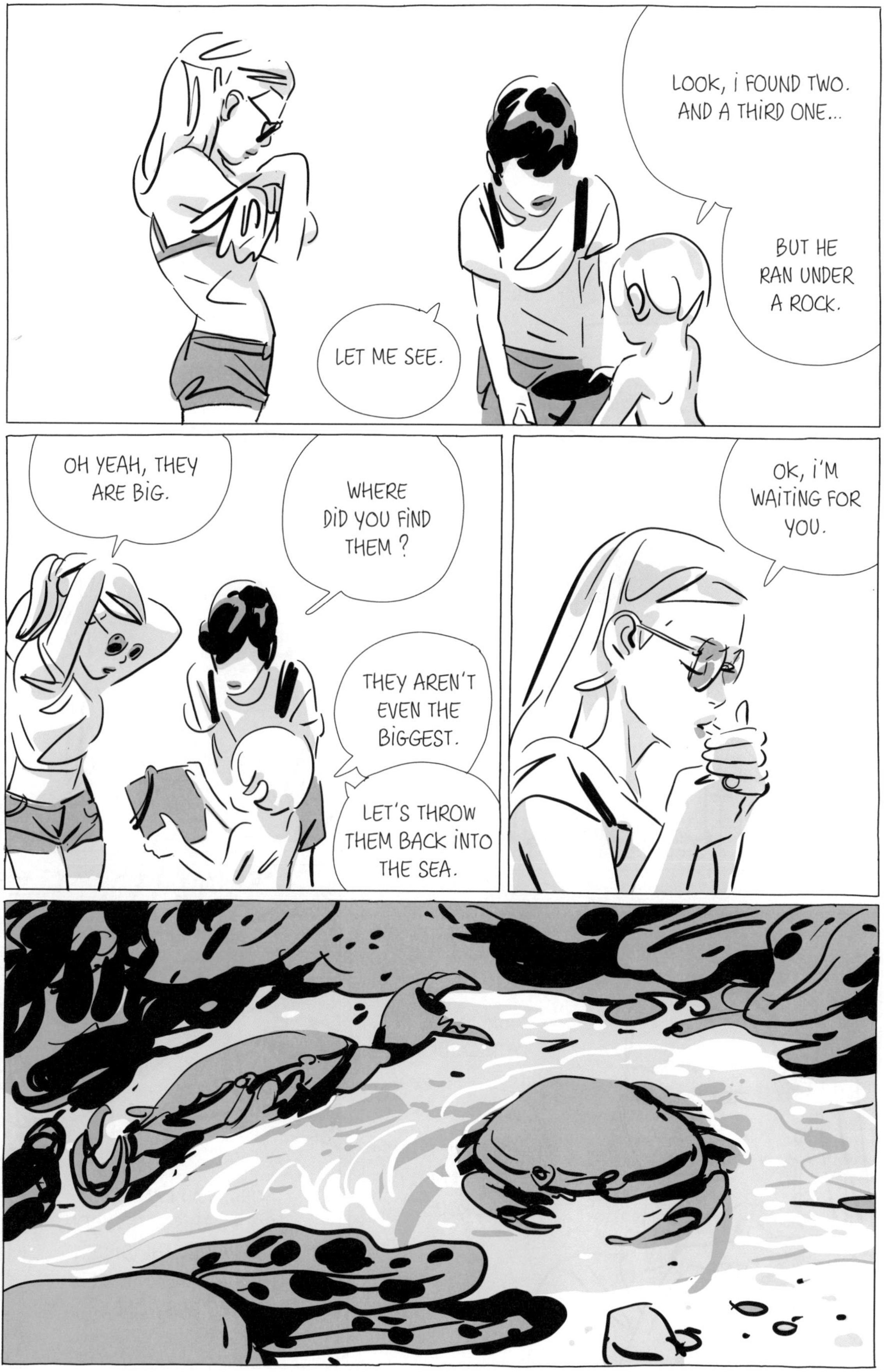
LOOK, i FOUND TWO. AND A THiRD ONE...
BUT HE RAN UNDER A ROCK.
LET ME SEE.
OH YEAH, THEY ARE BiG.
WHERE DiD YOU FiND THEM ?
THEY AREN'T EVEN THE BiGGEST.
LET'S THROW THEM BACK iNTO THE SEA.
OK, i'M WAiTiNG FOR YOU.

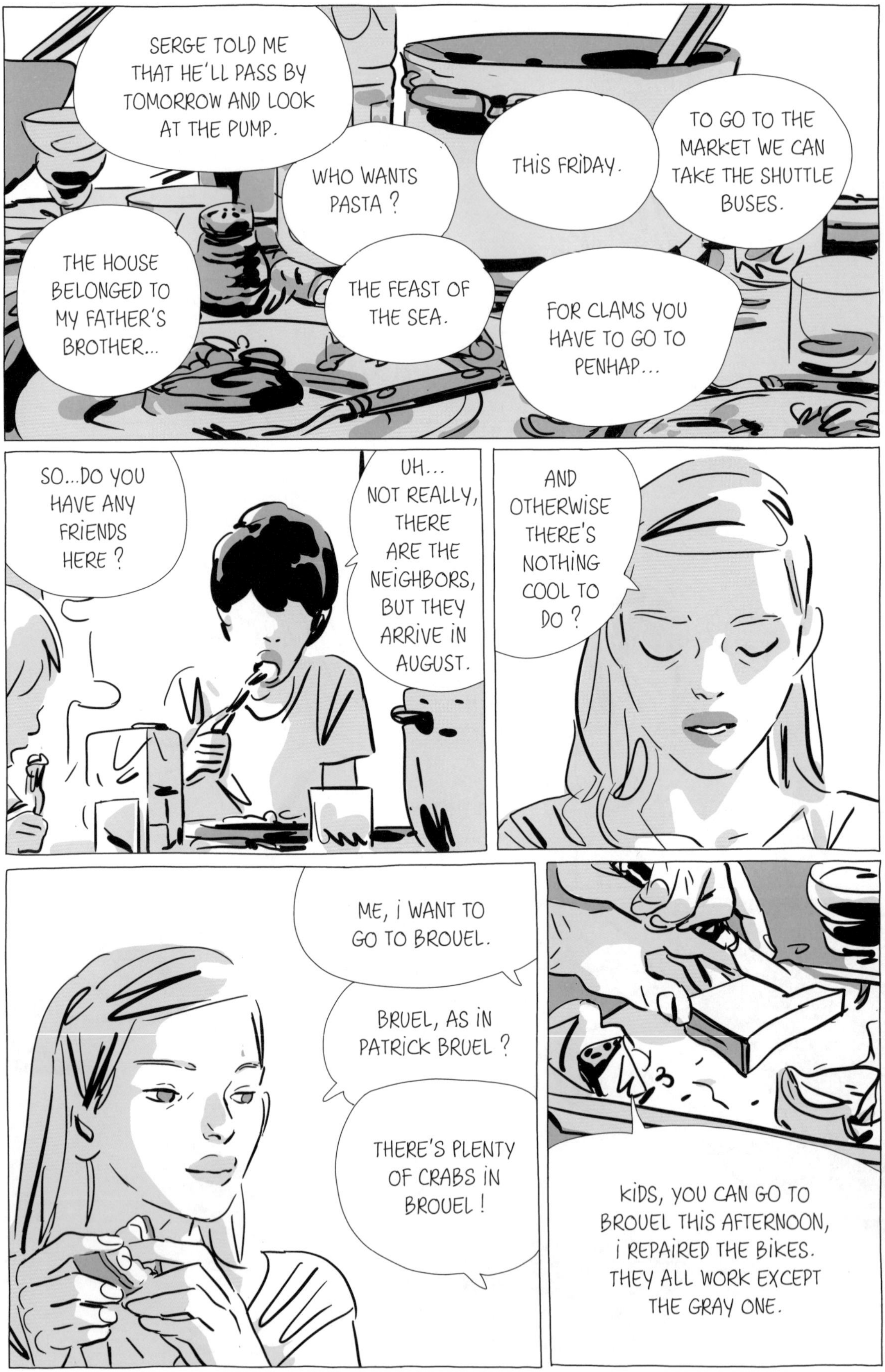
SERGE TOLD ME THAT HE'LL PASS BY TOMORROW AND LOOK AT THE PUMP.
WHO WANTS PASTA ?
THIS FRIDAY.
TO GO TO THE MARKET WE CAN TAKE THE SHUTTLE BUSES.
THE HOUSE BELONGED TO MY FATHER'S BROTHER...
THE FEAST OF THE SEA.
FOR CLAMS YOU HAVE TO GO TO PENHAP...
SO...DO YOU HAVE ANY FRIENDS HERE ?
UH... NOT REALLY, THERE ARE THE NEIGHBORS, BUT THEY ARRIVE IN AUGUST.
AND OTHERWISE THERE'S NOTHING COOL TO DO ?
ME, I WANT TO GO TO BROUEL.
BRUEL, AS IN PATRICK BRUEL ?
THERE'S PLENTY OF CRABS IN BROUEL !
KIDS, YOU CAN GO TO BROUEL THIS AFTERNOON, I REPAIRED THE BIKES. THEY ALL WORK EXCEPT THE GRAY ONE.

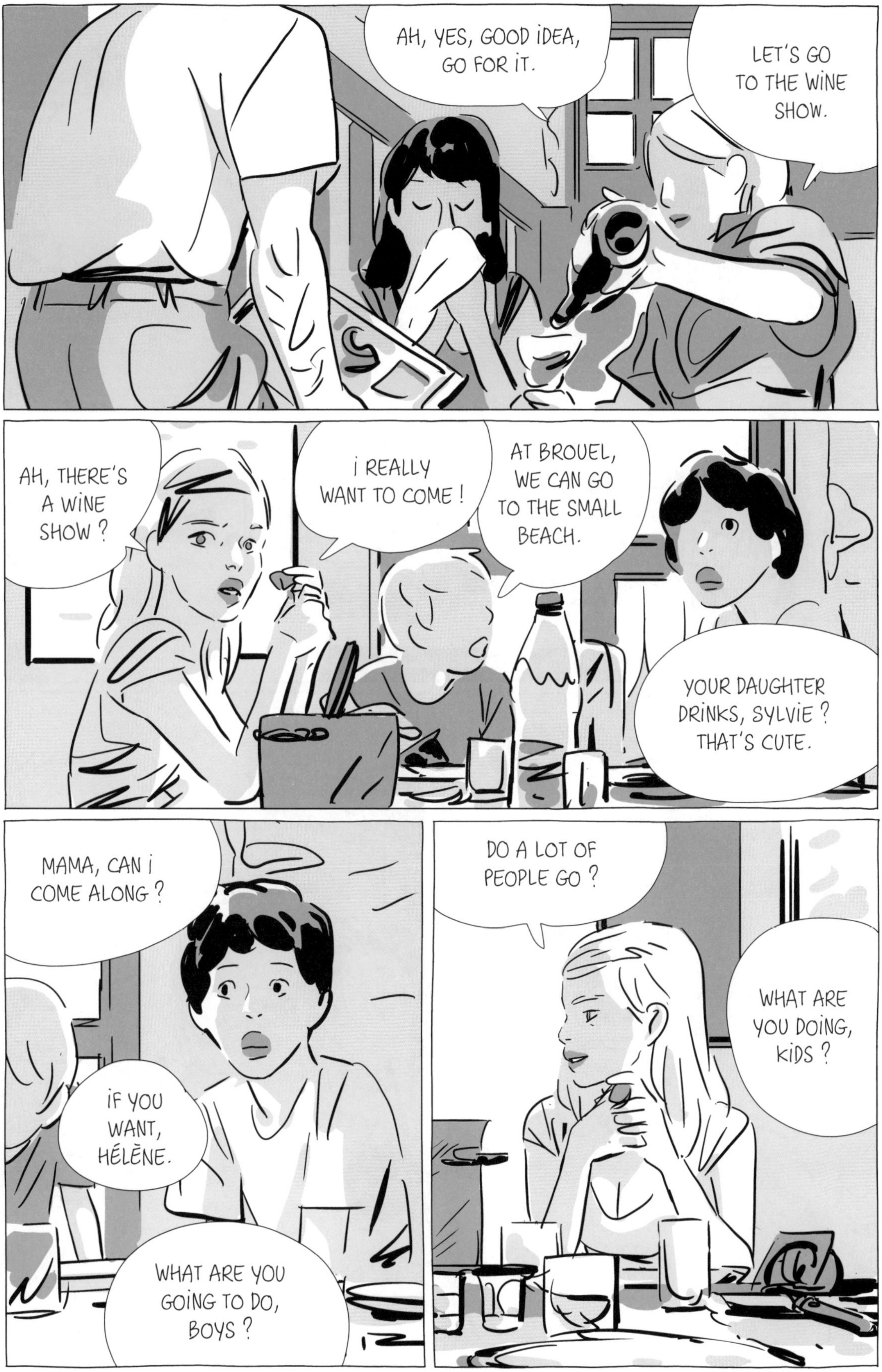
AH, YES, GOOD IDEA, GO FOR IT.
LET'S GO TO THE WINE SHOW.
AH, THERE'S A WINE SHOW ?
I REALLY WANT TO COME !
AT BROUEL, WE CAN GO TO THE SMALL BEACH.
YOUR DAUGHTER DRINKS, SYLVIE ? THAT'S CUTE.
MAMA, CAN I COME ALONG ?
IF YOU WANT, HÉLÈNE.
WHAT ARE YOU GOING TO DO, BOYS ?
DO A LOT OF PEOPLE GO ?
WHAT ARE YOU DOING, KIDS ?

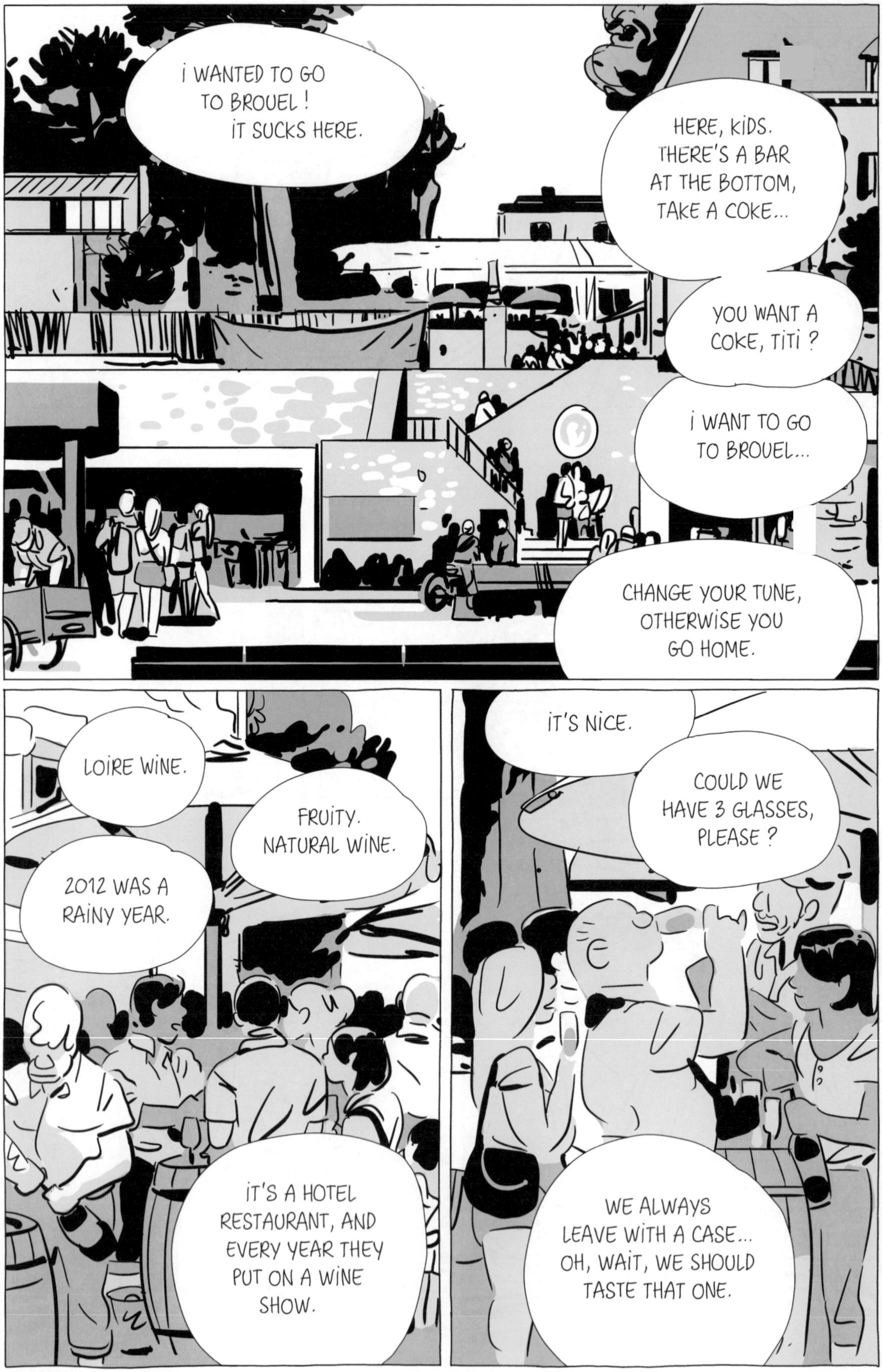

I WANTED TO GO TO BROUEL! IT SUCKS HERE.
HERE, KIDS. THERE'S A BAR AT THE BOTTOM, TAKE A COKE...
YOU WANT A COKE, TITI?
I WANT TO GO TO BROUEL...
CHANGE YOUR TUNE, OTHERWISE YOU GO HOME.
LOIRE WINE.
FRUITY. NATURAL WINE.
2012 WAS A RAINY YEAR.
IT'S A HOTEL RESTAURANT, AND EVERY YEAR THEY PUT ON A WINE SHOW.
IT'S NICE.
COULD WE HAVE 3 GLASSES, PLEASE?
WE ALWAYS LEAVE WITH A CASE... OH, WAIT, WE SHOULD TASTE THAT ONE.

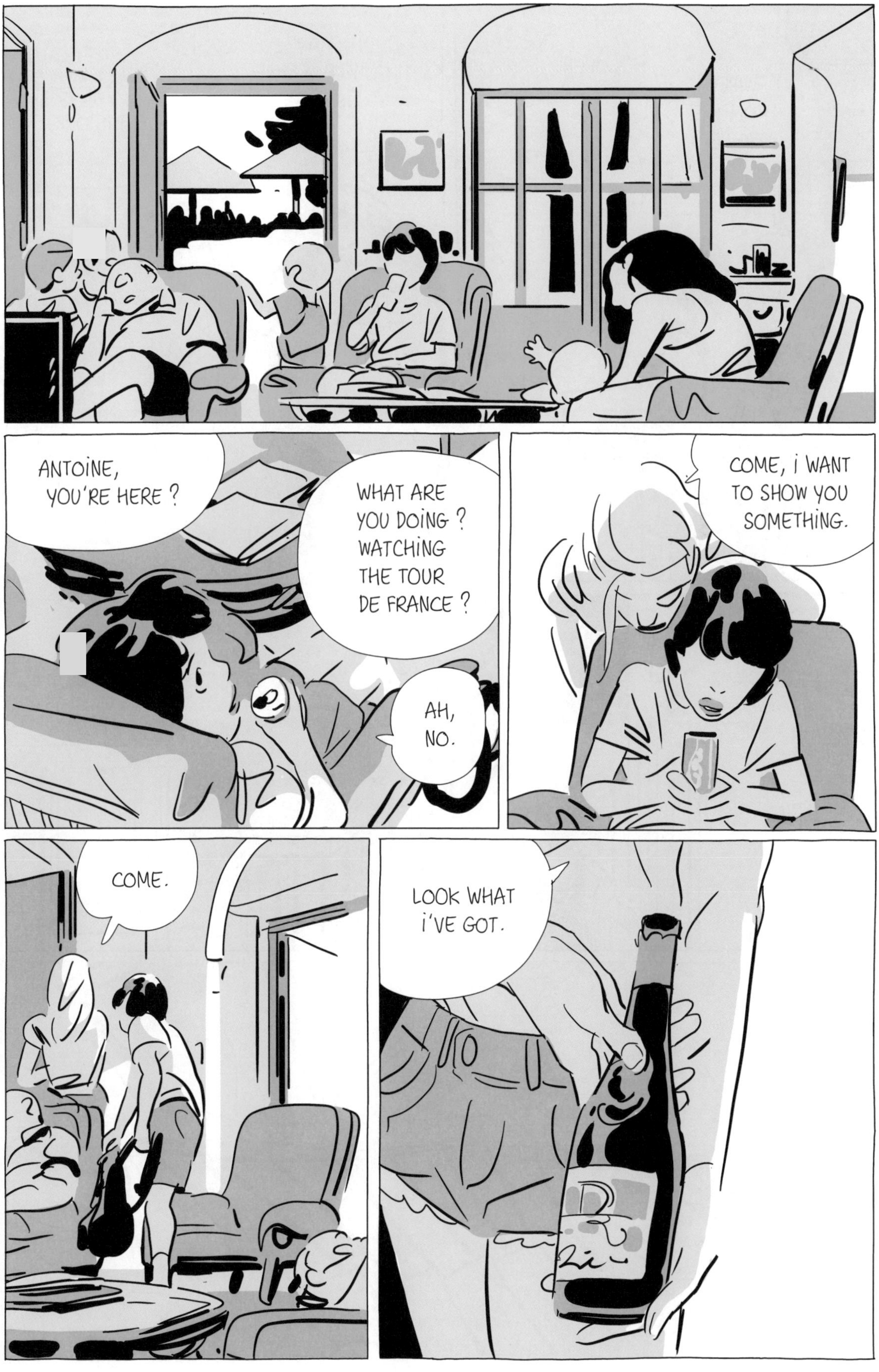
ANTOINE, YOU'RE HERE ?
WHAT ARE YOU DOING ? WATCHING THE TOUR DE FRANCE ?
AH, NO.
COME, I WANT TO SHOW YOU SOMETHING.
COME.
LOOK WHAT I'VE GOT.

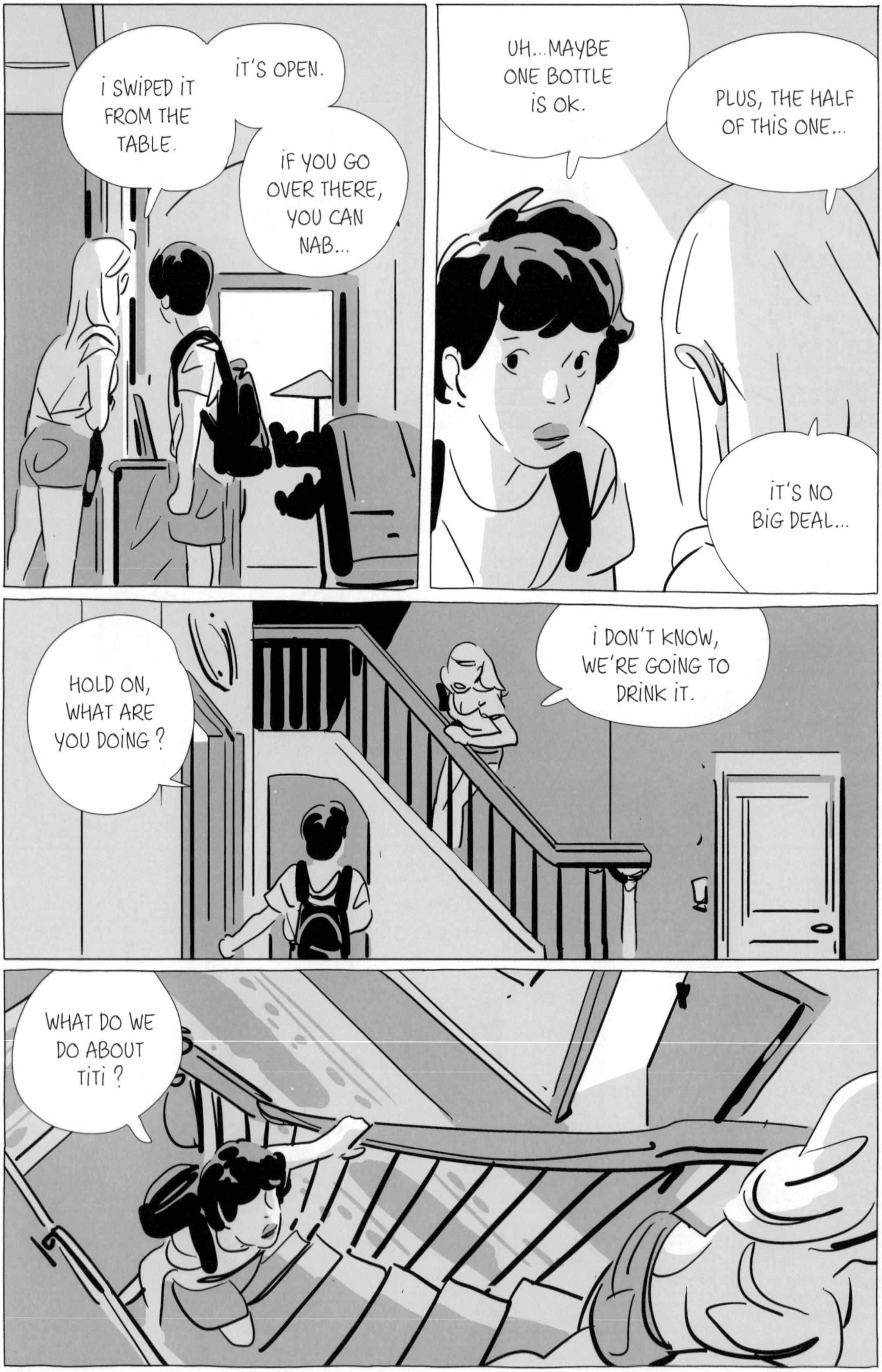
i SWiPED iT FROM THE TABLE.
iT'S OPEN.
iF YOU GO OVER THERE, YOU CAN NAB...
UH...MAYBE ONE BOTTLE iS OK.
PLUS, THE HALF OF THiS ONE...
iT'S NO BiG DEAL...
HOLD ON, WHAT ARE YOU DOiNG?
i DON'T KNOW, WE'RE GOiNG TO DRiNK iT.
WHAT DO WE DO ABOUT TiTi?

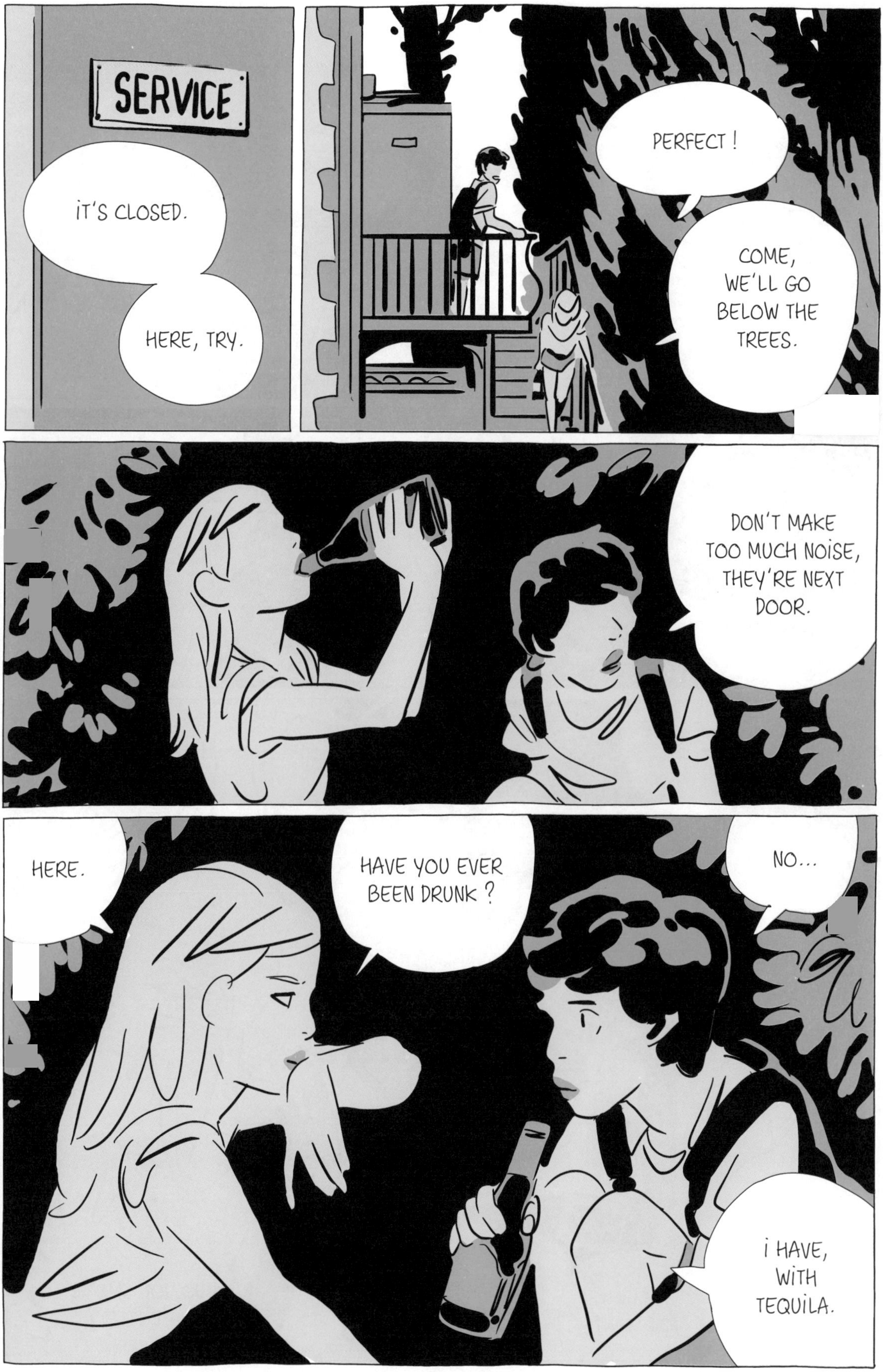
SERVICE
IT'S CLOSED.
HERE, TRY.
PERFECT !
COME, WE'LL GO BELOW THE TREES.
DON'T MAKE TOO MUCH NOISE, THEY'RE NEXT DOOR.
HERE.
HAVE YOU EVER BEEN DRUNK ?
NO...
I HAVE, WITH TEQUILA.

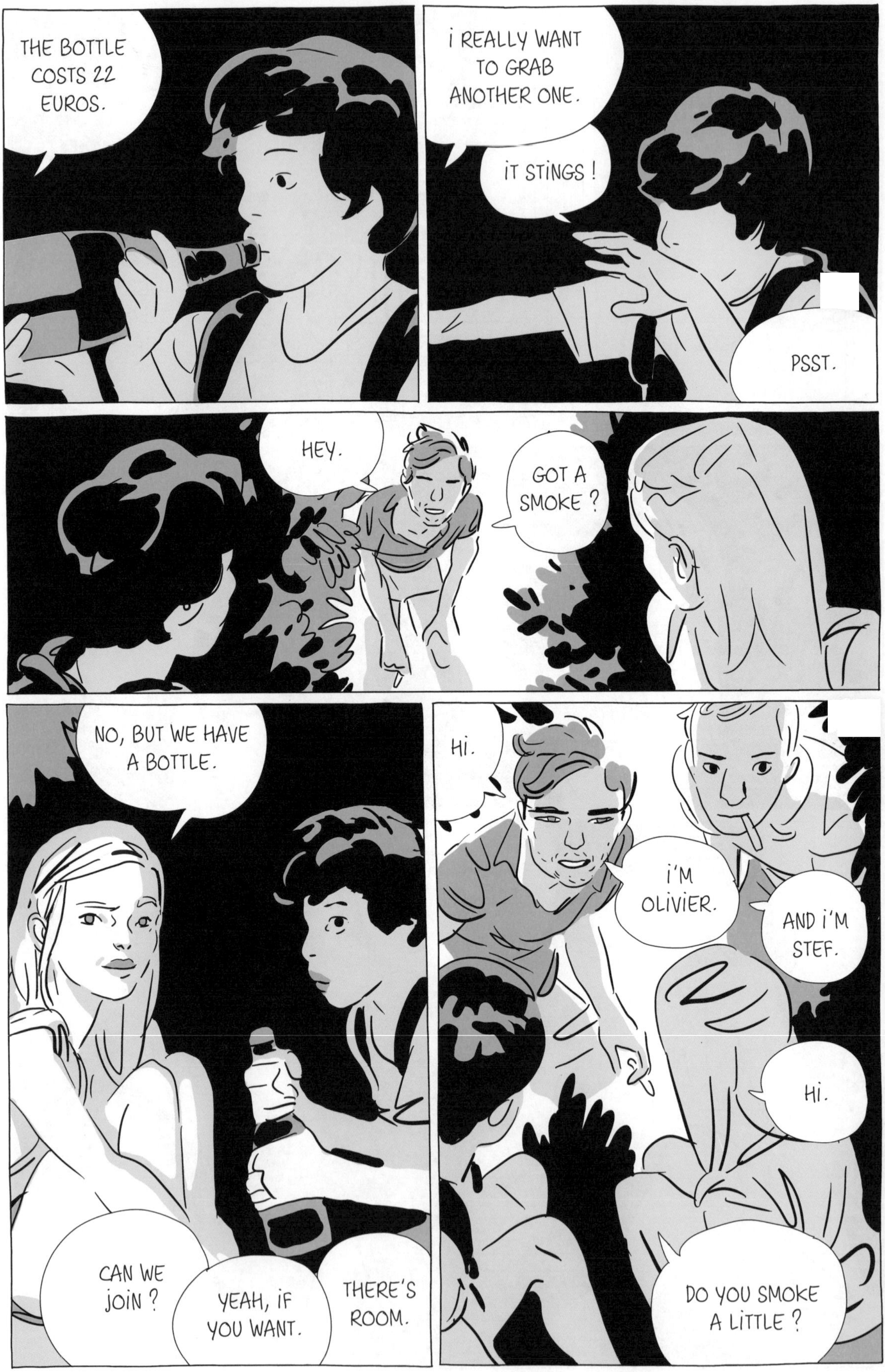
THE BOTTLE COSTS 22 EUROS.
i REALLY WANT TO GRAB ANOTHER ONE.
iT STiNGS !
PSST.
HEY.
GOT A SMOKE ?
NO, BUT WE HAVE A BOTTLE.
CAN WE JOiN ?
YEAH, iF YOU WANT.
THERE'S ROOM.
Hi.
i'M OLiViER.
AND i'M STEF.
Hi.
DO YOU SMOKE A LiTTLE ?

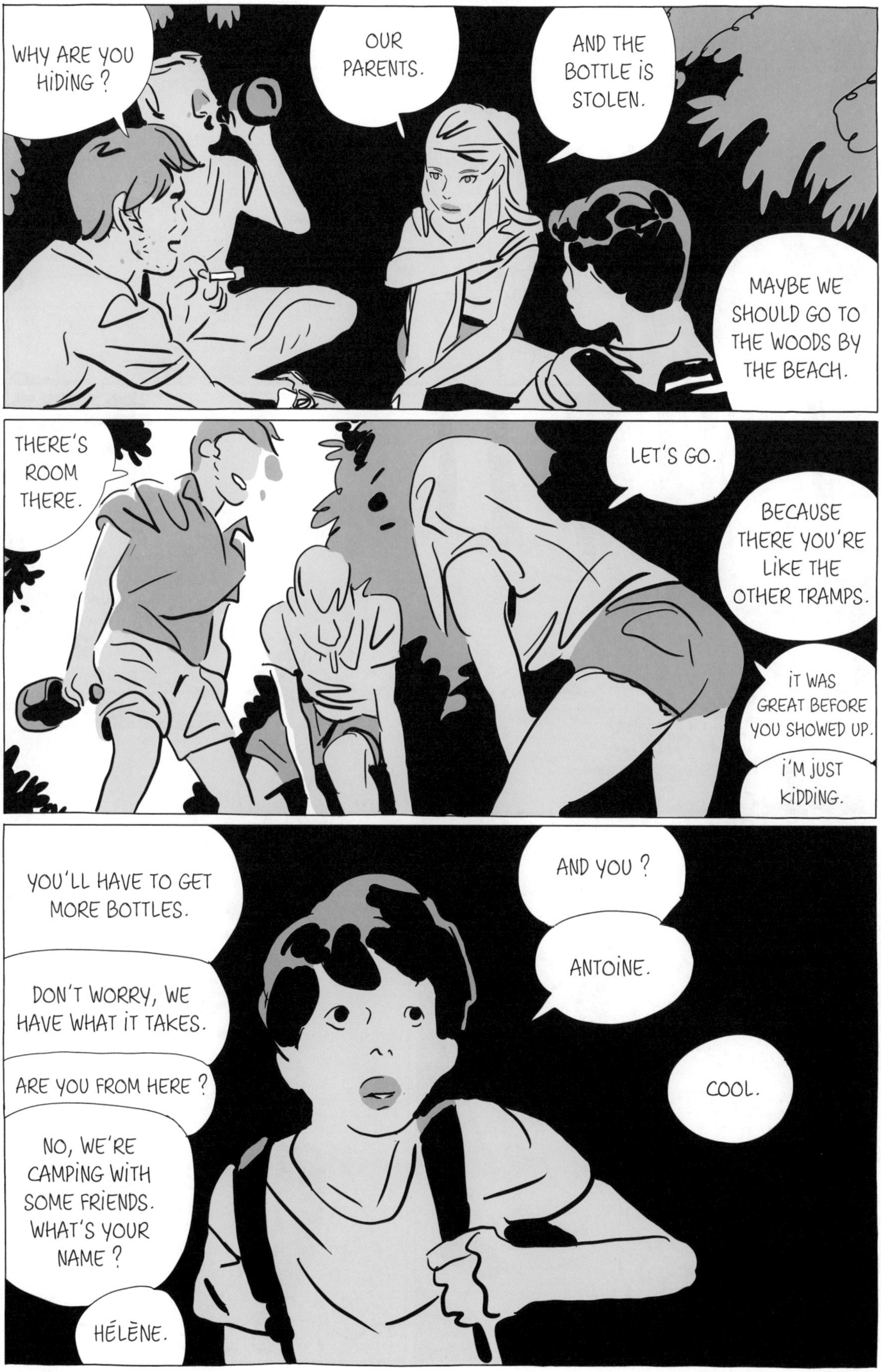
WHY ARE YOU HIDING ?
OUR PARENTS.
AND THE BOTTLE IS STOLEN.
MAYBE WE SHOULD GO TO THE WOODS BY THE BEACH.
THERE'S ROOM THERE.
LET'S GO.
BECAUSE THERE YOU'RE LIKE THE OTHER TRAMPS.
IT WAS GREAT BEFORE YOU SHOWED UP.
I'M JUST KIDDING.
YOU'LL HAVE TO GET MORE BOTTLES.
DON'T WORRY, WE HAVE WHAT IT TAKES.
ARE YOU FROM HERE ?
NO, WE'RE CAMPING WITH SOME FRIENDS. WHAT'S YOUR NAME ?
HÉLÈNE.
AND YOU ?
ANTOINE.
COOL.

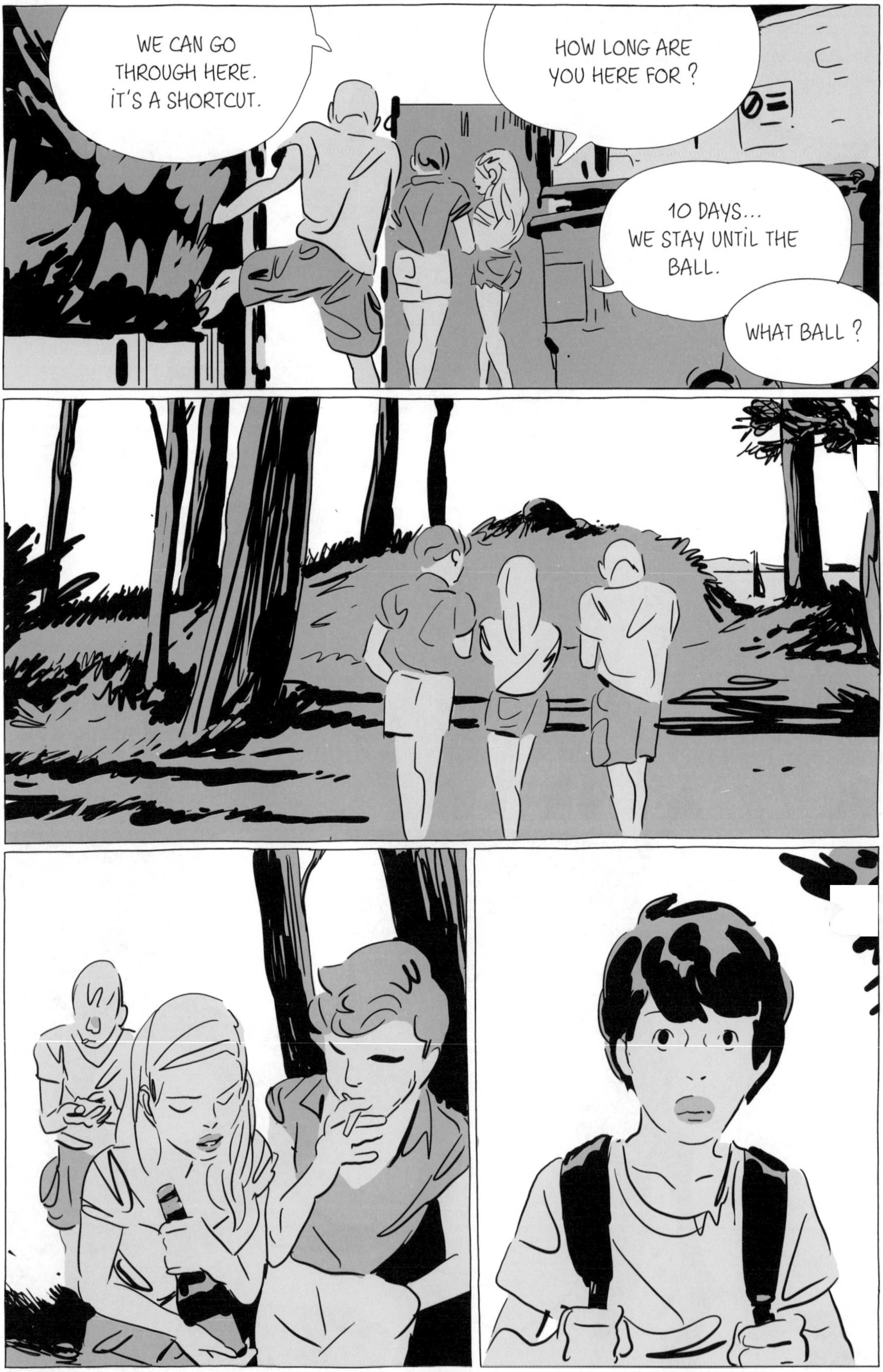
WE CAN GO THROUGH HERE. IT'S A SHORTCUT.
HOW LONG ARE YOU HERE FOR ?
10 DAYS... WE STAY UNTIL THE BALL.
WHAT BALL ?

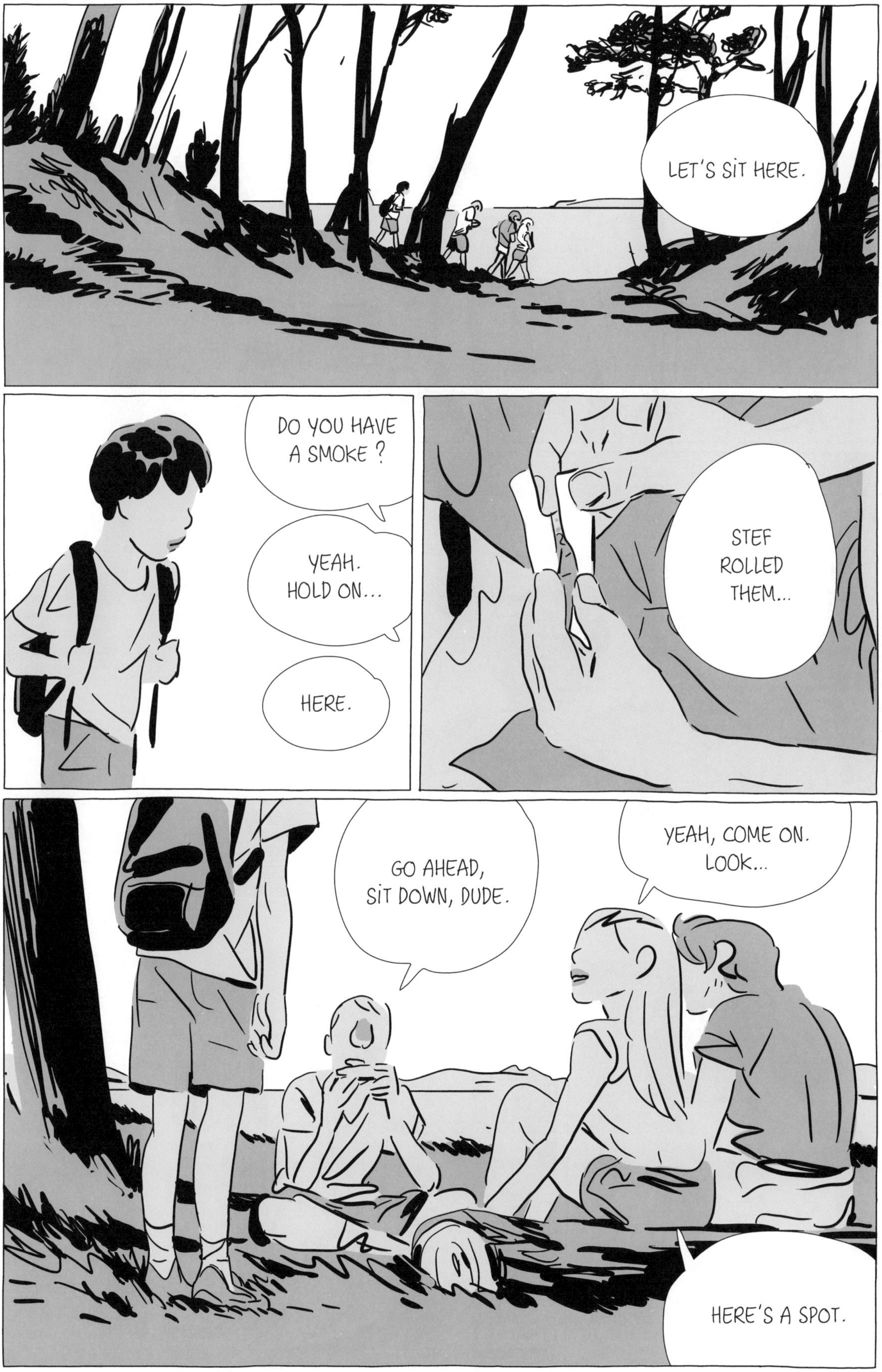
LET'S SIT HERE.
DO YOU HAVE A SMOKE ?
YEAH. HOLD ON...
HERE.
STEF ROLLED THEM...
GO AHEAD, SIT DOWN, DUDE.
YEAH, COME ON. LOOK...
HERE'S A SPOT.

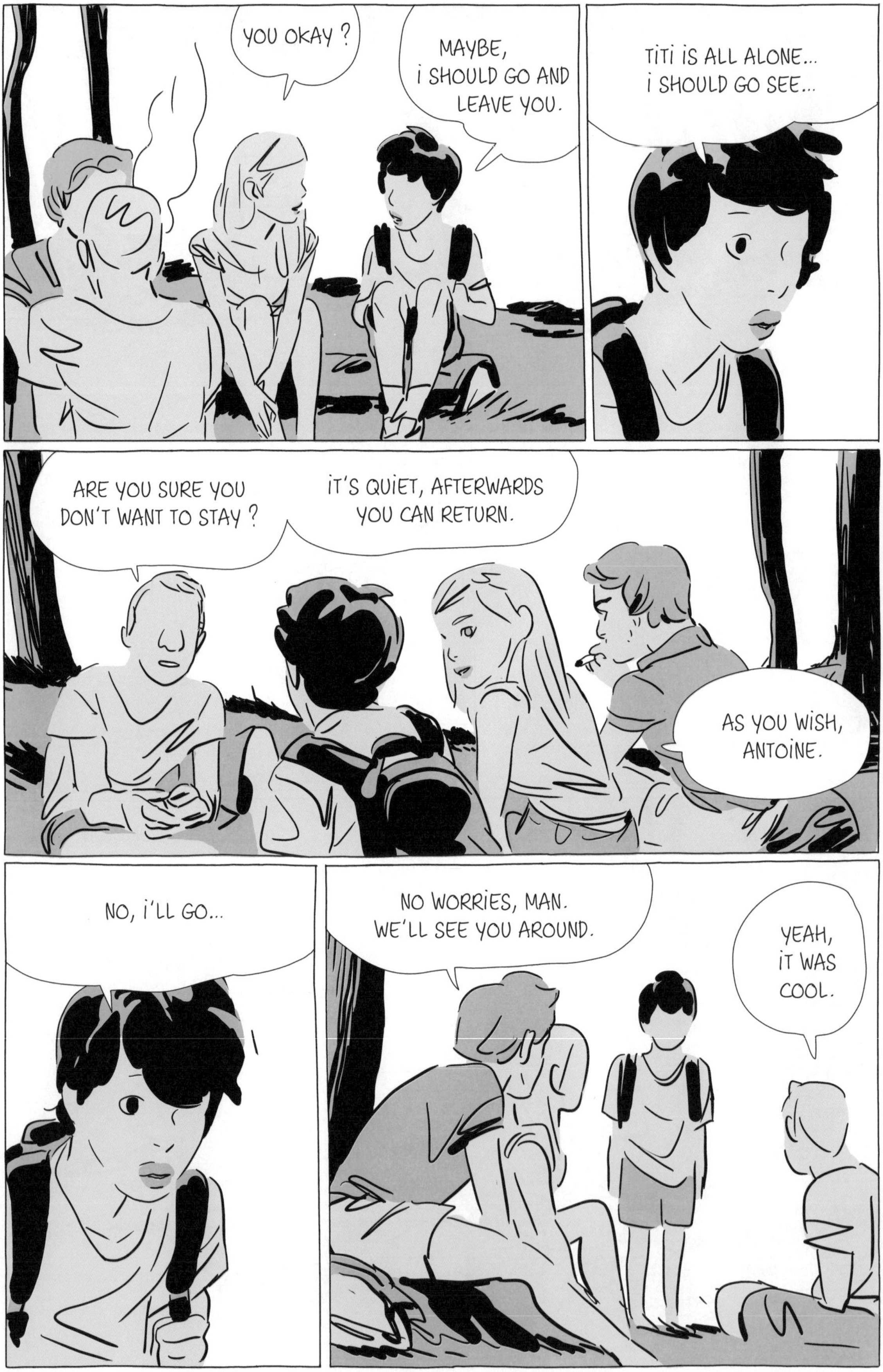
YOU OKAY ?
MAYBE, i SHOULD GO AND LEAVE YOU.
TiTi iS ALL ALONE... i SHOULD GO SEE...
ARE YOU SURE YOU DON'T WANT TO STAY ?
iT'S QUIET, AFTERWARDS YOU CAN RETURN.
AS YOU WiSH, ANTOiNE.
NO, i'LL GO...
NO WORRiES, MAN. WE'LL SEE YOU AROUND.
YEAH, iT WAS COOL.

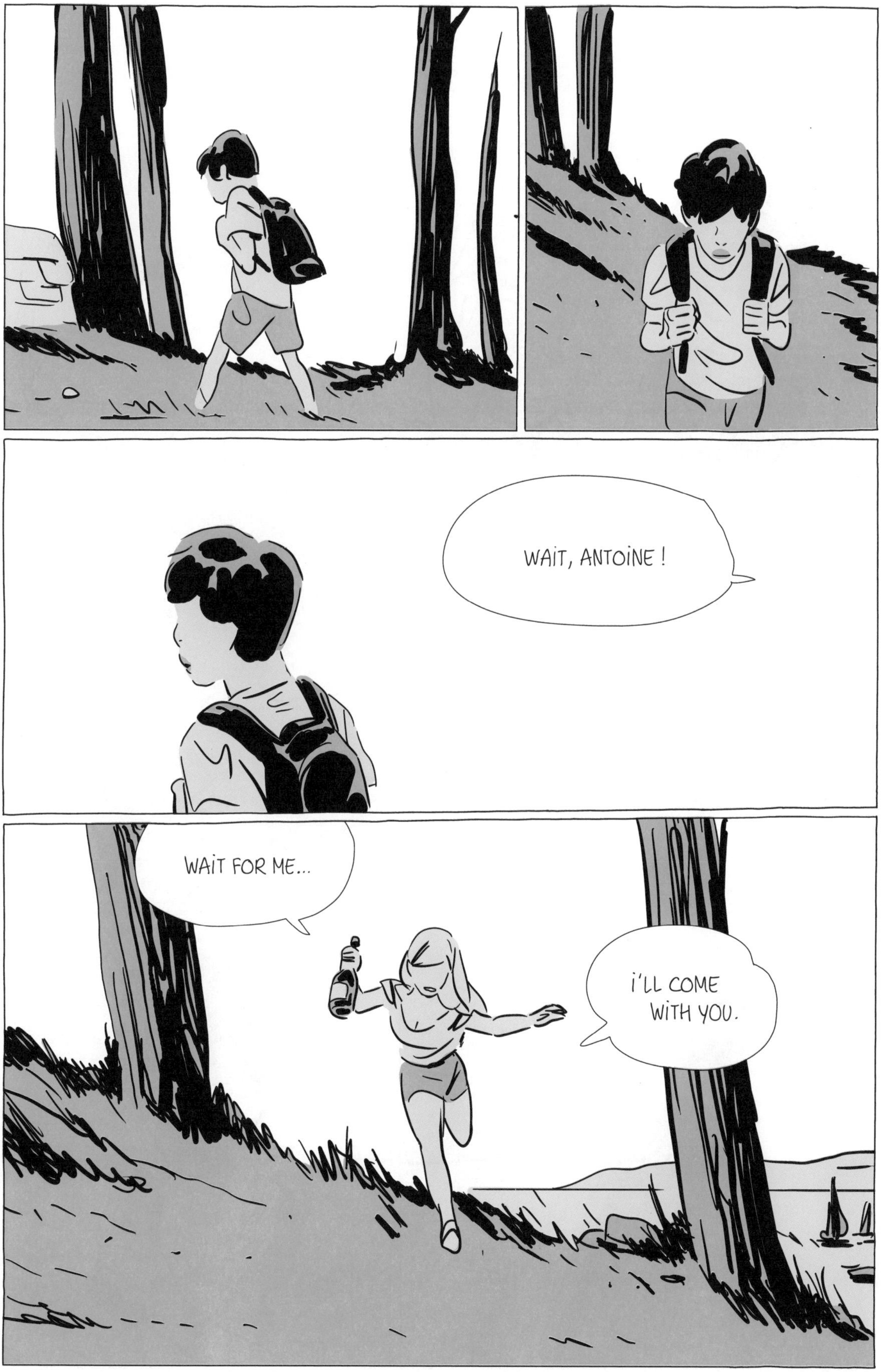
WAIT, ANTOINE !
WAIT FOR ME...
I'LL COME WITH YOU.

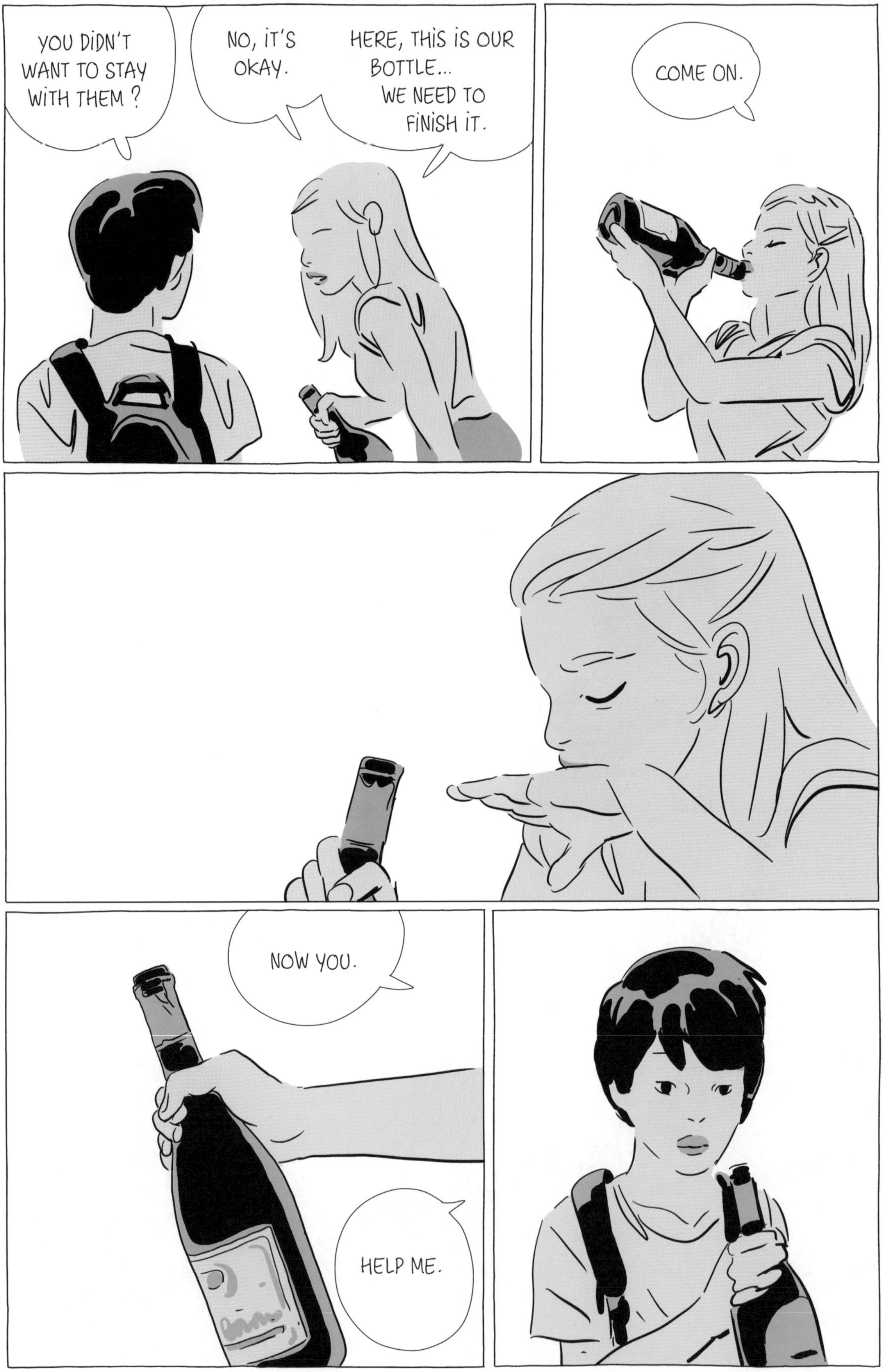
YOU DIDN'T WANT TO STAY WITH THEM ?
NO, IT'S OKAY.
HERE, THIS IS OUR BOTTLE... WE NEED TO FINISH IT.
COME ON.
NOW YOU.
HELP ME.

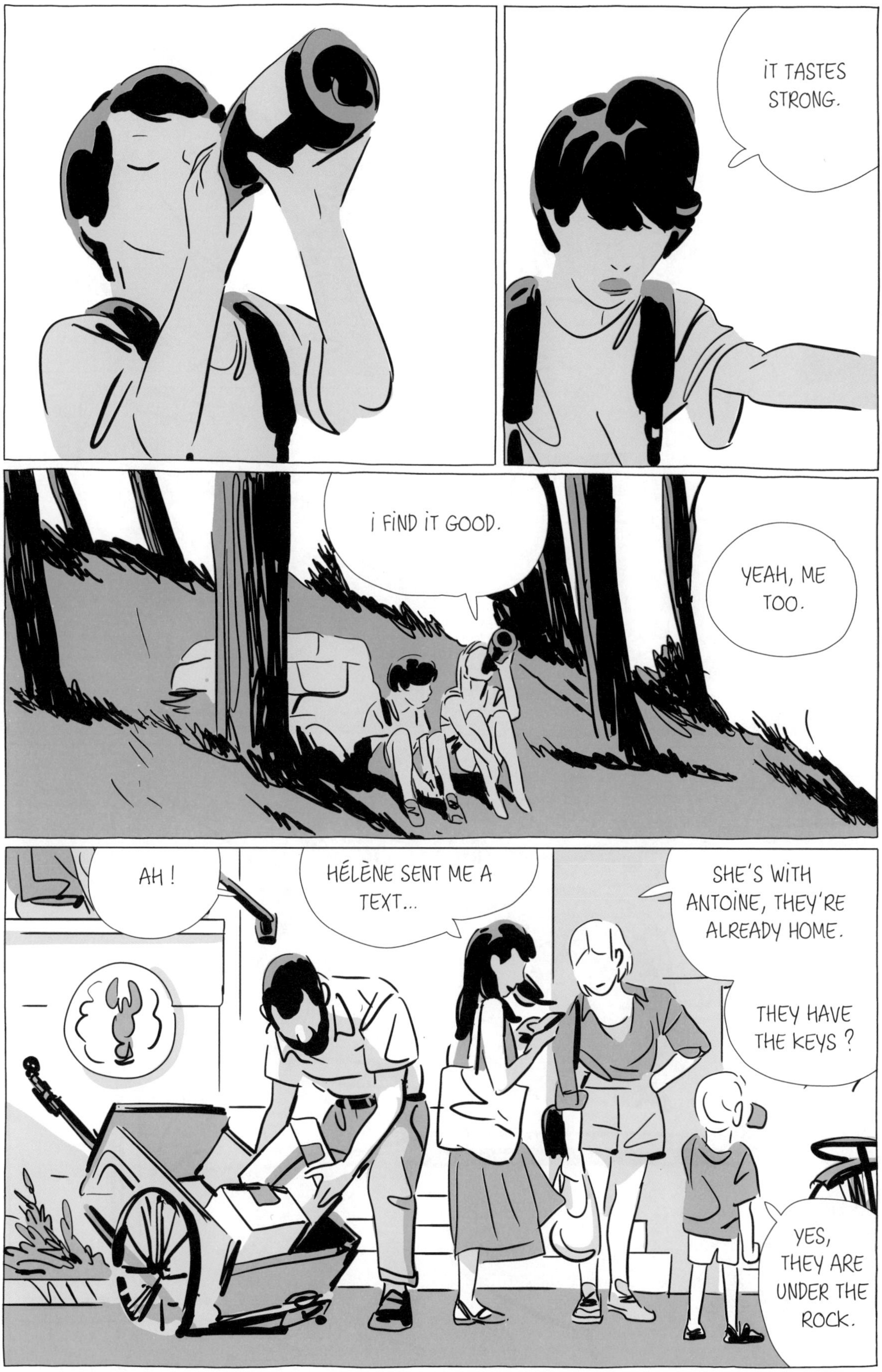
iT TASTES STRONG.
i FIND iT GOOD.
YEAH, ME TOO.
AH !
HÉLÈNE SENT ME A TEXT...
SHE'S WiTH ANTOiNE, THEY'RE ALREADY HOME.
THEY HAVE THE KEYS ?
YES, THEY ARE UNDER THE ROCK.

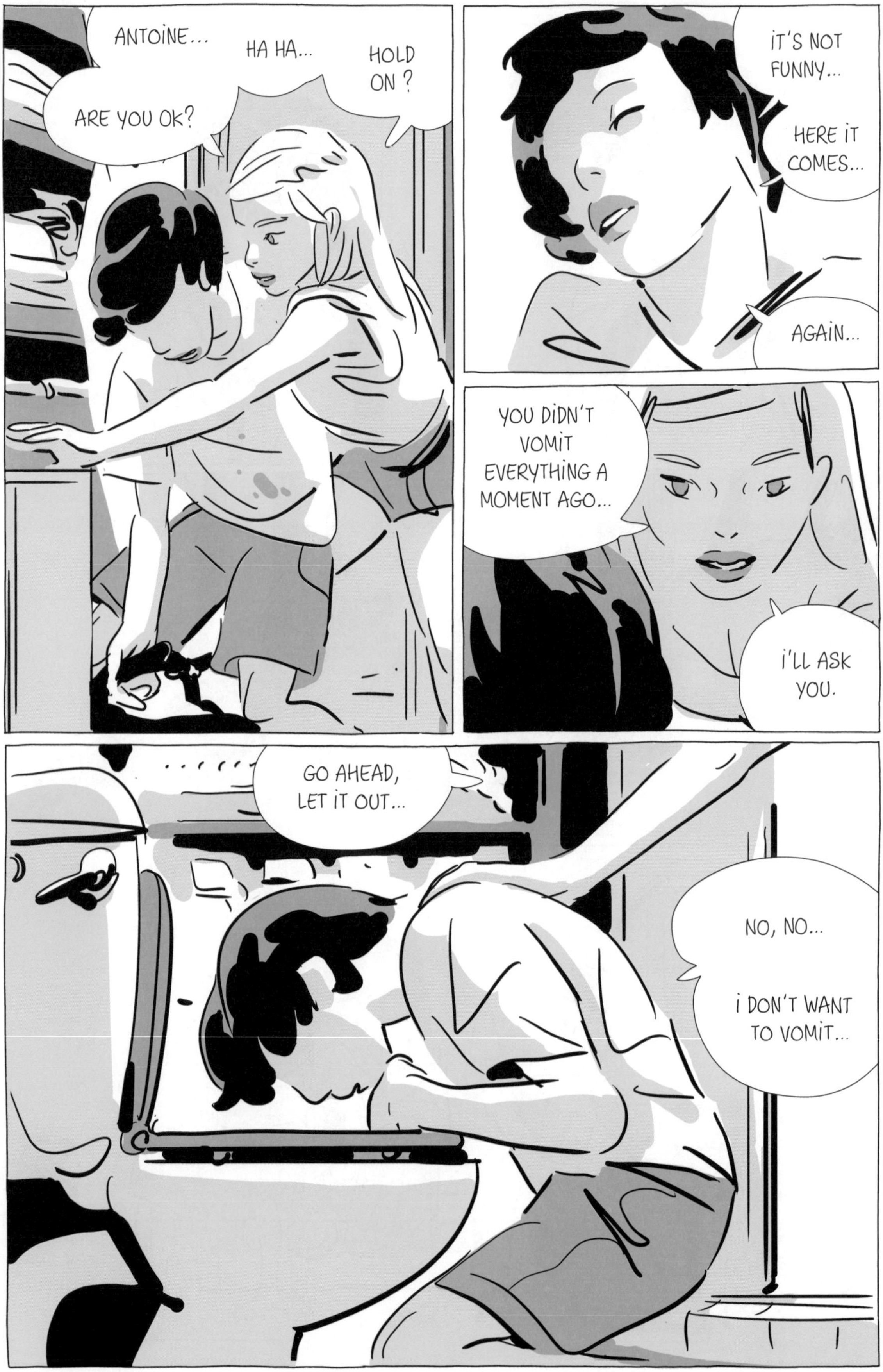
ANTOINE...
ARE YOU OK?
HA HA...
HOLD ON ?
IT'S NOT FUNNY...
HERE IT COMES...
AGAIN...
YOU DIDN'T VOMIT EVERYTHING A MOMENT AGO...
I'LL ASK YOU.
GO AHEAD, LET IT OUT...
NO, NO...
I DON'T WANT TO VOMIT...

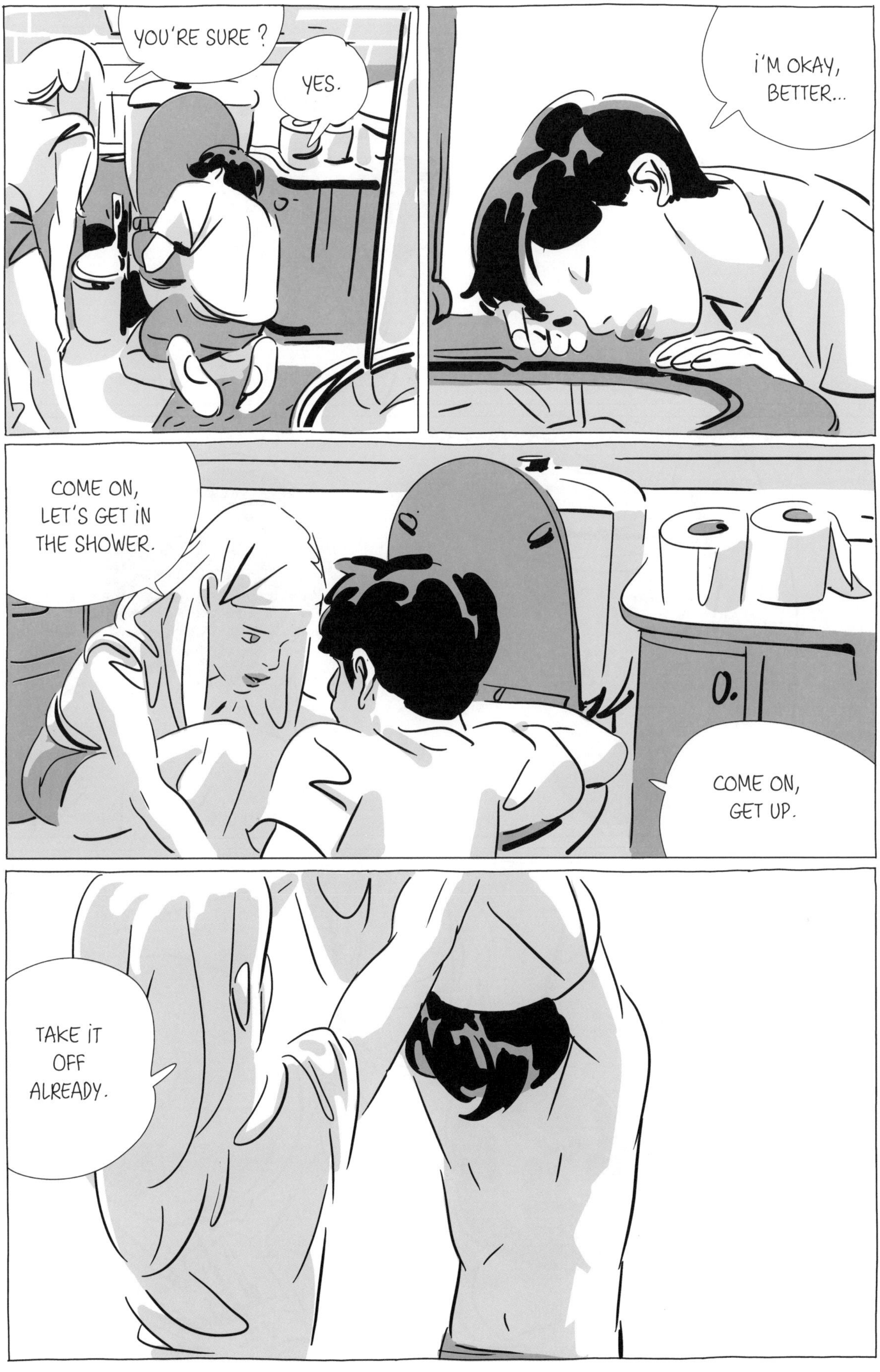
YOU'RE SURE ?
YES.
I'M OKAY, BETTER...
COME ON, LET'S GET IN THE SHOWER.
COME ON, GET UP.
TAKE IT OFF ALREADY.

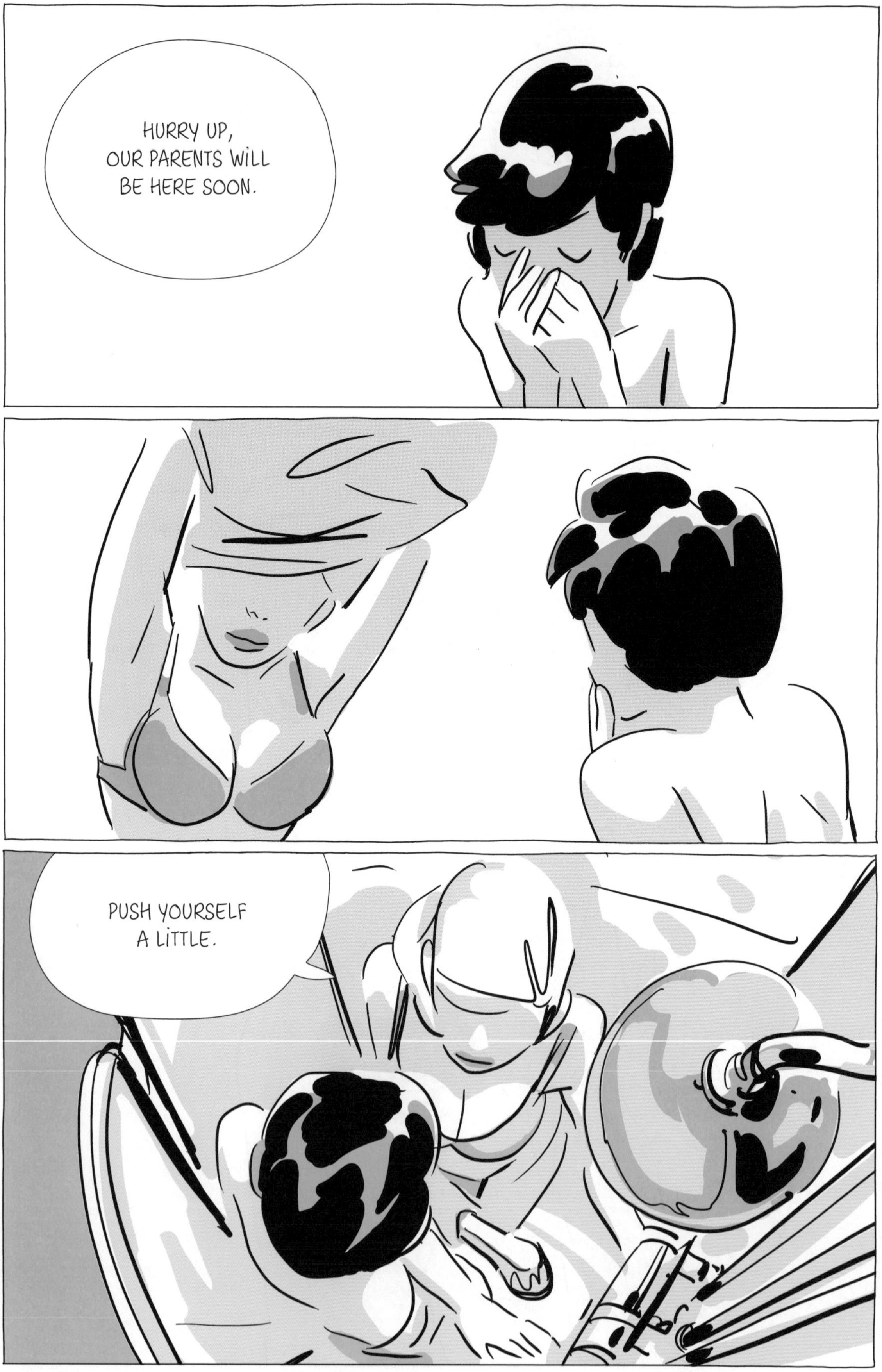
HURRY UP, OUR PARENTS WILL BE HERE SOON.
PUSH YOURSELF A LITTLE.

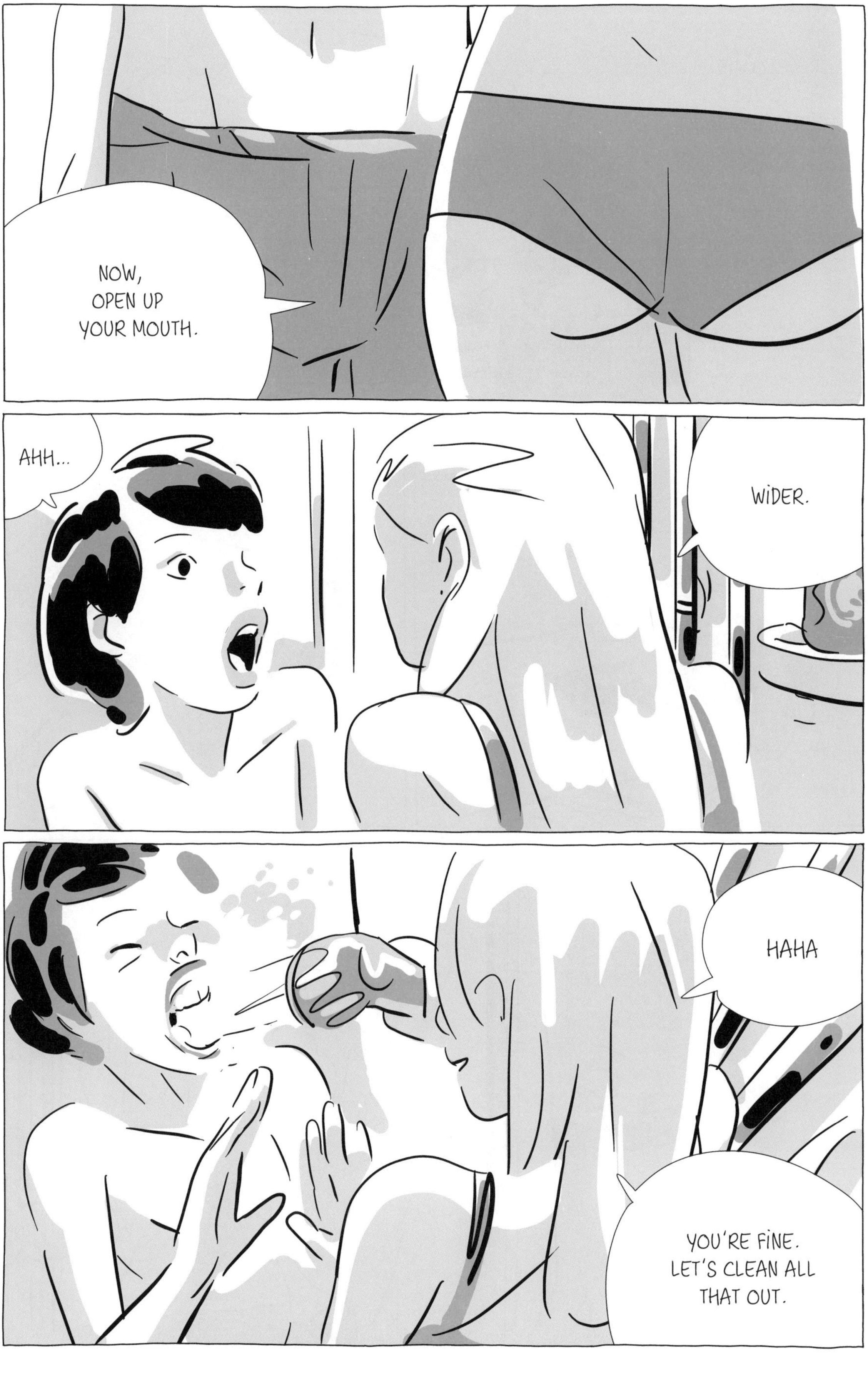
NOW, OPEN UP YOUR MOUTH.
AHH...
WIDER.
HAHA
YOU'RE FINE. LET'S CLEAN ALL THAT OUT.

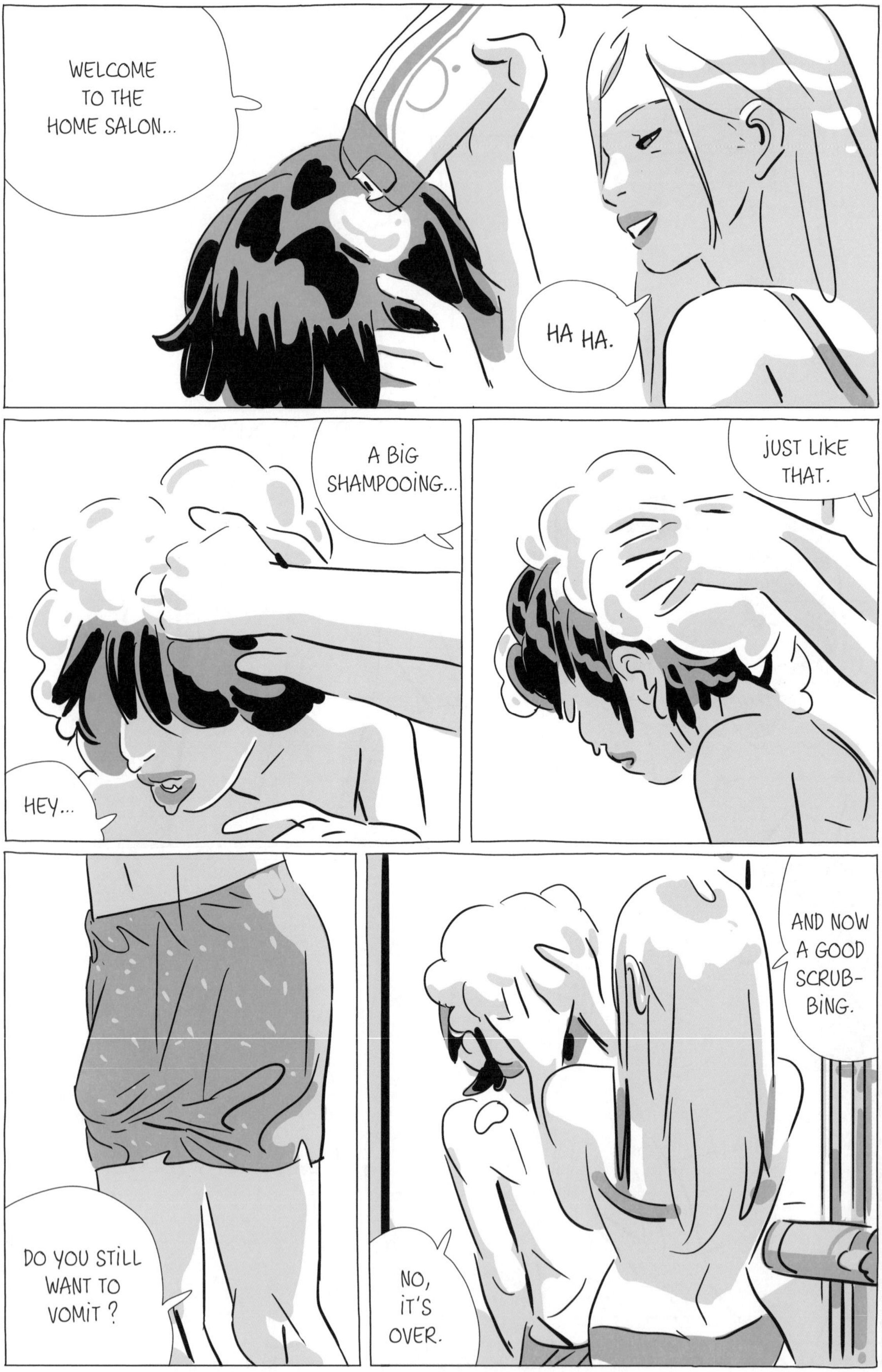
WELCOME TO THE HOME SALON...
HA HA.
A BIG SHAMPOOING...
HEY...
JUST LIKE THAT.
DO YOU STILL WANT TO VOMIT ?
AND NOW A GOOD SCRUB-BING.
NO, IT'S OVER.

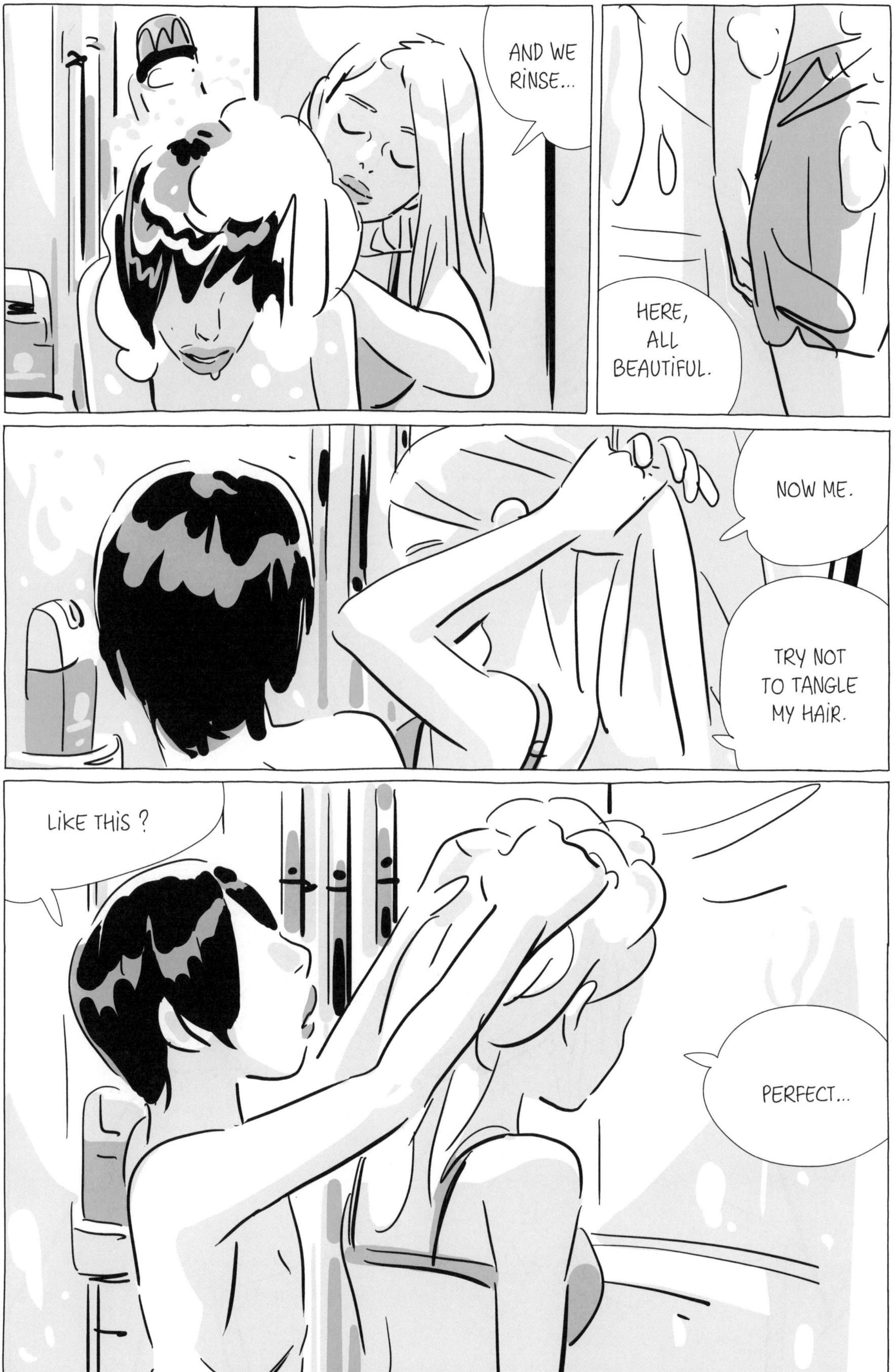
AND WE RINSE...
HERE, ALL BEAUTIFUL.
NOW ME.
TRY NOT TO TANGLE MY HAIR.
LIKE THIS ?
PERFECT...

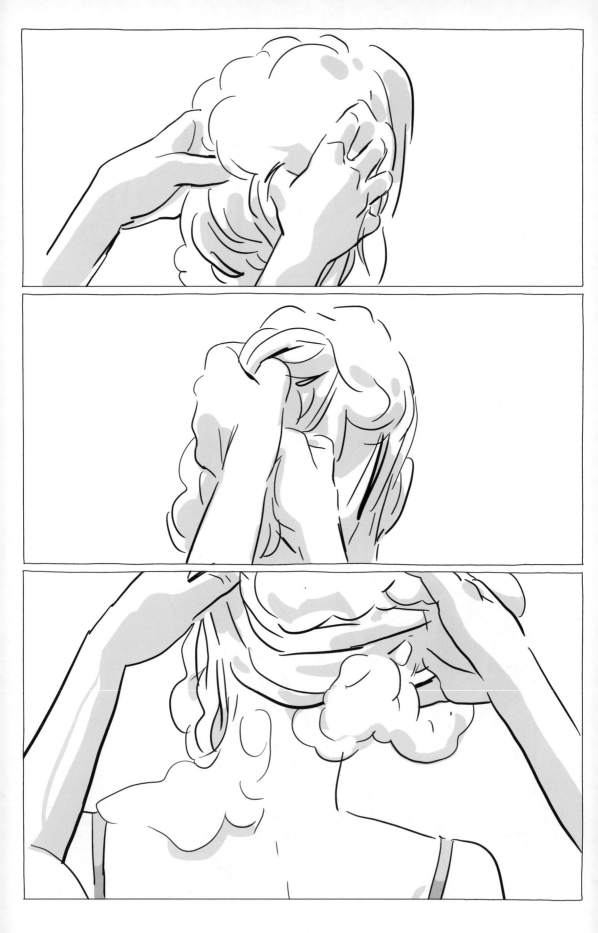

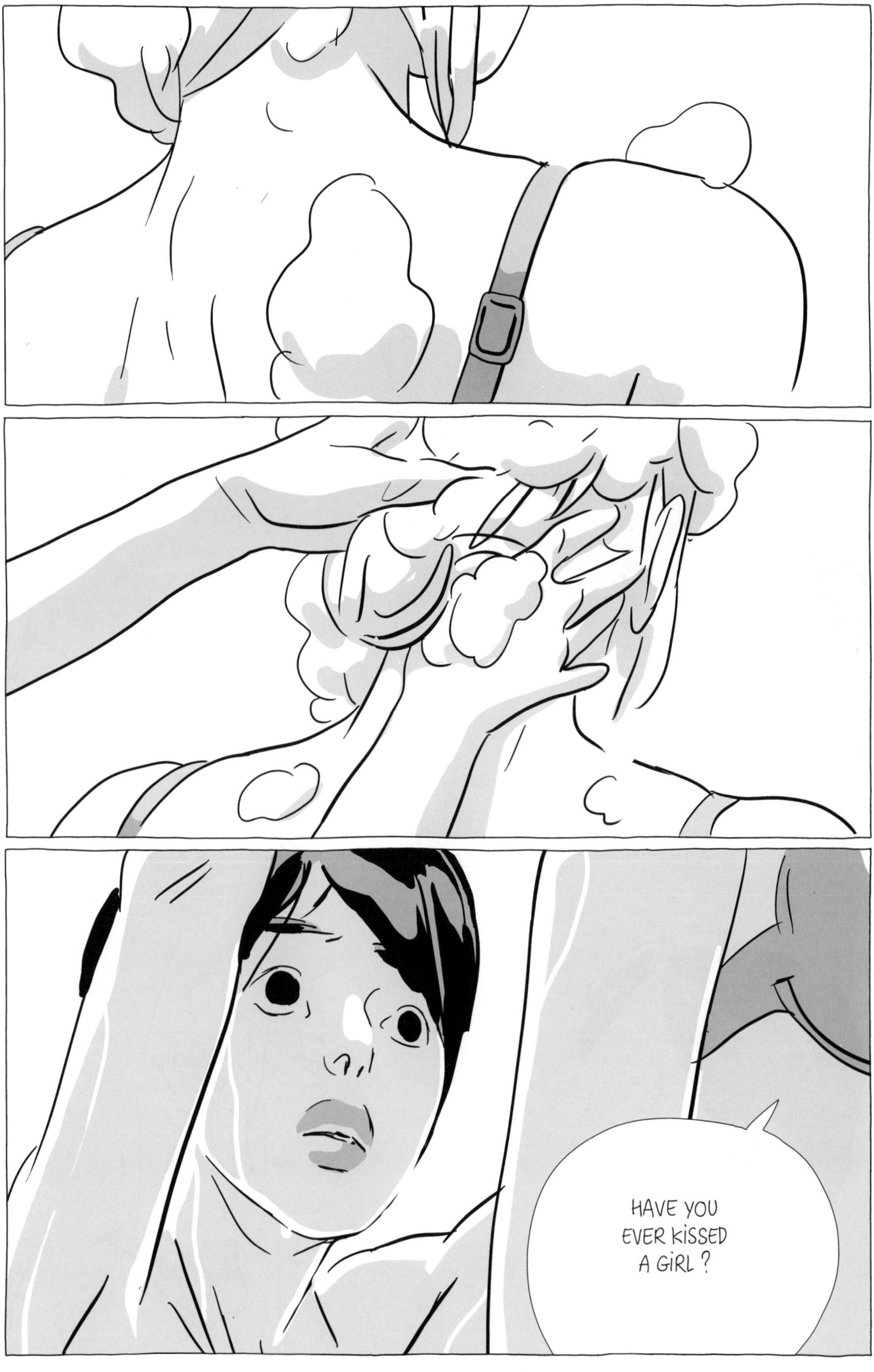
HAVE YOU EVER KISSED A GIRL ?

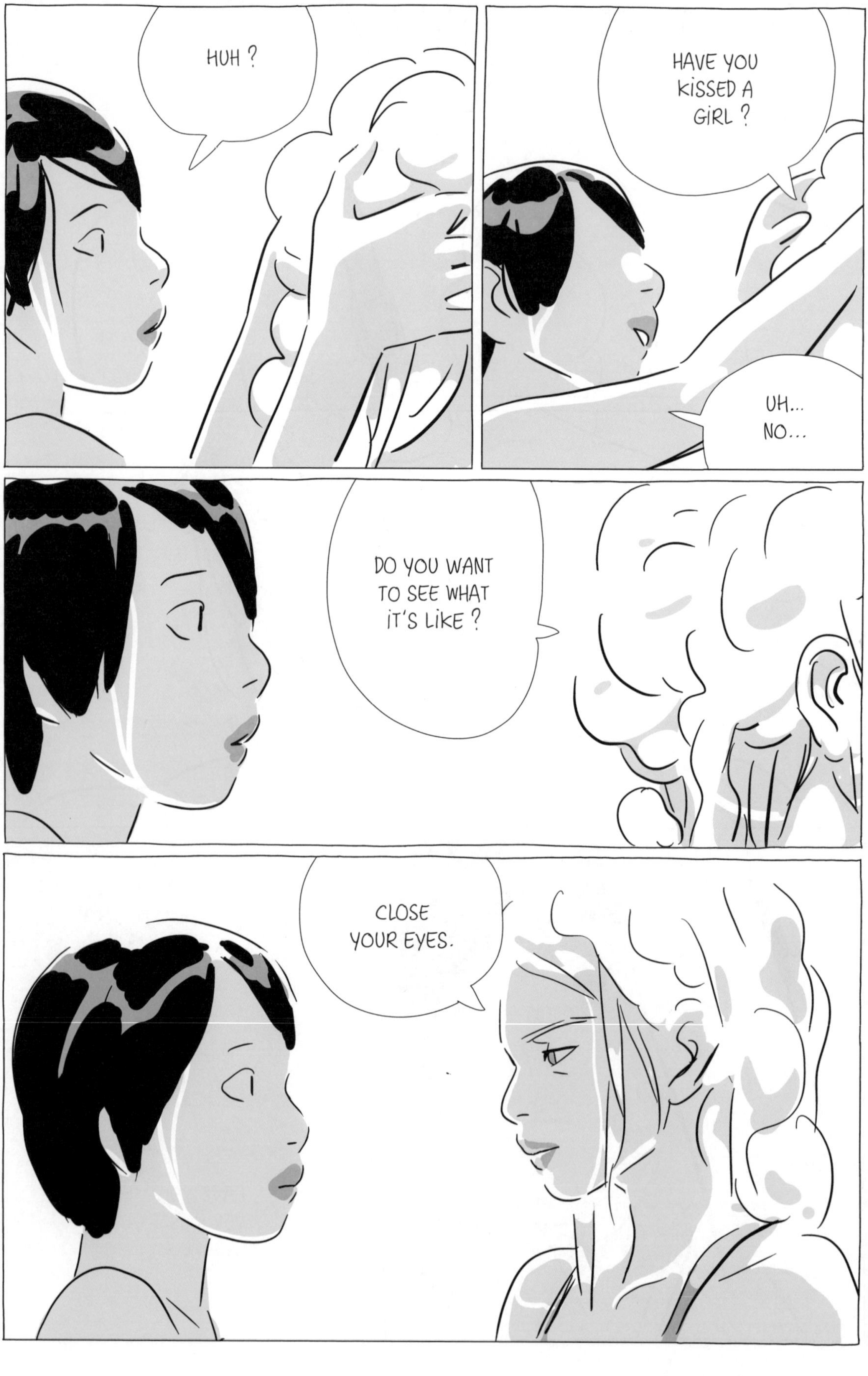
HUH ?
HAVE YOU KISSED A GIRL ?
UH... NO...
DO YOU WANT TO SEE WHAT IT'S LIKE ?
CLOSE YOUR EYES.

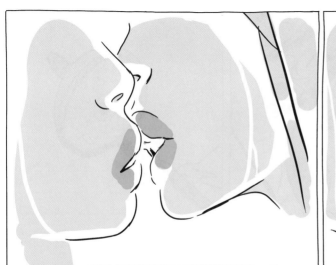
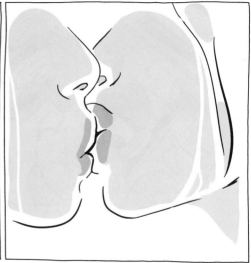

SO ?

UH...

AH...i THINK
THEY'VE
RETURNED...

WE SHOULD
RINSE QUICKLY.

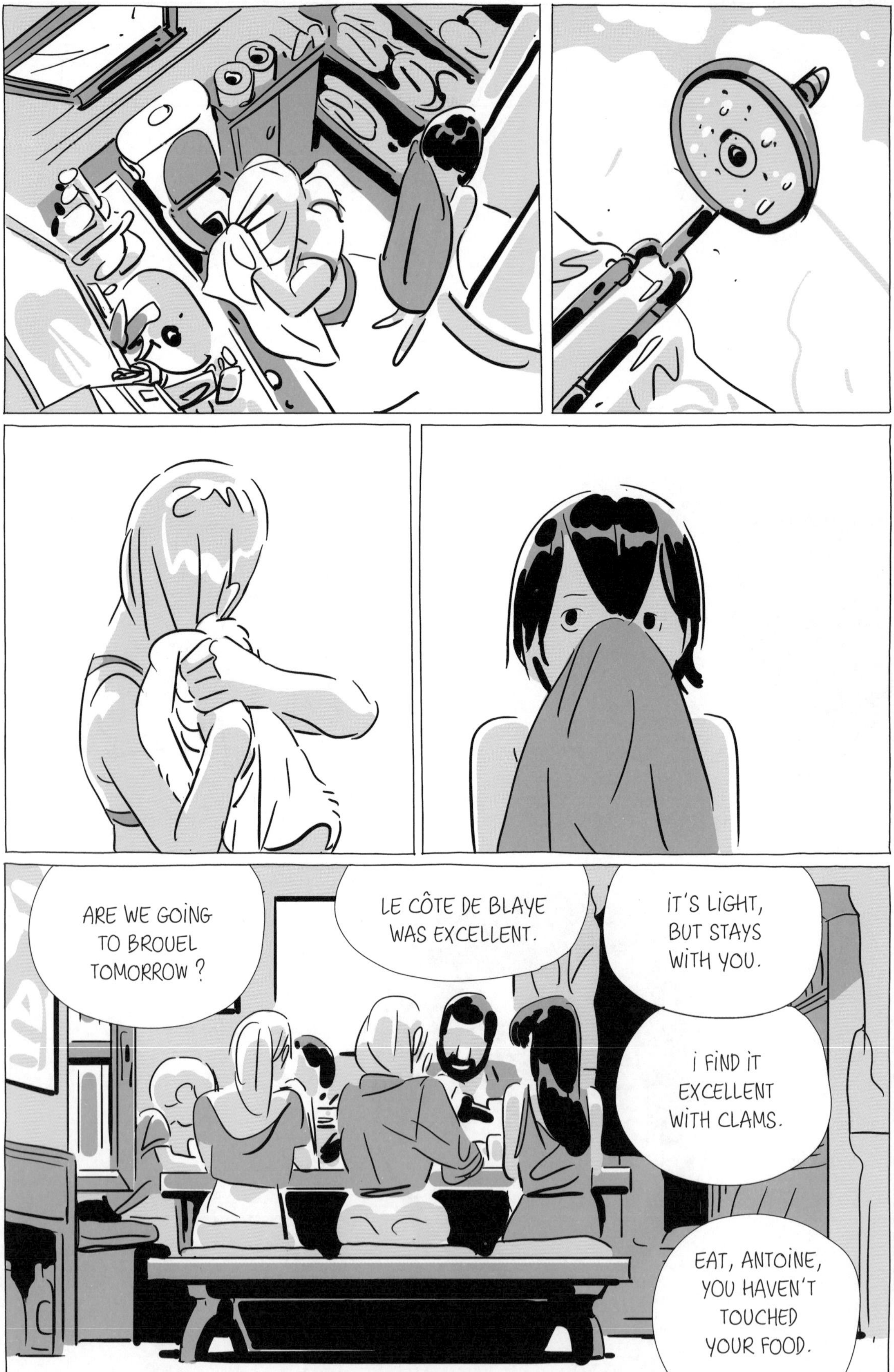
ARE WE GOING TO BROUEL TOMORROW ?
LE CÔTE DE BLAYE WAS EXCELLENT.
IT'S LIGHT, BUT STAYS WITH YOU.
I FIND IT EXCELLENT WITH CLAMS.
EAT, ANTOINE, YOU HAVEN'T TOUCHED YOUR FOOD.

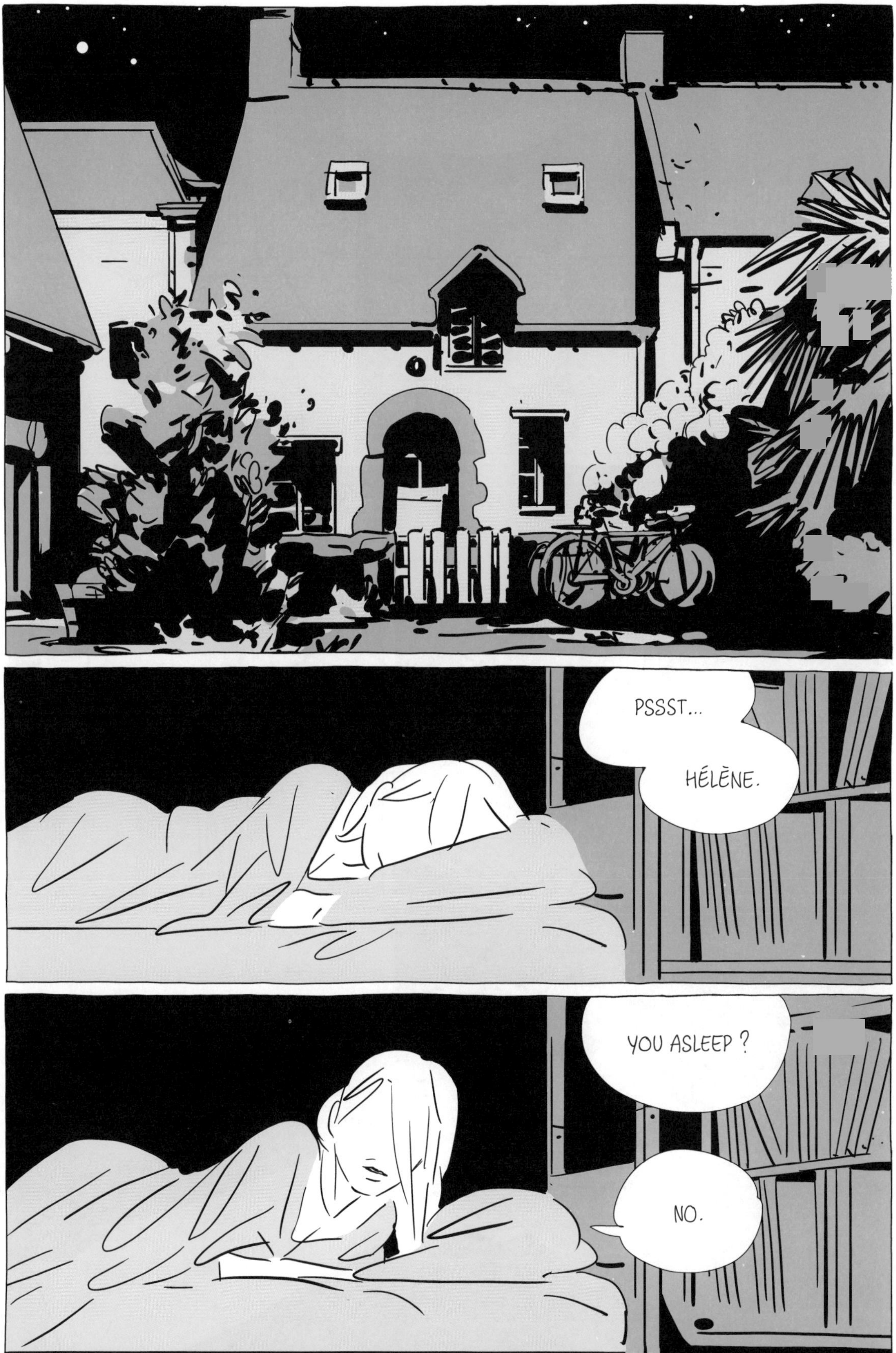
PSSST...
HÉLÈNE.
YOU ASLEEP ?
NO.

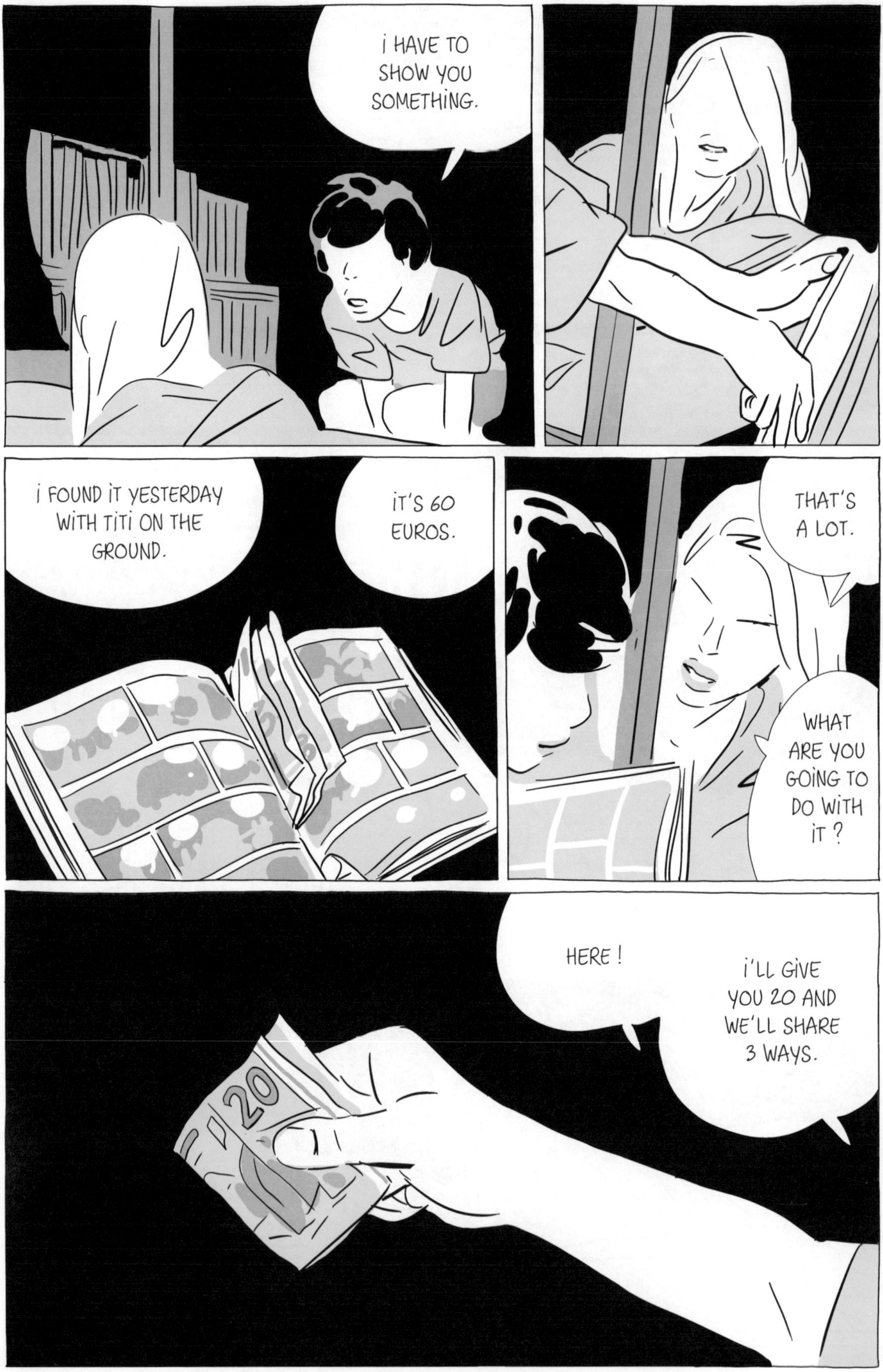
i HAVE TO SHOW YOU SOMETHiNG.
i FOUND iT YESTERDAY WiTH TiTi ON THE GROUND.
iT'S 60 EUROS.
THAT'S A LOT.
WHAT ARE YOU GOiNG TO DO WiTH iT ?
HERE !
i'LL GiVE YOU 20 AND WE'LL SHARE 3 WAYS.

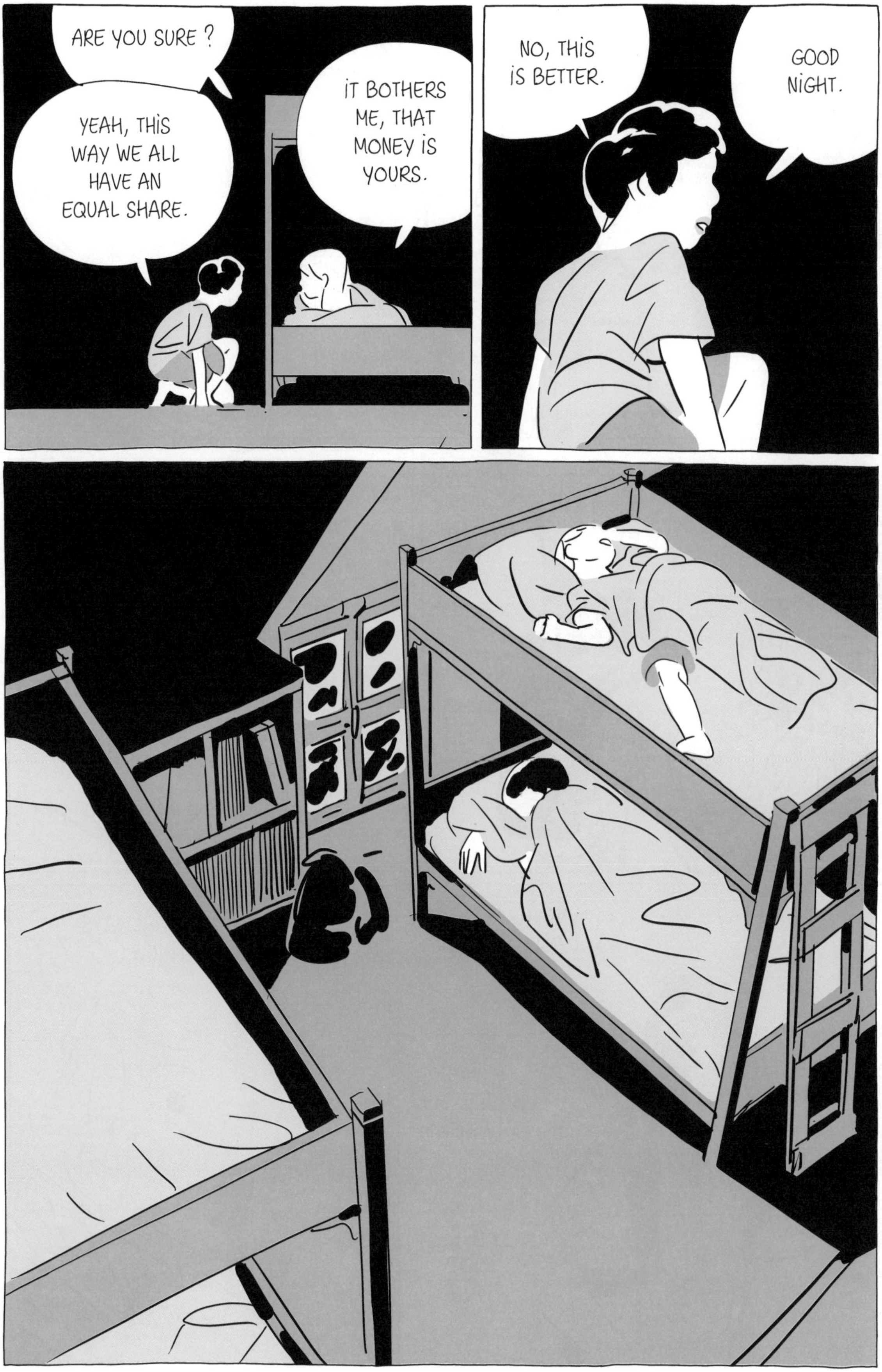
ARE YOU SURE ?
YEAH, THIS WAY WE ALL HAVE AN EQUAL SHARE.
IT BOTHERS ME, THAT MONEY IS YOURS.
NO, THIS IS BETTER.
GOOD NIGHT.

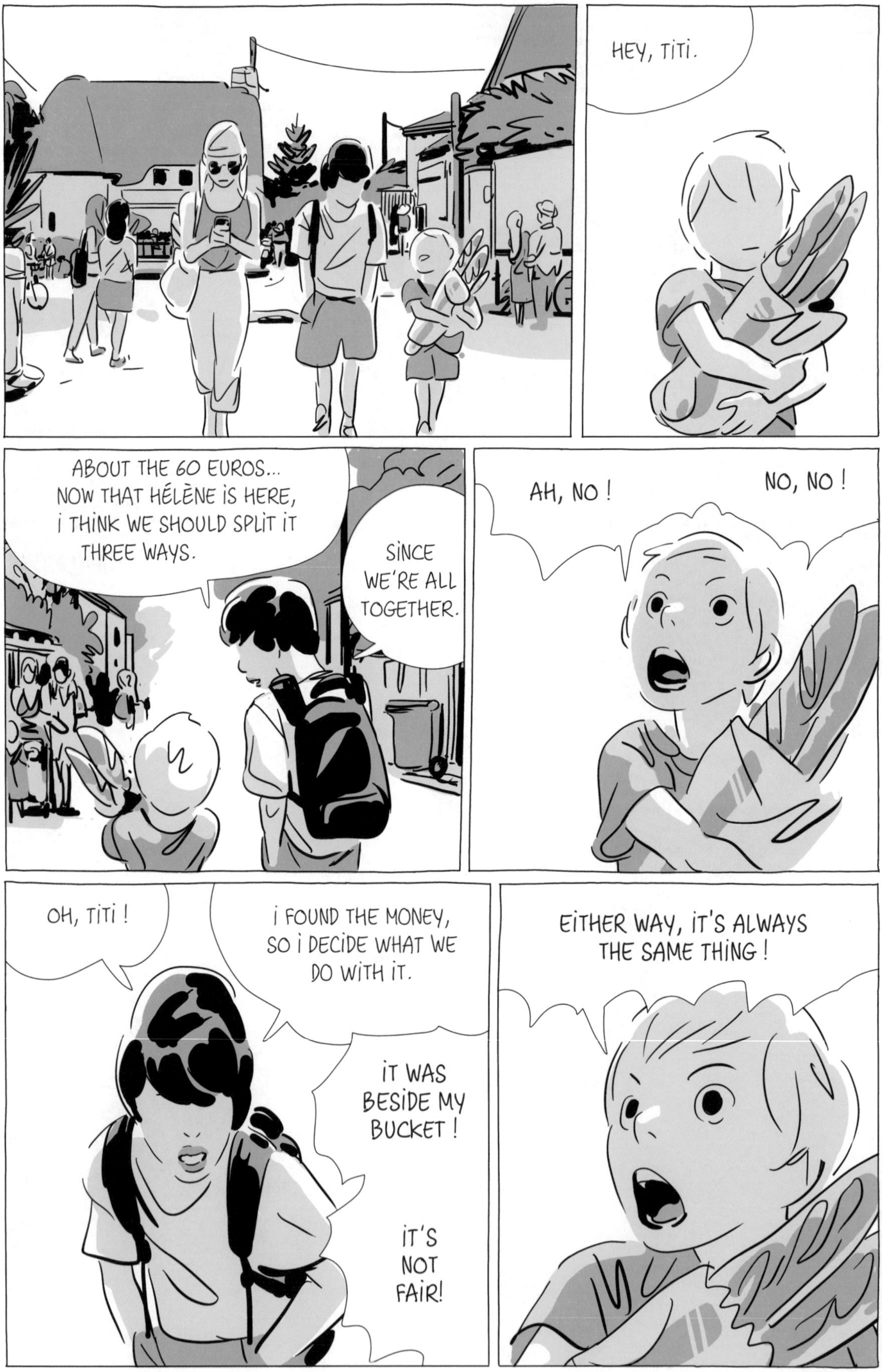
HEY, TITI.
ABOUT THE 60 EUROS... NOW THAT HÉLÈNE IS HERE, I THINK WE SHOULD SPLIT IT THREE WAYS.
SINCE WE'RE ALL TOGETHER.
AH, NO!
NO, NO!
OH, TITI!
I FOUND THE MONEY, SO I DECIDE WHAT WE DO WITH IT.
IT WAS BESIDE MY BUCKET!
IT'S NOT FAIR!
EITHER WAY, IT'S ALWAYS THE SAME THING!

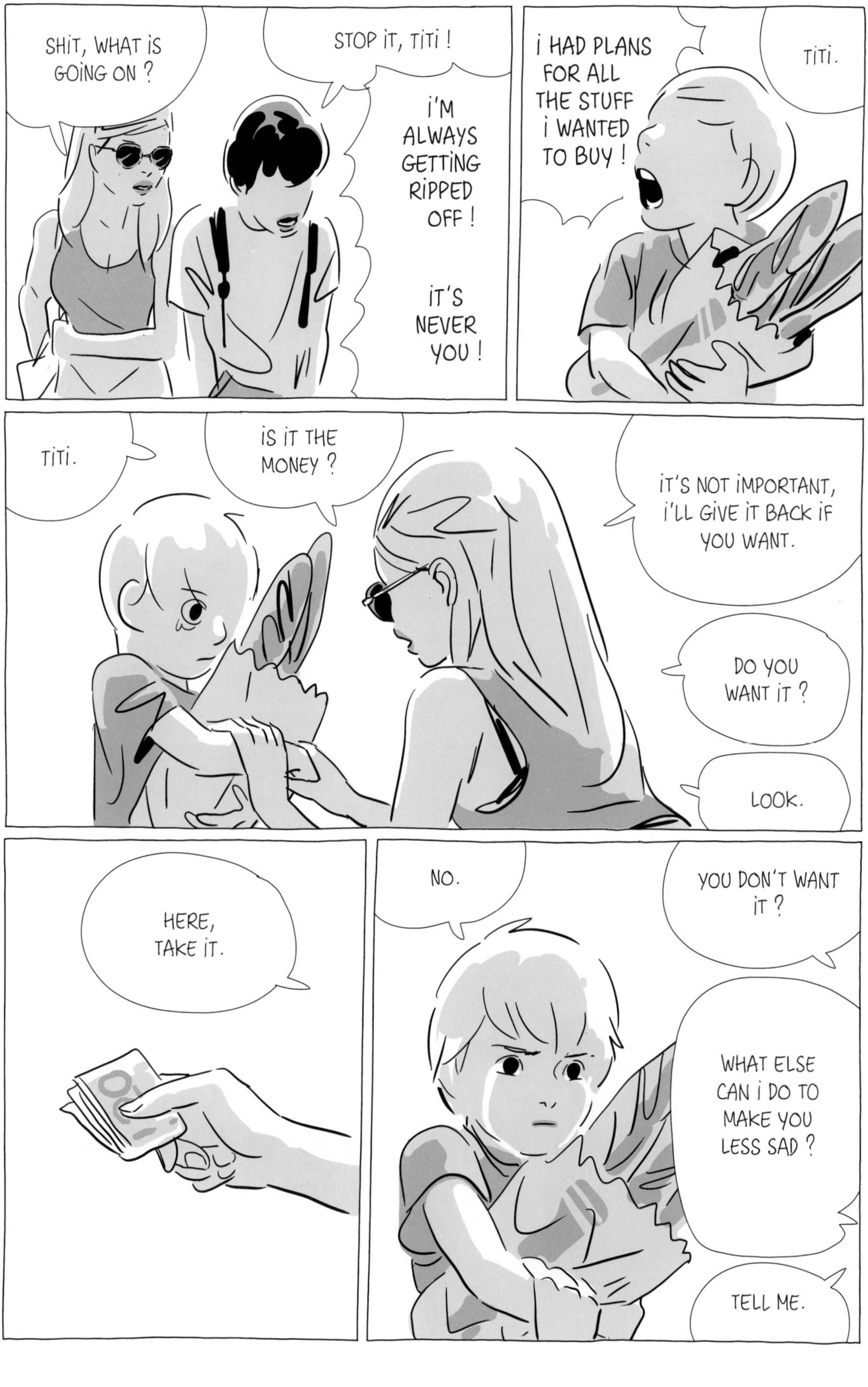
SHIT, WHAT IS GOING ON ?
STOP IT, TITI !
I'M ALWAYS GETTING RIPPED OFF !
IT'S NEVER YOU !
I HAD PLANS FOR ALL THE STUFF I WANTED TO BUY !
TITI.
TITI.
IS IT THE MONEY ?
IT'S NOT IMPORTANT, I'LL GIVE IT BACK IF YOU WANT.
DO YOU WANT IT ?
LOOK.
HERE, TAKE IT.
NO.
YOU DON'T WANT IT ?
WHAT ELSE CAN I DO TO MAKE YOU LESS SAD ?
TELL ME.

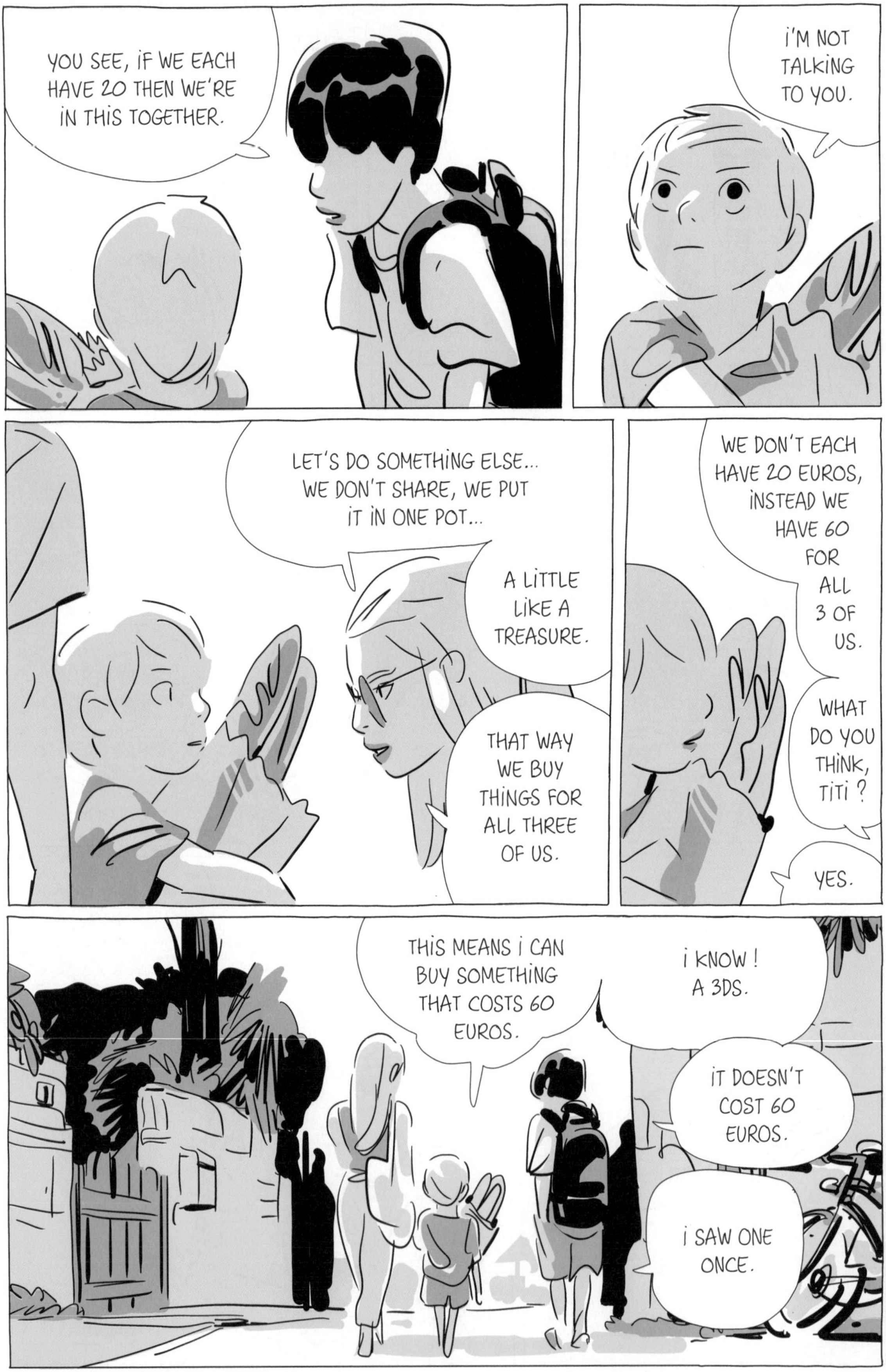
YOU SEE, IF WE EACH HAVE 20 THEN WE'RE IN THIS TOGETHER.
I'M NOT TALKING TO YOU.
LET'S DO SOMETHING ELSE... WE DON'T SHARE, WE PUT IT IN ONE POT...
A LITTLE LIKE A TREASURE.
THAT WAY WE BUY THINGS FOR ALL THREE OF US.
WE DON'T EACH HAVE 20 EUROS, INSTEAD WE HAVE 60 FOR ALL 3 OF US.
WHAT DO YOU THINK, TITI ?
YES.
THIS MEANS I CAN BUY SOMETHING THAT COSTS 60 EUROS.
I KNOW ! A 3DS.
IT DOESN'T COST 60 EUROS.
I SAW ONE ONCE.

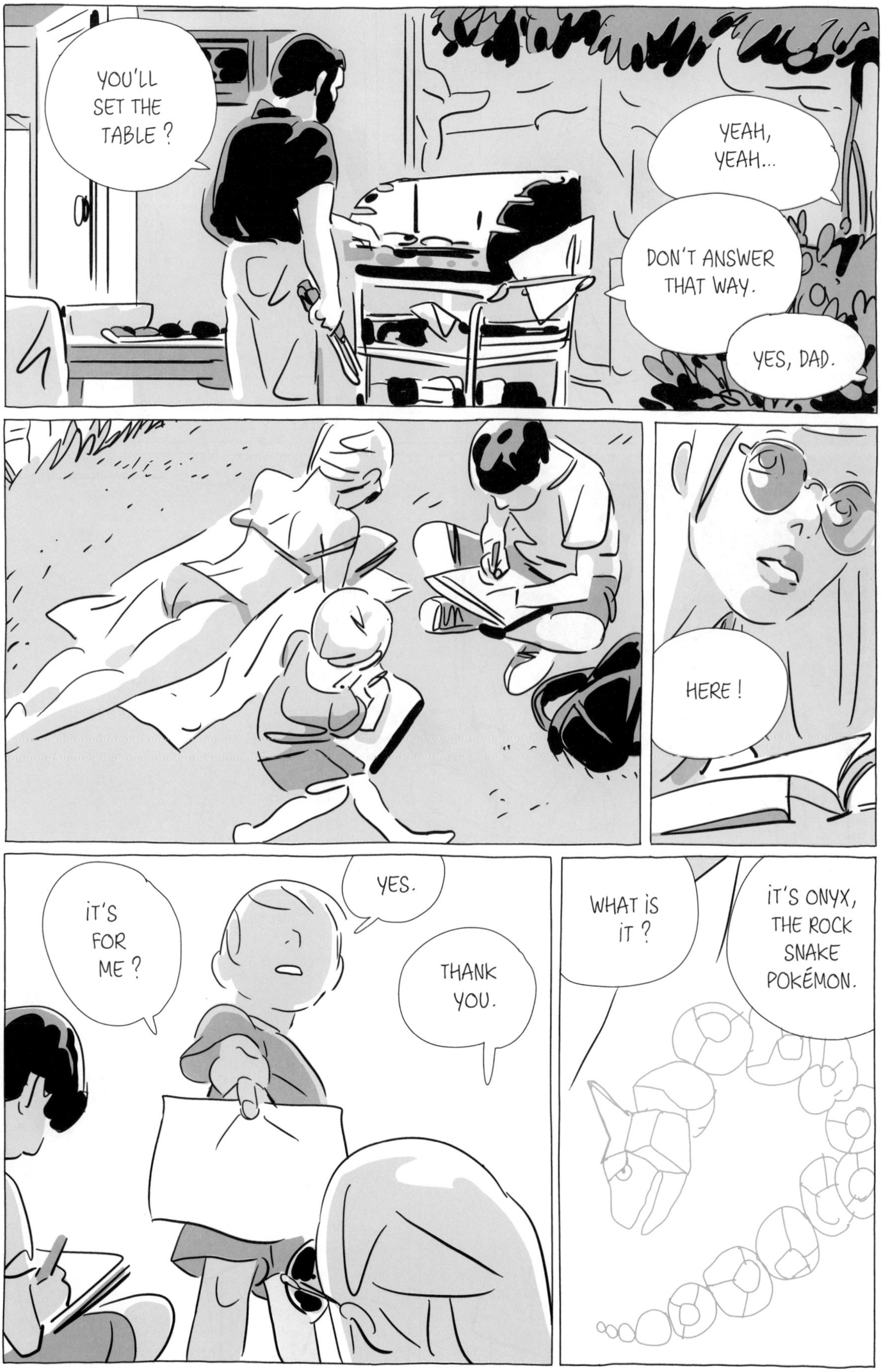
YOU'LL SET THE TABLE ?
YEAH, YEAH...
DON'T ANSWER THAT WAY.
YES, DAD.
HERE !
iT'S FOR ME ?
YES.
THANK YOU.
WHAT iS iT ?
iT'S ONYX, THE ROCK SNAKE POKÉMON.

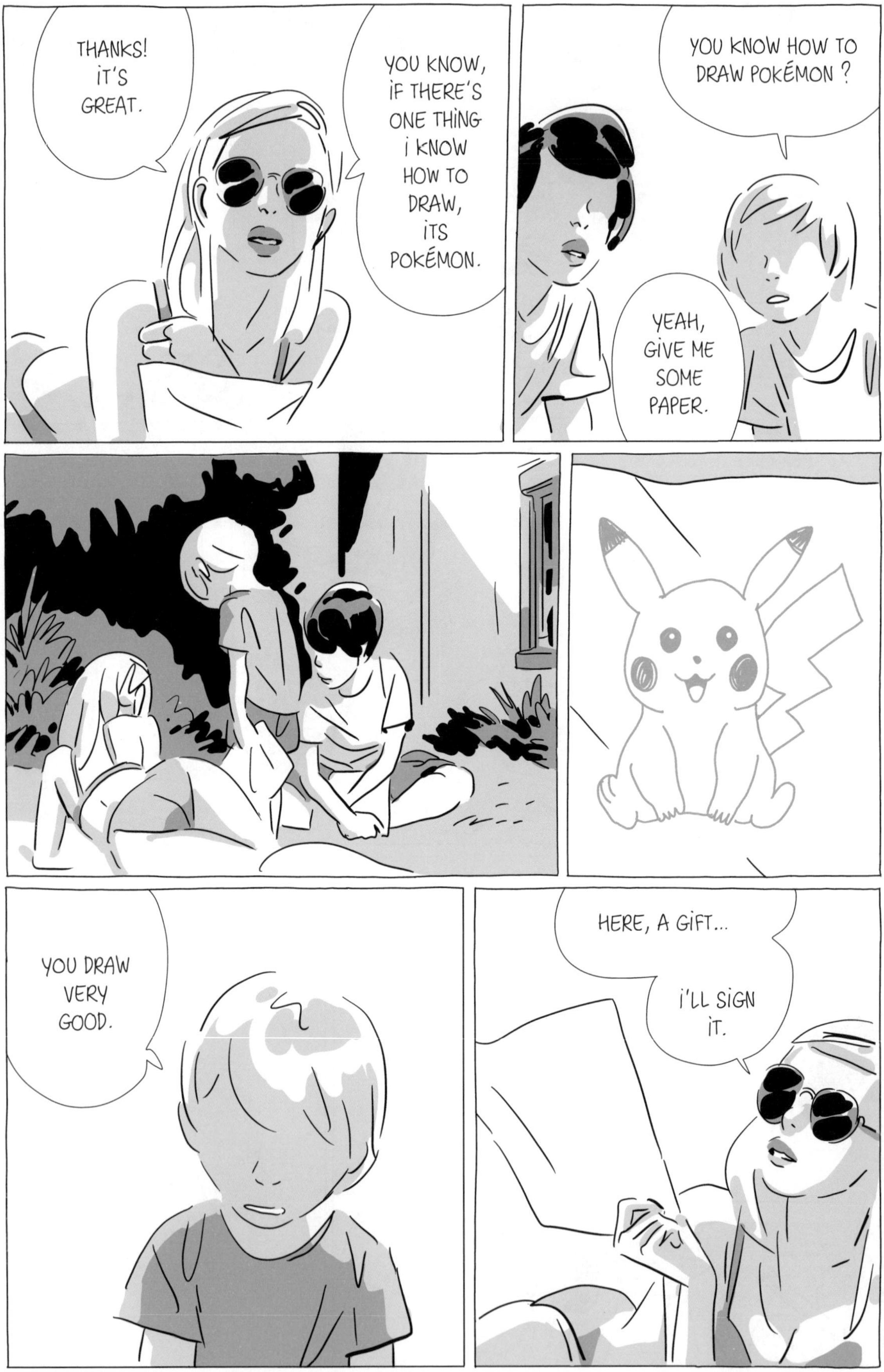
THANKS! IT'S GREAT.
YOU KNOW, IF THERE'S ONE THING I KNOW HOW TO DRAW, ITS POKÉMON.
YOU KNOW HOW TO DRAW POKÉMON ?
YEAH, GIVE ME SOME PAPER.
YOU DRAW VERY GOOD.
HERE, A GIFT...
I'LL SIGN IT.

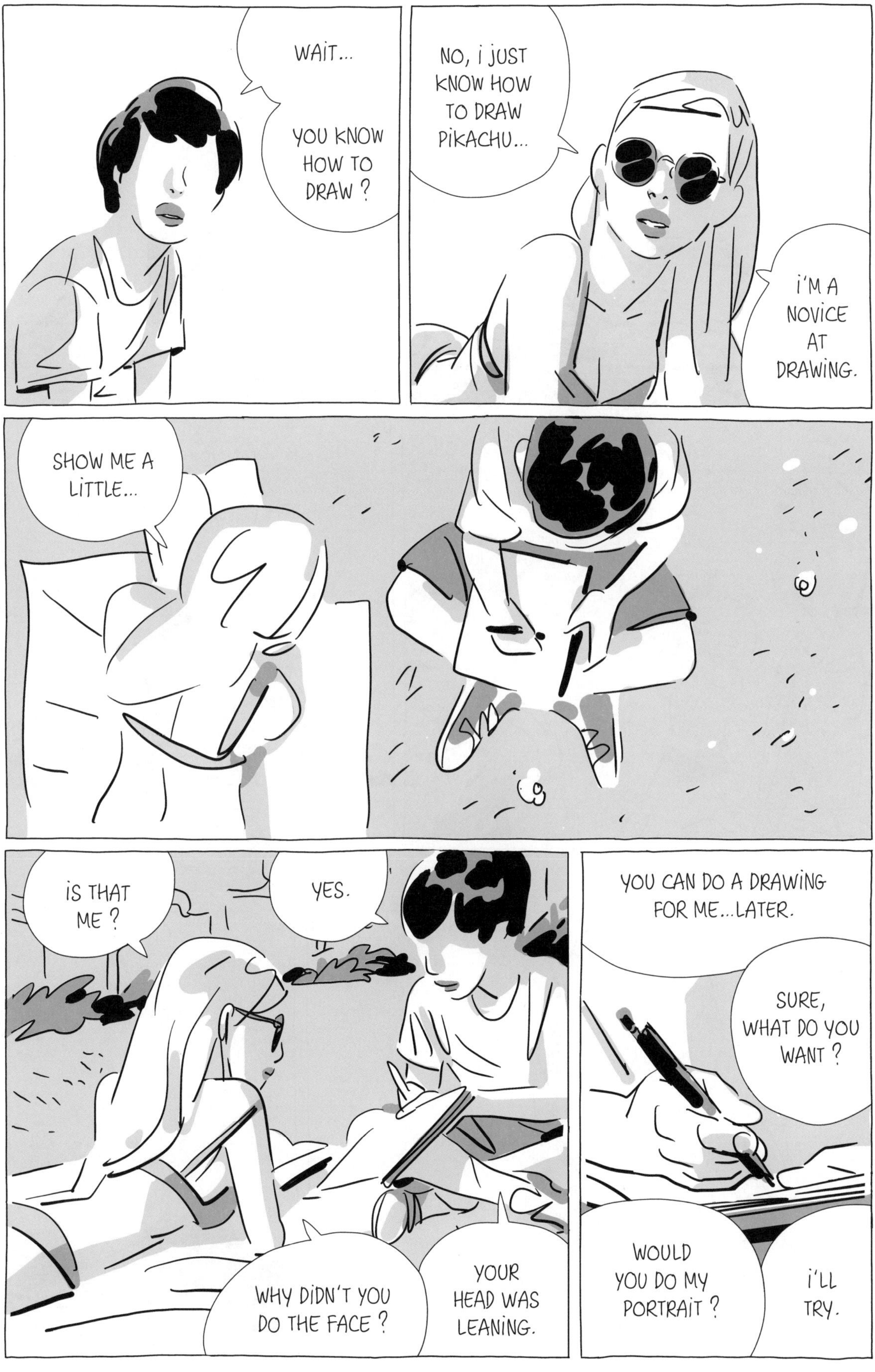
WAIT...
YOU KNOW HOW TO DRAW ?
NO, i JUST KNOW HOW TO DRAW PiKACHU...
i'M A NOVICE AT DRAWING.
SHOW ME A LITTLE...
iS THAT ME ?
YES.
WHY DiDN'T YOU DO THE FACE ?
YOUR HEAD WAS LEANiNG.
YOU CAN DO A DRAWiNG FOR ME...LATER.
SURE, WHAT DO YOU WANT ?
WOULD YOU DO MY PORTRAiT ?
i'LL TRY.

WOW!

i ALMOST GOT iT.

iT'S ENORMOUS.

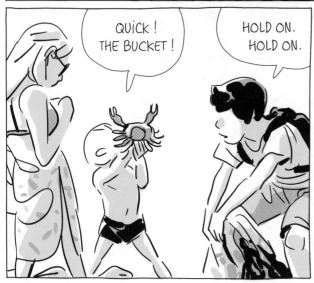

QUICK! THE BUCKET!

HOLD ON. HOLD ON.

iT'S CRAZY...

BROUEL iS THE BEST BEACH FOR CRABS.

iT'S THE ALGAE ON THE ROCKS, WHERE THERE iS A LiTTLE BiT OF WATER NEXT TO iT...

LiKE THiS ONE... ONCE WE FOUND A SPIDER CRAB.

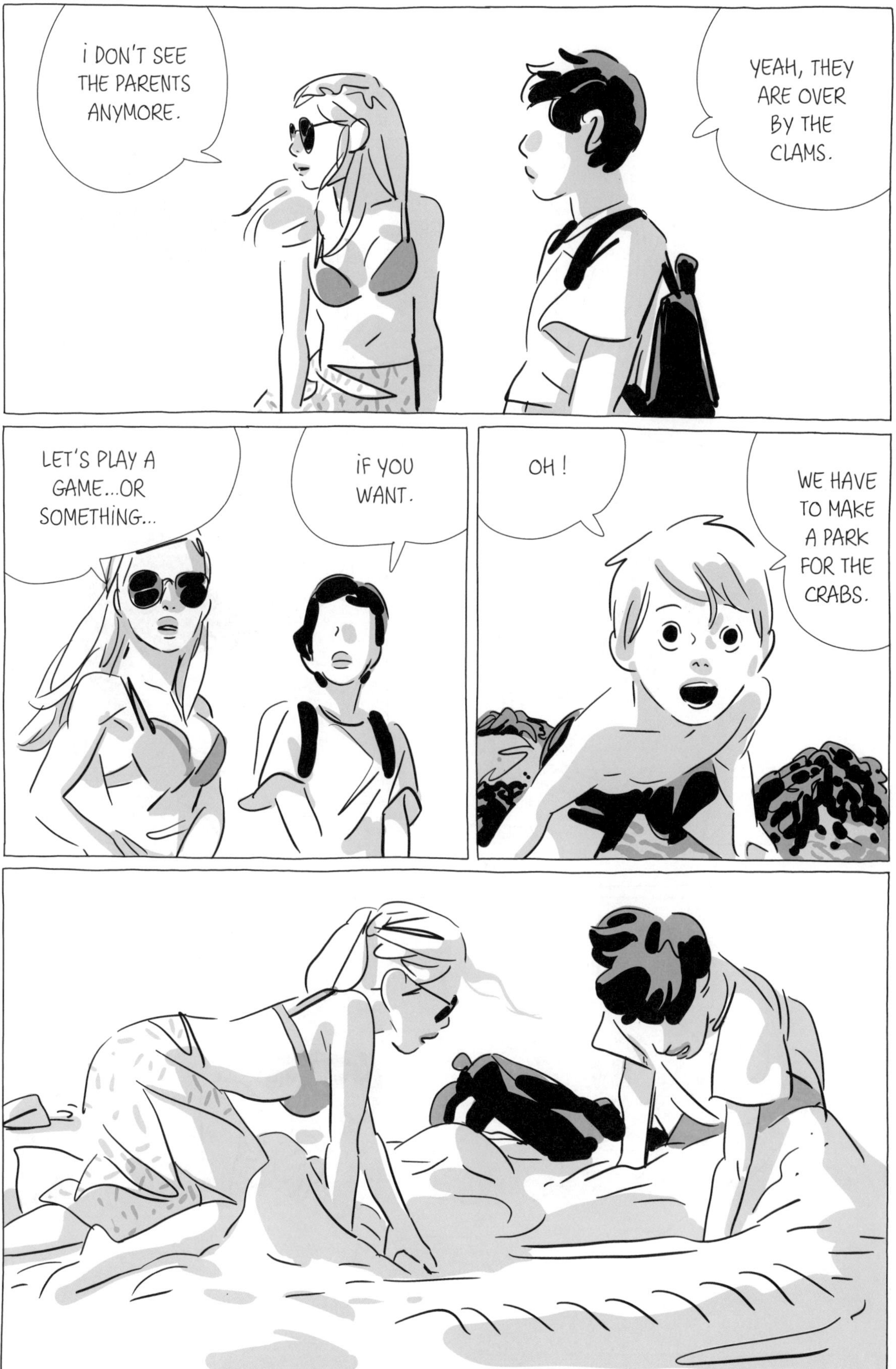
I DON'T SEE THE PARENTS ANYMORE.
YEAH, THEY ARE OVER BY THE CLAMS.
LET'S PLAY A GAME...OR SOMETHING...
IF YOU WANT.
OH!
WE HAVE TO MAKE A PARK FOR THE CRABS.

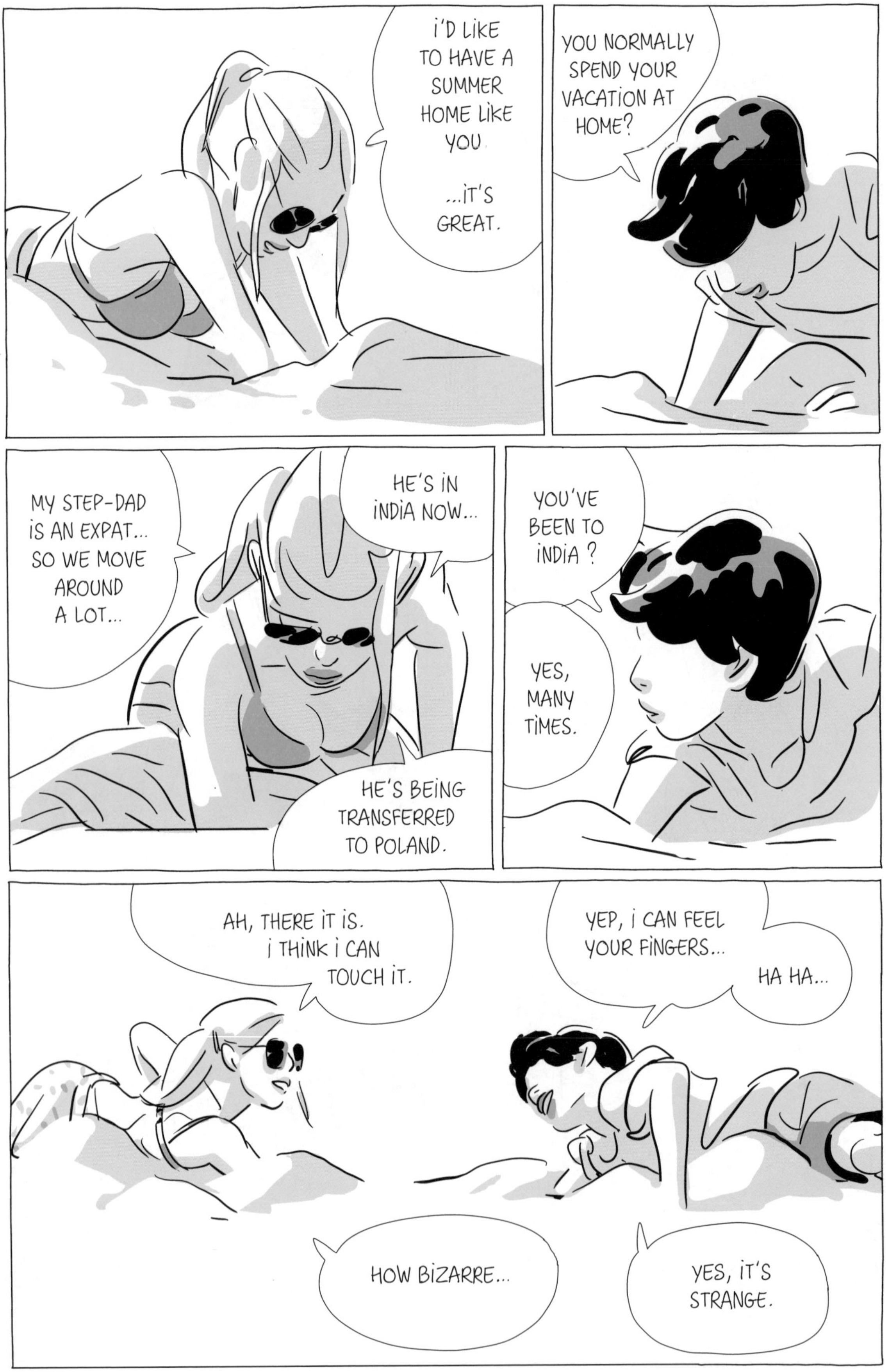
I'D LIKE TO HAVE A SUMMER HOME LIKE YOU.
...IT'S GREAT.
YOU NORMALLY SPEND YOUR VACATION AT HOME?
MY STEP-DAD IS AN EXPAT... SO WE MOVE AROUND A LOT...
HE'S IN INDIA NOW...
HE'S BEING TRANSFERRED TO POLAND.
YOU'VE BEEN TO INDIA ?
YES, MANY TIMES.
AH, THERE IT IS. I THINK I CAN TOUCH IT.
YEP, I CAN FEEL YOUR FINGERS...
HA HA...
HOW BIZARRE...
YES, IT'S STRANGE.

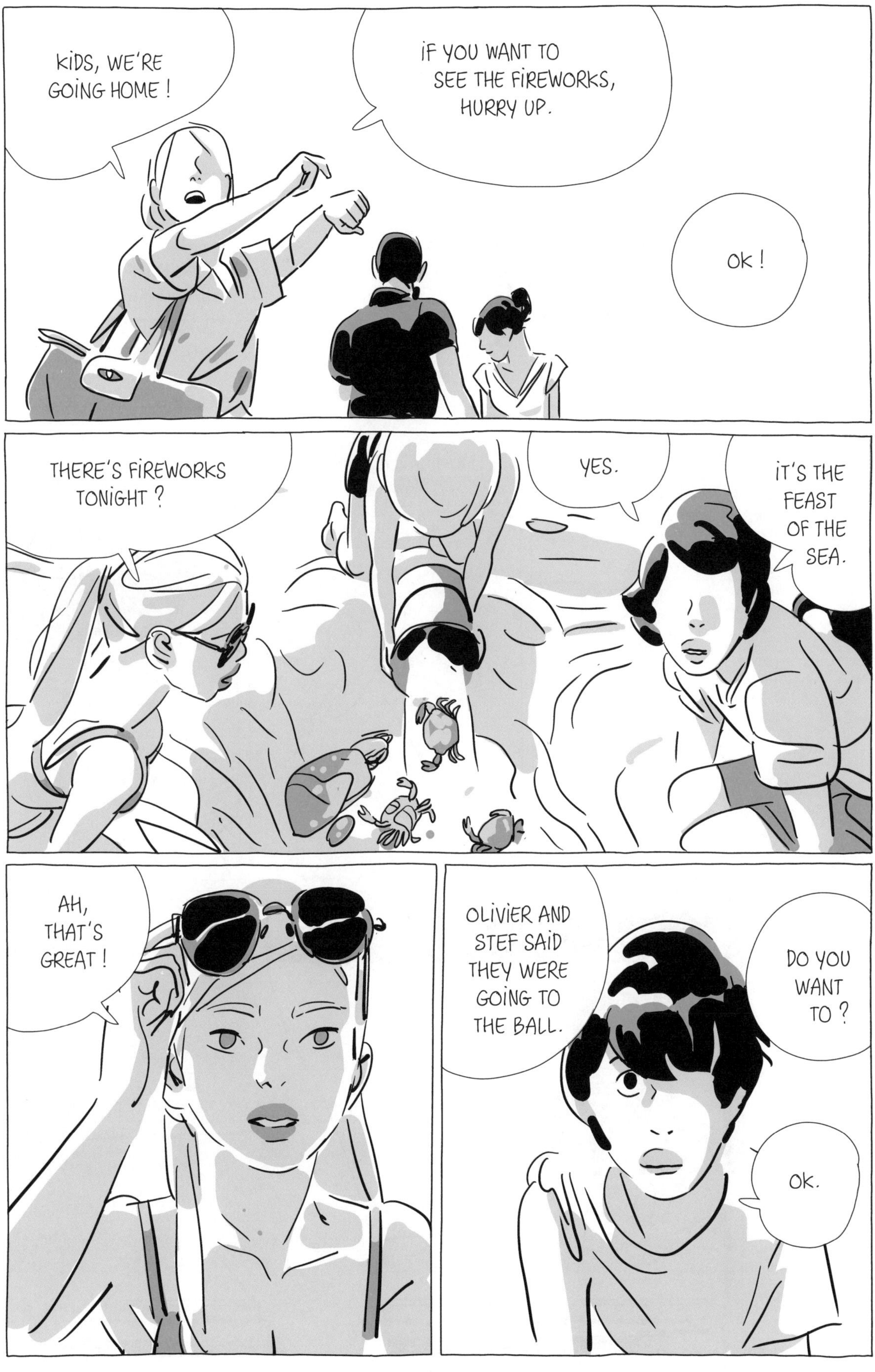
KIDS, WE'RE GOING HOME !
IF YOU WANT TO SEE THE FIREWORKS, HURRY UP.
OK !
THERE'S FIREWORKS TONIGHT ?
YES.
IT'S THE FEAST OF THE SEA.
AH, THAT'S GREAT !
OLIVIER AND STEF SAID THEY WERE GOING TO THE BALL.
DO YOU WANT TO ?
OK.

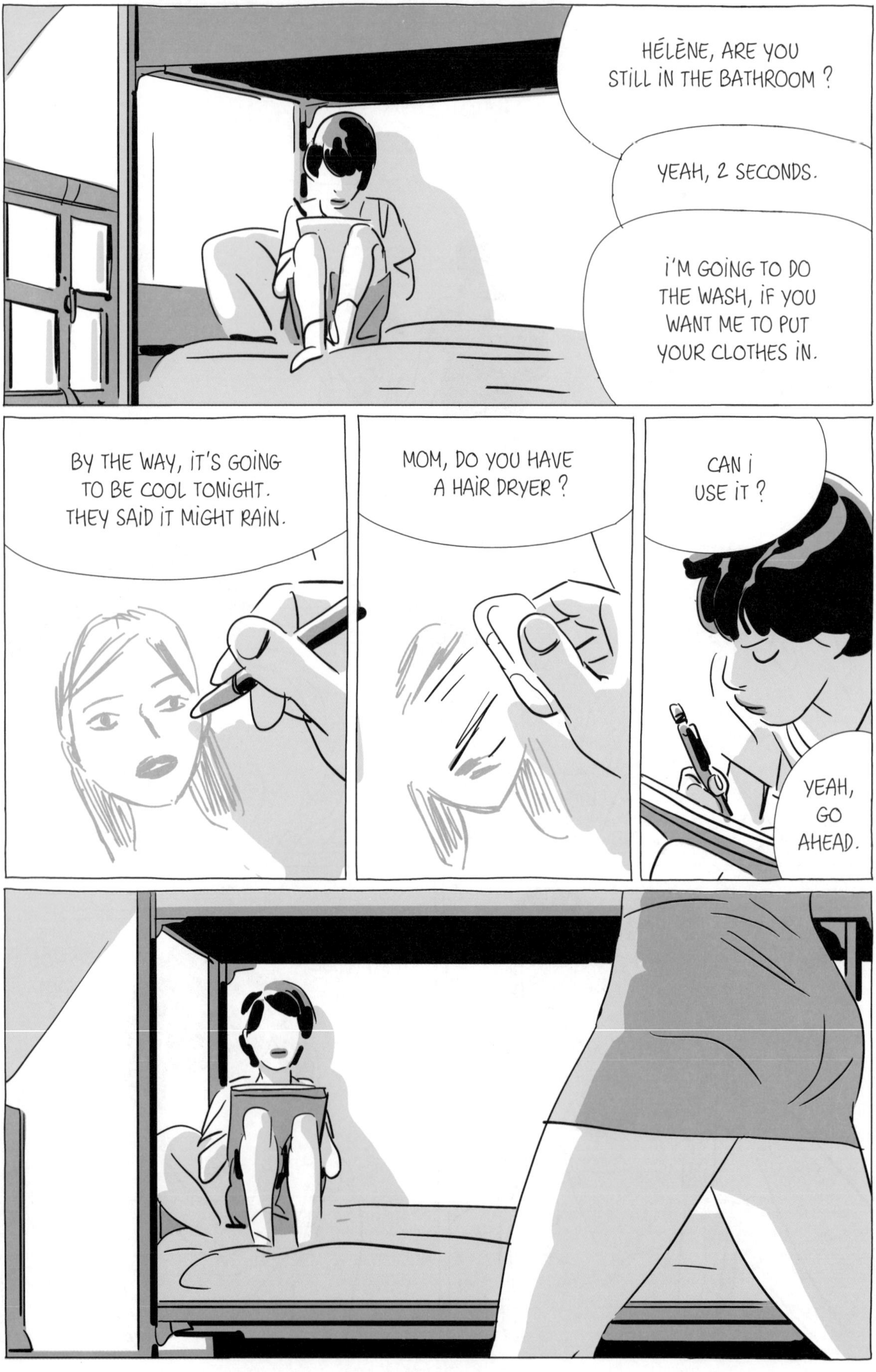
HÉLÈNE, ARE YOU STILL IN THE BATHROOM ?
YEAH, 2 SECONDS.
I'M GOING TO DO THE WASH, IF YOU WANT ME TO PUT YOUR CLOTHES IN.
BY THE WAY, IT'S GOING TO BE COOL TONIGHT. THEY SAID IT MIGHT RAIN.
MOM, DO YOU HAVE A HAIR DRYER ?
CAN I USE IT ?
YEAH, GO AHEAD.

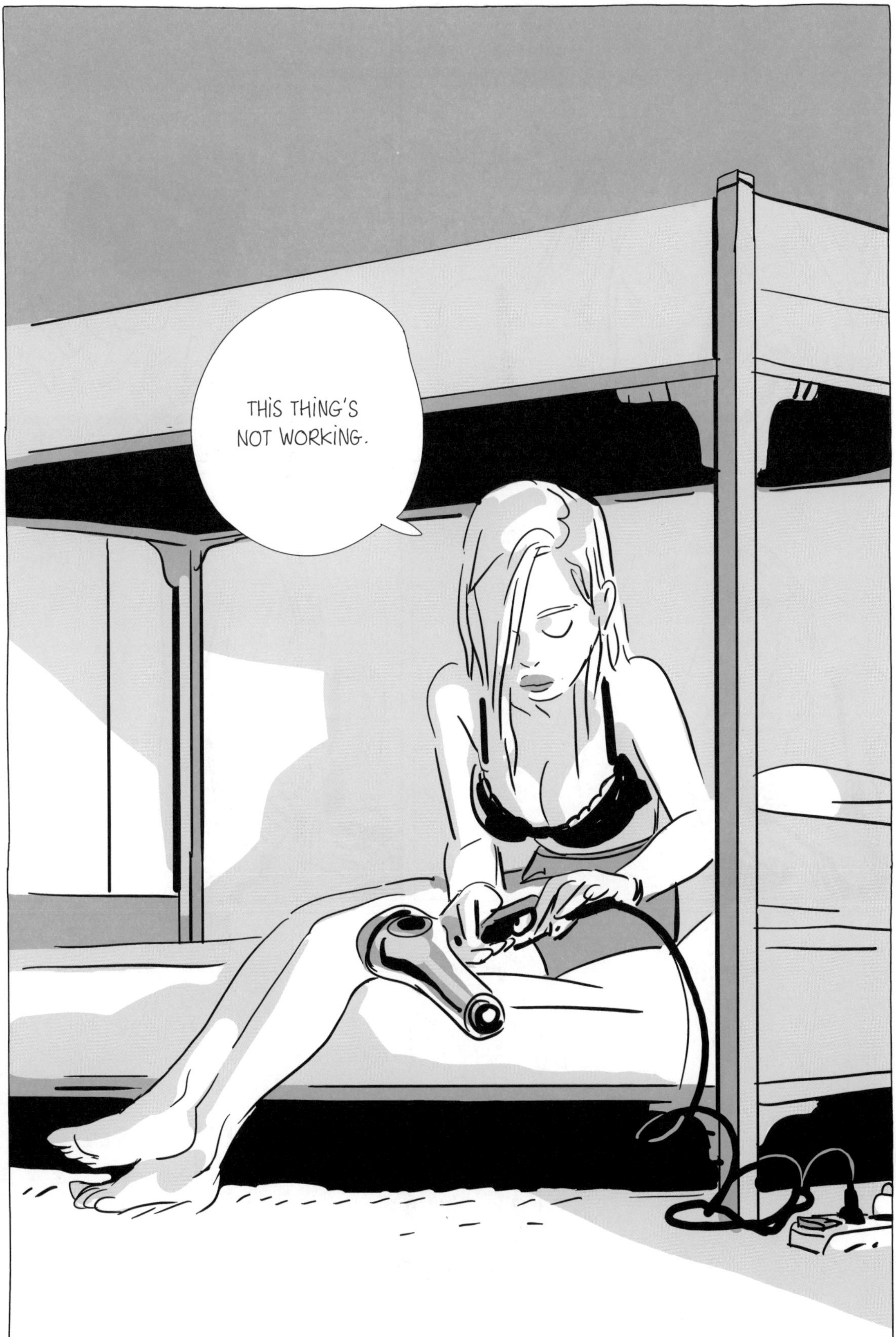
THIS THING'S NOT WORKING.

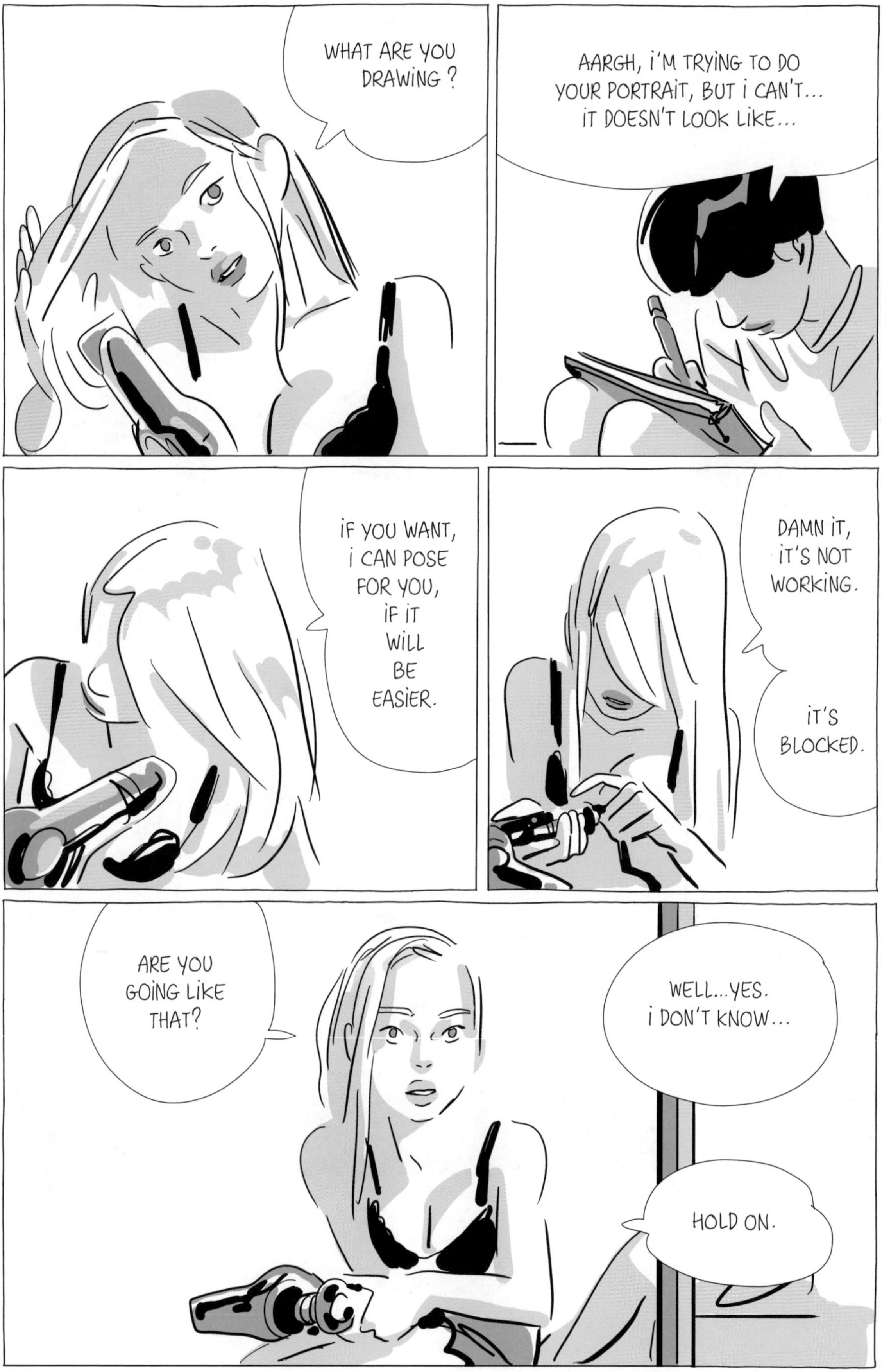

WHAT ARE YOU DRAWING ?
AARGH, I'M TRYING TO DO YOUR PORTRAIT, BUT I CAN'T... IT DOESN'T LOOK LIKE...
IF YOU WANT, I CAN POSE FOR YOU, IF IT WILL BE EASIER.
DAMN IT, IT'S NOT WORKING.
IT'S BLOCKED.
ARE YOU GOING LIKE THAT?
WELL...YES. I DON'T KNOW...
HOLD ON.

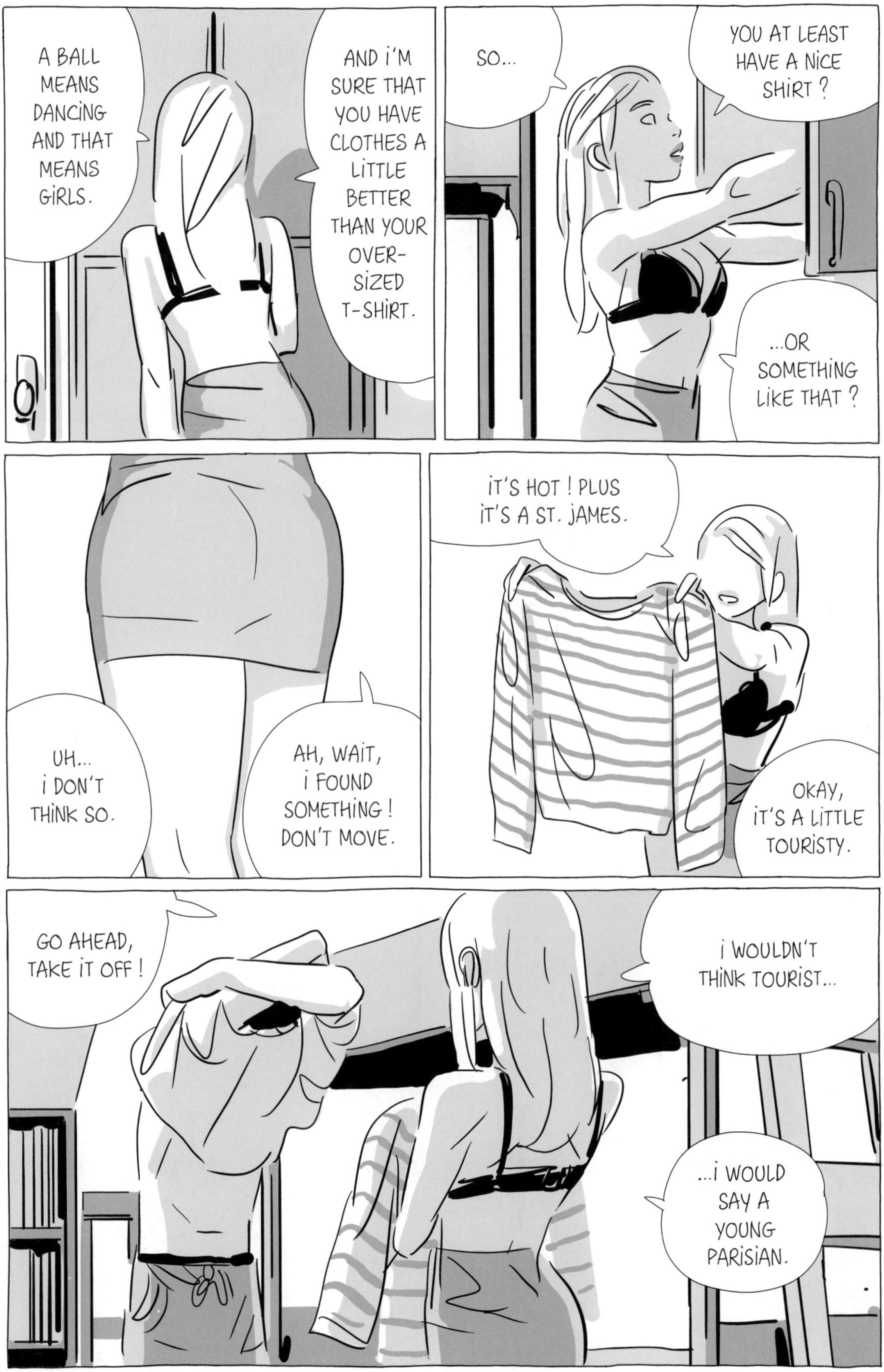
A BALL MEANS DANCING AND THAT MEANS GIRLS.
AND I'M SURE THAT YOU HAVE CLOTHES A LITTLE BETTER THAN YOUR OVER-SIZED T-SHIRT.
SO...
YOU AT LEAST HAVE A NICE SHIRT?
...OR SOMETHING LIKE THAT?
UH... I DON'T THINK SO.
AH, WAIT, I FOUND SOMETHING! DON'T MOVE.
IT'S HOT! PLUS IT'S A ST. JAMES.
OKAY, IT'S A LITTLE TOURISTY.
GO AHEAD, TAKE IT OFF!
I WOULDN'T THINK TOURIST...
...I WOULD SAY A YOUNG PARISIAN.

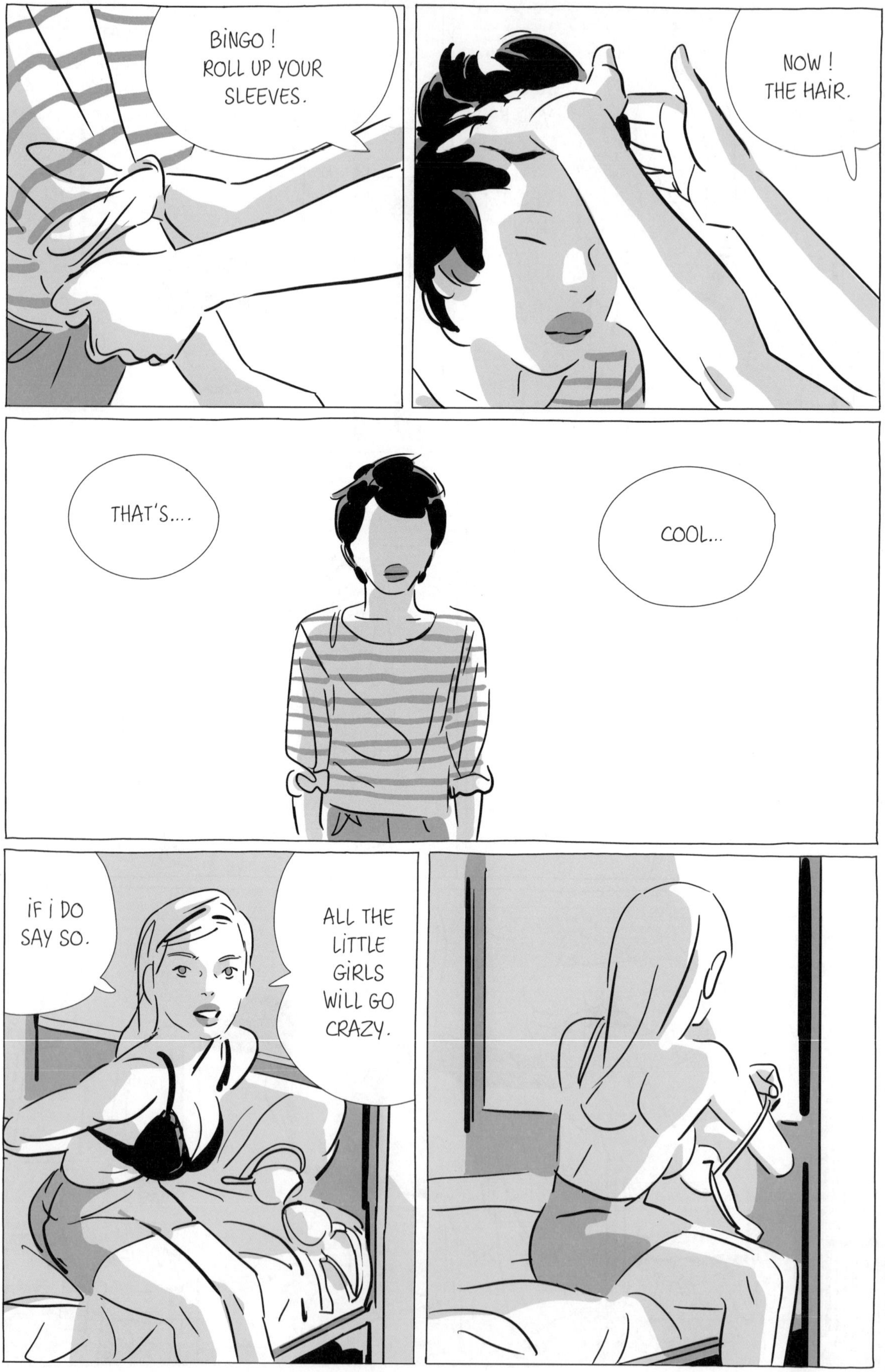
BINGO !
ROLL UP YOUR SLEEVES.
NOW !
THE HAIR.
THAT'S....
COOL...
IF I DO SAY SO.
ALL THE LITTLE GIRLS WILL GO CRAZY.

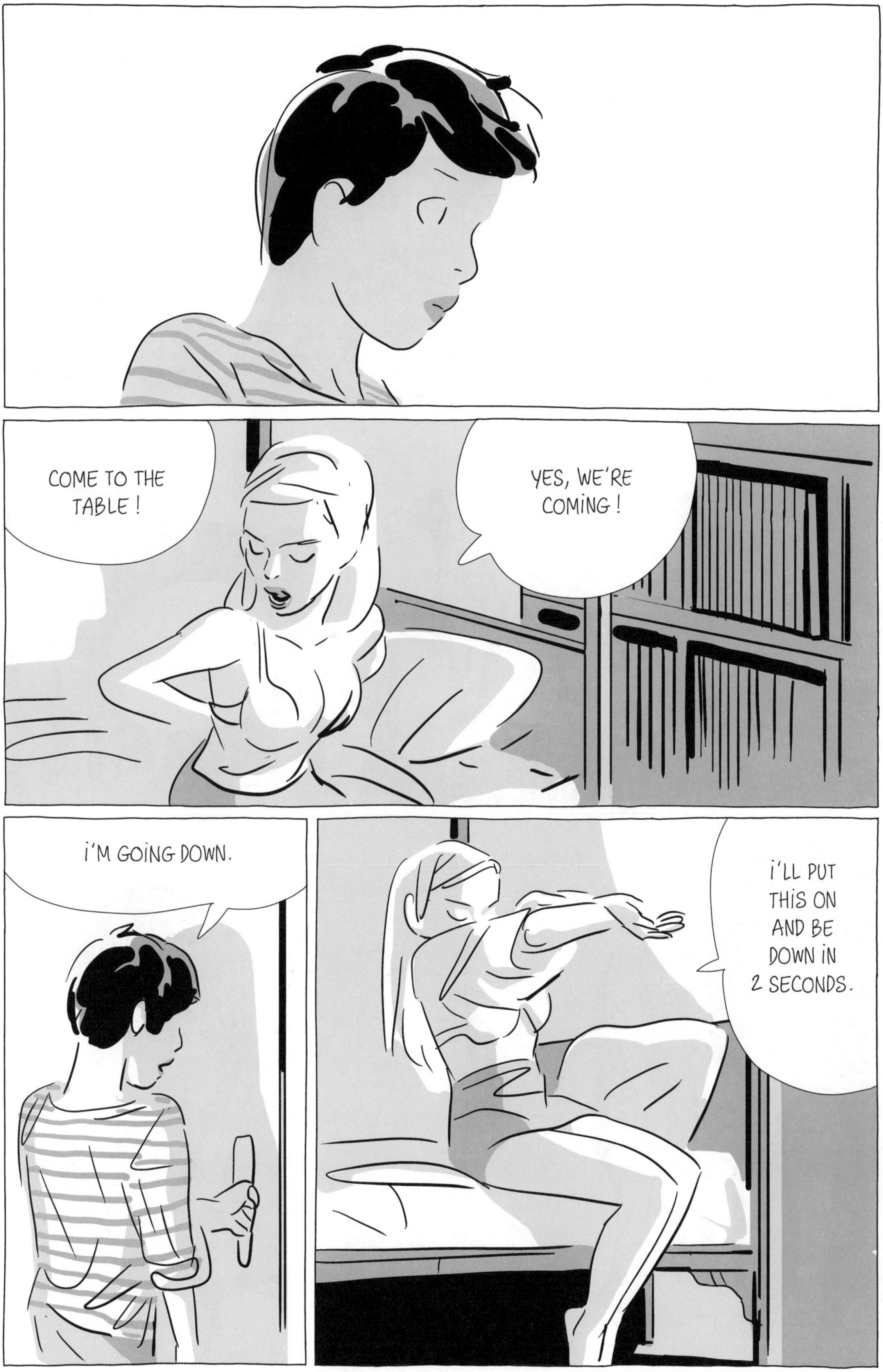
COME TO THE TABLE !
YES, WE'RE COMING !
I'M GOING DOWN.
I'LL PUT THIS ON AND BE DOWN IN 2 SECONDS.

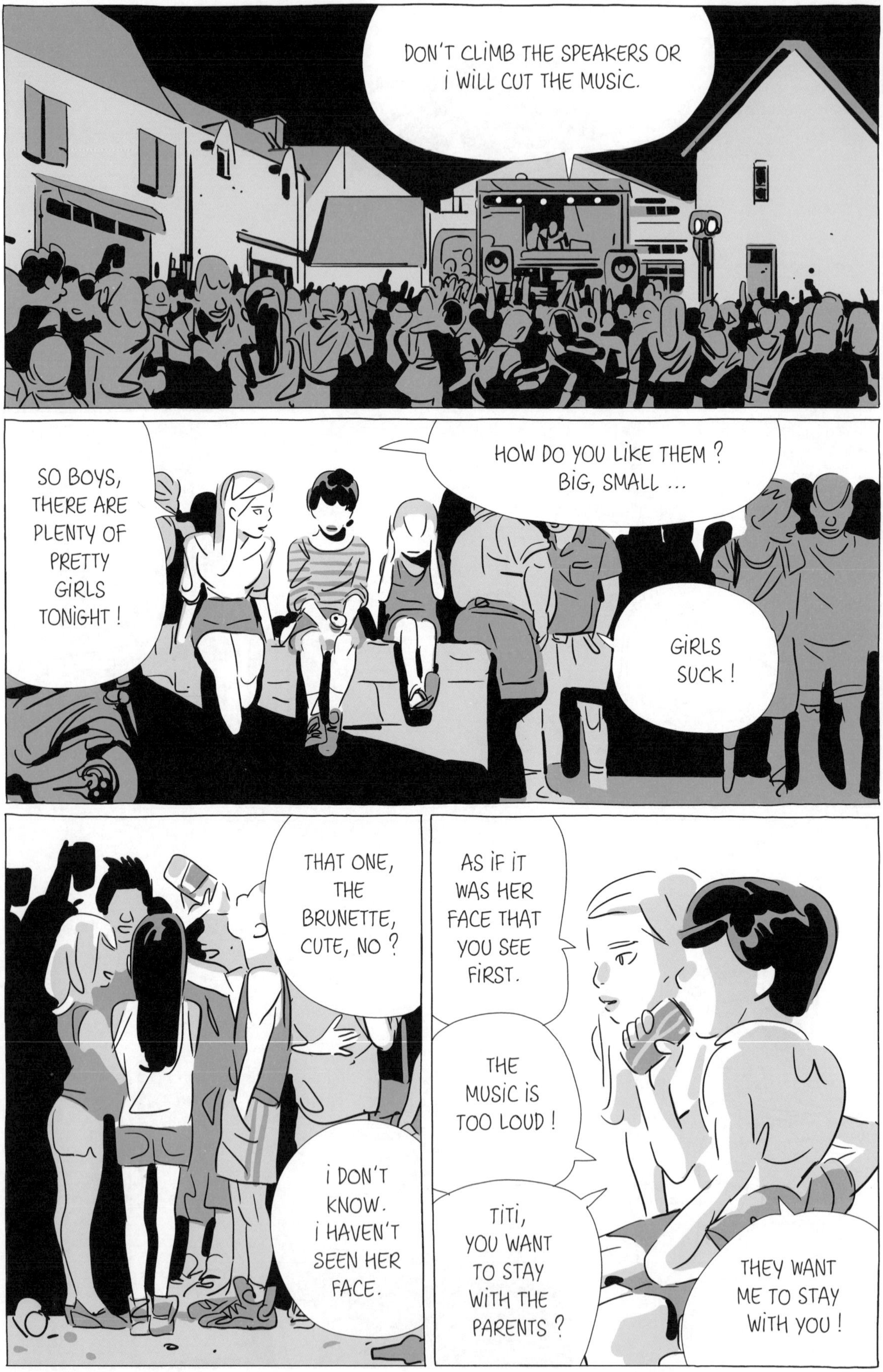
DON'T CLIMB THE SPEAKERS OR i WILL CUT THE MUSIC.
SO BOYS, THERE ARE PLENTY OF PRETTY GIRLS TONIGHT !
HOW DO YOU LIKE THEM ? BIG, SMALL ...
GIRLS SUCK !
THAT ONE, THE BRUNETTE, CUTE, NO ?
i DON'T KNOW. i HAVEN'T SEEN HER FACE.
AS iF iT WAS HER FACE THAT YOU SEE FiRST.
THE MUSiC iS TOO LOUD !
TiTi, YOU WANT TO STAY WiTH THE PARENTS ?
THEY WANT ME TO STAY WiTH YOU !

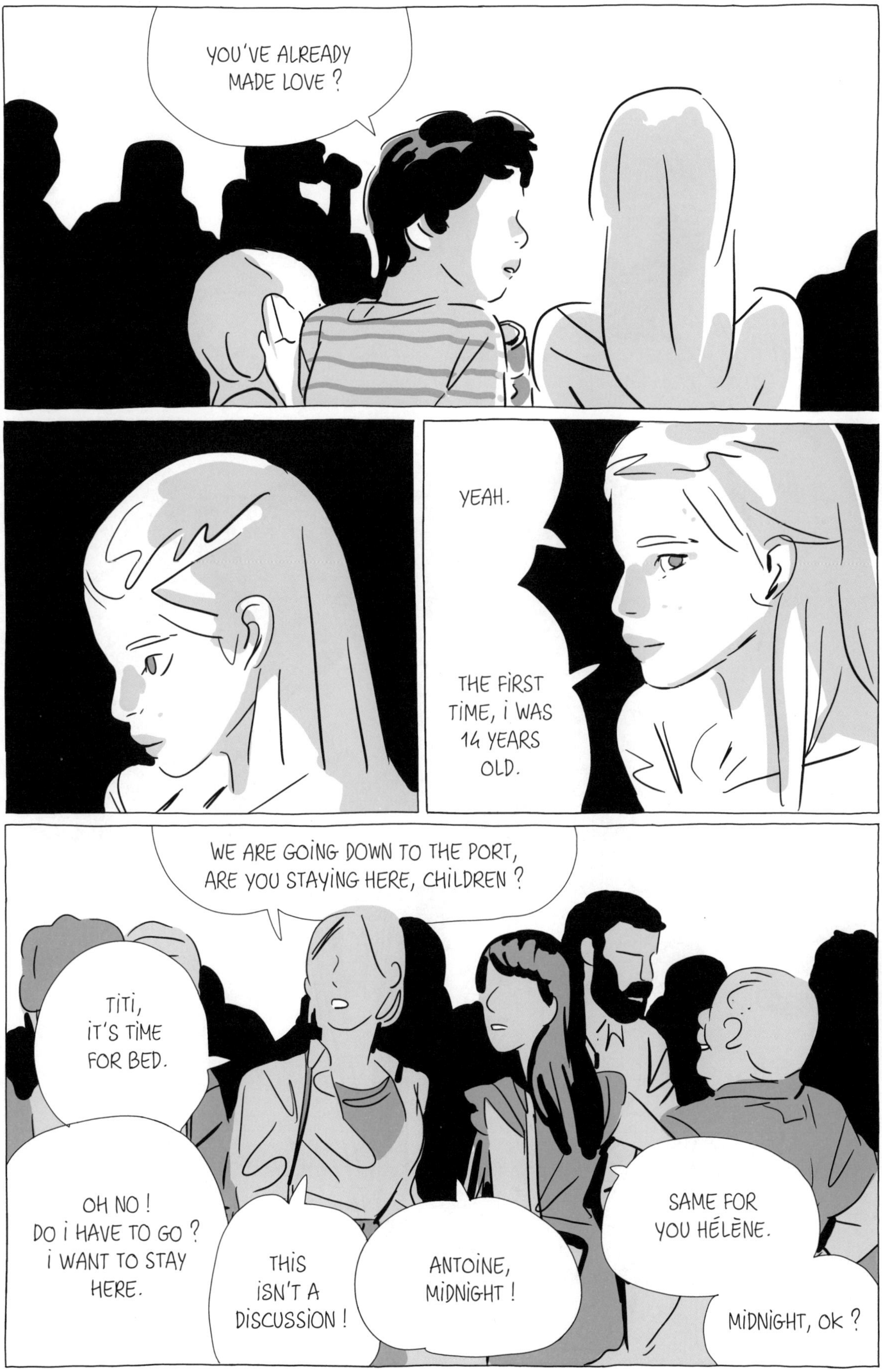
YOU'VE ALREADY MADE LOVE ?
YEAH.
THE FIRST TIME, I WAS 14 YEARS OLD.
WE ARE GOING DOWN TO THE PORT, ARE YOU STAYING HERE, CHILDREN ?
TITI, IT'S TIME FOR BED.
OH NO ! DO I HAVE TO GO ? I WANT TO STAY HERE.
THIS ISN'T A DISCUSSION !
ANTOINE, MIDNIGHT !
SAME FOR YOU HÉLÈNE.
MIDNIGHT, OK ?

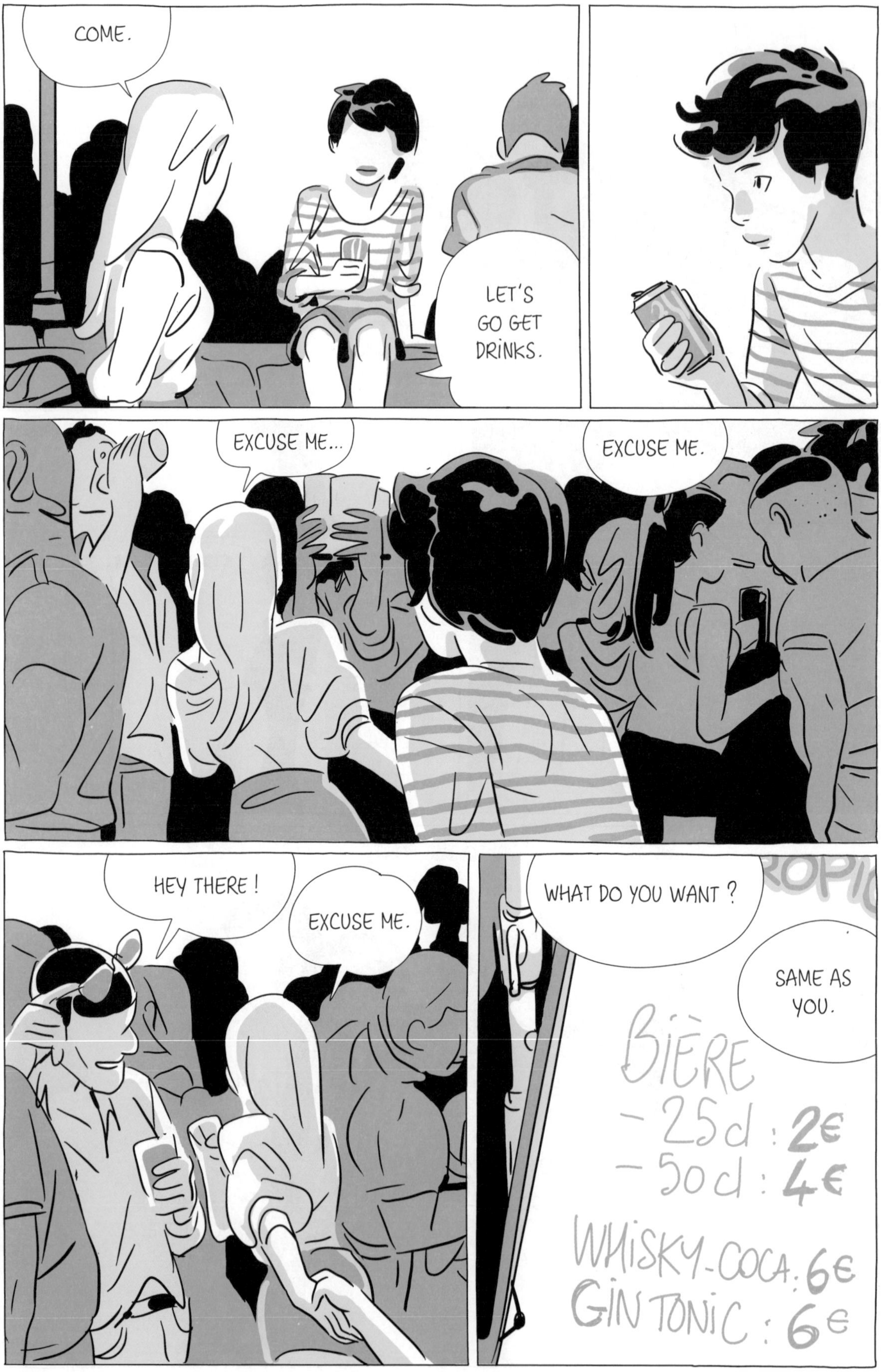
COME.
LET'S GO GET DRINKS.
EXCUSE ME...
EXCUSE ME.
HEY THERE !
EXCUSE ME.
WHAT DO YOU WANT ?
SAME AS YOU.
BIÈRE
- 25cl : 2€
- 50cl : 4€
WHISKY-COCA : 6€
GIN TONIC : 6€

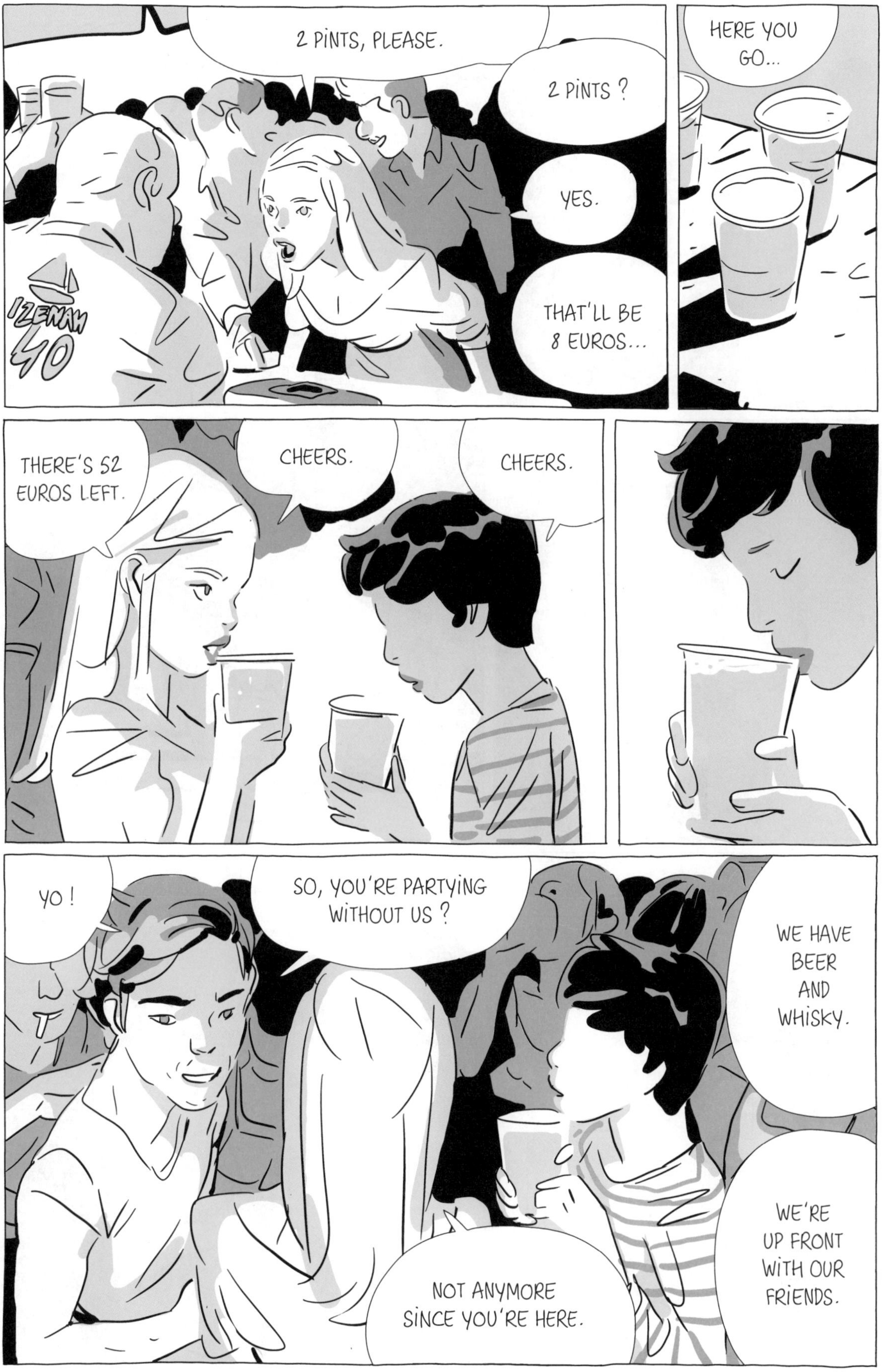
2 PINTS, PLEASE.
2 PINTS ?
YES.
THAT'LL BE 8 EUROS...
HERE YOU GO...
THERE'S 52 EUROS LEFT.
CHEERS.
CHEERS.
YO !
SO, YOU'RE PARTYING WITHOUT US ?
WE HAVE BEER AND WHISKY.
NOT ANYMORE SINCE YOU'RE HERE.
WE'RE UP FRONT WITH OUR FRIENDS.

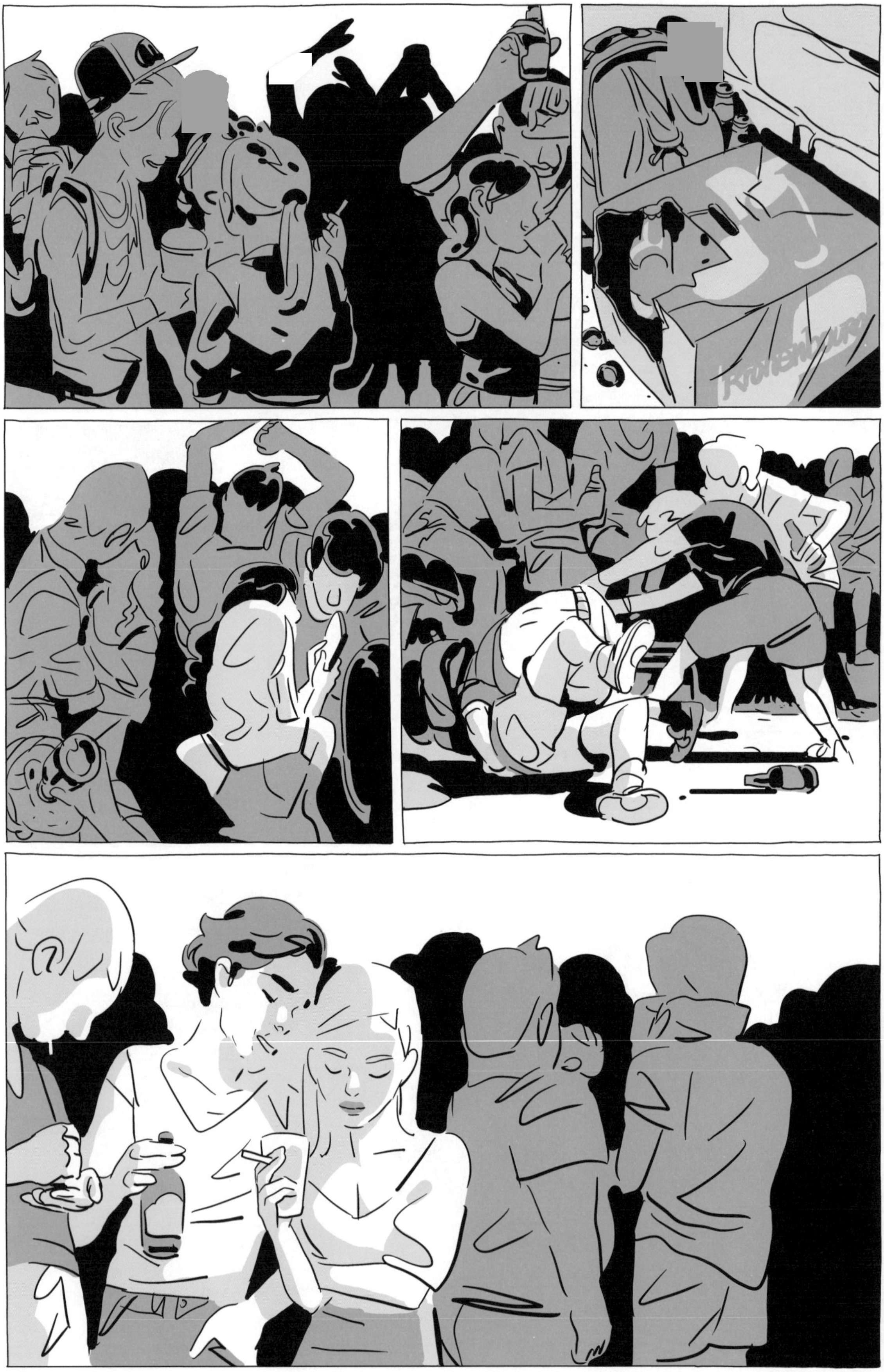
Kronenbourg

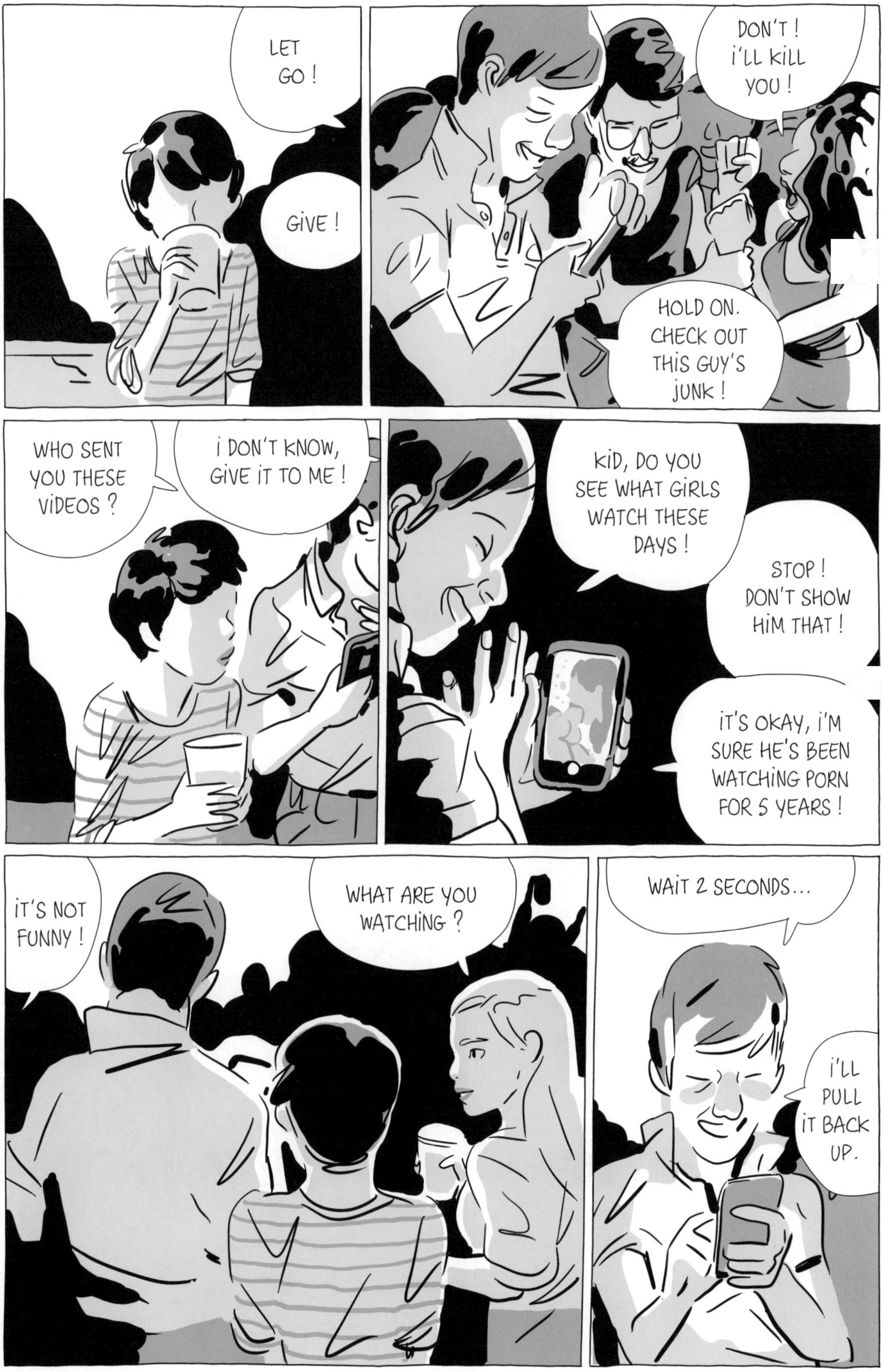
LET GO !
GIVE !
DON'T ! i'LL KiLL YOU !
HOLD ON. CHECK OUT THIS GUY'S JUNK !
WHO SENT YOU THESE ViDEOS ?
i DON'T KNOW, GiVE iT TO ME !
KiD, DO YOU SEE WHAT GiRLS WATCH THESE DAYS !
STOP ! DON'T SHOW HiM THAT !
iT'S OKAY, i'M SURE HE'S BEEN WATCHiNG PORN FOR 5 YEARS !
iT'S NOT FUNNY !
WHAT ARE YOU WATCHiNG ?
WAiT 2 SECONDS...
i'LL PULL iT BACK UP.

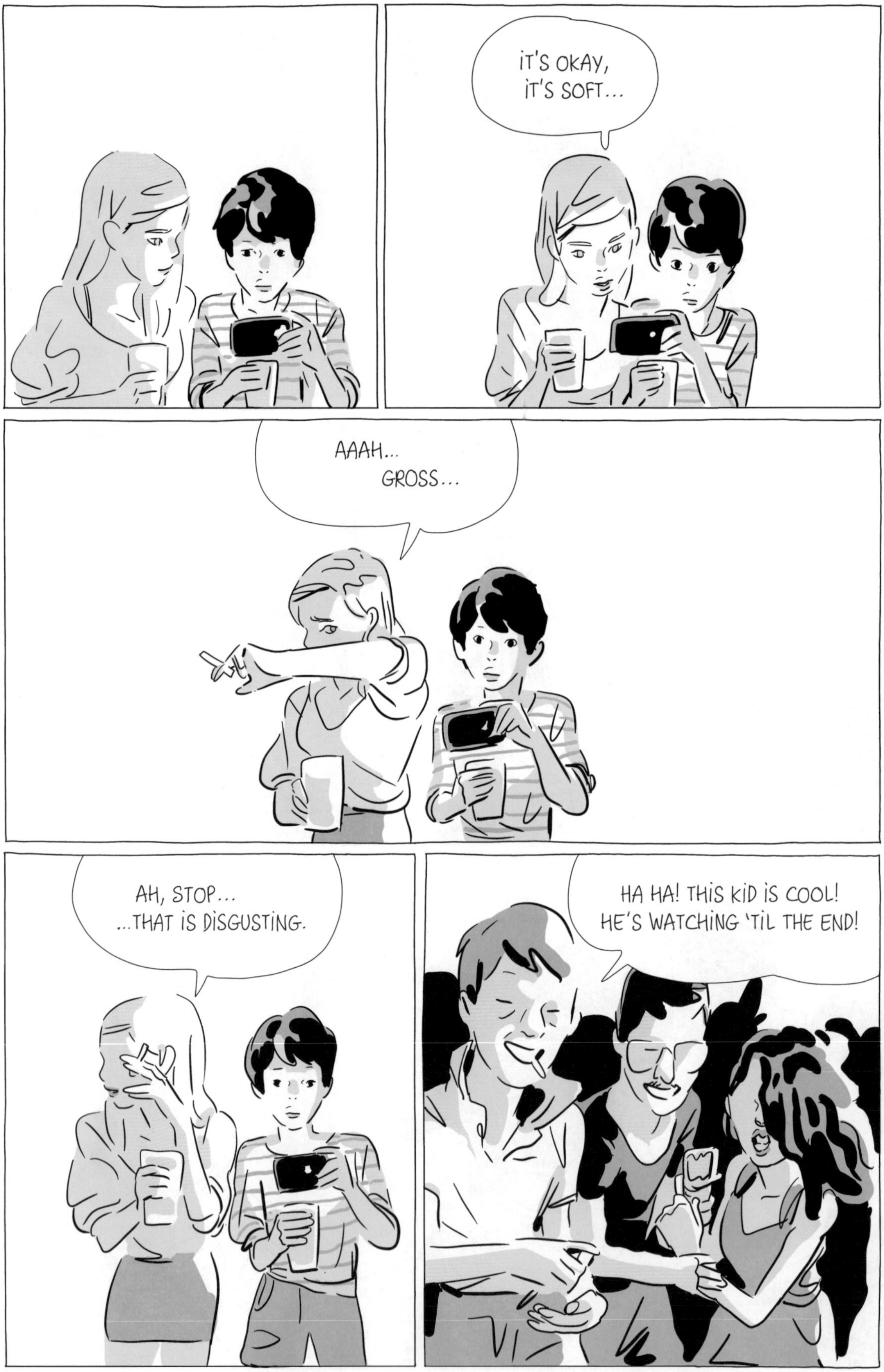
IT'S OKAY,
IT'S SOFT...
AAAH...
GROSS...
AH, STOP...
...THAT IS DISGUSTING.
HA HA! THIS KID IS COOL!
HE'S WATCHING 'TIL THE END!

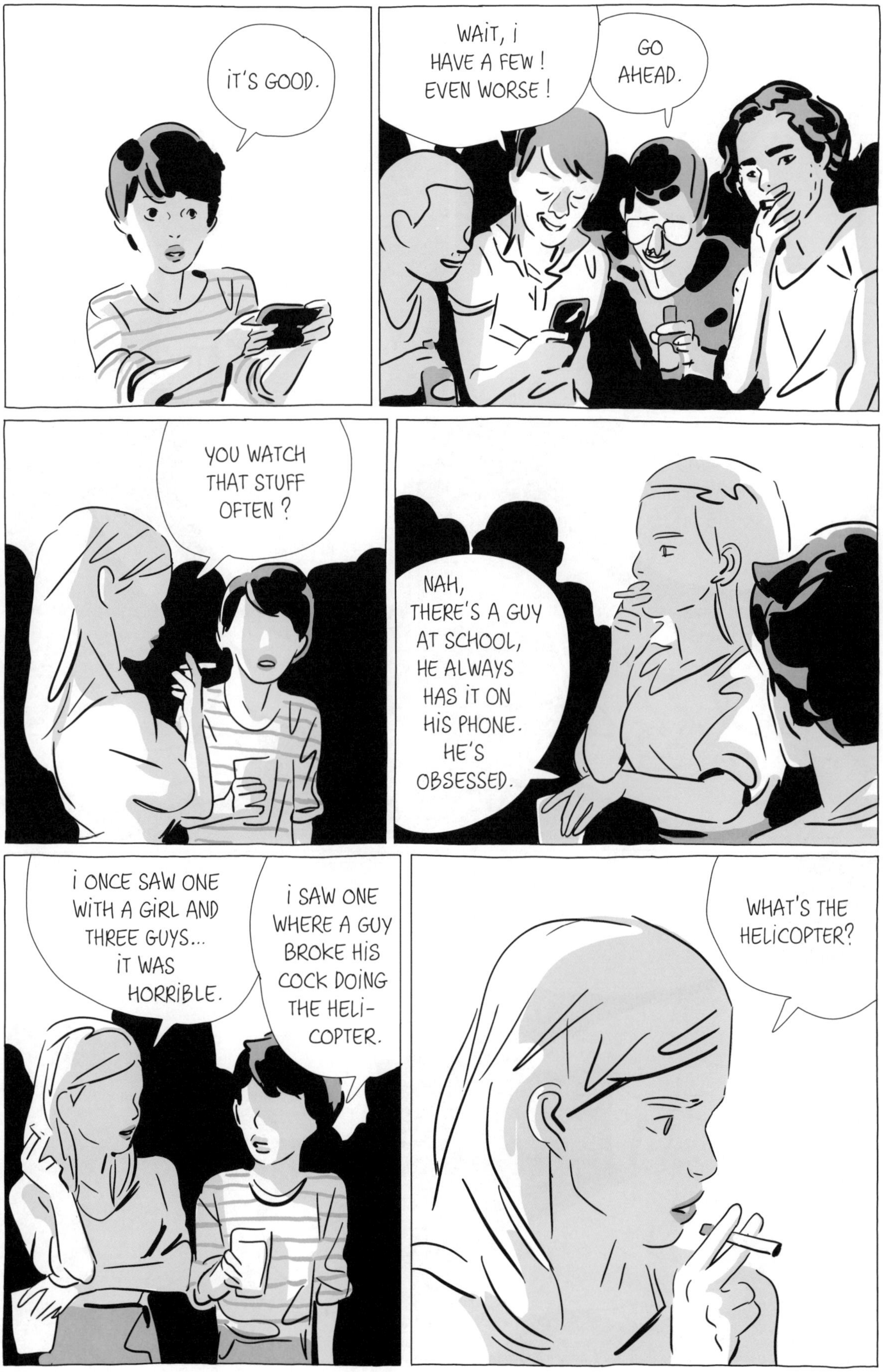
IT'S GOOD.
WAIT, I HAVE A FEW! EVEN WORSE!
GO AHEAD.
YOU WATCH THAT STUFF OFTEN?
NAH, THERE'S A GUY AT SCHOOL, HE ALWAYS HAS IT ON HIS PHONE. HE'S OBSESSED.
I ONCE SAW ONE WITH A GIRL AND THREE GUYS... IT WAS HORRIBLE.
I SAW ONE WHERE A GUY BROKE HIS COCK DOING THE HELI- COPTER.
WHAT'S THE HELICOPTER?

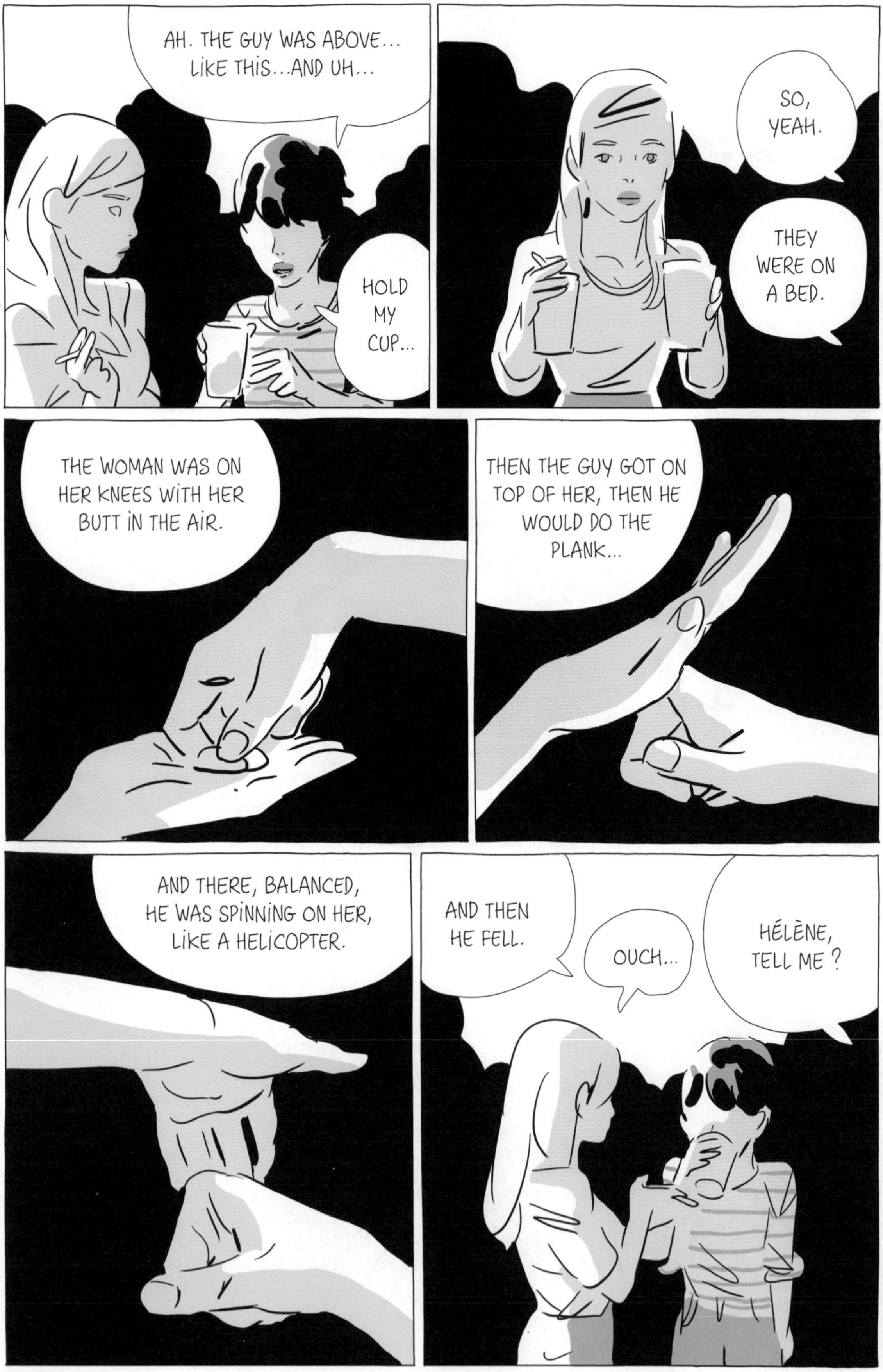
AH. THE GUY WAS ABOVE... LIKE THIS...AND UH...
HOLD MY CUP...
SO, YEAH.
THEY WERE ON A BED.
THE WOMAN WAS ON HER KNEES WITH HER BUTT IN THE AIR.
THEN THE GUY GOT ON TOP OF HER, THEN HE WOULD DO THE PLANK...
AND THERE, BALANCED, HE WAS SPINNING ON HER, LIKE A HELICOPTER.
AND THEN HE FELL.
OUCH...
HÉLÈNE, TELL ME ?

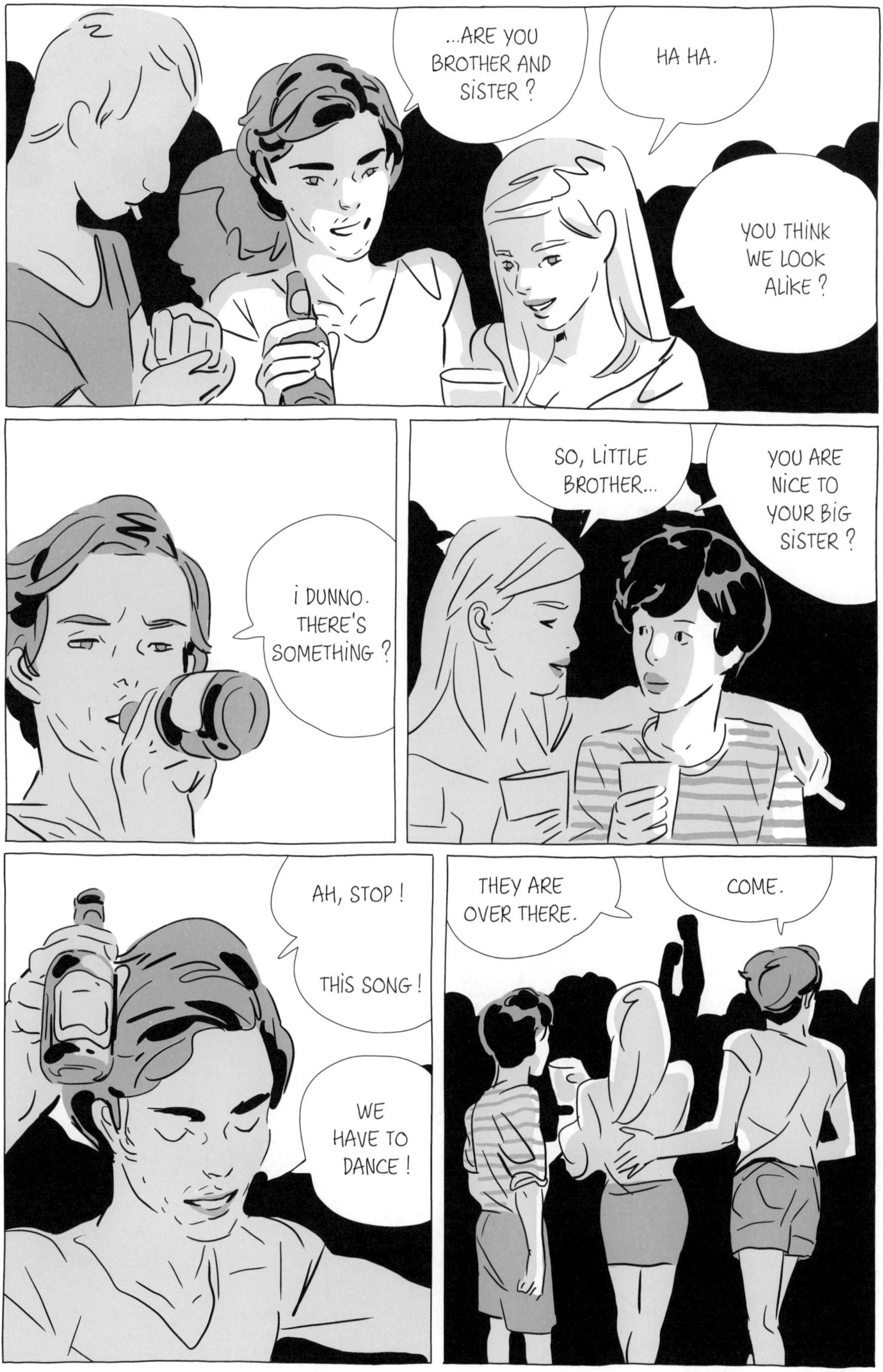
...ARE YOU BROTHER AND SISTER ?
HA HA.
YOU THINK WE LOOK ALIKE ?
I DUNNO. THERE'S SOMETHING ?
SO, LITTLE BROTHER...
YOU ARE NICE TO YOUR BIG SISTER ?
AH, STOP !
THIS SONG !
WE HAVE TO DANCE !
THEY ARE OVER THERE.
COME.

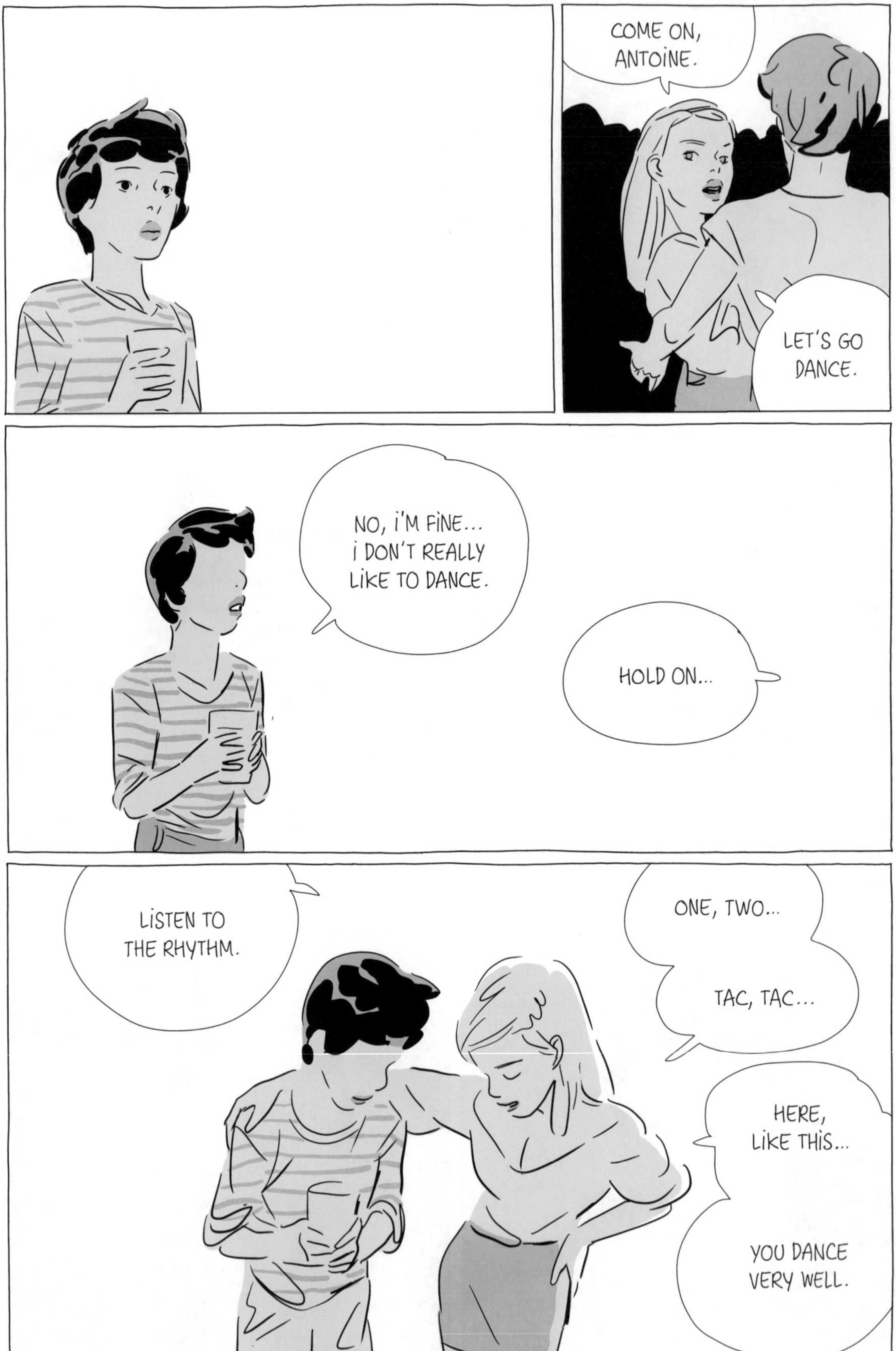
COME ON, ANTOINE.
LET'S GO DANCE.
NO, I'M FINE... I DON'T REALLY LIKE TO DANCE.
HOLD ON...
LISTEN TO THE RHYTHM.
ONE, TWO...
TAC, TAC...
HERE, LIKE THIS...
YOU DANCE VERY WELL.

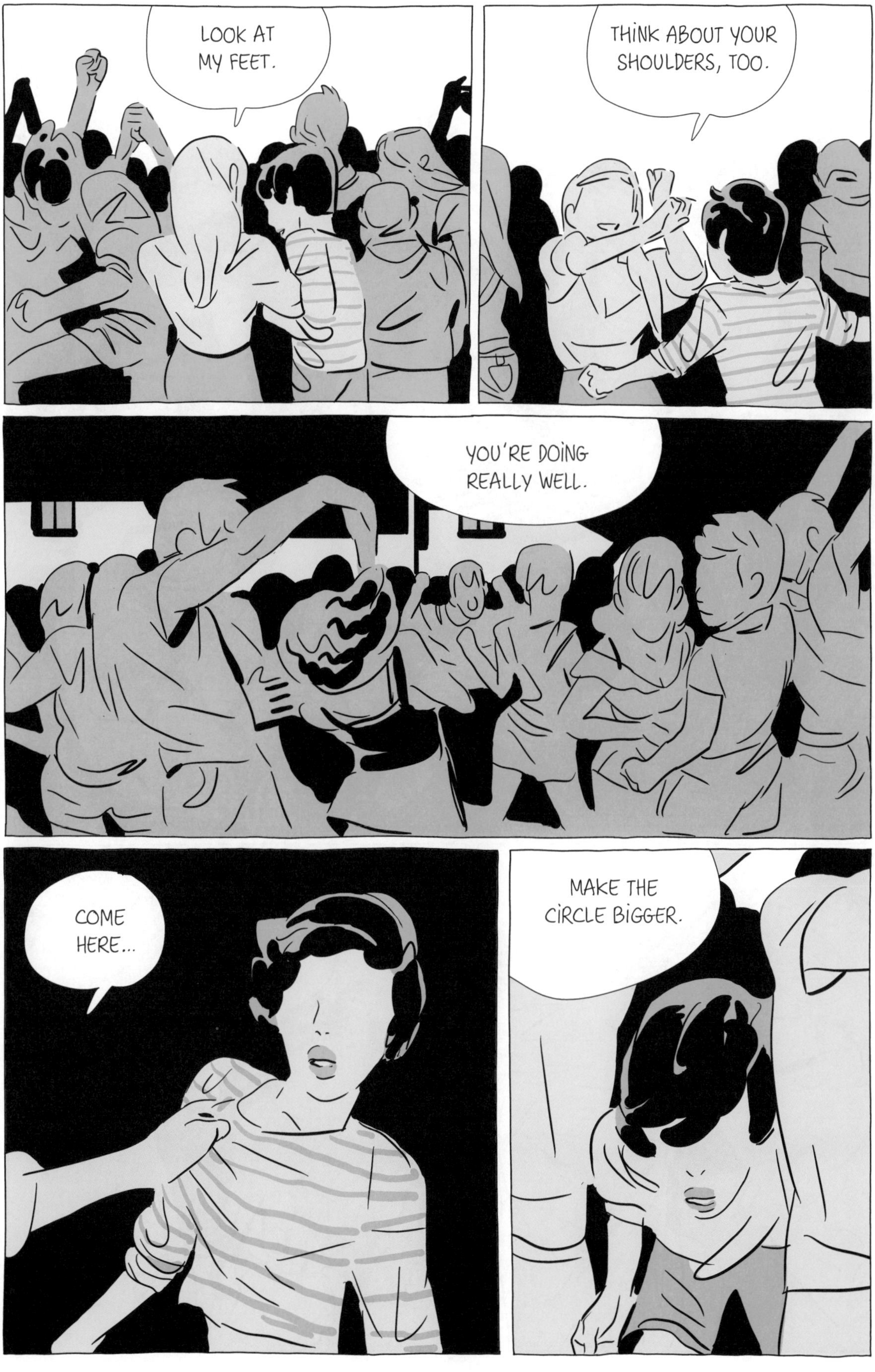
LOOK AT MY FEET.
THINK ABOUT YOUR SHOULDERS, TOO.
YOU'RE DOING REALLY WELL.
COME HERE...
MAKE THE CIRCLE BIGGER.

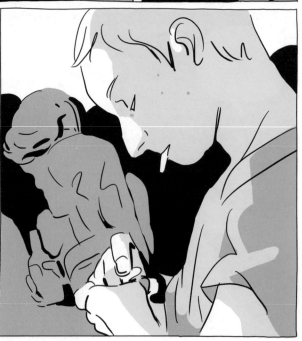

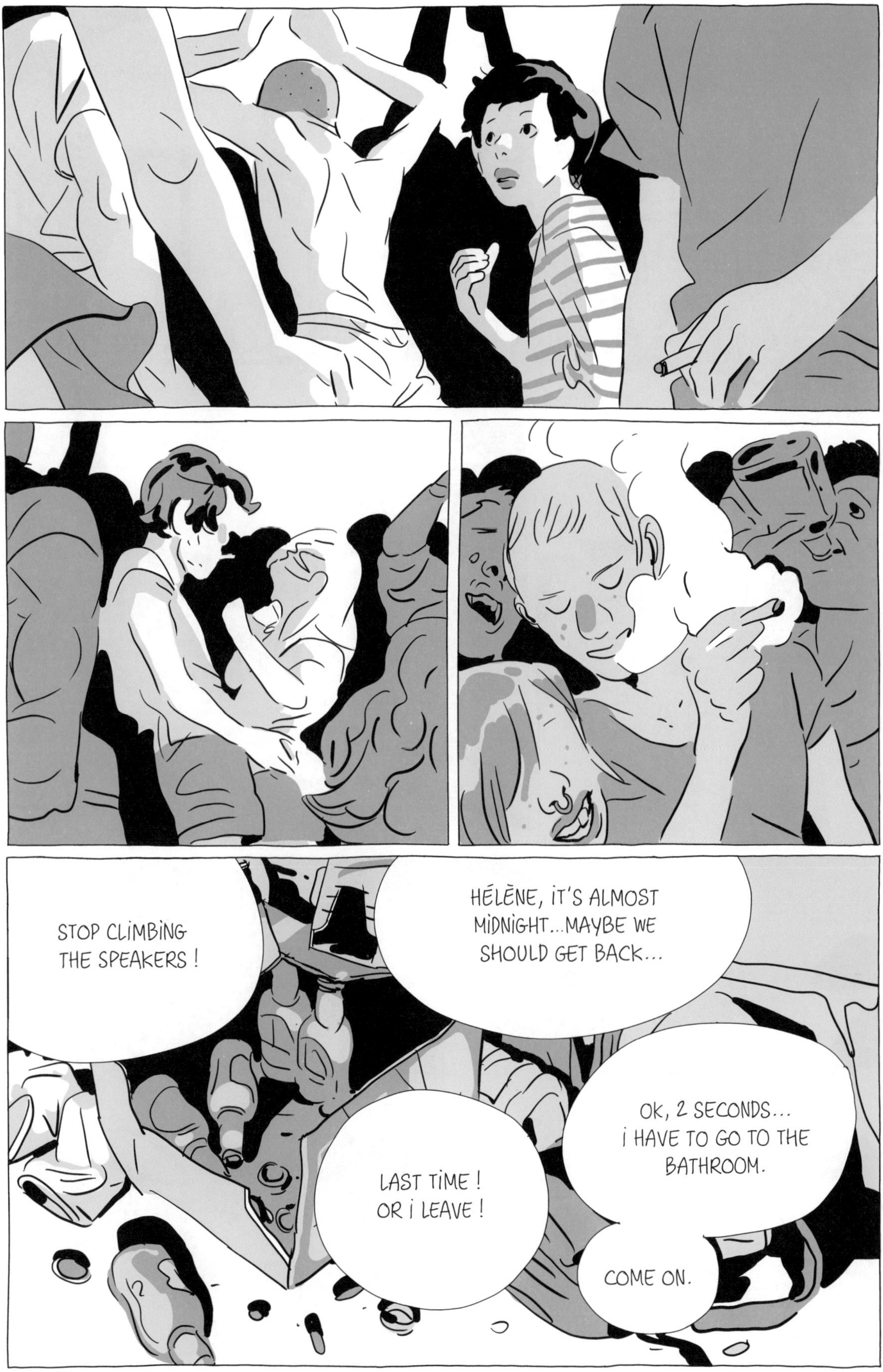
STOP CLiMBiNG THE SPEAKERS !
HÉLÈNE, iT'S ALMOST MiDNiGHT...MAYBE WE SHOULD GET BACK...
OK, 2 SECONDS... i HAVE TO GO TO THE BATHROOM.
LAST TiME ! OR i LEAVE !
COME ON.

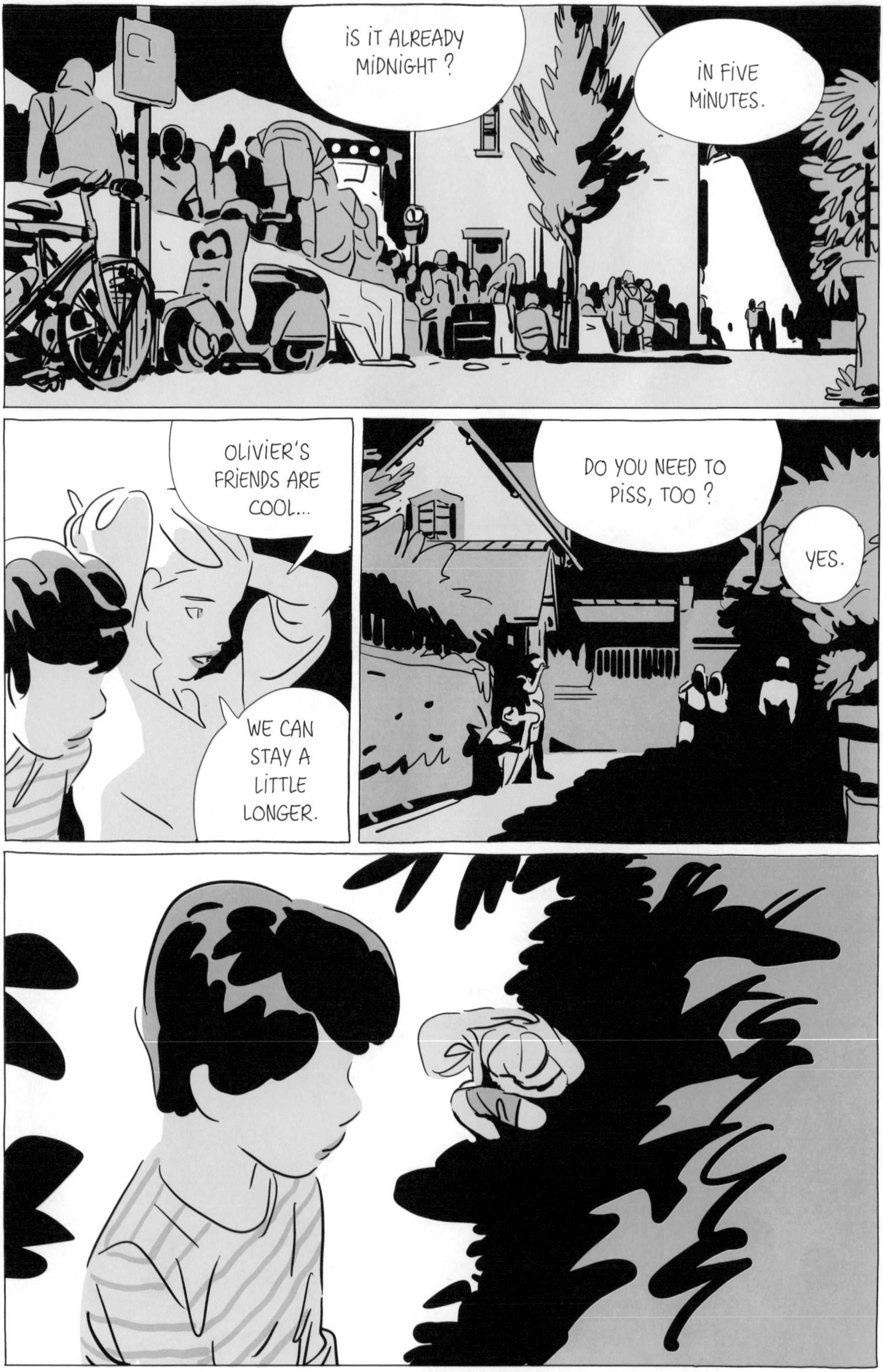
IS IT ALREADY MIDNIGHT ?
IN FIVE MINUTES.
OLIVIER'S FRIENDS ARE COOL...
WE CAN STAY A LITTLE LONGER.
DO YOU NEED TO PISS, TOO ?
YES.

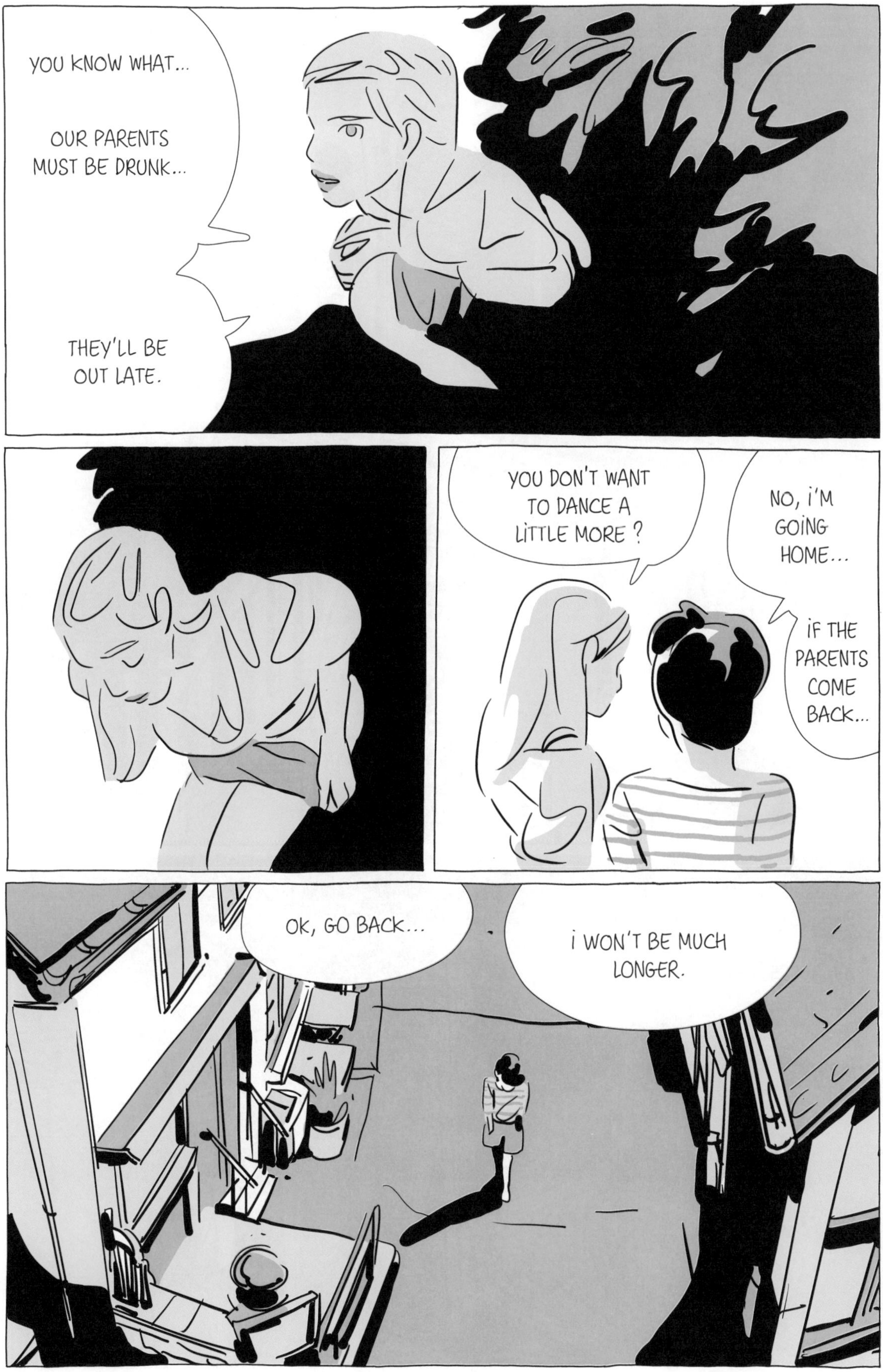

YOU KNOW WHAT...
OUR PARENTS MUST BE DRUNK...
THEY'LL BE OUT LATE.
YOU DON'T WANT TO DANCE A LITTLE MORE ?
NO, I'M GOING HOME...
IF THE PARENTS COME BACK...
OK, GO BACK...
I WON'T BE MUCH LONGER.

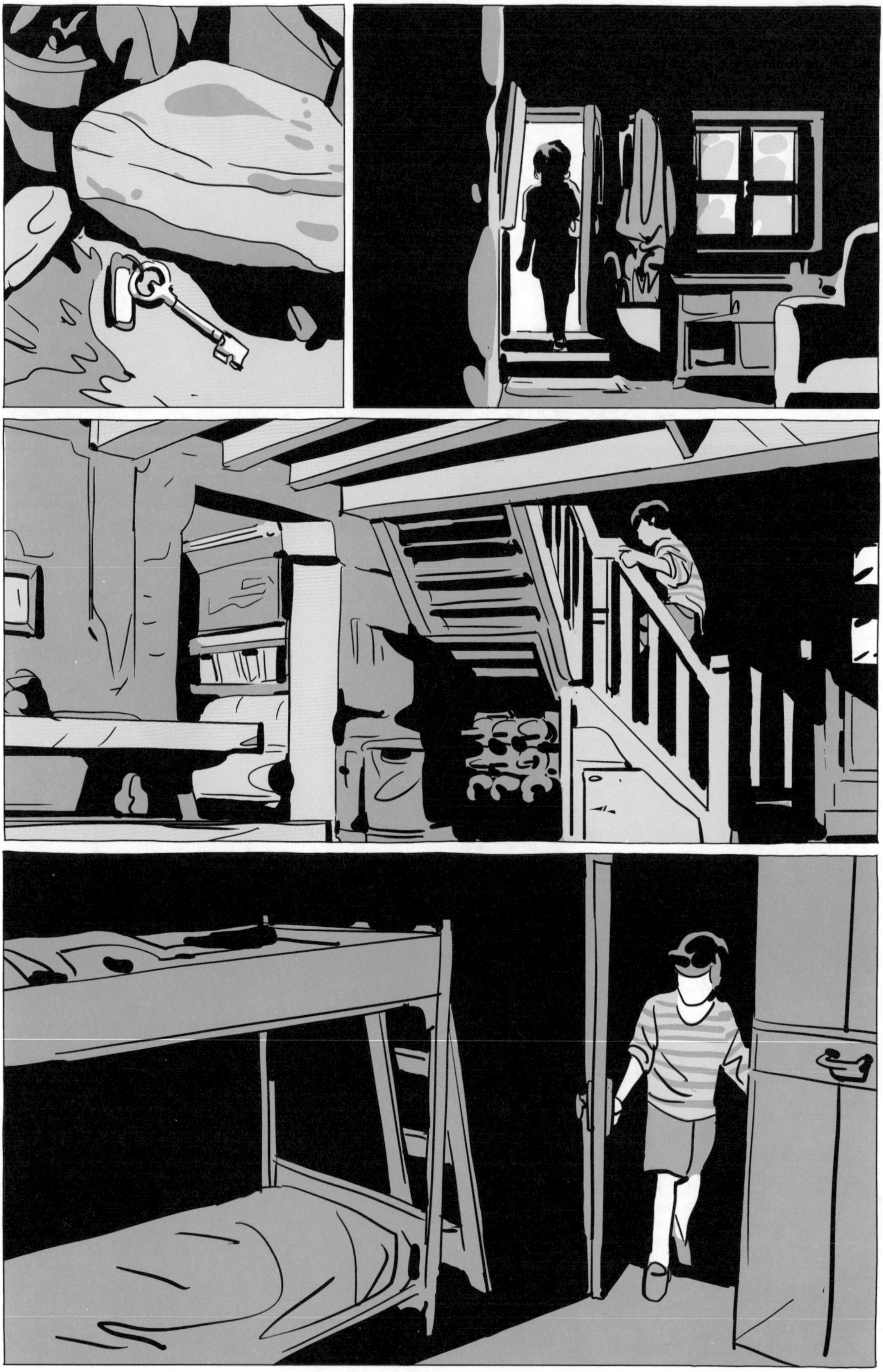

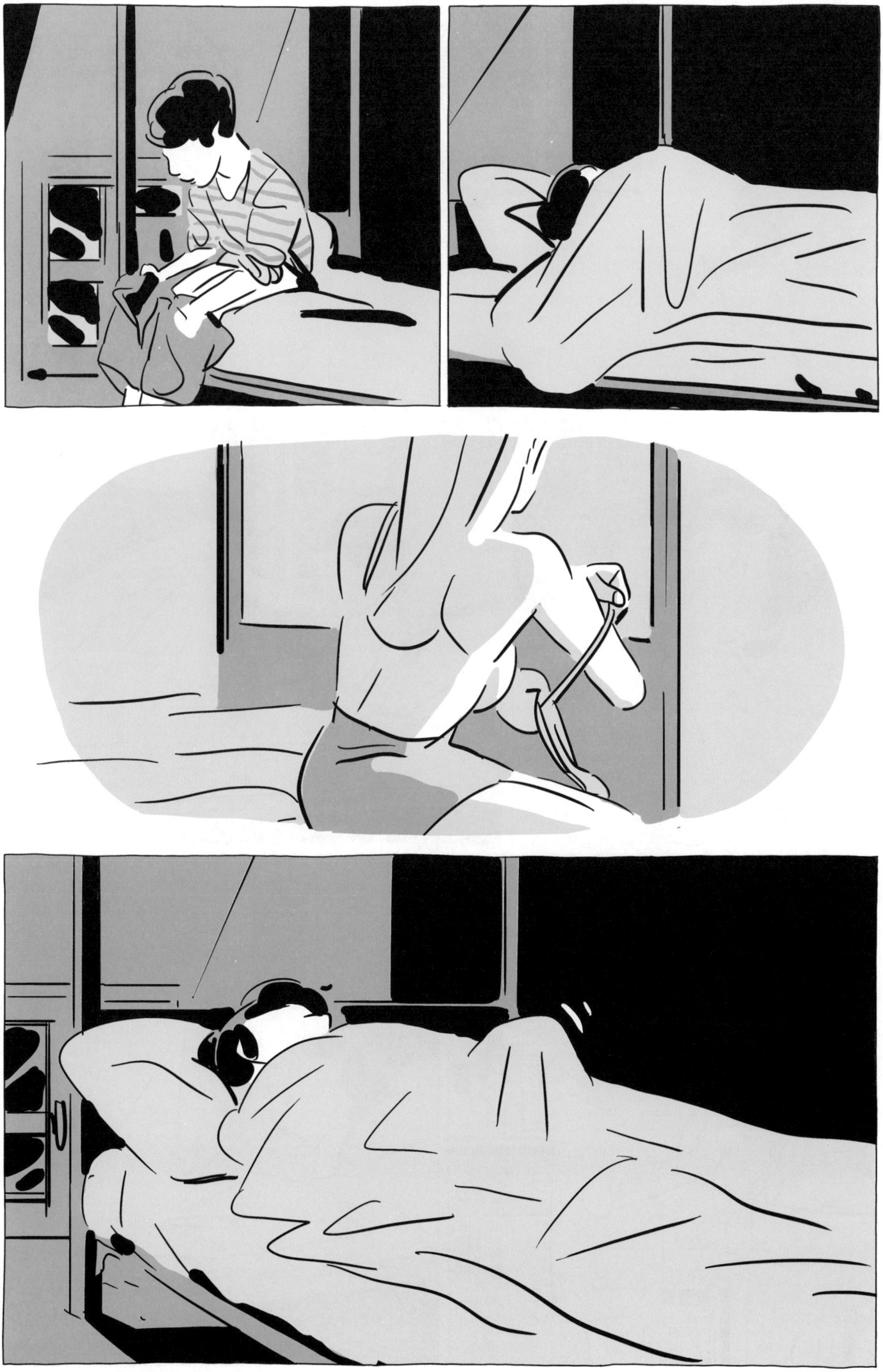

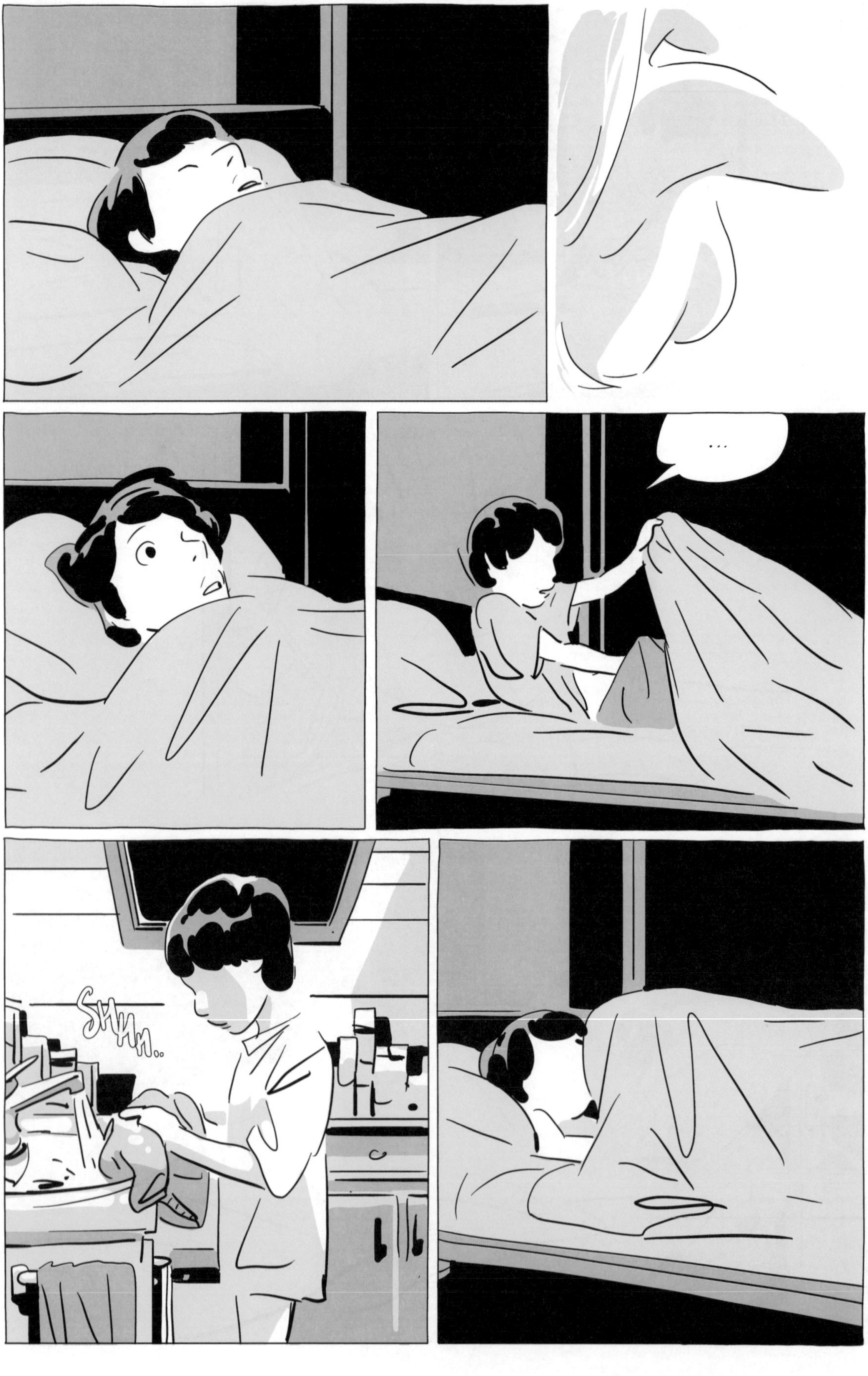
...
SHHH..

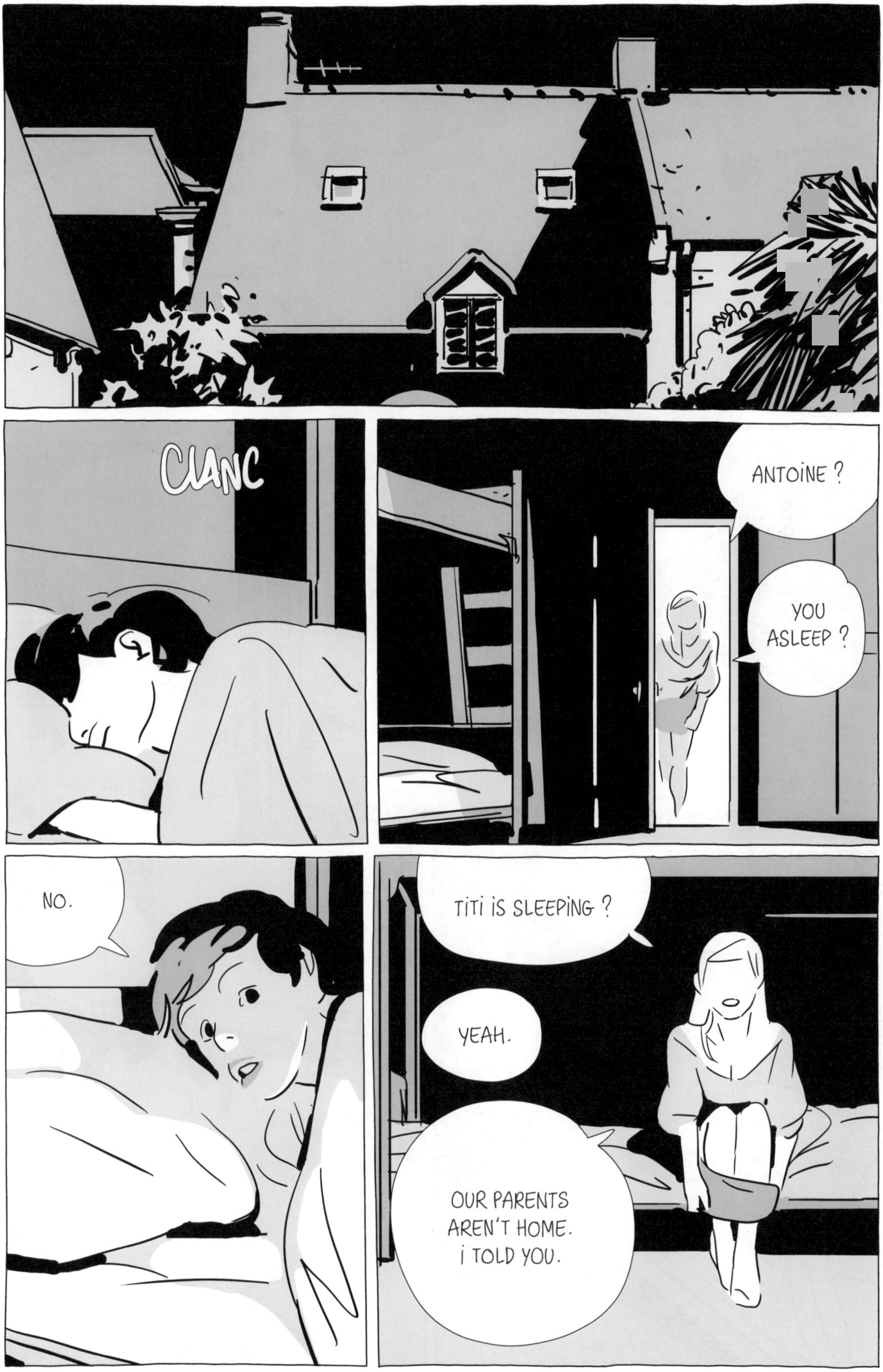
CLANC
ANTOINE ?
YOU ASLEEP ?
NO.
TITI IS SLEEPING ?
YEAH.
OUR PARENTS AREN'T HOME. I TOLD YOU.

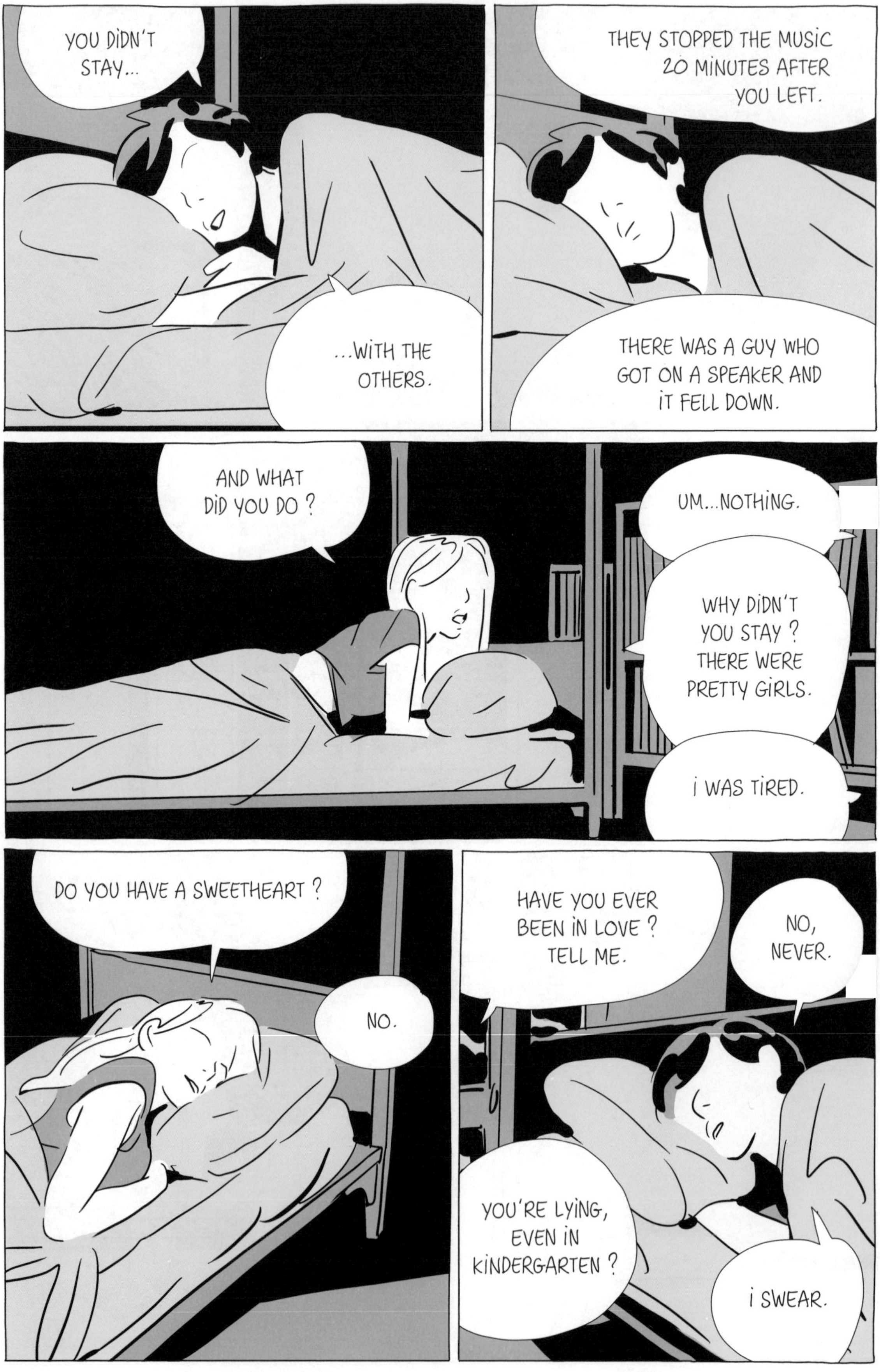
YOU DIDN'T STAY...
...WITH THE OTHERS.
THEY STOPPED THE MUSIC 20 MINUTES AFTER YOU LEFT.
THERE WAS A GUY WHO GOT ON A SPEAKER AND IT FELL DOWN.
AND WHAT DID YOU DO ?
UM...NOTHING.
WHY DIDN'T YOU STAY ? THERE WERE PRETTY GIRLS.
I WAS TIRED.
DO YOU HAVE A SWEETHEART ?
NO.
HAVE YOU EVER BEEN IN LOVE ? TELL ME.
NO, NEVER.
YOU'RE LYING, EVEN IN KINDERGARTEN ?
I SWEAR.

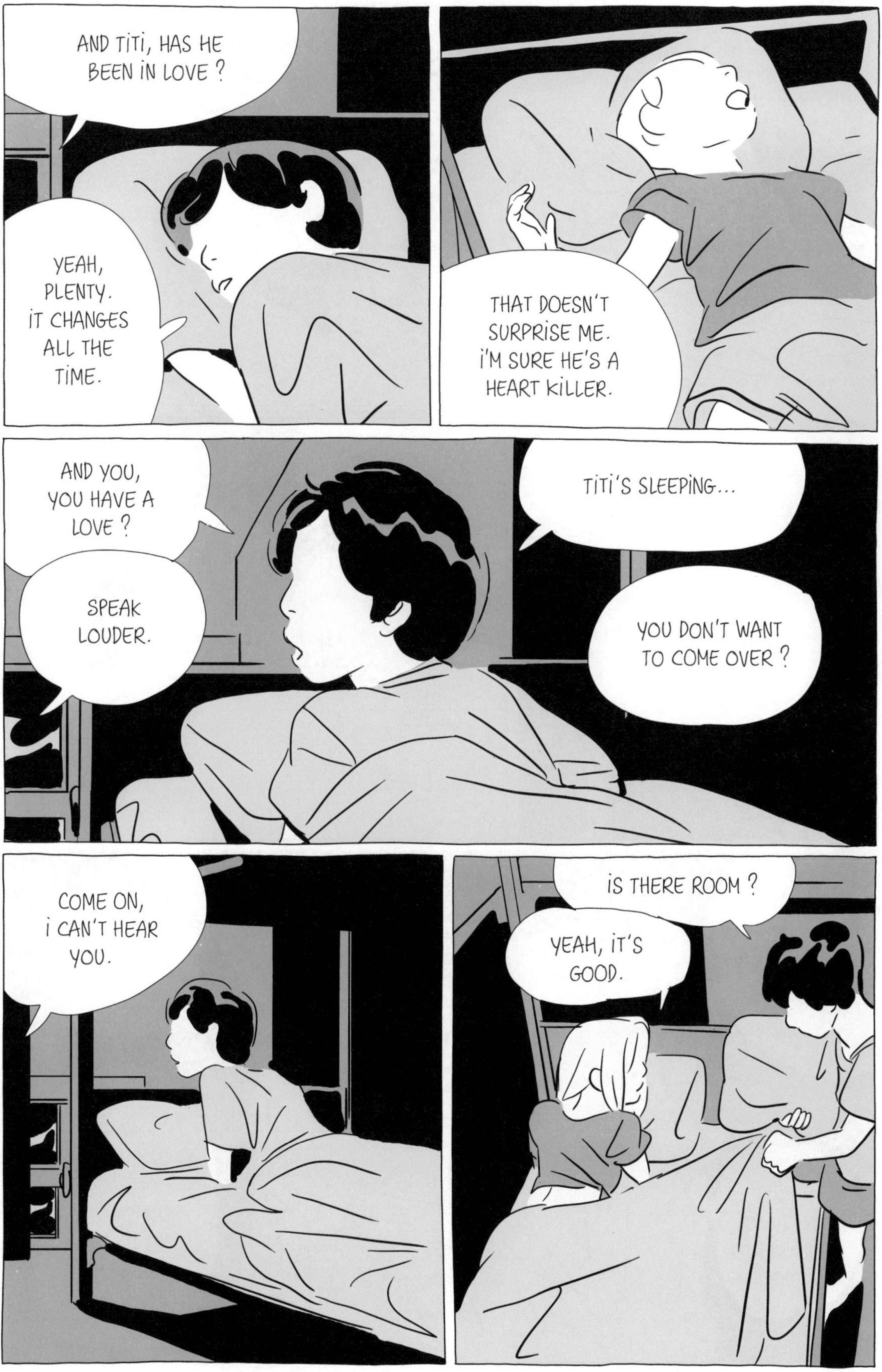
AND TITI, HAS HE BEEN IN LOVE ?
YEAH, PLENTY. IT CHANGES ALL THE TIME.
THAT DOESN'T SURPRISE ME. I'M SURE HE'S A HEART KILLER.
AND YOU, YOU HAVE A LOVE ?
SPEAK LOUDER.
TITI'S SLEEPING...
YOU DON'T WANT TO COME OVER ?
COME ON, I CAN'T HEAR YOU.
IS THERE ROOM ?
YEAH, IT'S GOOD.

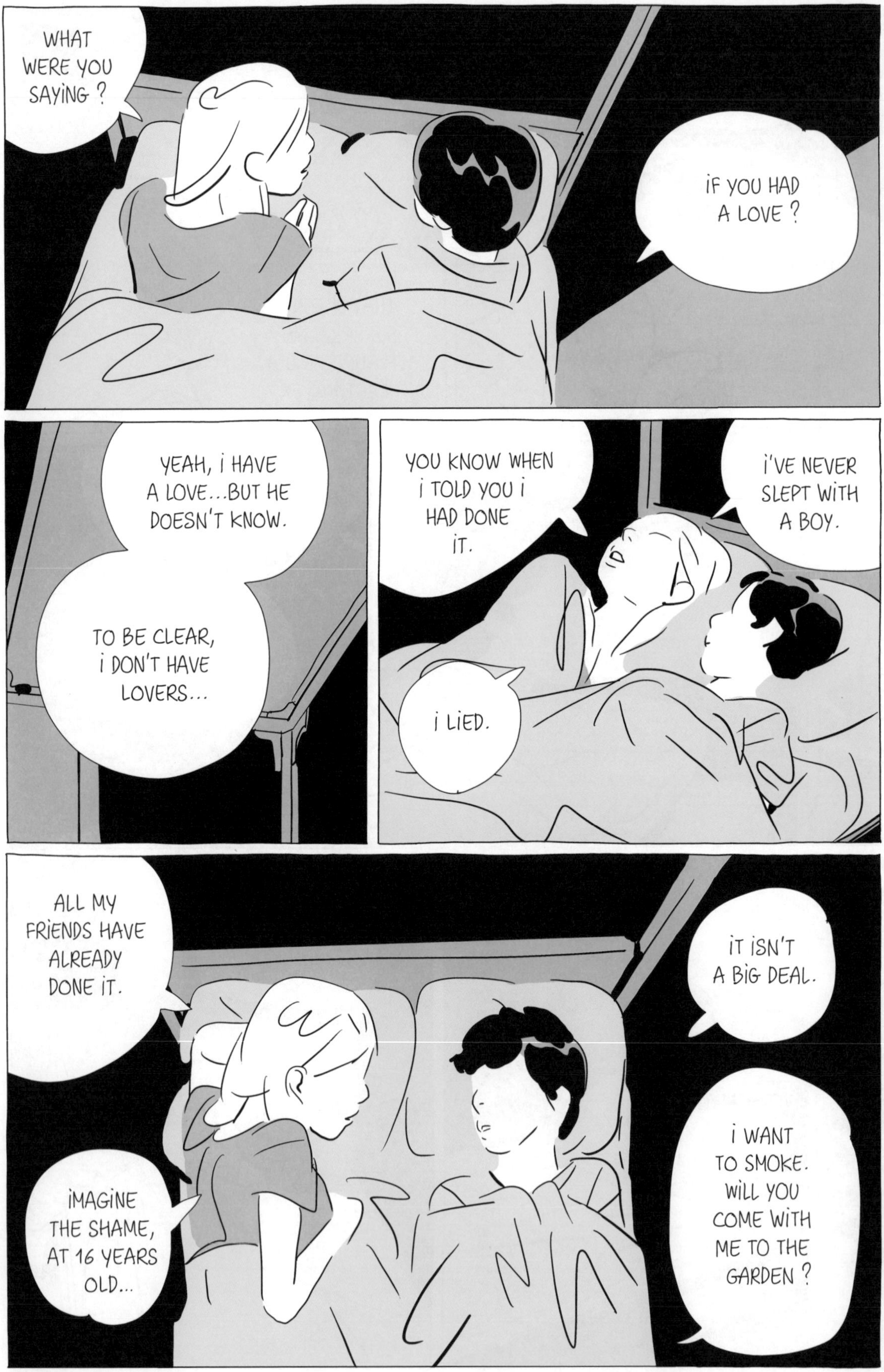
WHAT WERE YOU SAYING ?
iF YOU HAD A LOVE ?
YEAH, i HAVE A LOVE...BUT HE DOESN'T KNOW.
TO BE CLEAR, i DON'T HAVE LOVERS...
YOU KNOW WHEN i TOLD YOU i HAD DONE iT.
i'VE NEVER SLEPT WiTH A BOY.
i LiED.
ALL MY FRiENDS HAVE ALREADY DONE iT.
iT iSN'T A BiG DEAL.
iMAGiNE THE SHAME, AT 16 YEARS OLD...
i WANT TO SMOKE. WiLL YOU COME WiTH ME TO THE GARDEN ?

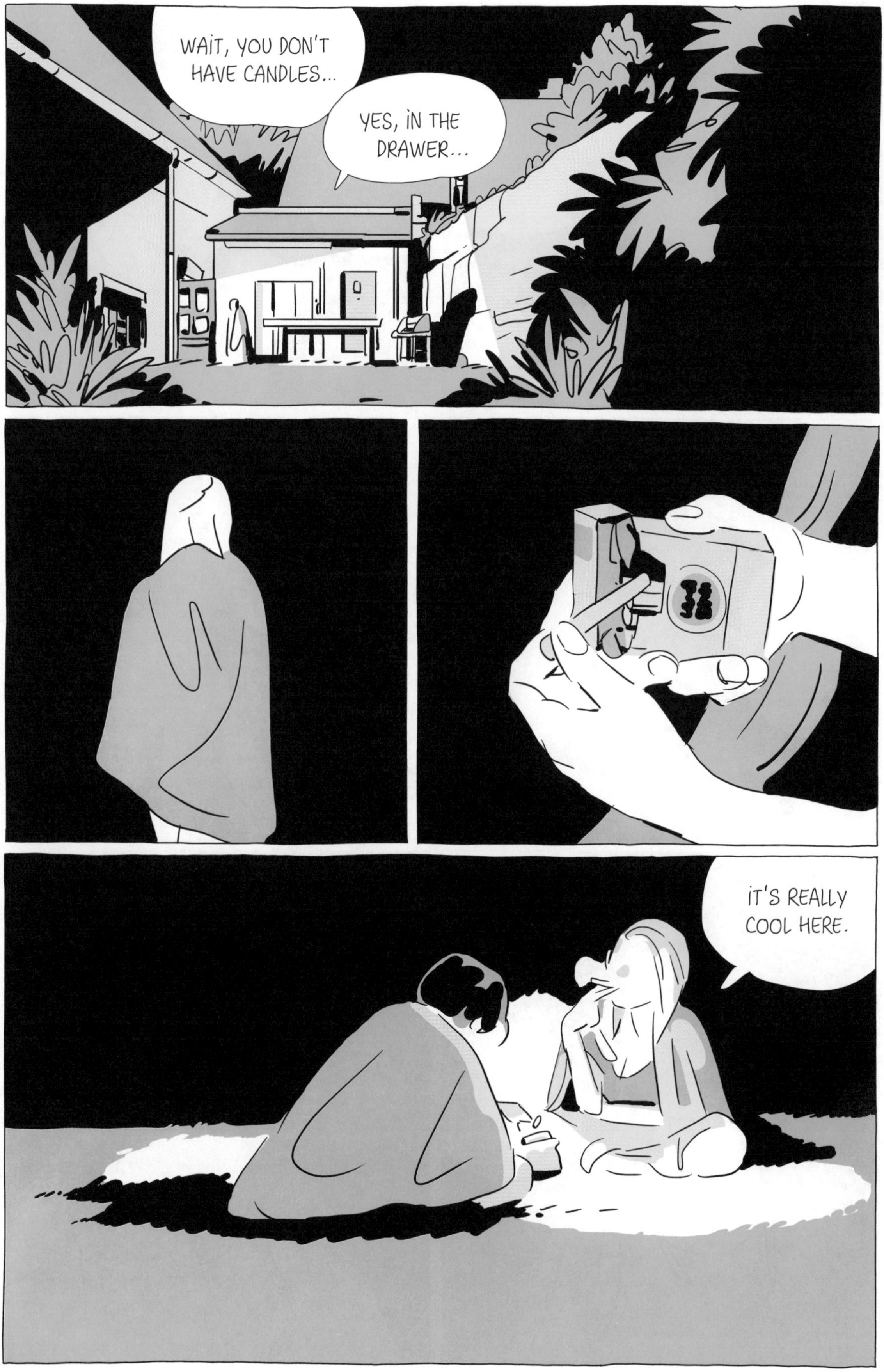
WAIT, YOU DON'T HAVE CANDLES...
YES, IN THE DRAWER...
IT'S REALLY COOL HERE.

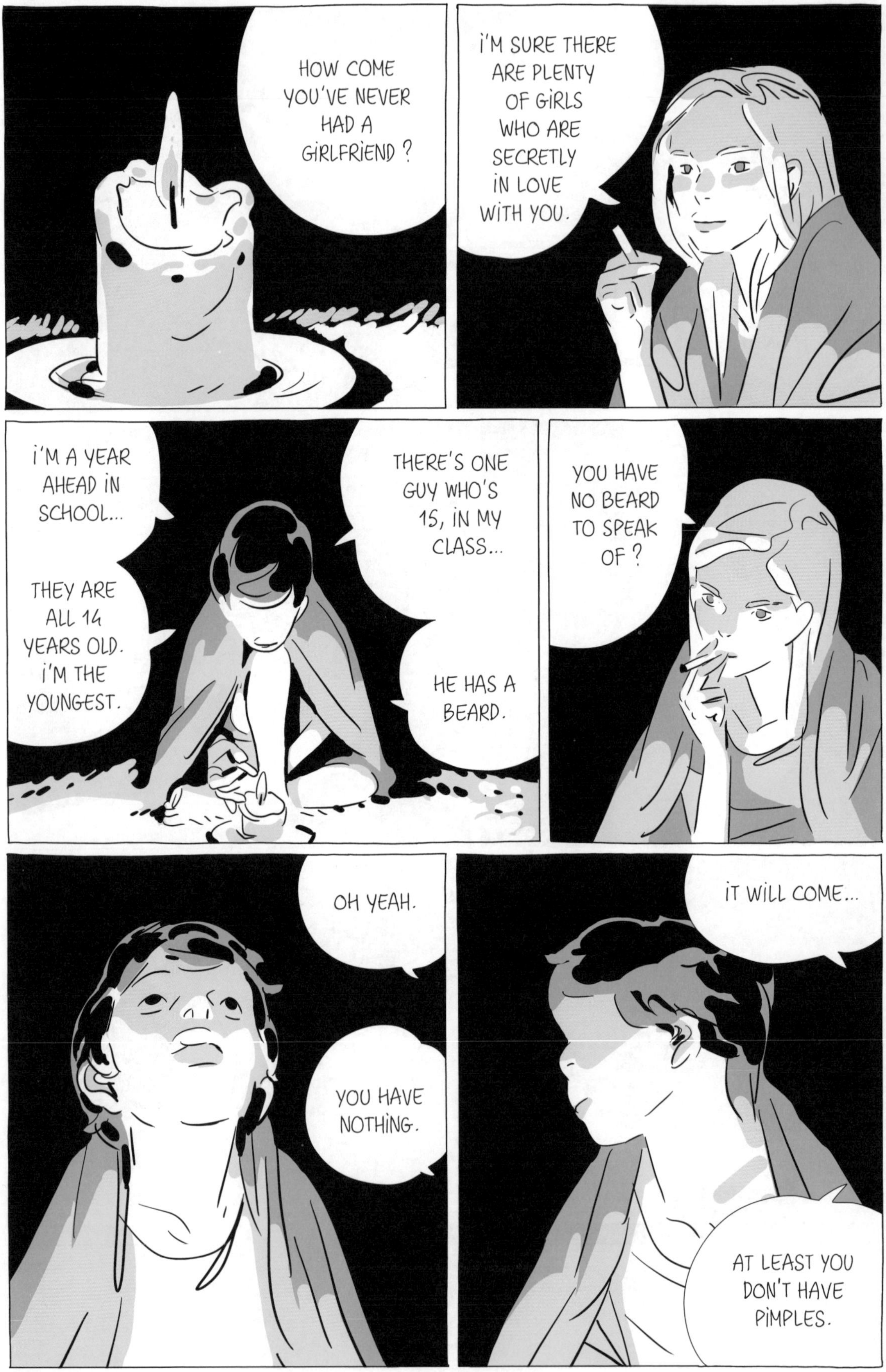
HOW COME YOU'VE NEVER HAD A GIRLFRIEND?
I'M SURE THERE ARE PLENTY OF GIRLS WHO ARE SECRETLY IN LOVE WITH YOU.
I'M A YEAR AHEAD IN SCHOOL...
THEY ARE ALL 14 YEARS OLD. I'M THE YOUNGEST.
THERE'S ONE GUY WHO'S 15, IN MY CLASS...
HE HAS A BEARD.
YOU HAVE NO BEARD TO SPEAK OF?
OH YEAH.
YOU HAVE NOTHING.
IT WILL COME...
AT LEAST YOU DON'T HAVE PIMPLES.

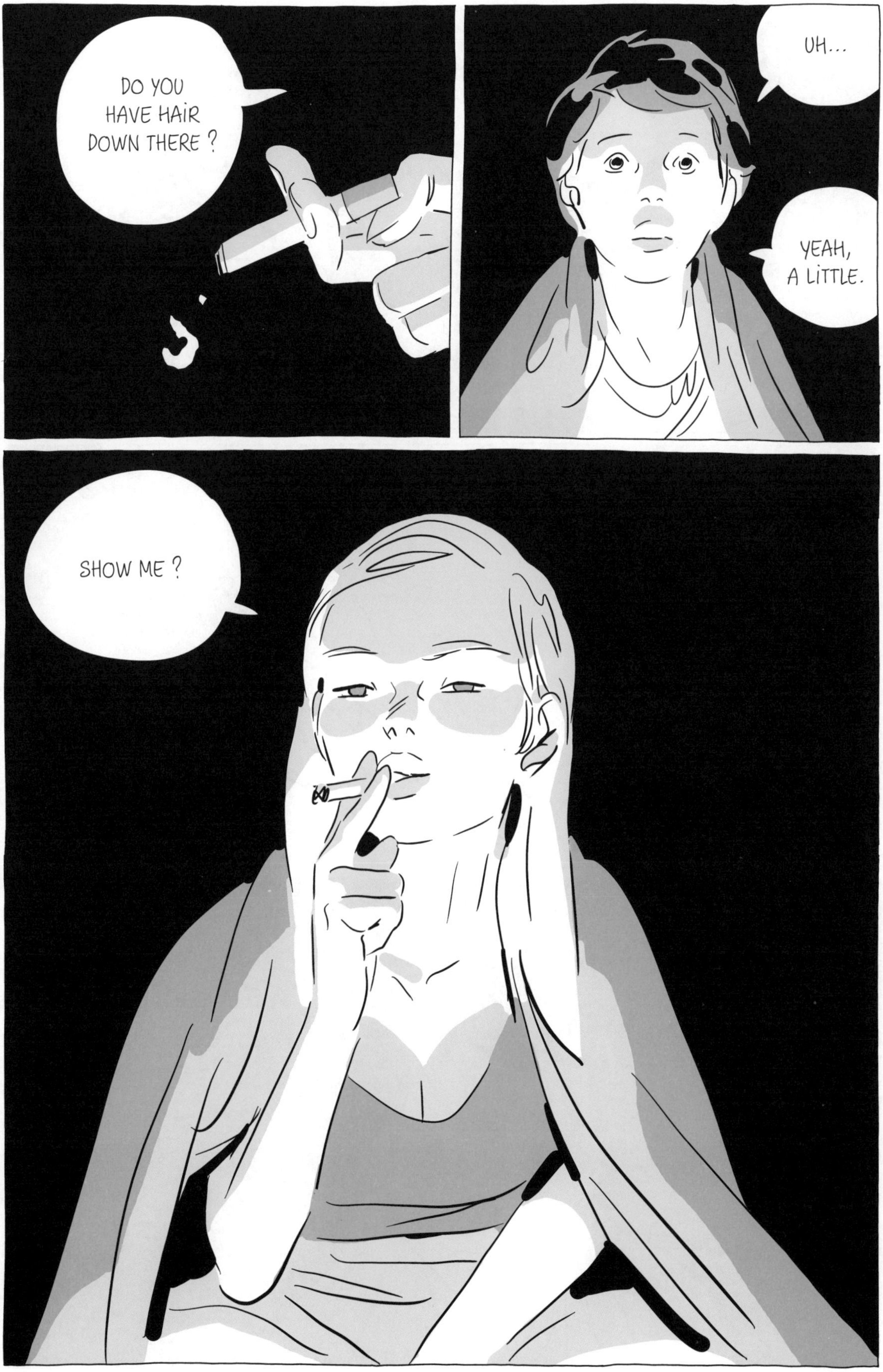
DO YOU HAVE HAIR DOWN THERE ?
UH...
YEAH, A LITTLE.
SHOW ME ?

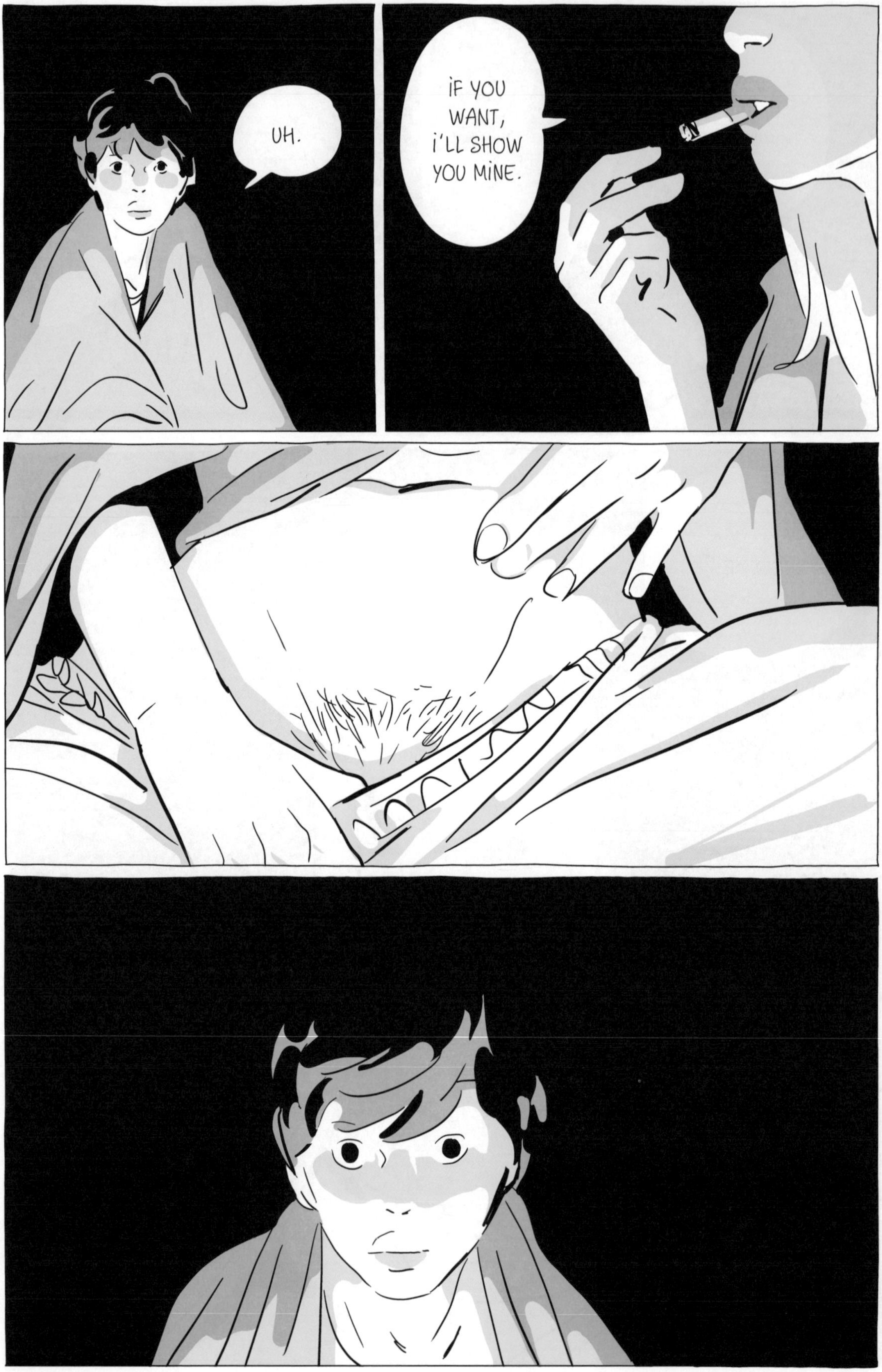
UH.
IF YOU WANT, I'LL SHOW YOU MINE.

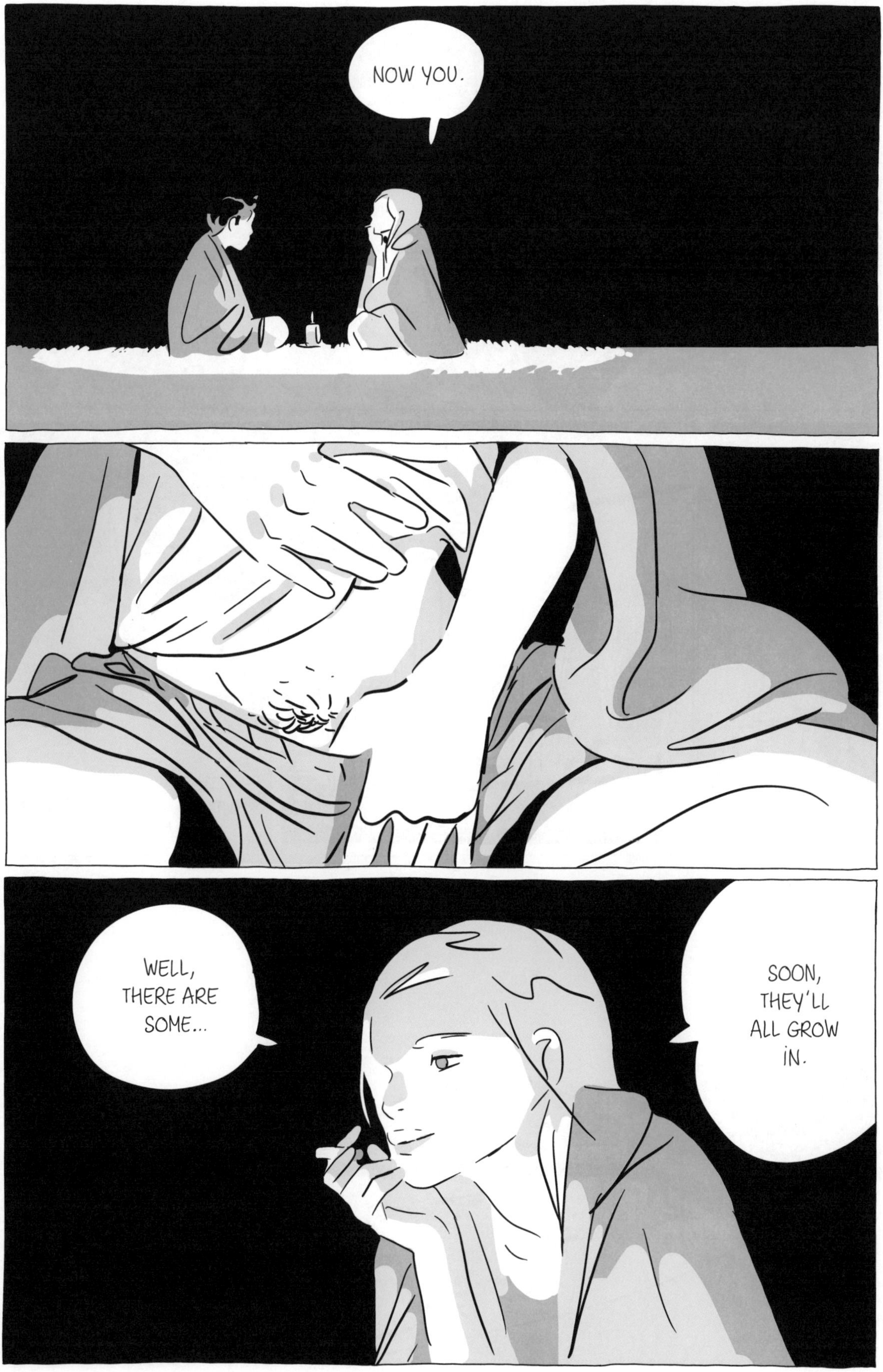
NOW YOU.
WELL, THERE ARE SOME...
SOON, THEY'LL ALL GROW IN.

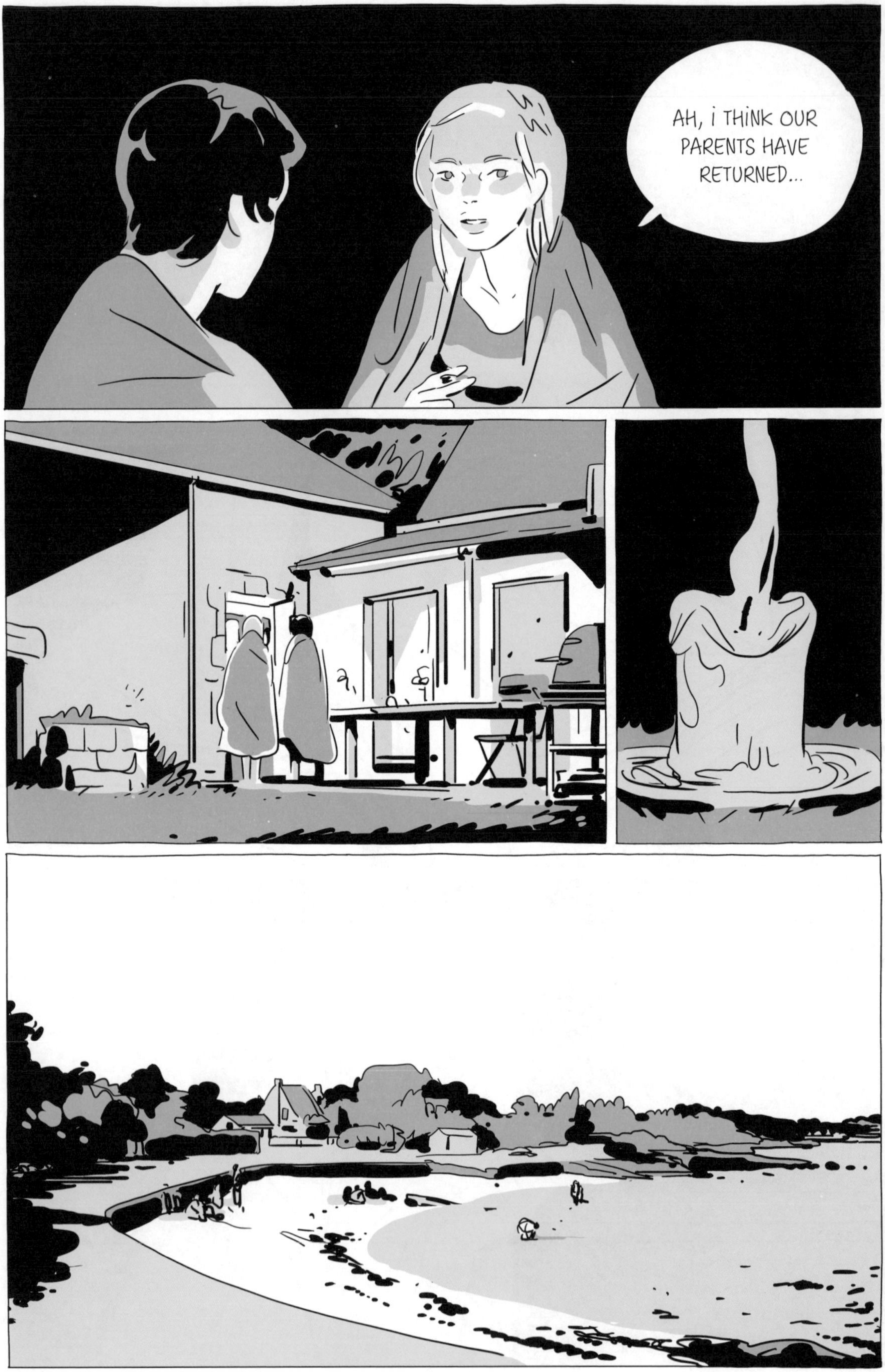
AH, I THINK OUR PARENTS HAVE RETURNED...

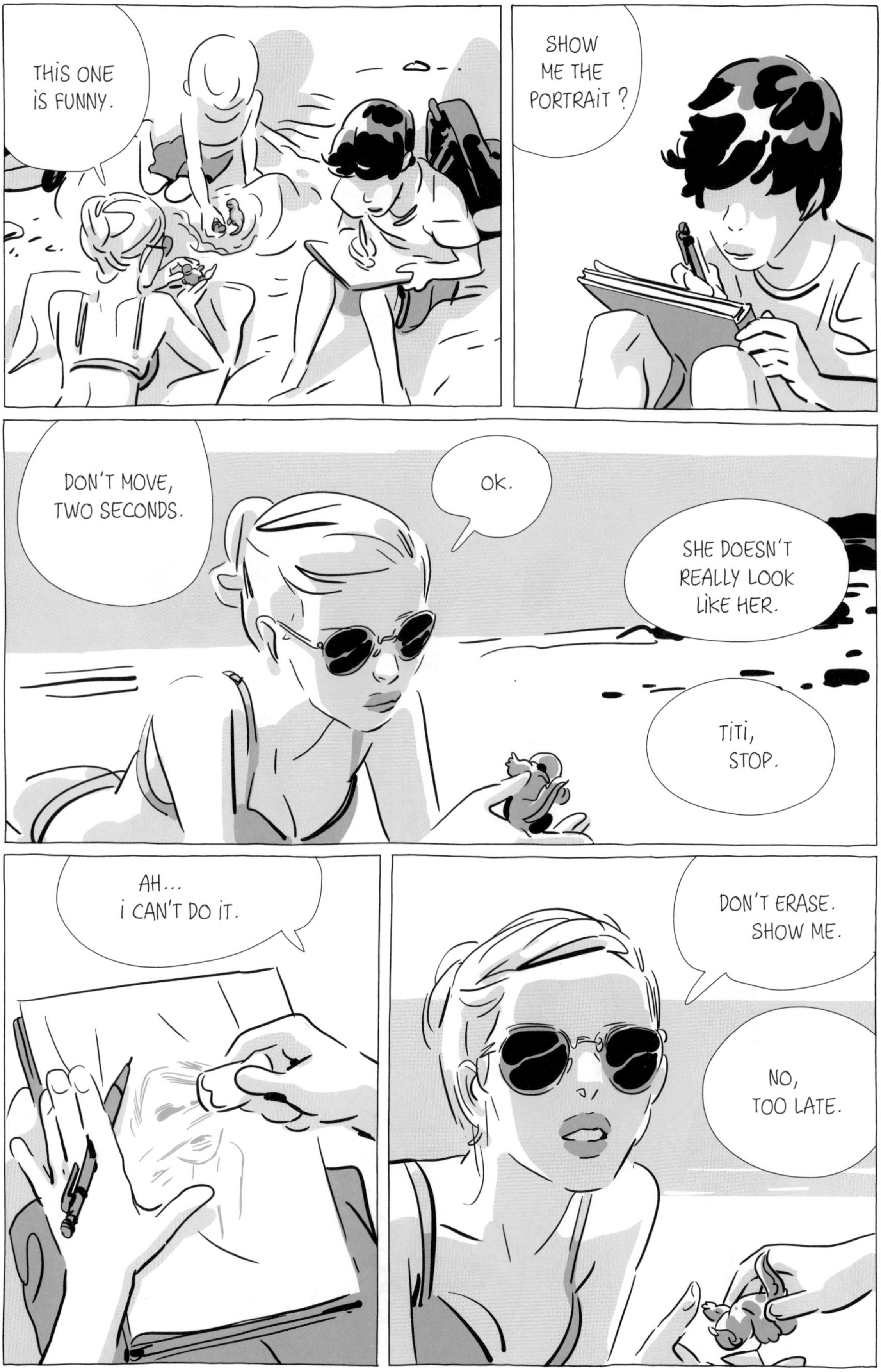
THIS ONE IS FUNNY.
SHOW ME THE PORTRAIT ?
DON'T MOVE, TWO SECONDS.
OK.
SHE DOESN'T REALLY LOOK LIKE HER.
TITI, STOP.
AH... I CAN'T DO IT.
DON'T ERASE. SHOW ME.
NO, TOO LATE.

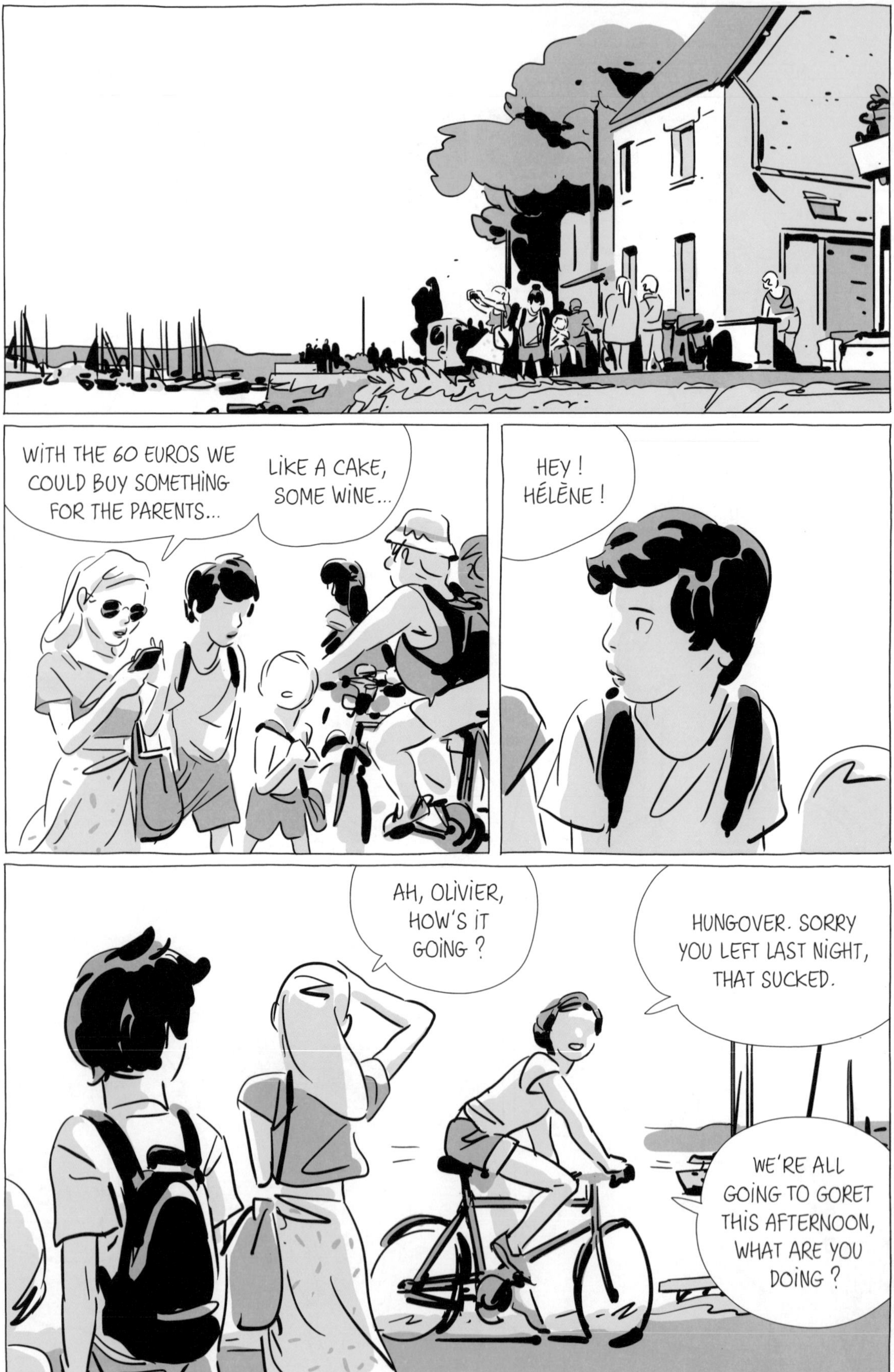
WITH THE 60 EUROS WE COULD BUY SOMETHING FOR THE PARENTS...
LIKE A CAKE, SOME WINE...
HEY ! HÉLÈNE !
AH, OLIVIER, HOW'S IT GOING ?
HUNGOVER. SORRY YOU LEFT LAST NIGHT, THAT SUCKED.
WE'RE ALL GOING TO GORET THIS AFTERNOON, WHAT ARE YOU DOING ?

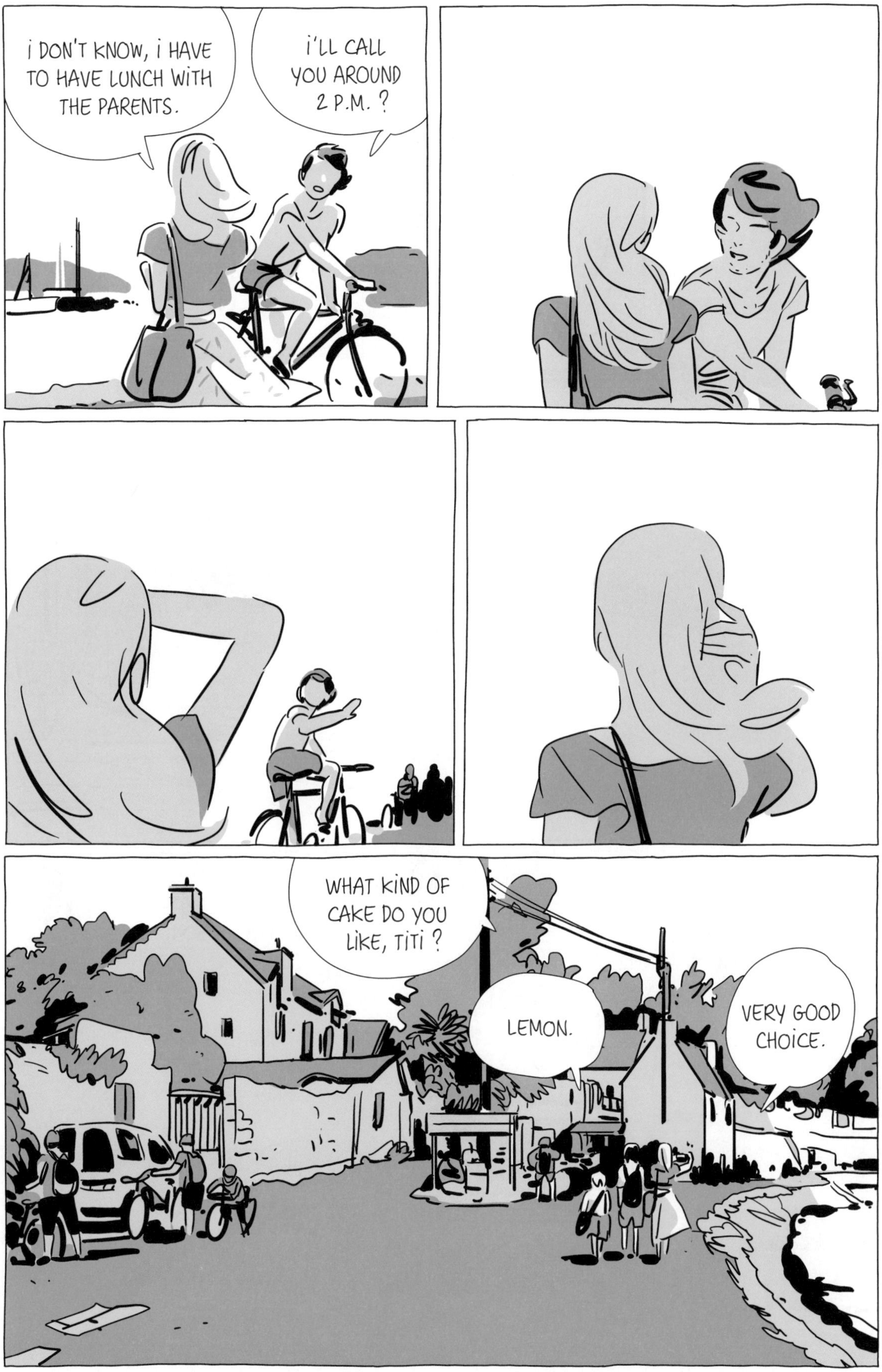
I DON'T KNOW, I HAVE TO HAVE LUNCH WITH THE PARENTS.
I'LL CALL YOU AROUND 2 P.M. ?
WHAT KIND OF CAKE DO YOU LIKE, TITI ?
LEMON.
VERY GOOD CHOICE.

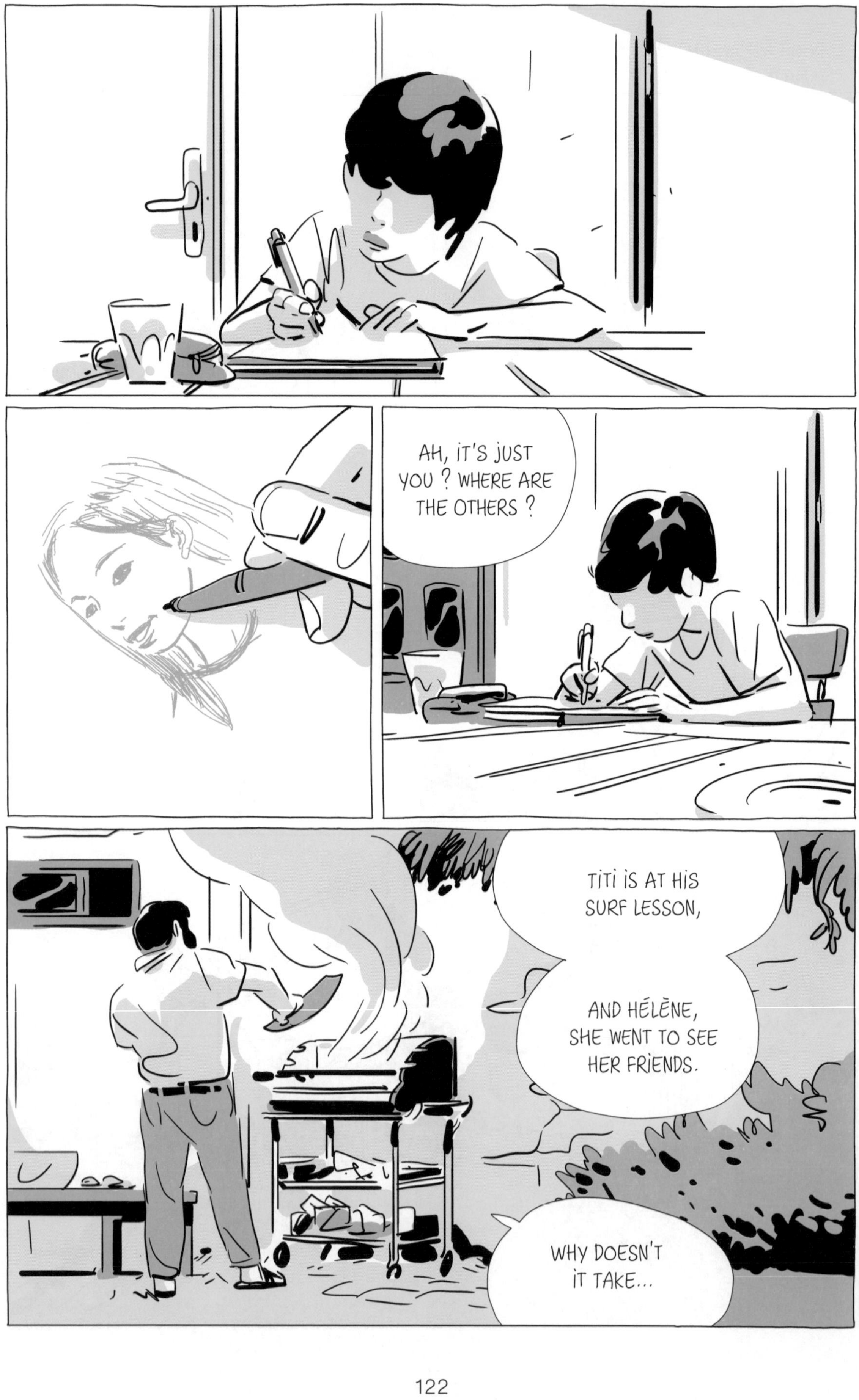
AH, IT'S JUST YOU ? WHERE ARE THE OTHERS ?
TITI IS AT HIS SURF LESSON,
AND HÉLÈNE, SHE WENT TO SEE HER FRIENDS.
WHY DOESN'T IT TAKE...

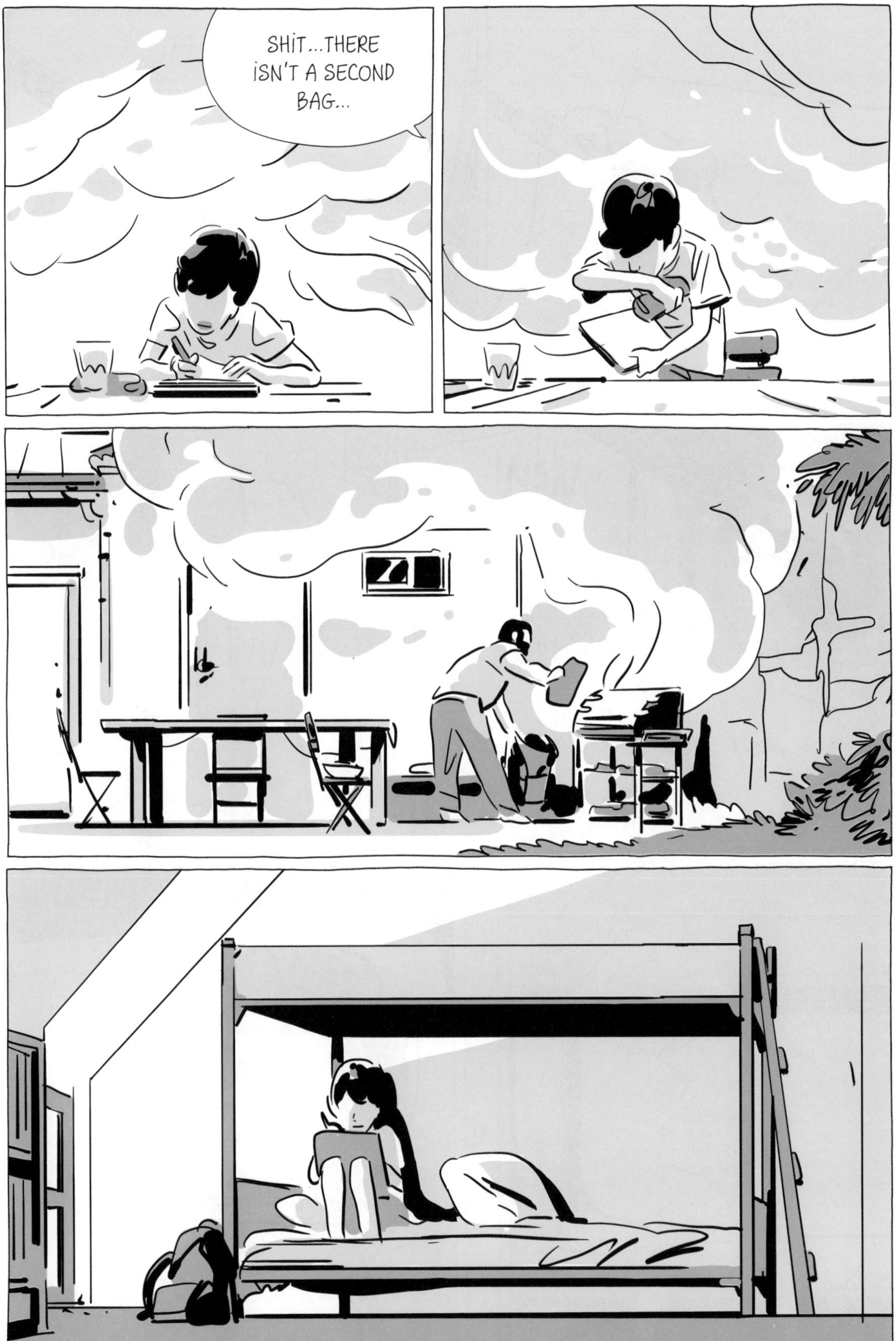
SHIT...THERE ISN'T A SECOND BAG...

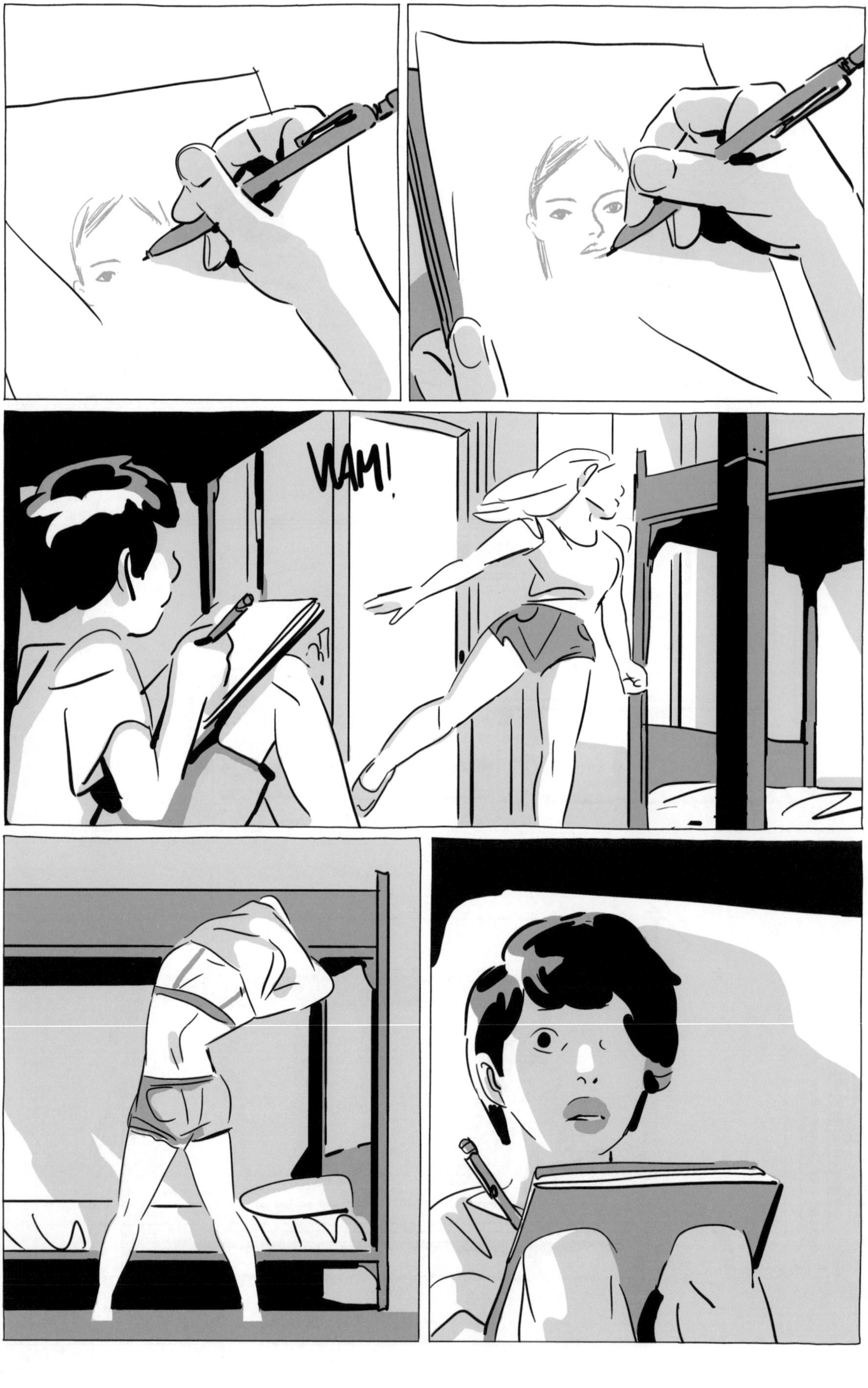
WAM!

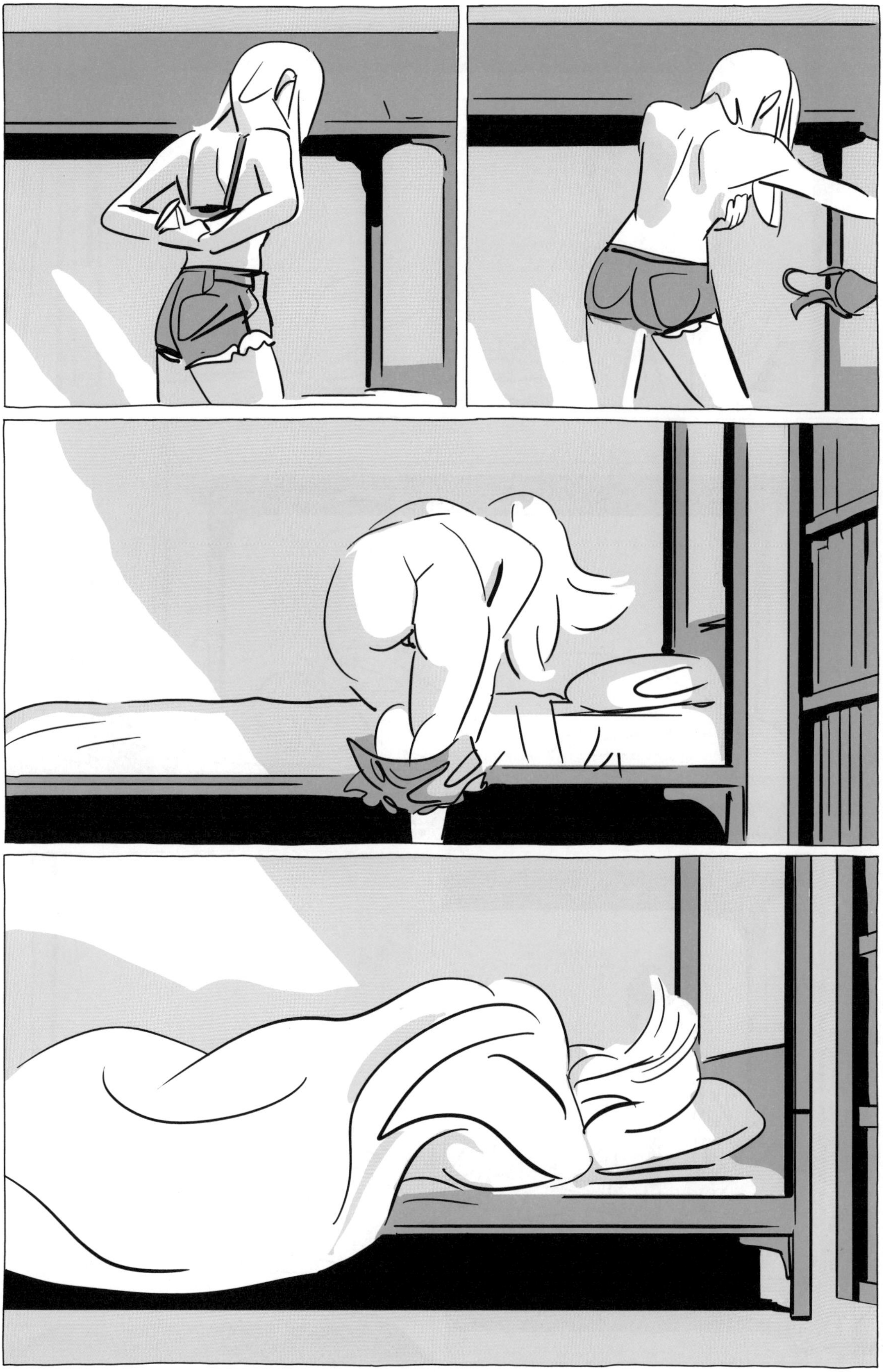

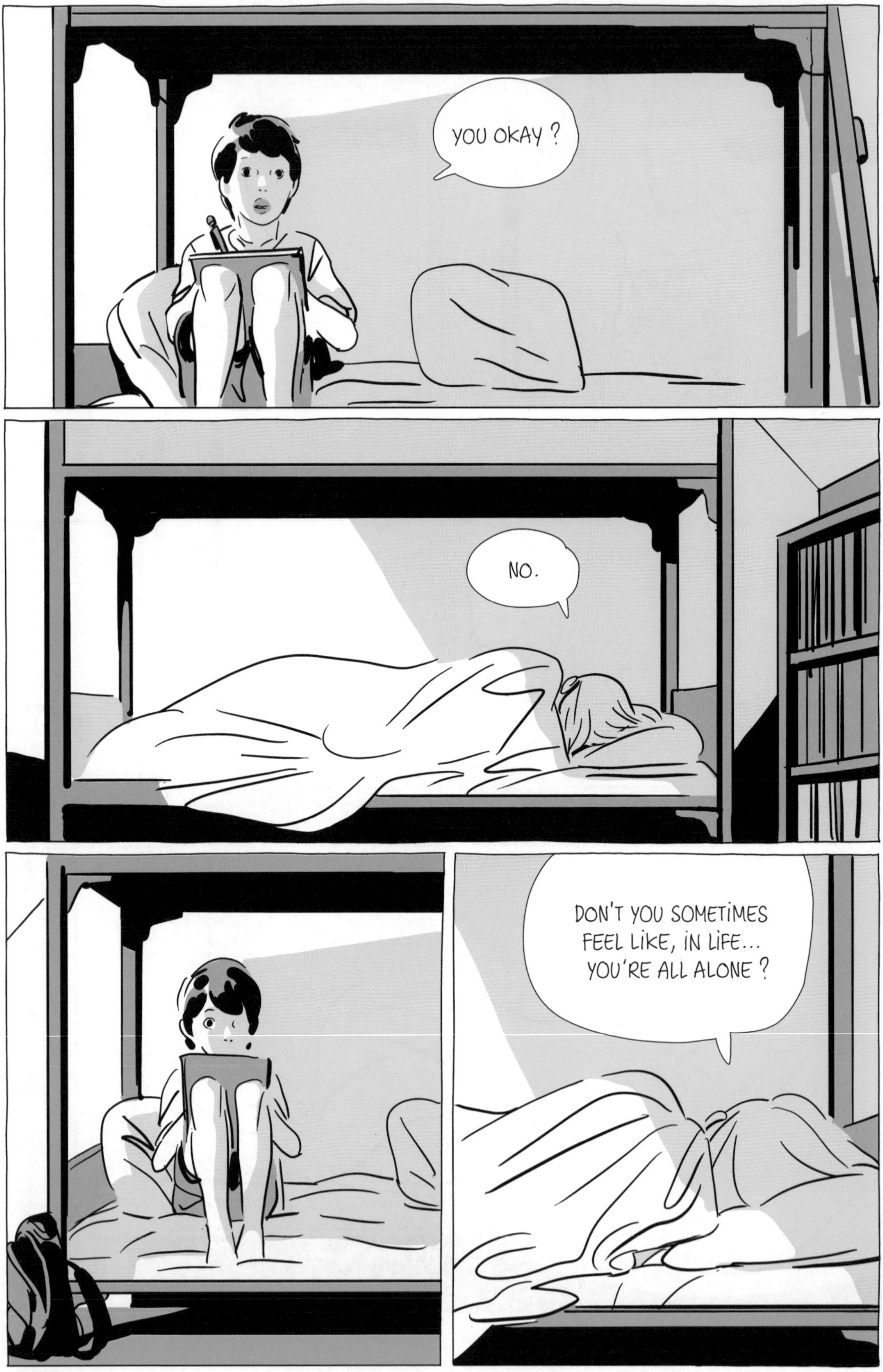
YOU OKAY ?
NO.
DON'T YOU SOMETIMES FEEL LIKE, IN LIFE... YOU'RE ALL ALONE ?

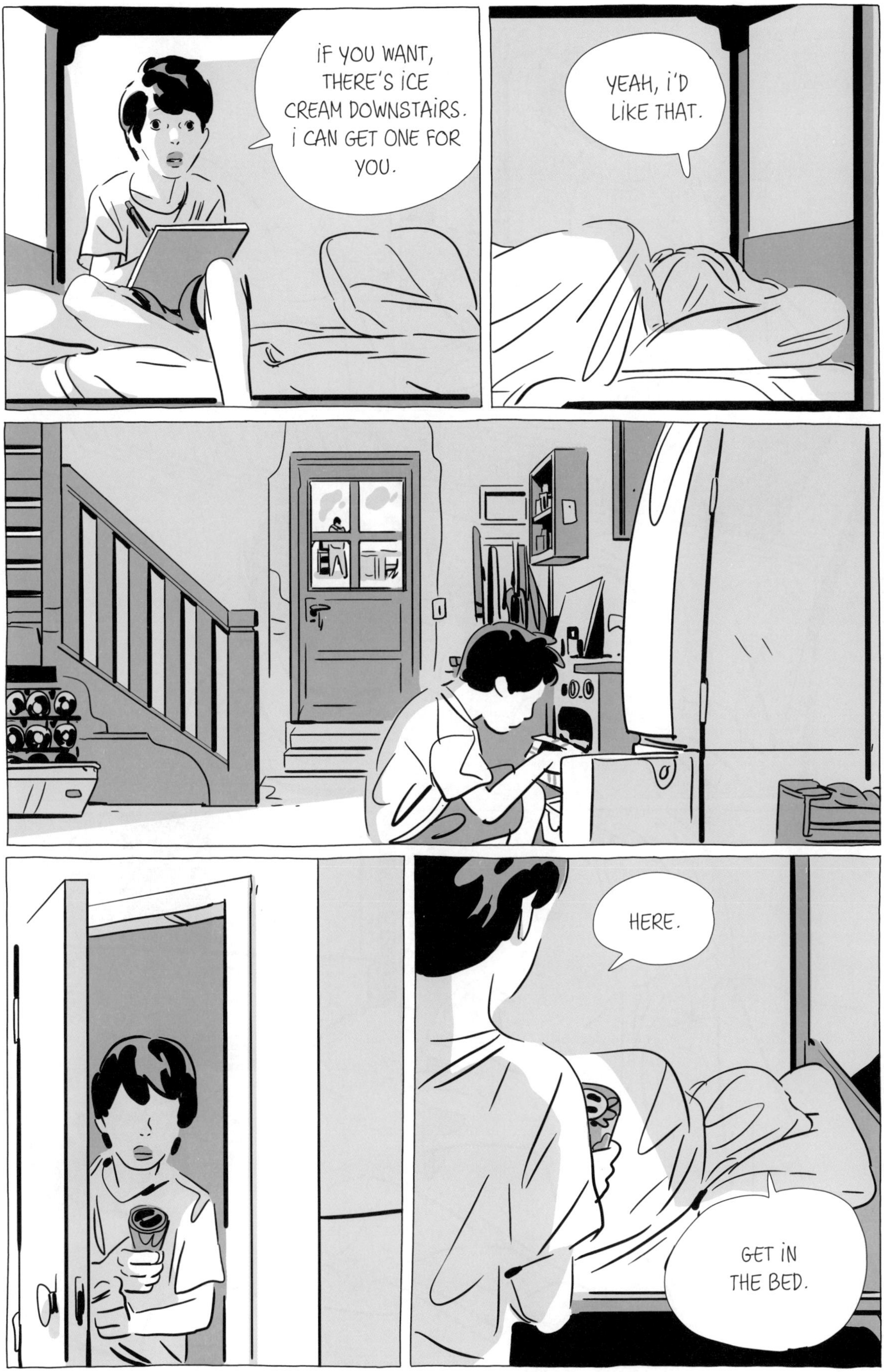
IF YOU WANT, THERE'S ICE CREAM DOWNSTAIRS. I CAN GET ONE FOR YOU.
YEAH, I'D LIKE THAT.
HERE.
GET IN THE BED.

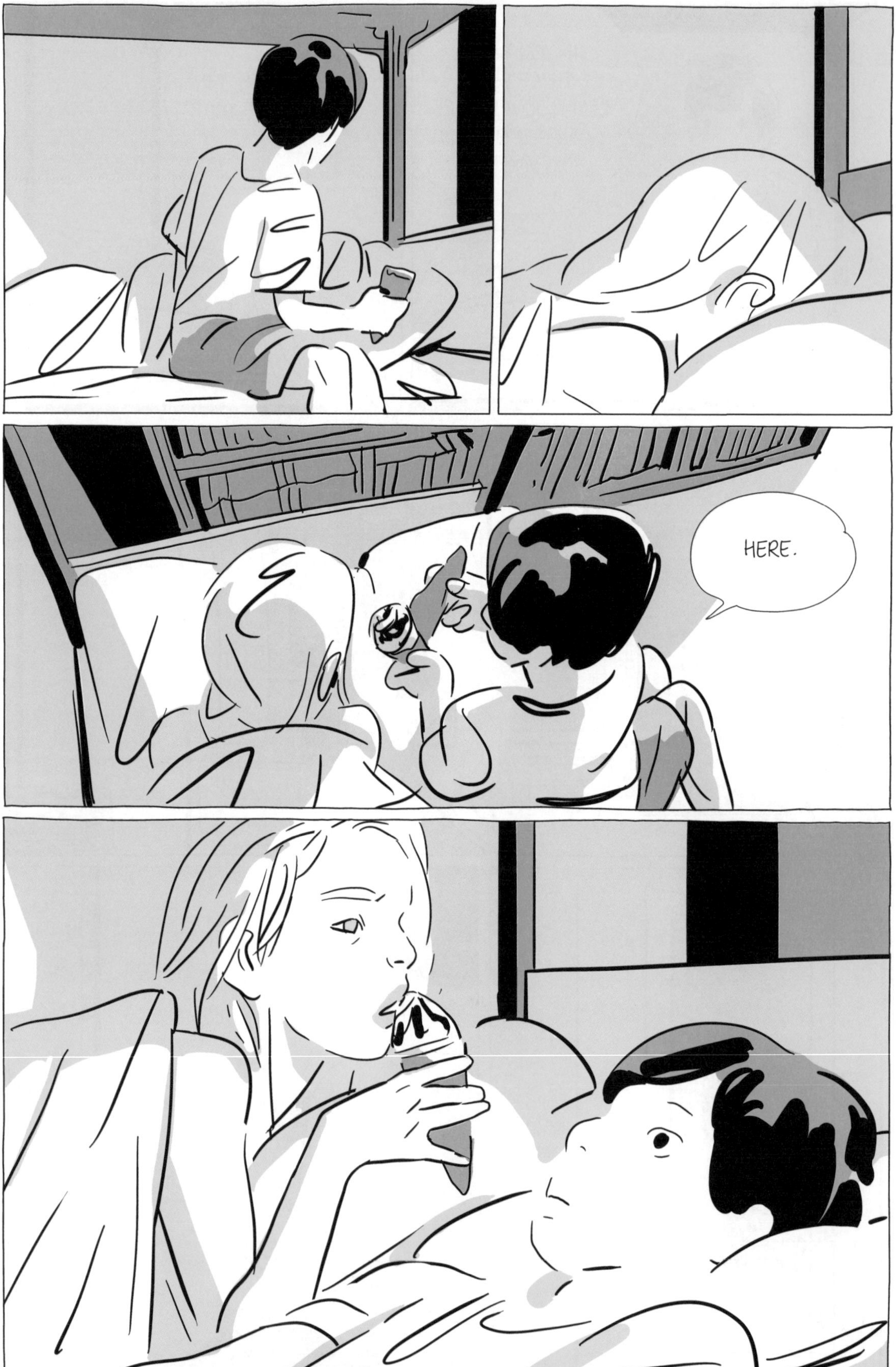
HERE.

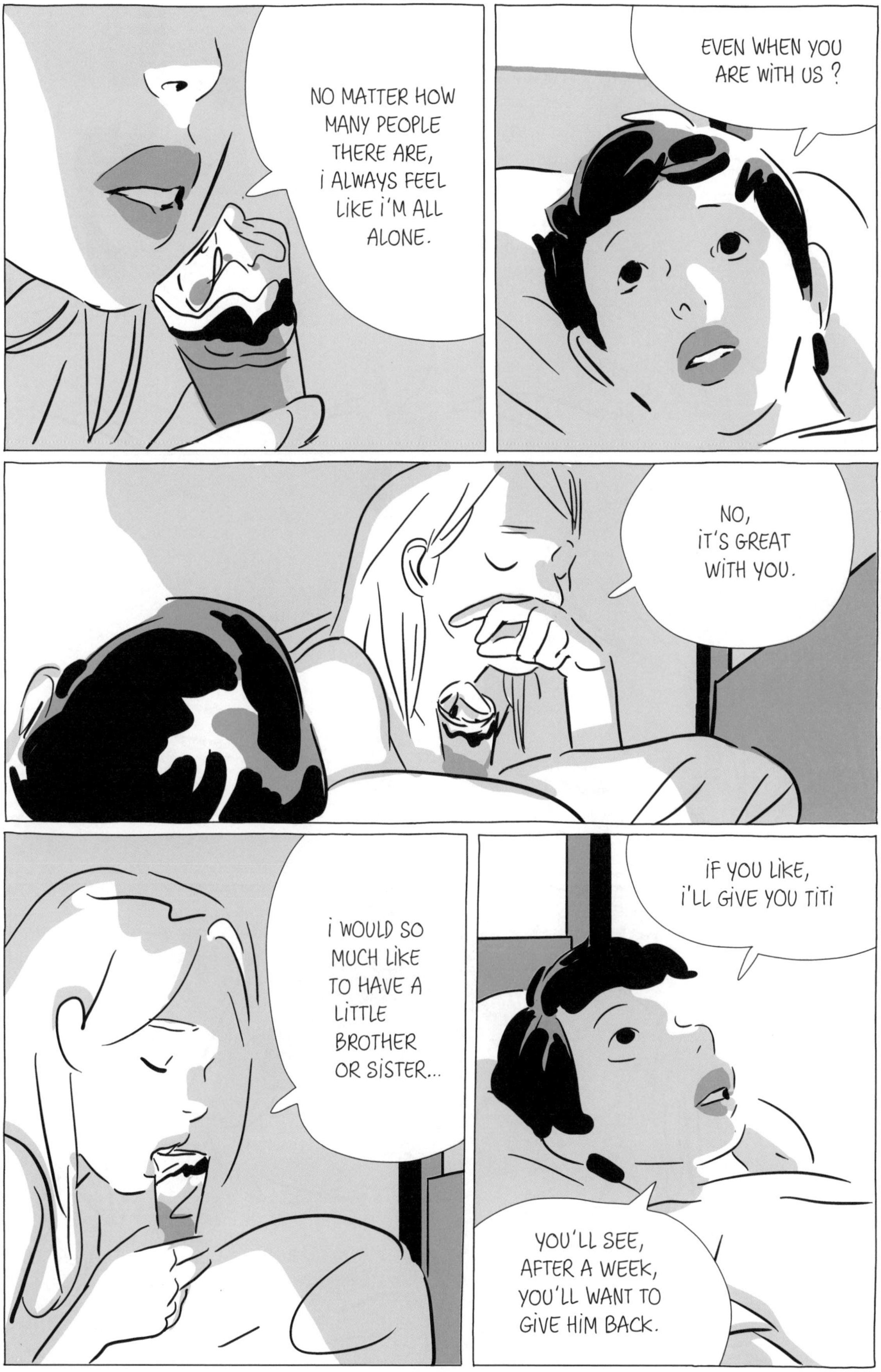
NO MATTER HOW MANY PEOPLE THERE ARE, I ALWAYS FEEL LIKE I'M ALL ALONE.
EVEN WHEN YOU ARE WITH US ?
NO, IT'S GREAT WITH YOU.
I WOULD SO MUCH LIKE TO HAVE A LITTLE BROTHER OR SISTER...
IF YOU LIKE, I'LL GIVE YOU TITI
YOU'LL SEE, AFTER A WEEK, YOU'LL WANT TO GIVE HIM BACK.

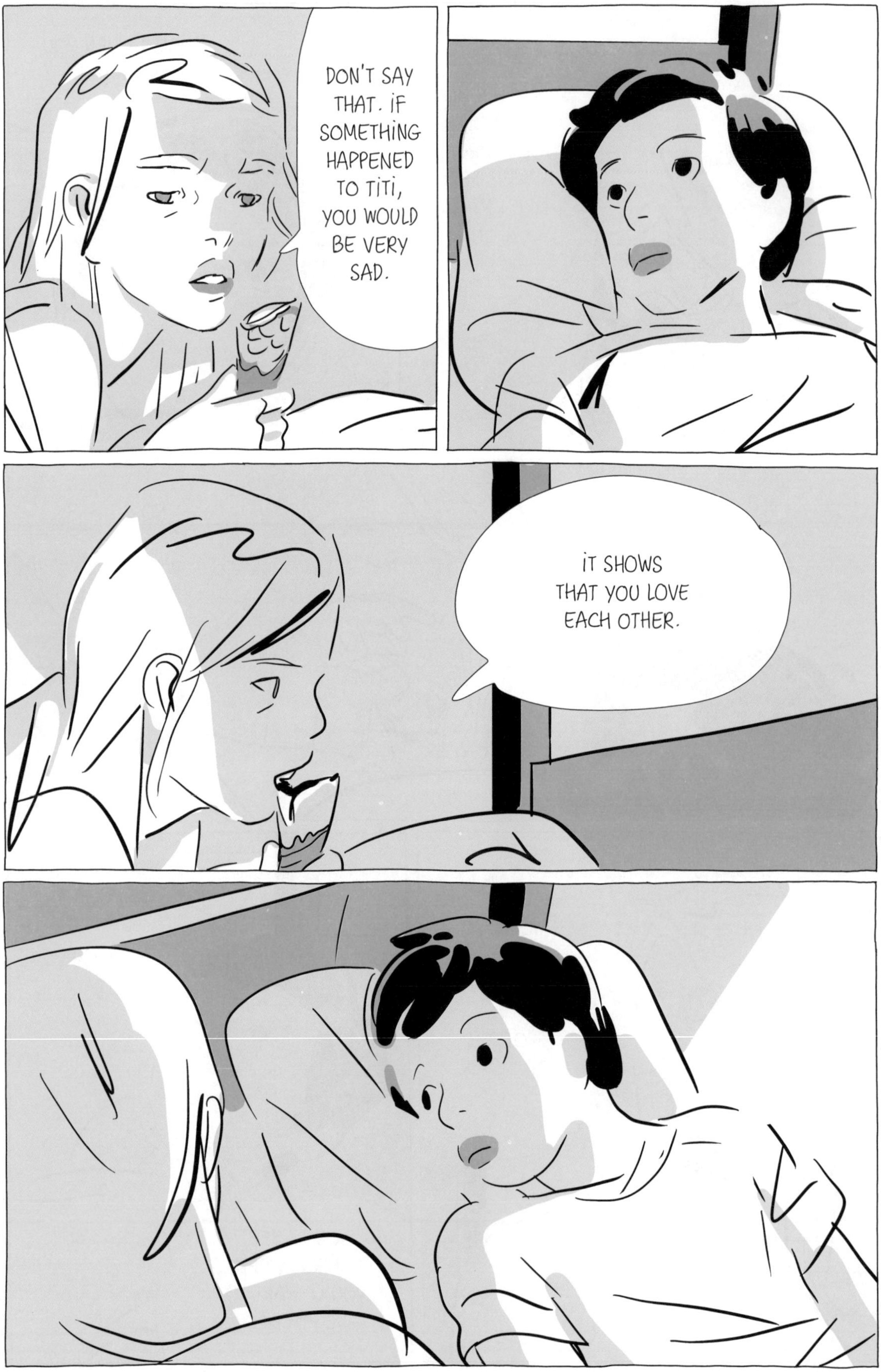
DON'T SAY THAT. IF SOMETHING HAPPENED TO TITI, YOU WOULD BE VERY SAD.
IT SHOWS THAT YOU LOVE EACH OTHER.

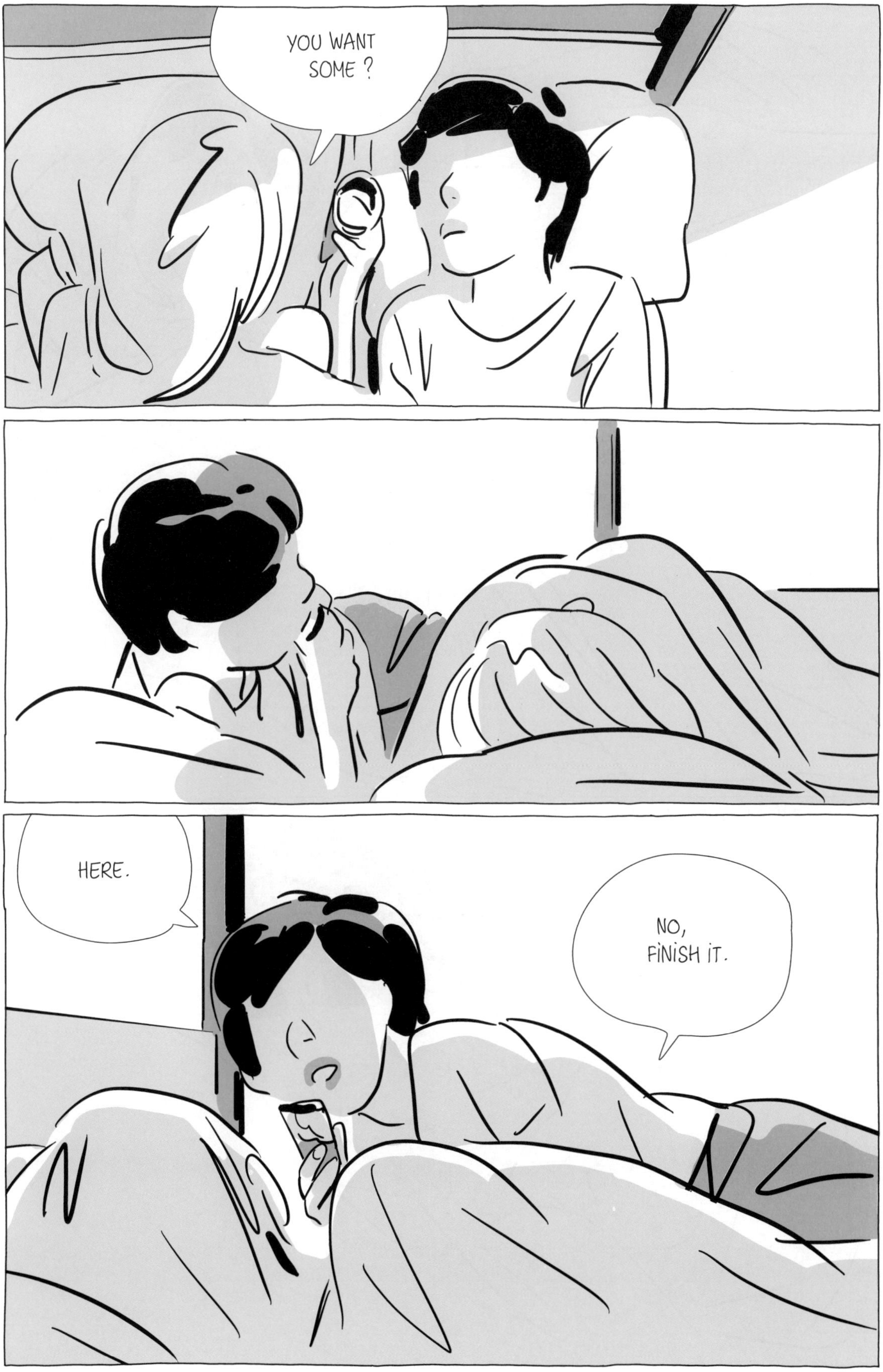
YOU WANT SOME ?
HERE.
NO, FINISH IT.

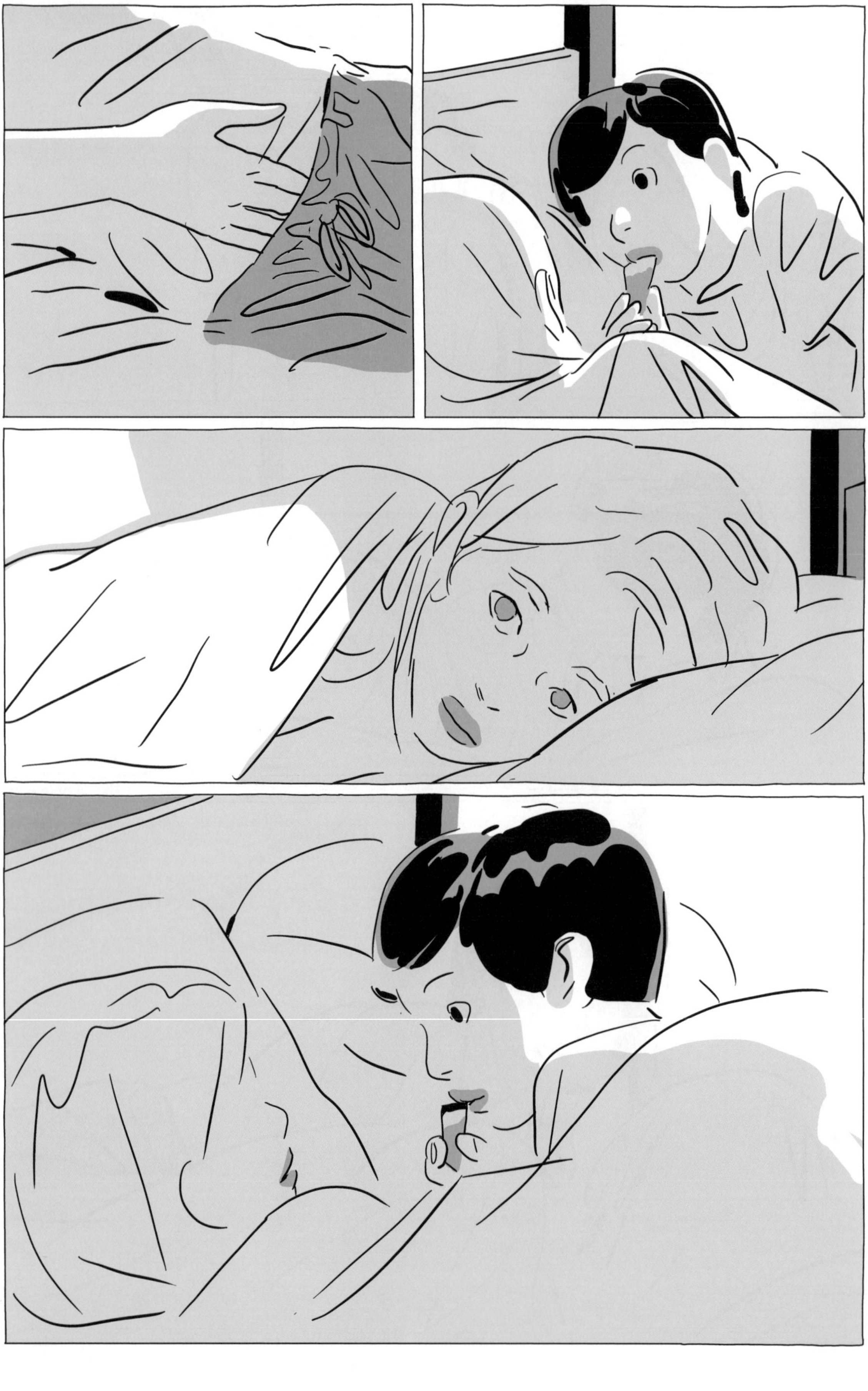

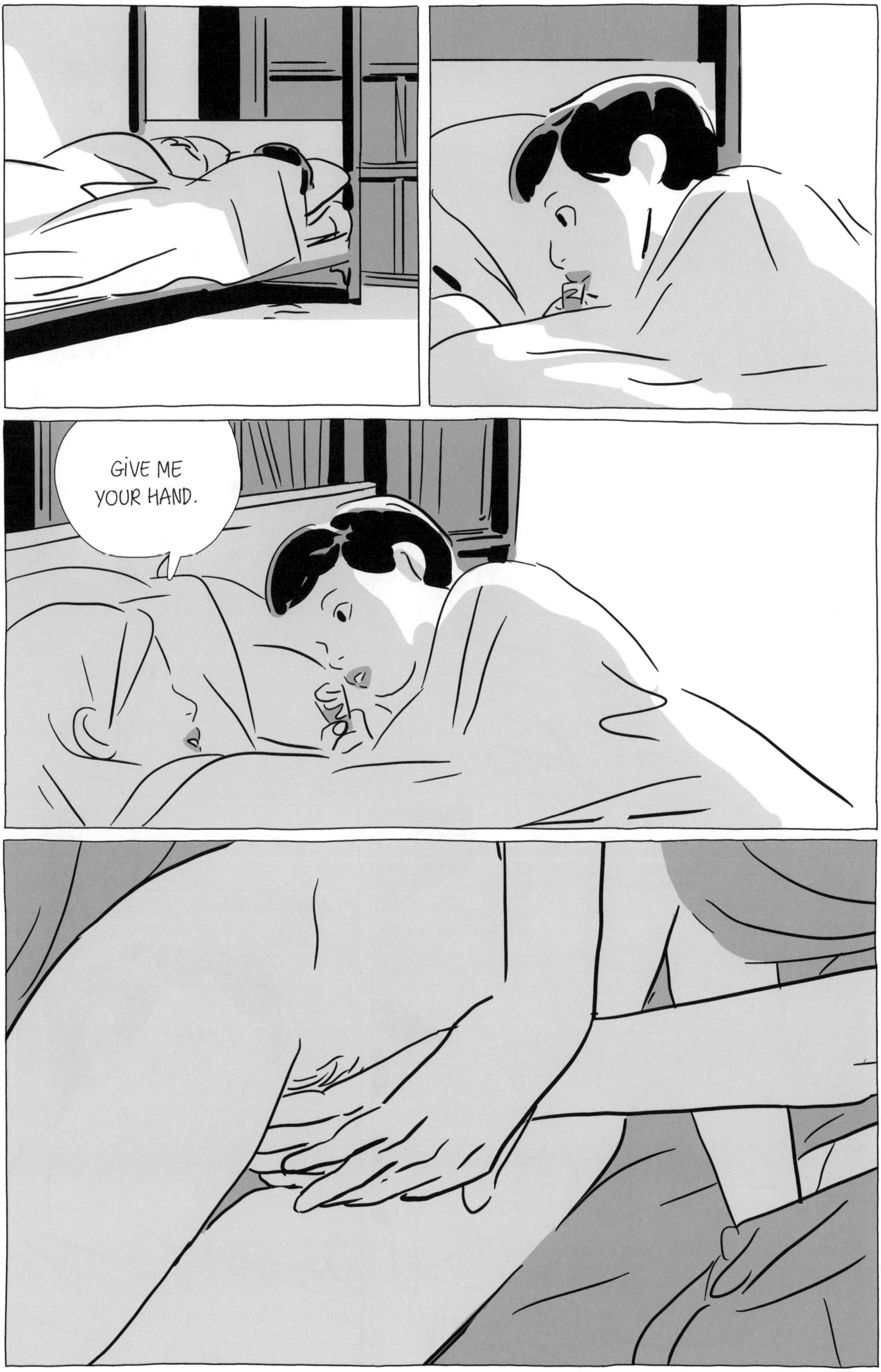
GIVE ME YOUR HAND.

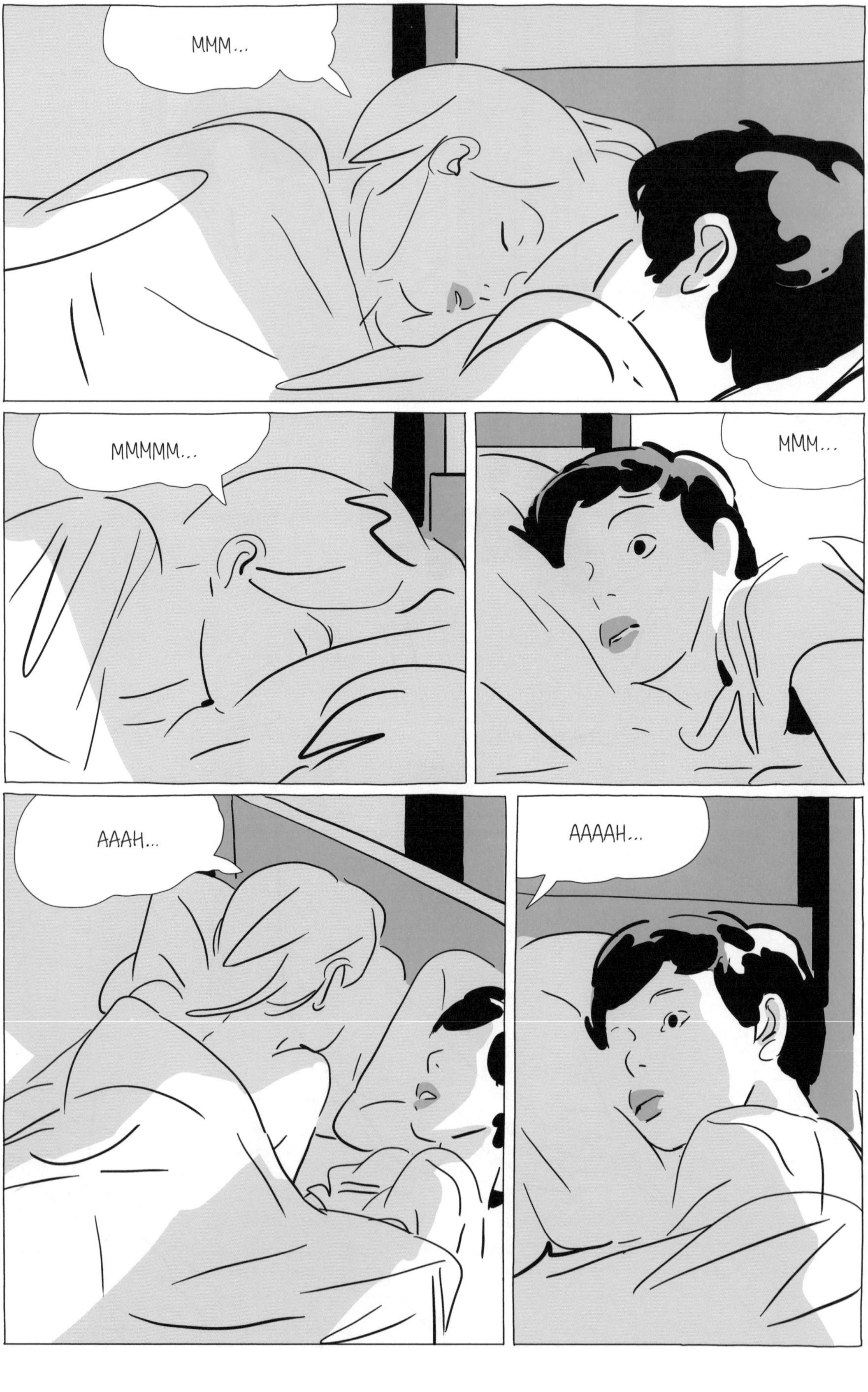
MMM...
MMMMM...
MMM...
AAAH...
AAAAH...

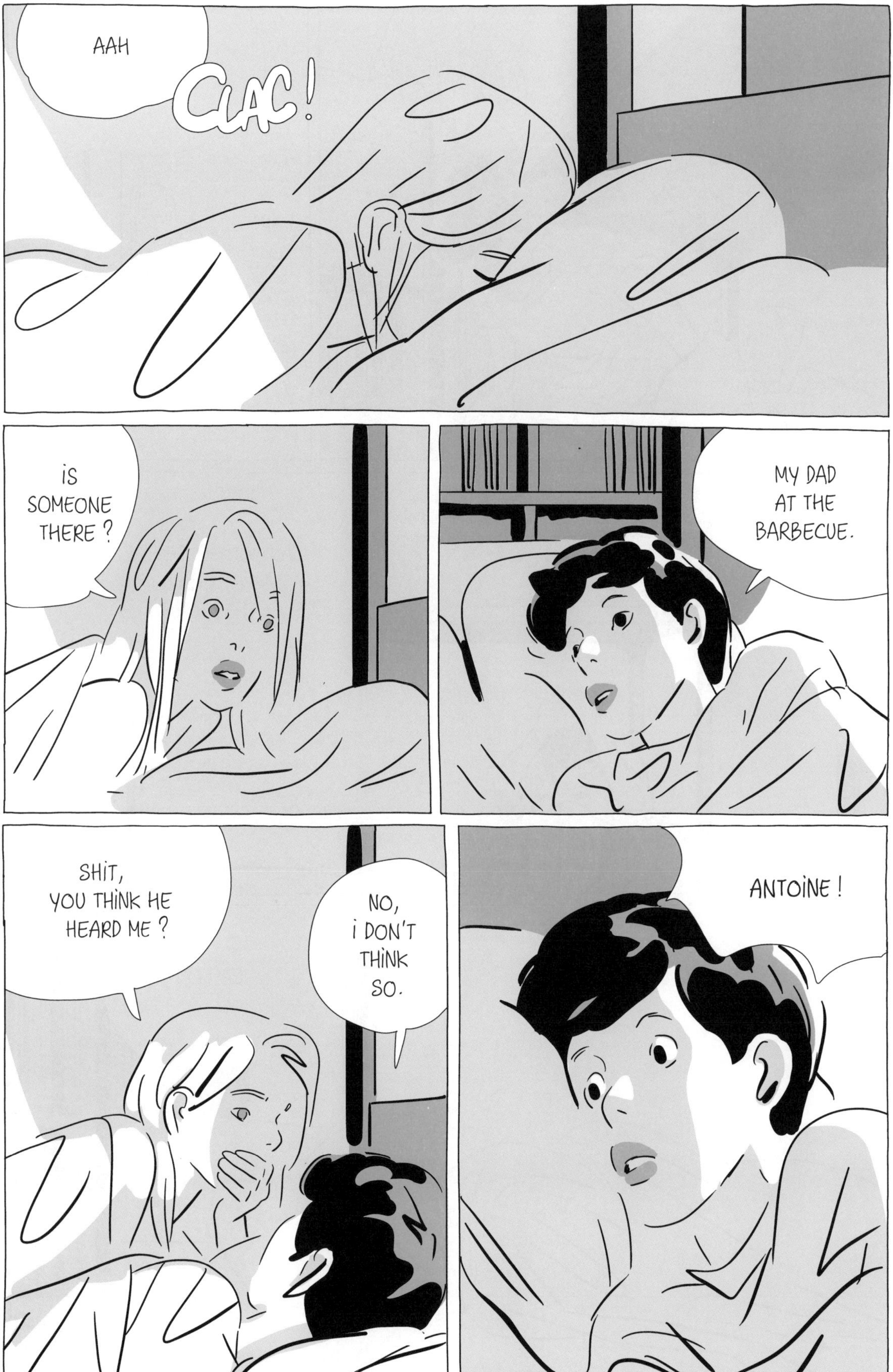
AAH
CLAC!
IS SOMEONE THERE?
MY DAD AT THE BARBECUE.
SHIT, YOU THINK HE HEARD ME?
NO, I DON'T THINK SO.
ANTOINE!

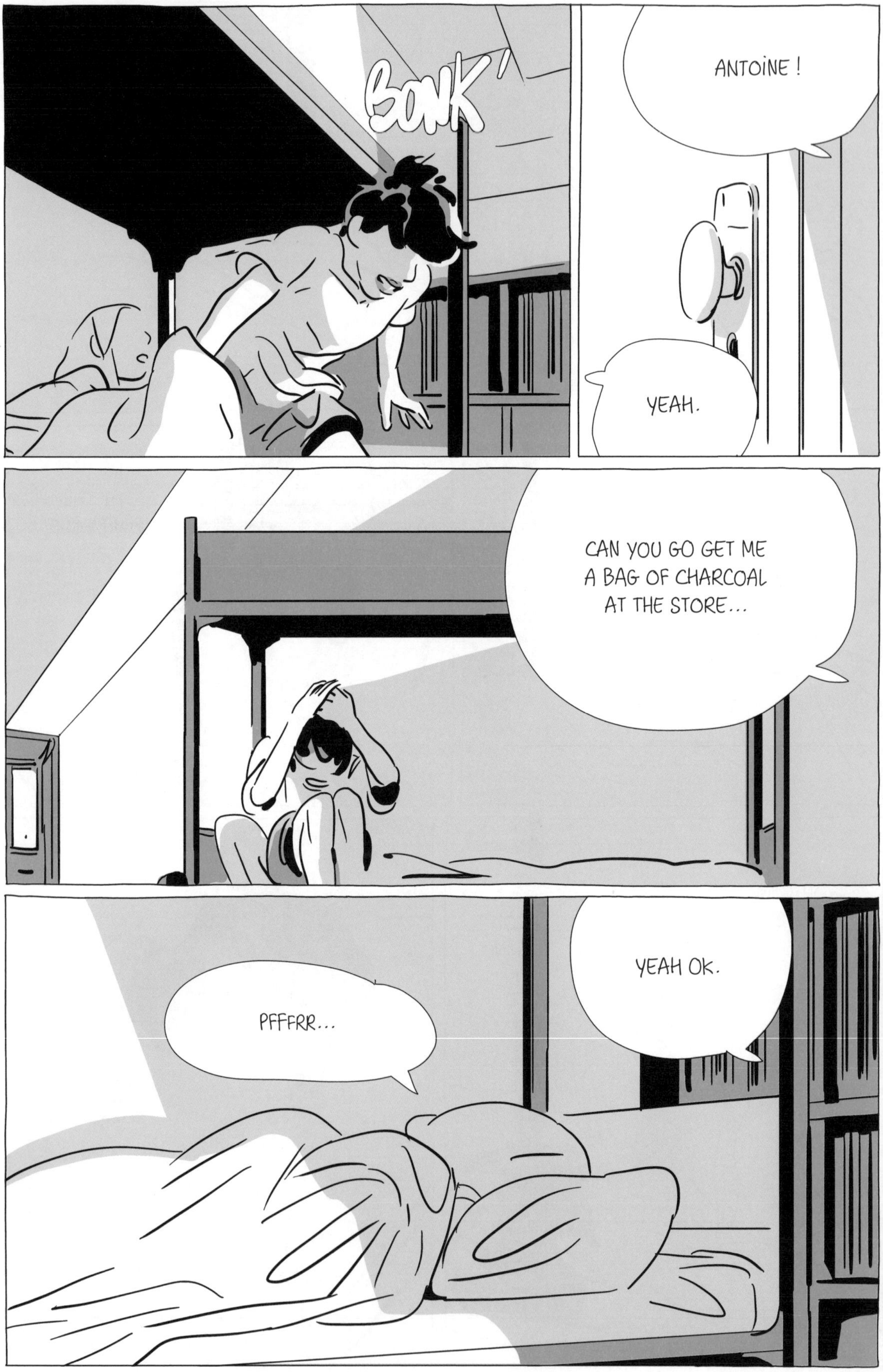
BONK!
ANTOINE!
YEAH.
CAN YOU GO GET ME A BAG OF CHARCOAL AT THE STORE...
YEAH OK.
PFFFRR...

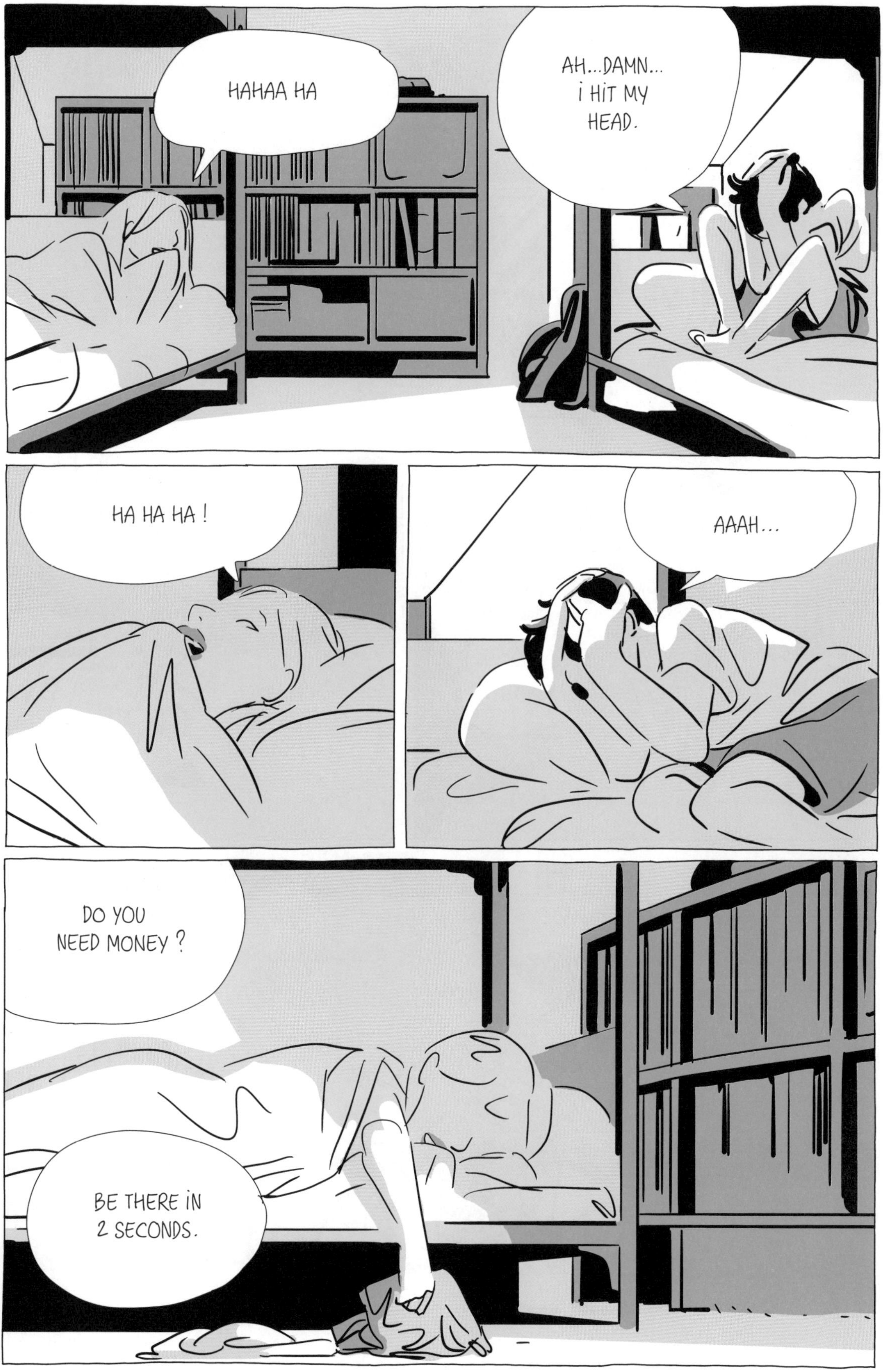
HAHAA HA
AH...DAMN... I HIT MY HEAD.
HA HA HA !
AAAH...
DO YOU NEED MONEY ?
BE THERE IN 2 SECONDS.

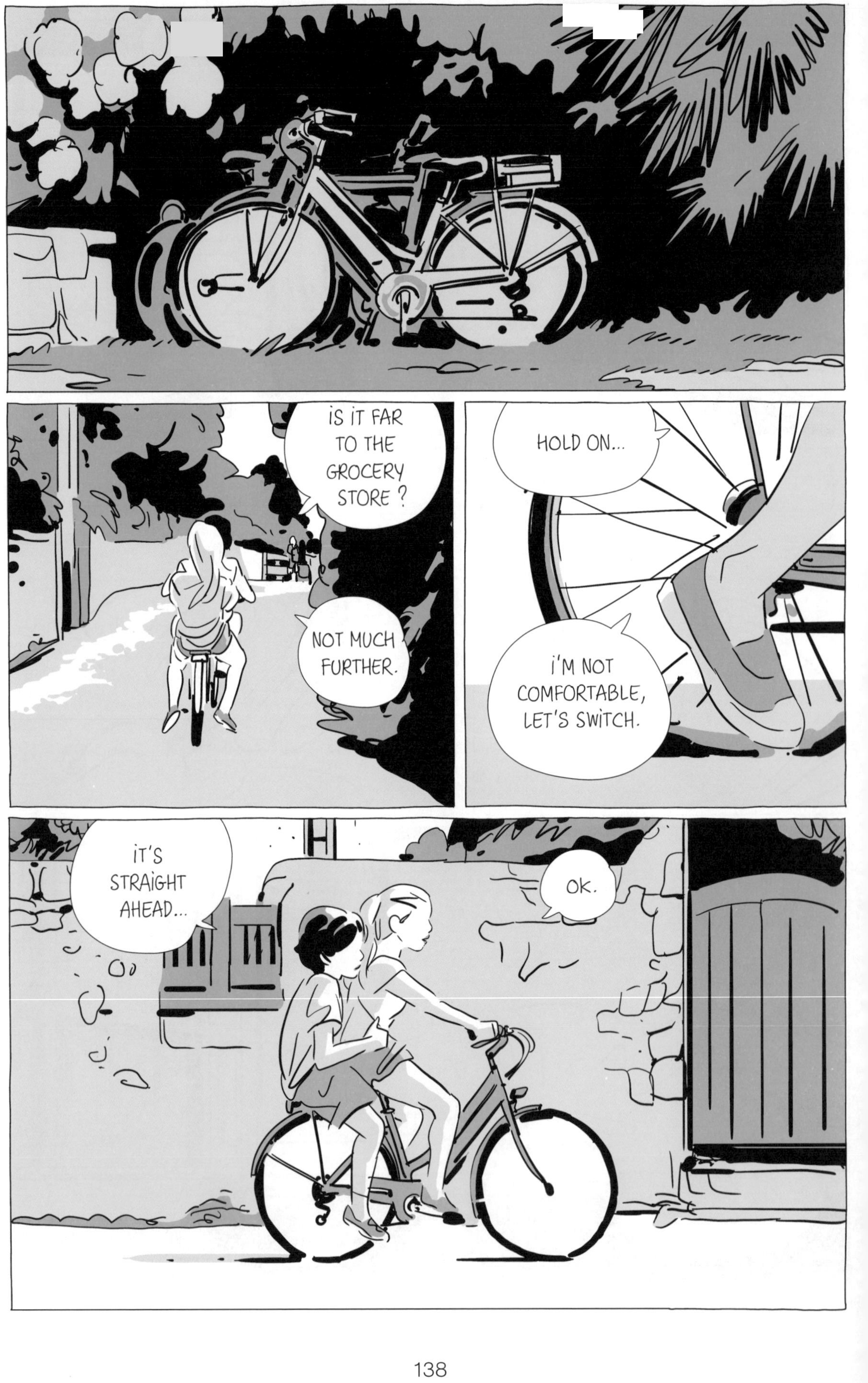
IS IT FAR TO THE GROCERY STORE ?
NOT MUCH FURTHER.
HOLD ON...
I'M NOT COMFORTABLE, LET'S SWITCH.
IT'S STRAIGHT AHEAD...
OK.

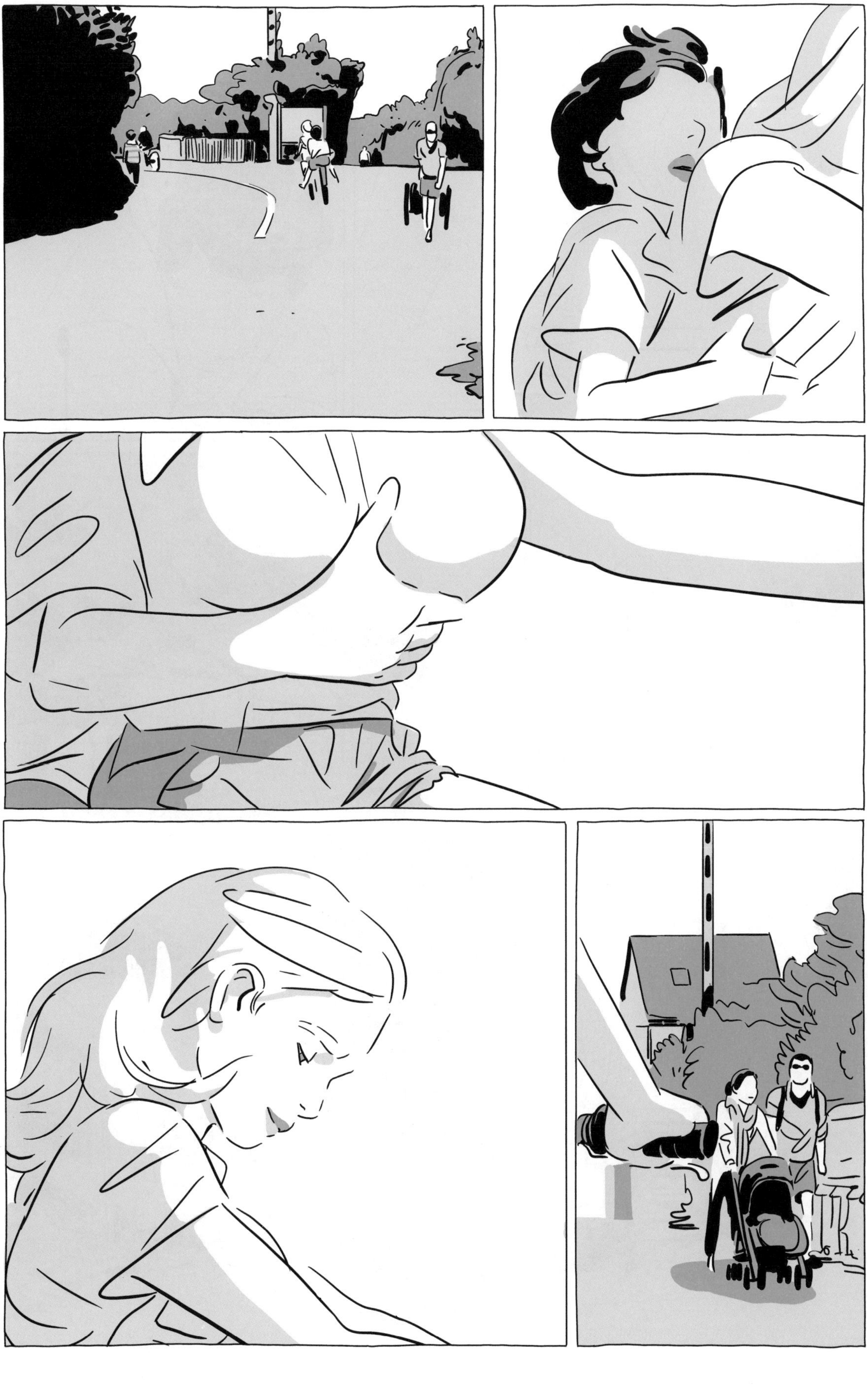

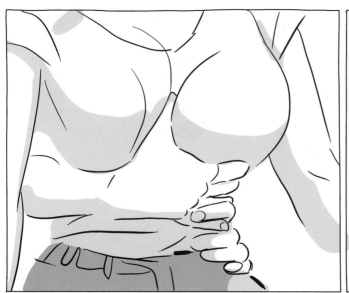

WILL WE BE THERE SOON ?

YEAH, JUST DOWN THE HILL.

OK. WAIT.

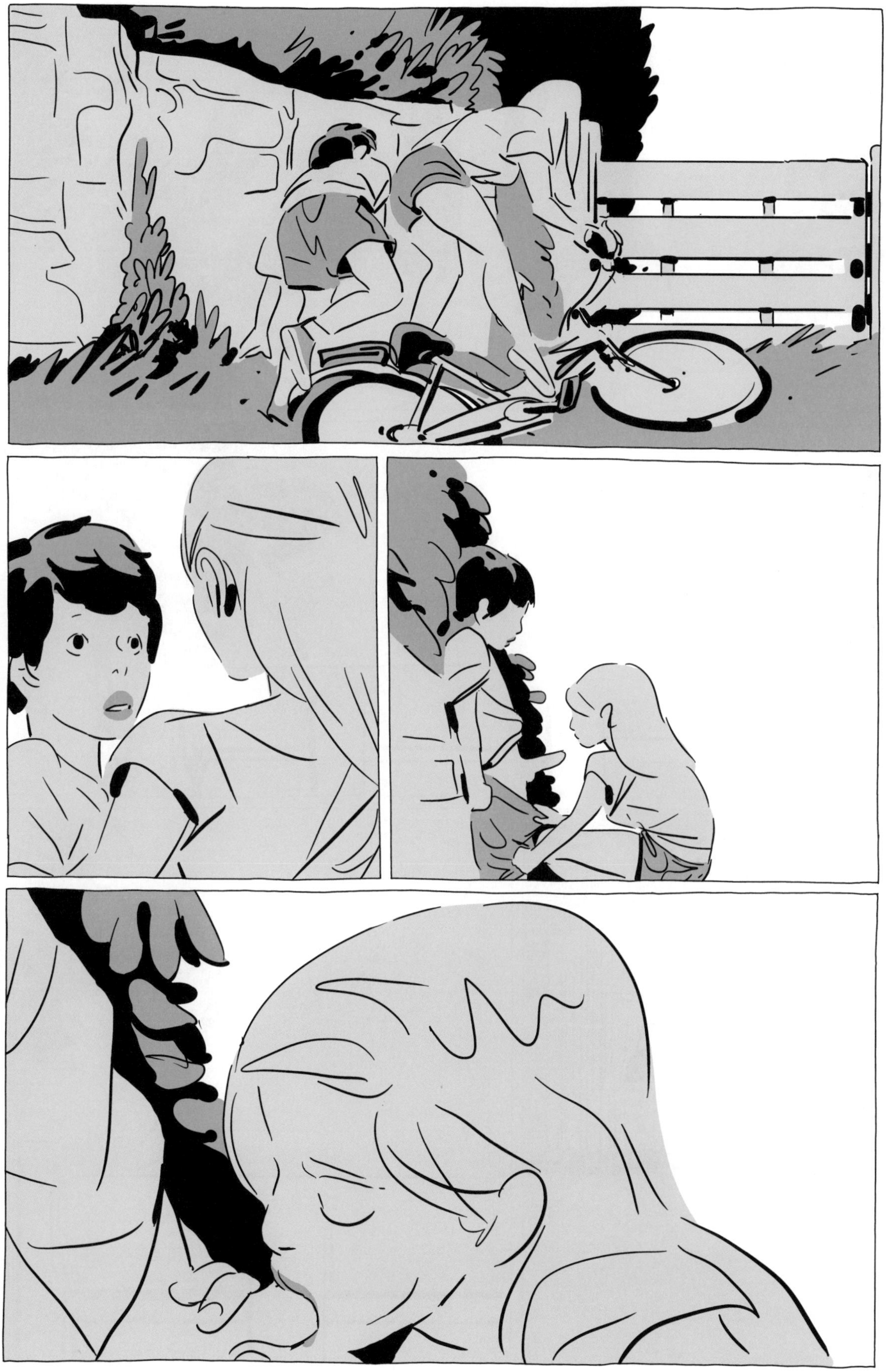

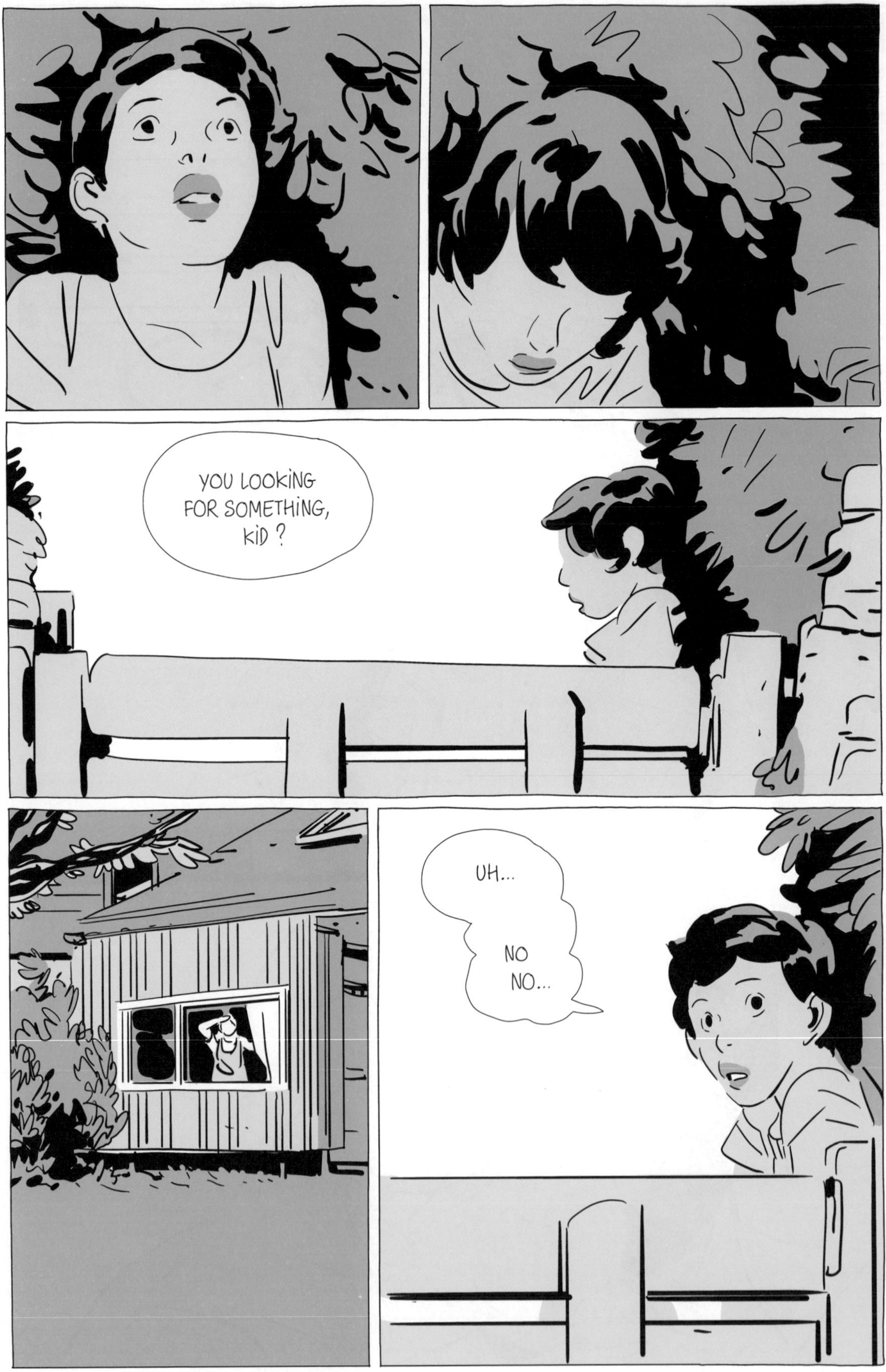
YOU LOOKING FOR SOMETHING, KID ?
UH...
NO NO...

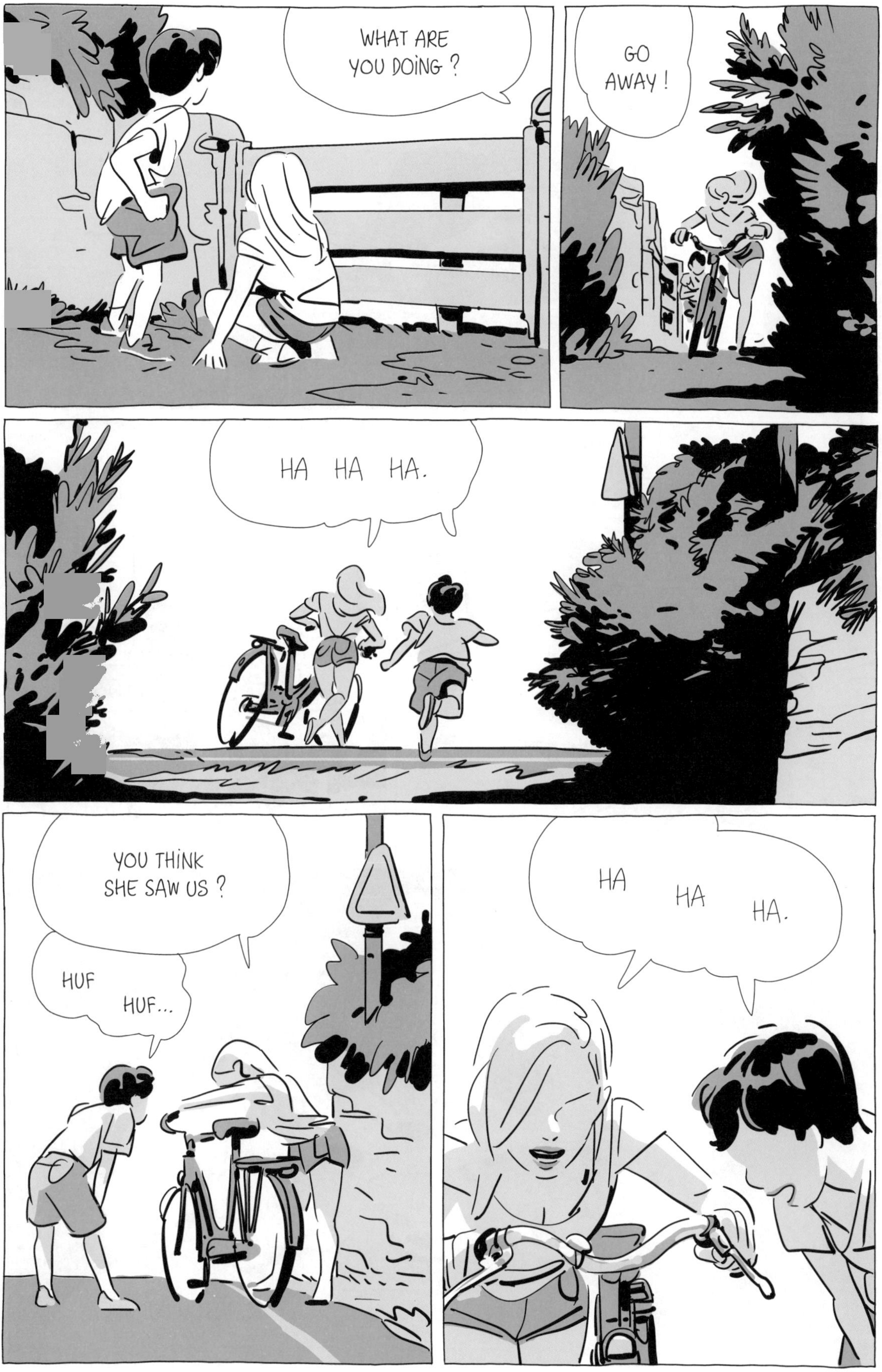
WHAT ARE YOU DOING ?
GO AWAY !
HA HA HA.
YOU THINK SHE SAW US ?
HUF HUF...
HA HA HA.

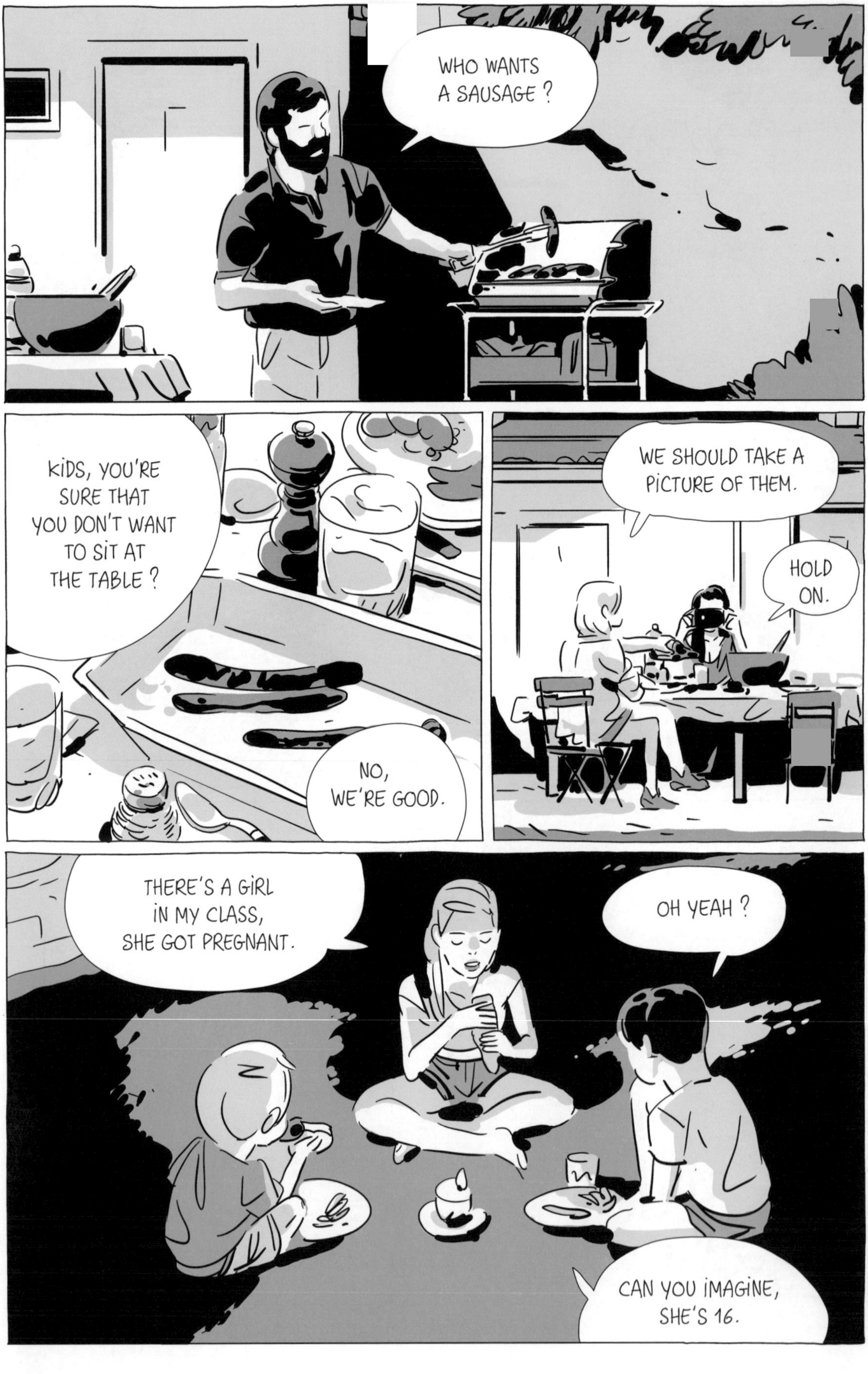
WHO WANTS A SAUSAGE ?
KIDS, YOU'RE SURE THAT YOU DON'T WANT TO SIT AT THE TABLE ?
NO, WE'RE GOOD.
WE SHOULD TAKE A PICTURE OF THEM.
HOLD ON.
THERE'S A GIRL IN MY CLASS, SHE GOT PREGNANT.
OH YEAH ?
CAN YOU IMAGINE, SHE'S 16.

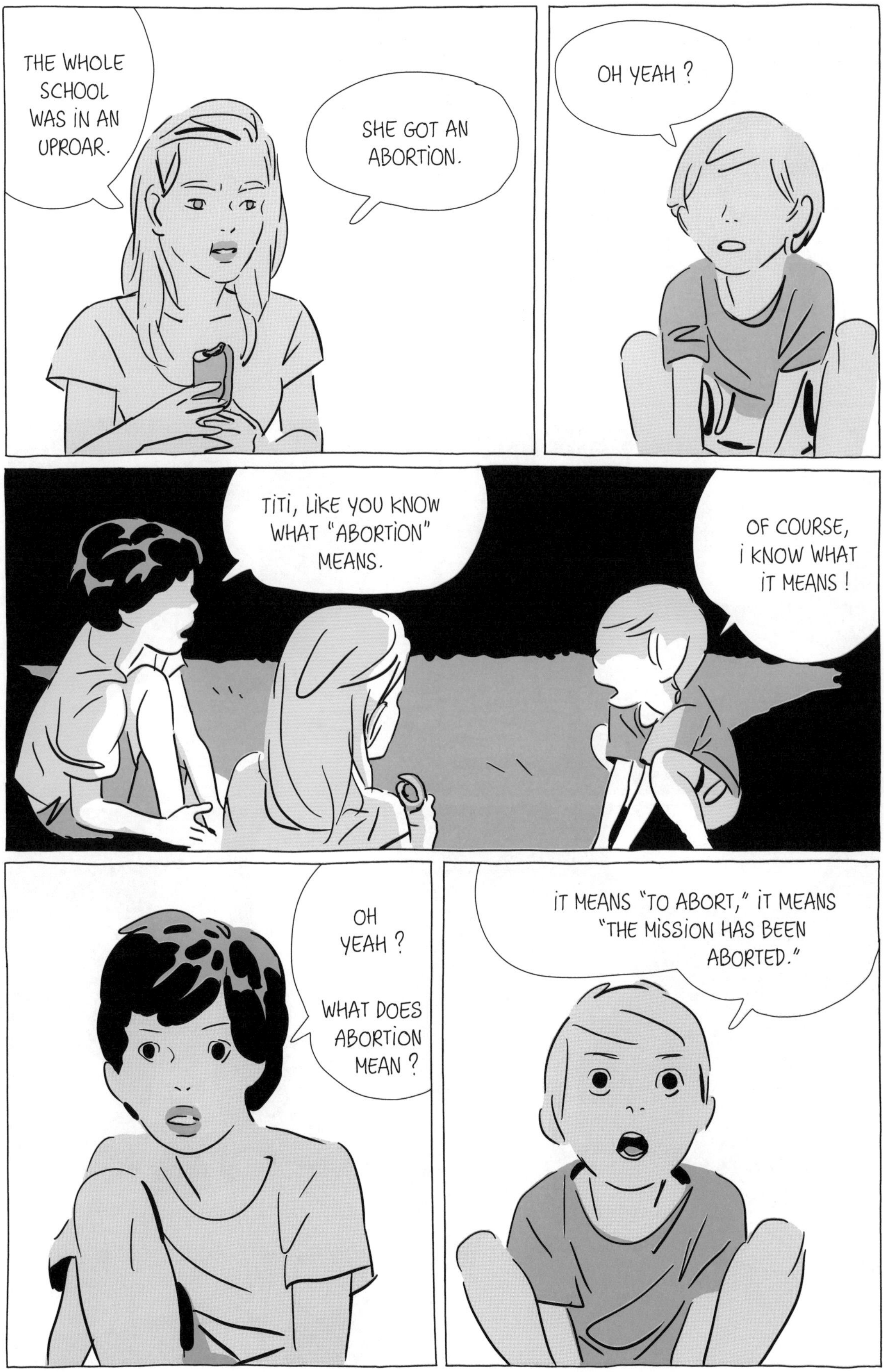
THE WHOLE SCHOOL WAS IN AN UPROAR.
SHE GOT AN ABORTION.
OH YEAH ?
TITI, LIKE YOU KNOW WHAT "ABORTION" MEANS.
OF COURSE, I KNOW WHAT IT MEANS !
OH YEAH ?
WHAT DOES ABORTION MEAN ?
IT MEANS "TO ABORT," IT MEANS "THE MISSION HAS BEEN ABORTED."

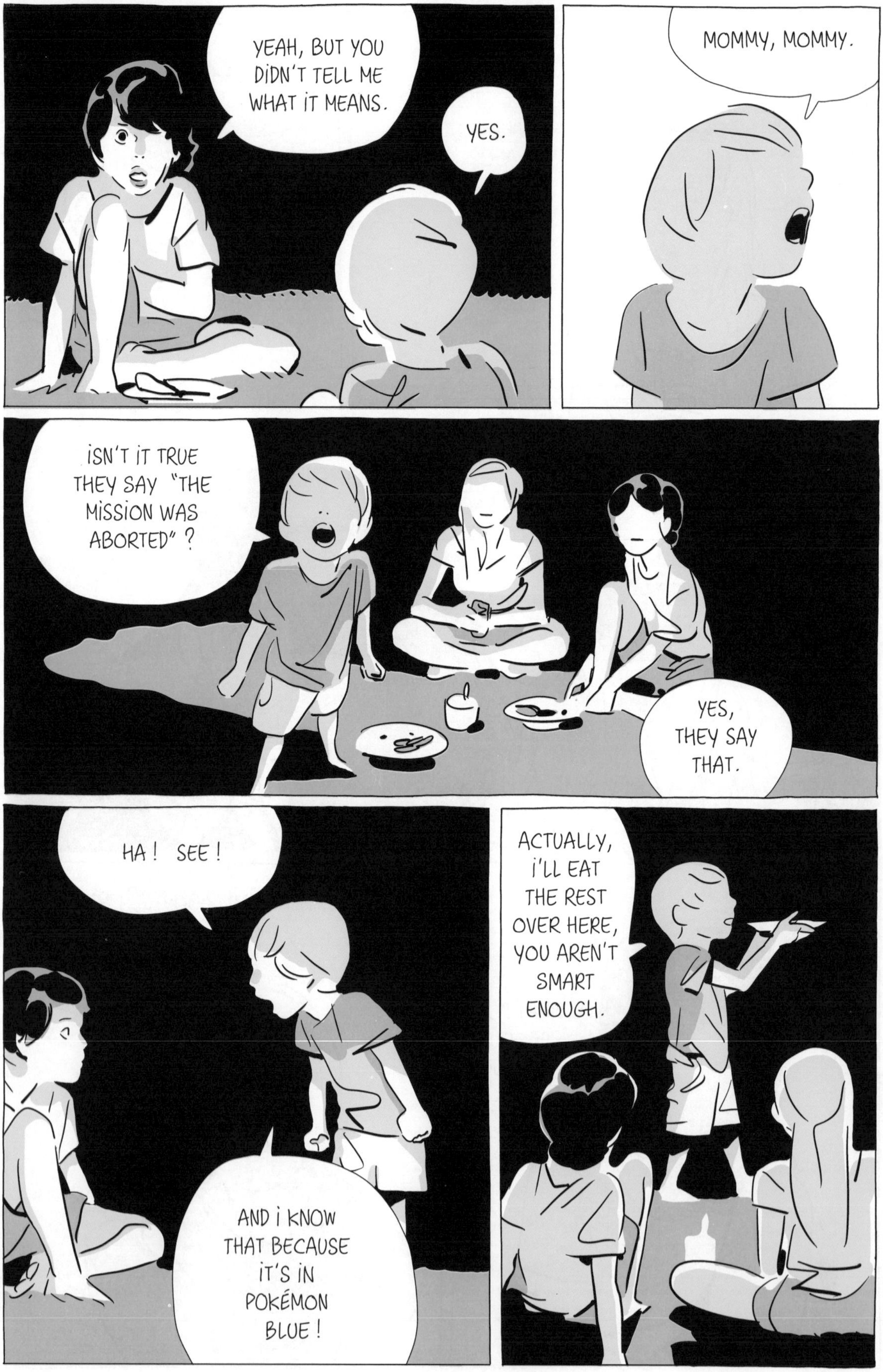
YEAH, BUT YOU DIDN'T TELL ME WHAT IT MEANS.
YES.
MOMMY, MOMMY.
ISN'T IT TRUE THEY SAY "THE MISSION WAS ABORTED"?
YES, THEY SAY THAT.
HA! SEE!
AND I KNOW THAT BECAUSE IT'S IN POKÉMON BLUE!
ACTUALLY, I'LL EAT THE REST OVER HERE, YOU AREN'T SMART ENOUGH.

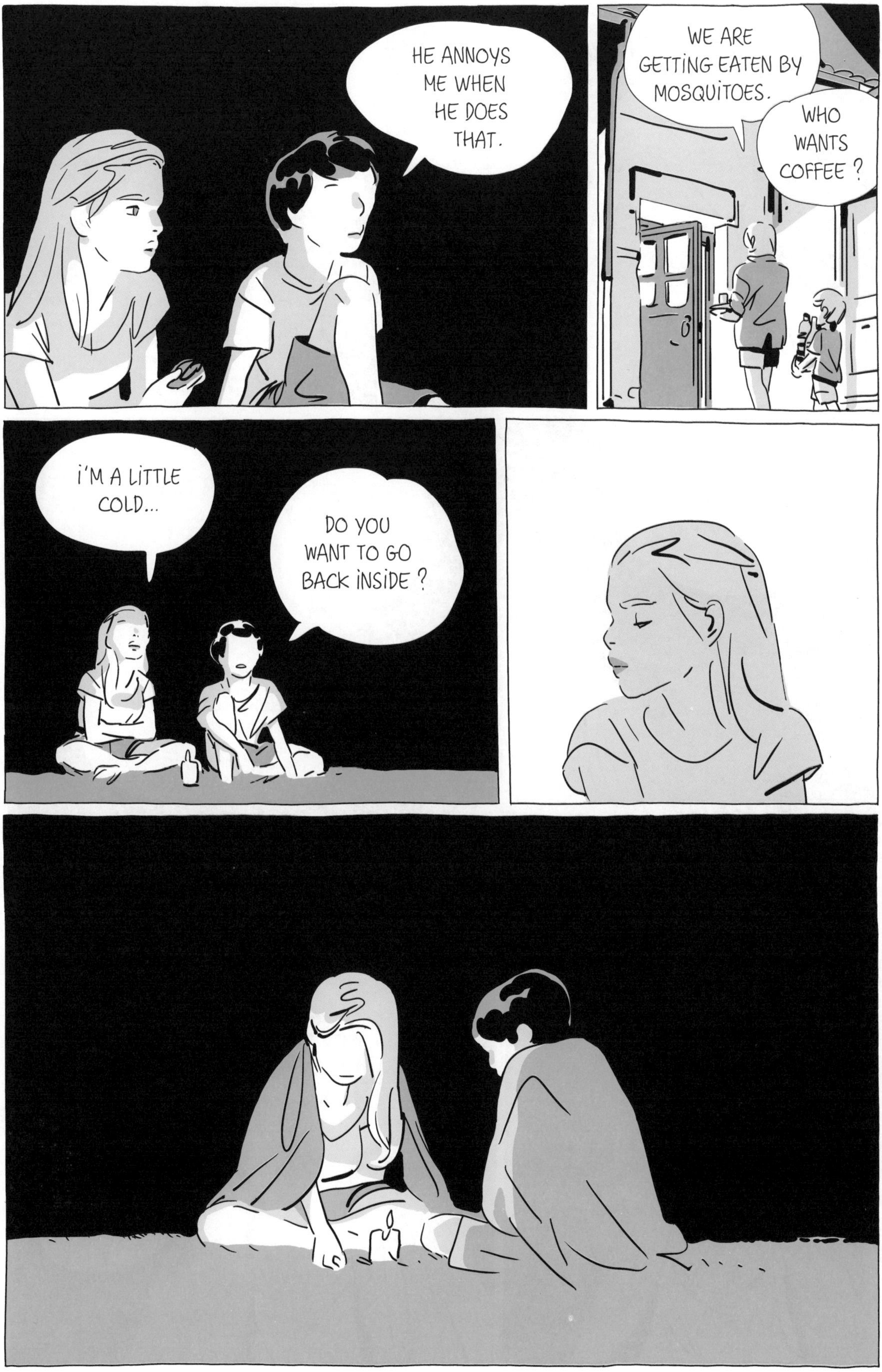
HE ANNOYS ME WHEN HE DOES THAT.
WE ARE GETTING EATEN BY MOSQUITOES.
WHO WANTS COFFEE ?
I'M A LITTLE COLD...
DO YOU WANT TO GO BACK INSIDE ?

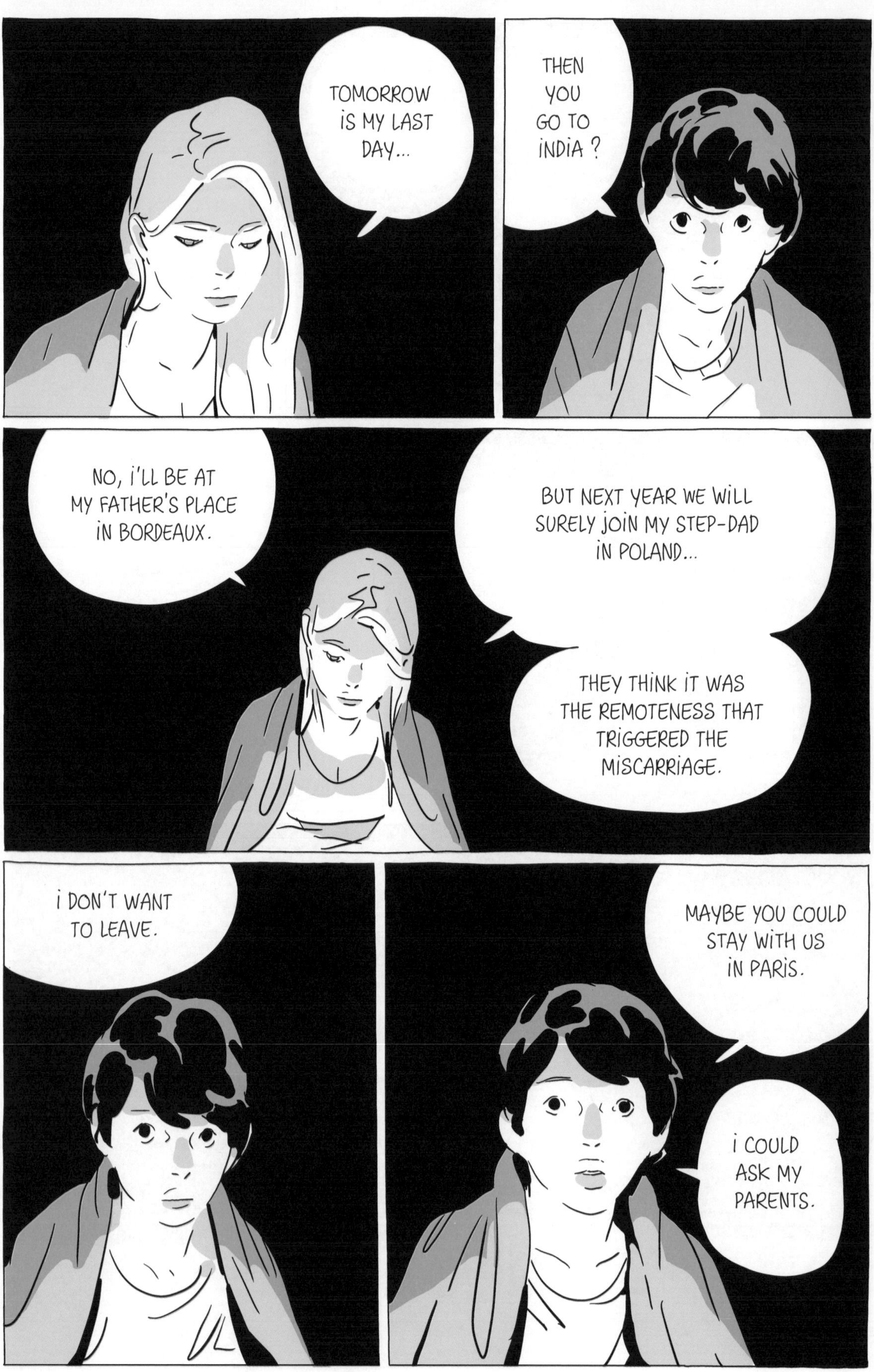
TOMORROW IS MY LAST DAY...
THEN YOU GO TO INDIA ?
NO, I'LL BE AT MY FATHER'S PLACE IN BORDEAUX.
BUT NEXT YEAR WE WILL SURELY JOIN MY STEP-DAD IN POLAND...
THEY THINK IT WAS THE REMOTENESS THAT TRIGGERED THE MISCARRIAGE.
I DON'T WANT TO LEAVE.
MAYBE YOU COULD STAY WITH US IN PARIS.
I COULD ASK MY PARENTS.

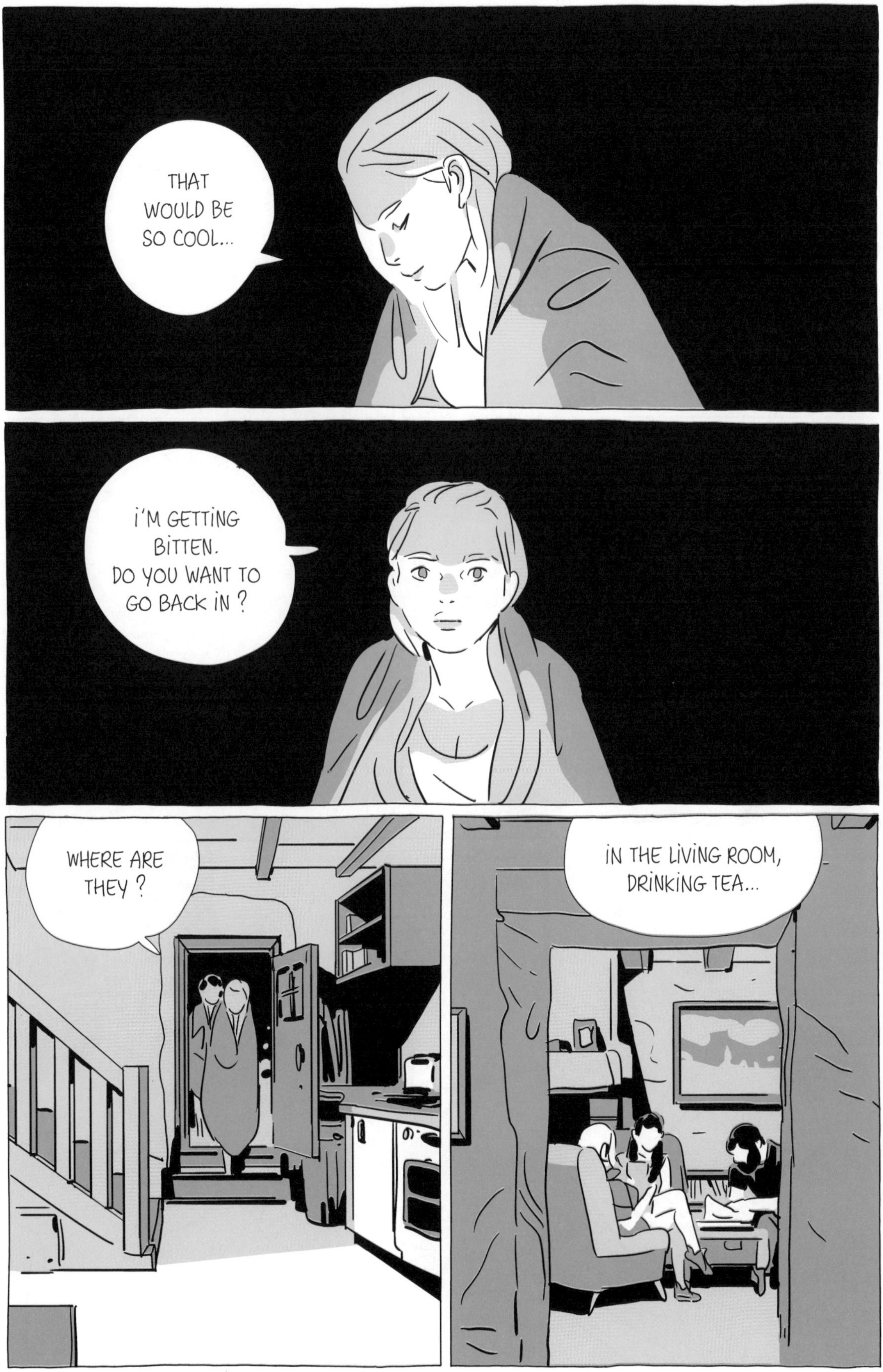
THAT WOULD BE SO COOL...
I'M GETTING BITTEN. DO YOU WANT TO GO BACK IN ?
WHERE ARE THEY ?
IN THE LIVING ROOM, DRINKING TEA...

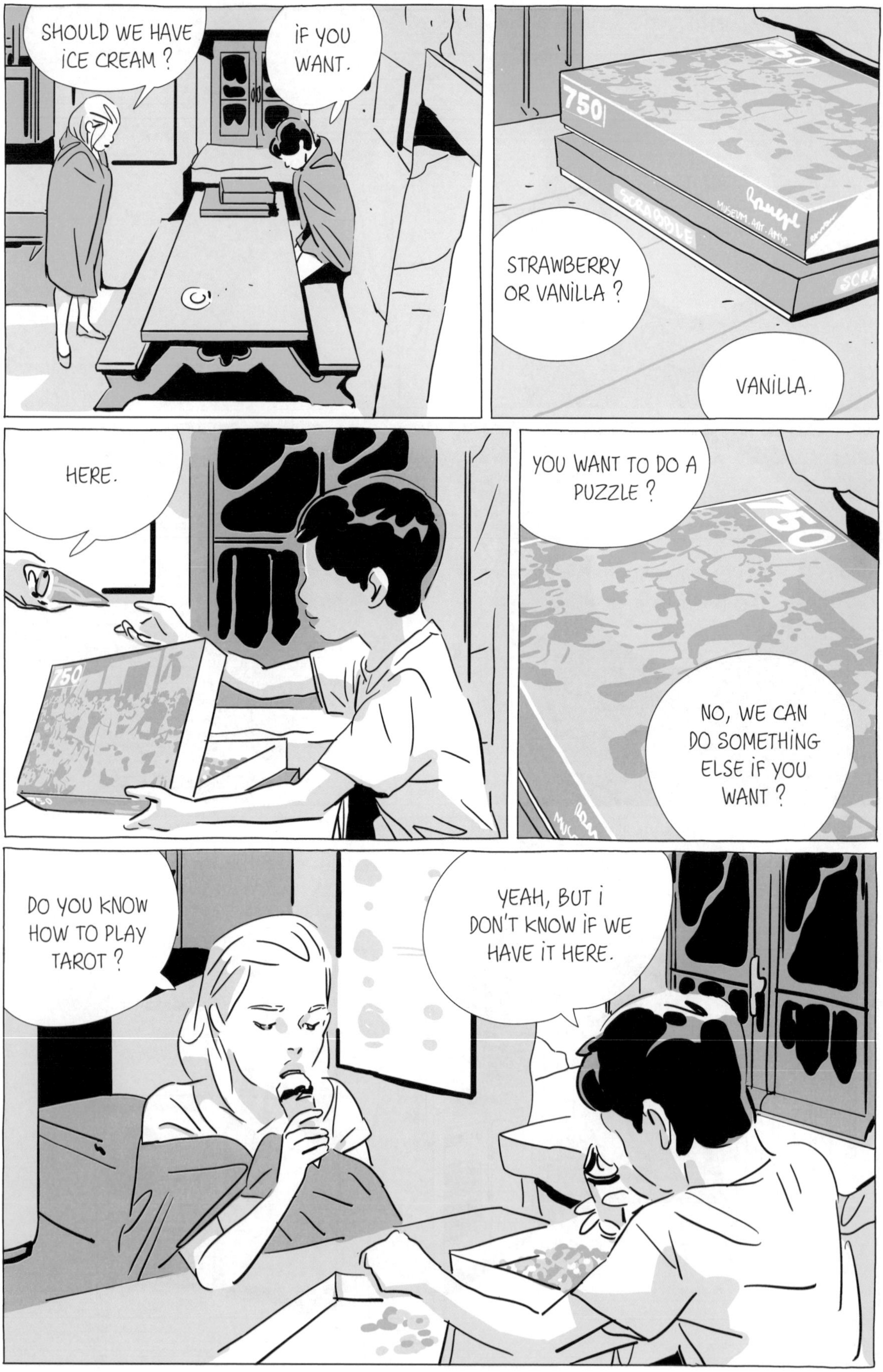
SHOULD WE HAVE ICE CREAM ?
IF YOU WANT.
STRAWBERRY OR VANILLA ?
VANILLA.
HERE.
YOU WANT TO DO A PUZZLE ?
NO, WE CAN DO SOMETHING ELSE IF YOU WANT ?
DO YOU KNOW HOW TO PLAY TAROT ?
YEAH, BUT I DON'T KNOW IF WE HAVE IT HERE.

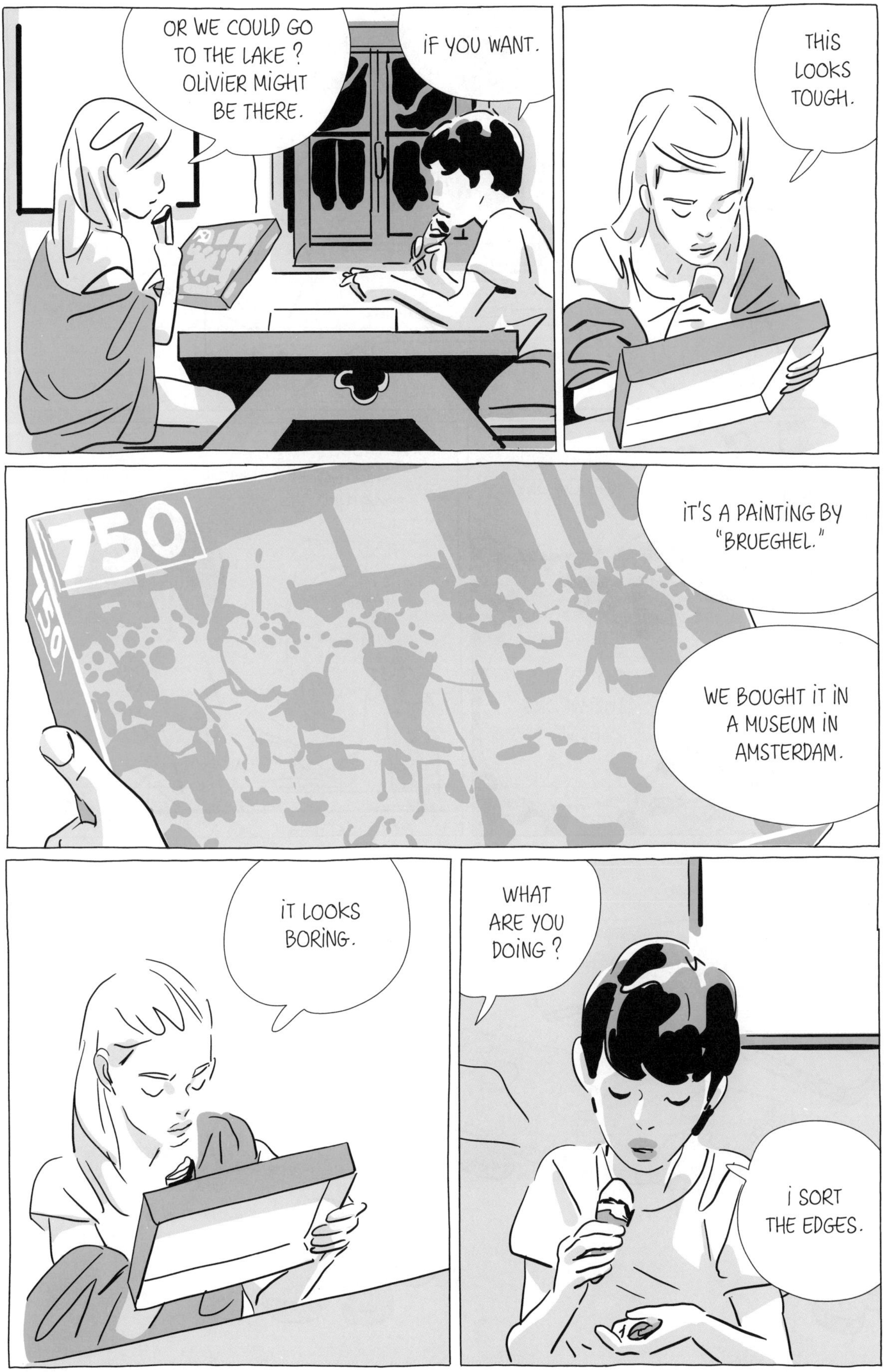
OR WE COULD GO TO THE LAKE? OLIVIER MIGHT BE THERE.
IF YOU WANT.
THIS LOOKS TOUGH.
750
IT'S A PAINTING BY "BRUEGHEL."
WE BOUGHT IT IN A MUSEUM IN AMSTERDAM.
IT LOOKS BORING.
WHAT ARE YOU DOING?
I SORT THE EDGES.

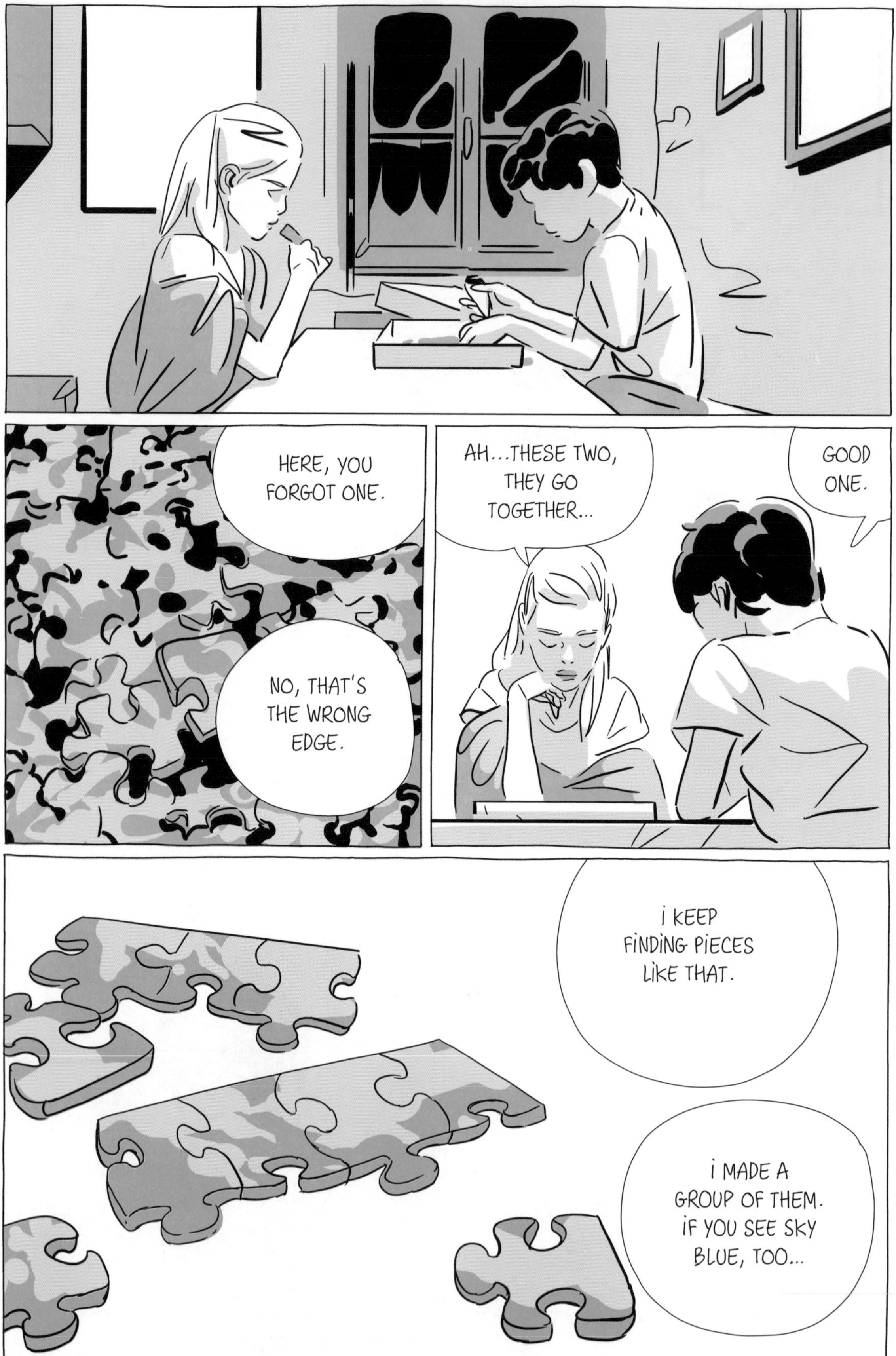
HERE, YOU FORGOT ONE.
NO, THAT'S THE WRONG EDGE.
AH...THESE TWO, THEY GO TOGETHER...
GOOD ONE.
I KEEP FINDING PIECES LIKE THAT.
I MADE A GROUP OF THEM. IF YOU SEE SKY BLUE, TOO...

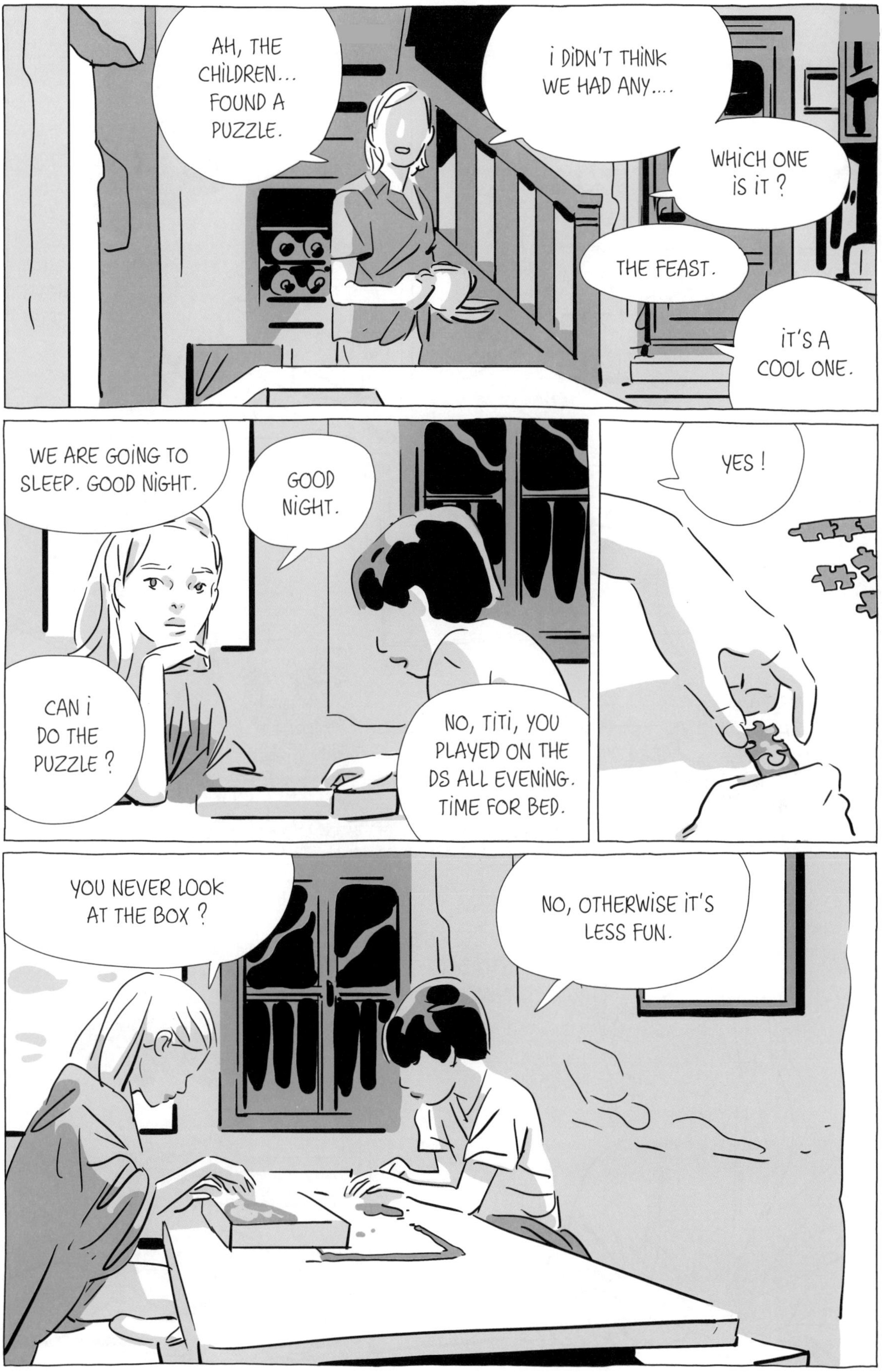
AH, THE CHILDREN... FOUND A PUZZLE.
i DIDN'T THiNK WE HAD ANY....
WHiCH ONE iS iT ?
THE FEAST.
iT'S A COOL ONE.
WE ARE GOiNG TO SLEEP. GOOD NiGHT.
GOOD NiGHT.
CAN i DO THE PUZZLE ?
NO, TiTi, YOU PLAYED ON THE DS ALL EVENiNG. TiME FOR BED.
YES !
YOU NEVER LOOK AT THE BOX ?
NO, OTHERWiSE iT'S LESS FUN.

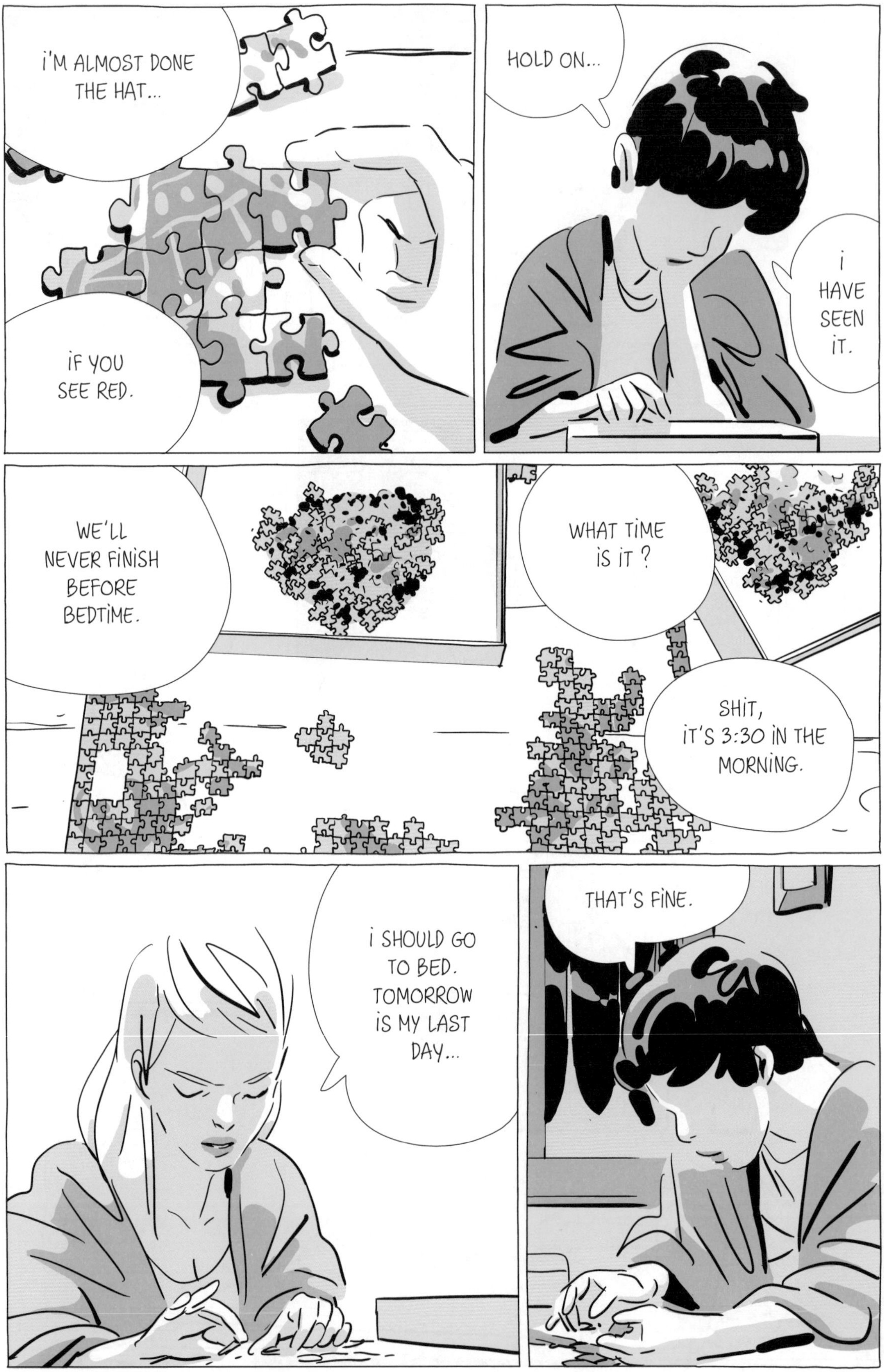
I'M ALMOST DONE THE HAT...
IF YOU SEE RED.
HOLD ON...
I HAVE SEEN IT.
WE'LL NEVER FINISH BEFORE BEDTIME.
WHAT TIME IS IT ?
SHIT, IT'S 3:30 IN THE MORNING.
I SHOULD GO TO BED. TOMORROW IS MY LAST DAY...
THAT'S FINE.

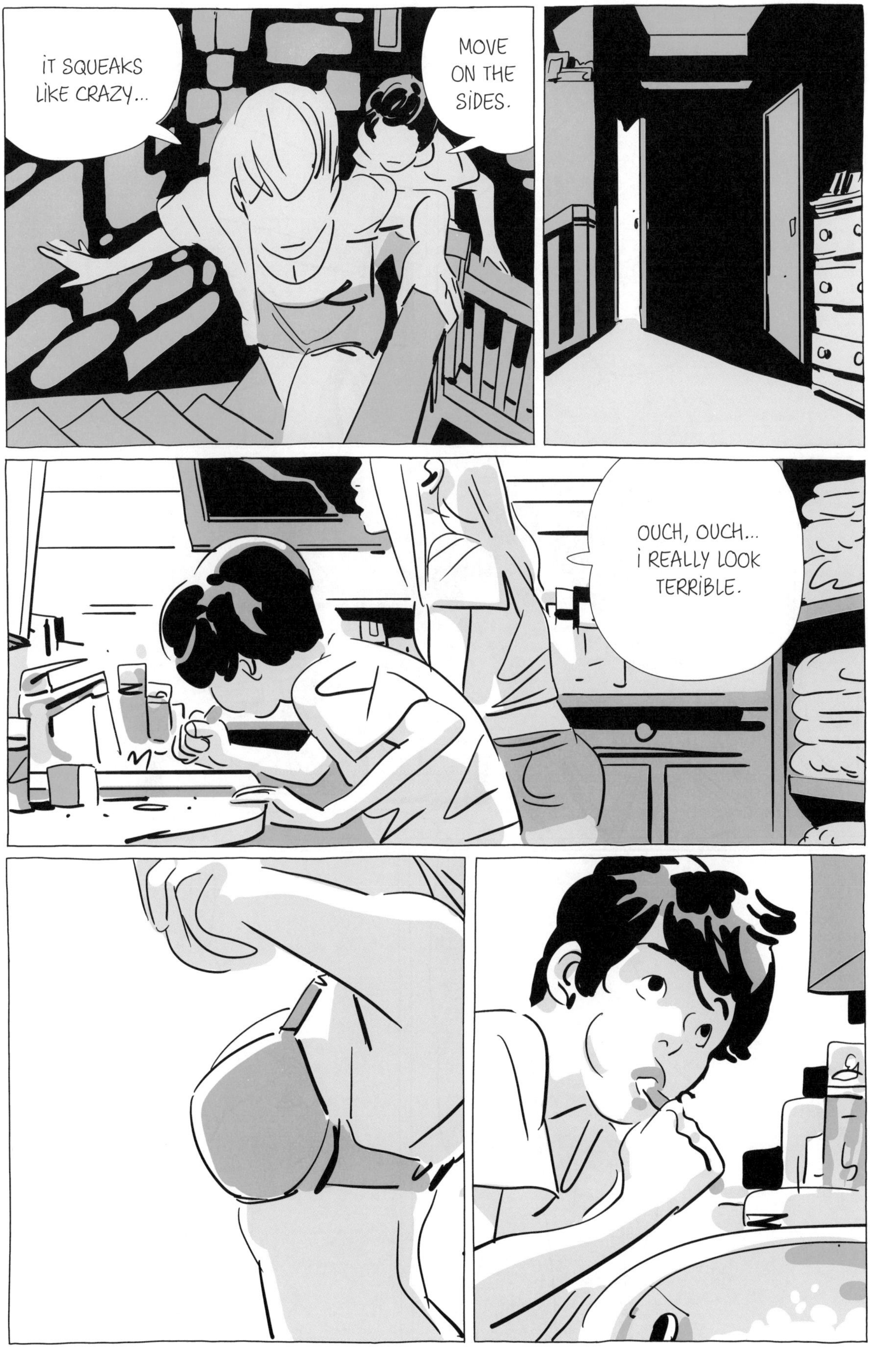

IT SQUEAKS LIKE CRAZY...
MOVE ON THE SIDES.
OUCH, OUCH... I REALLY LOOK TERRIBLE.

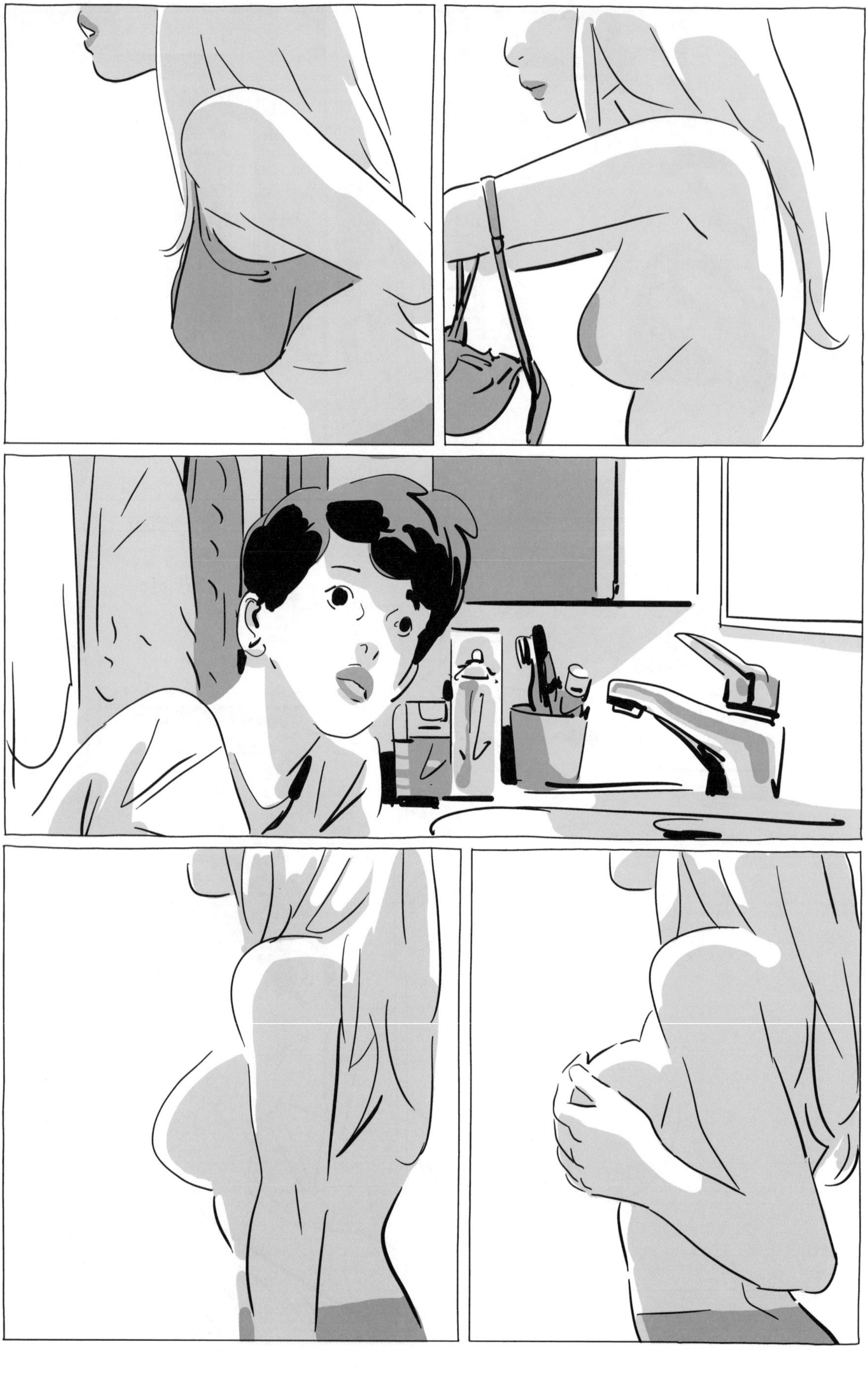

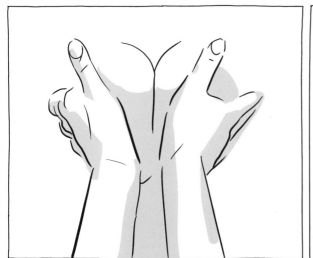

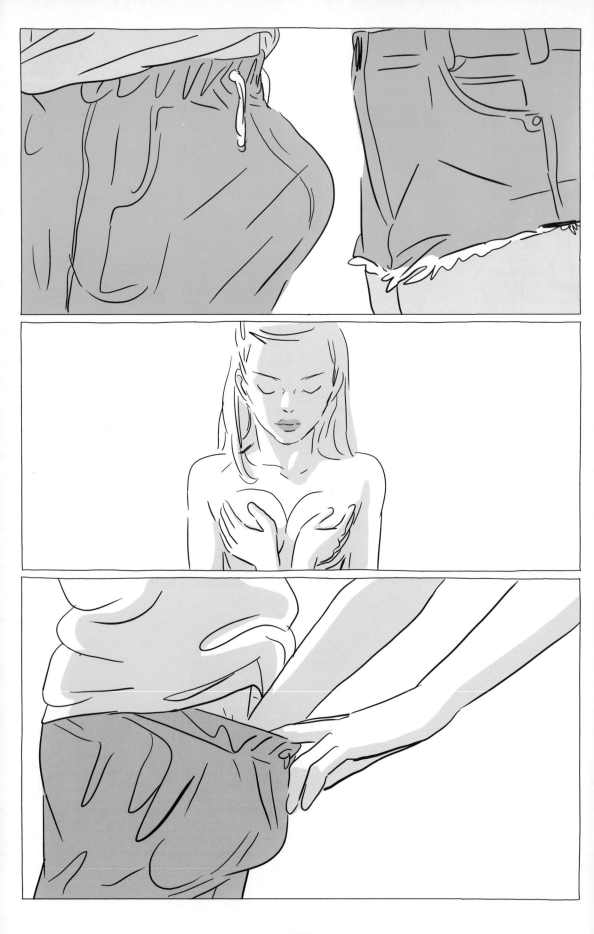

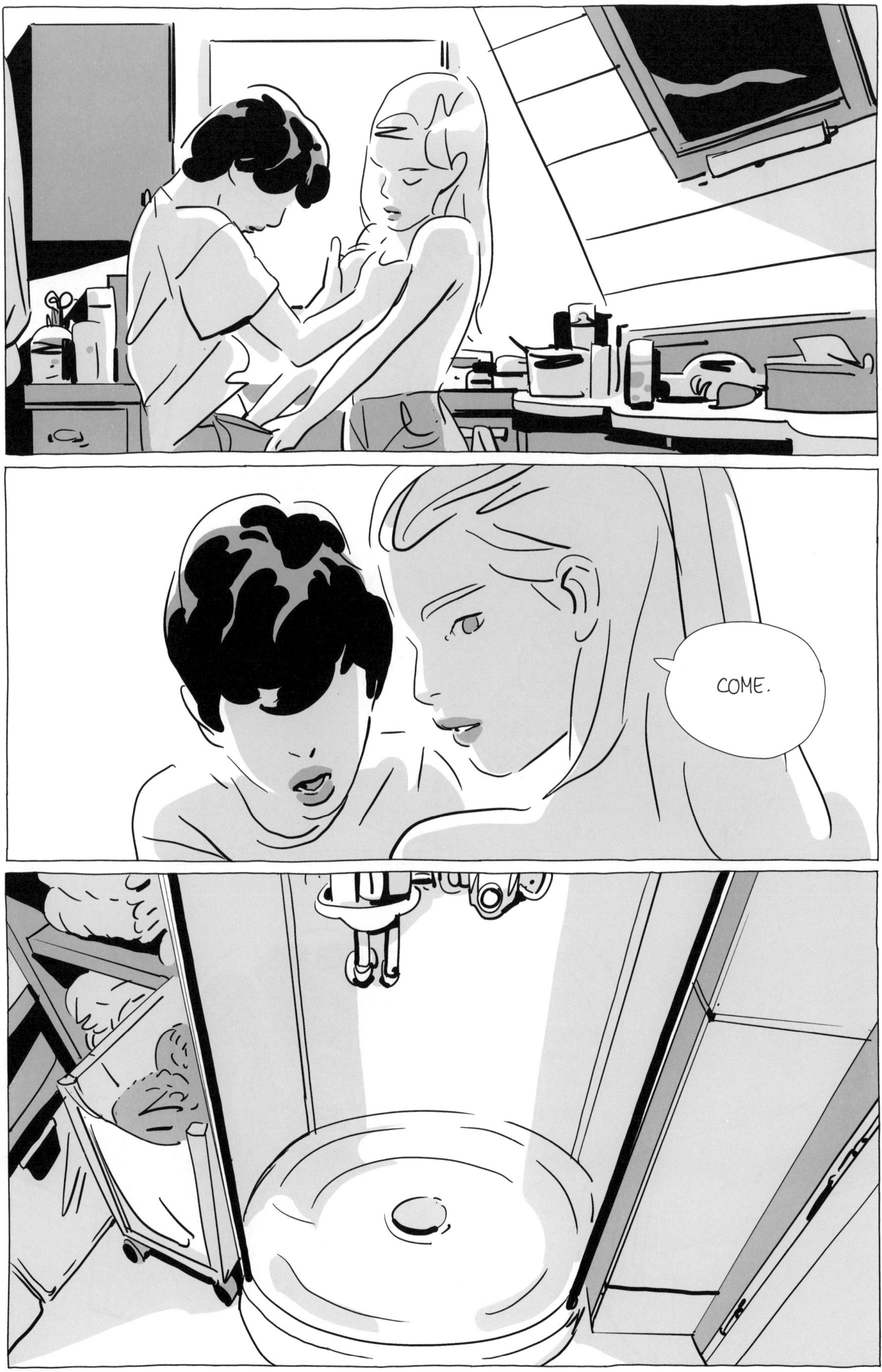
COME.

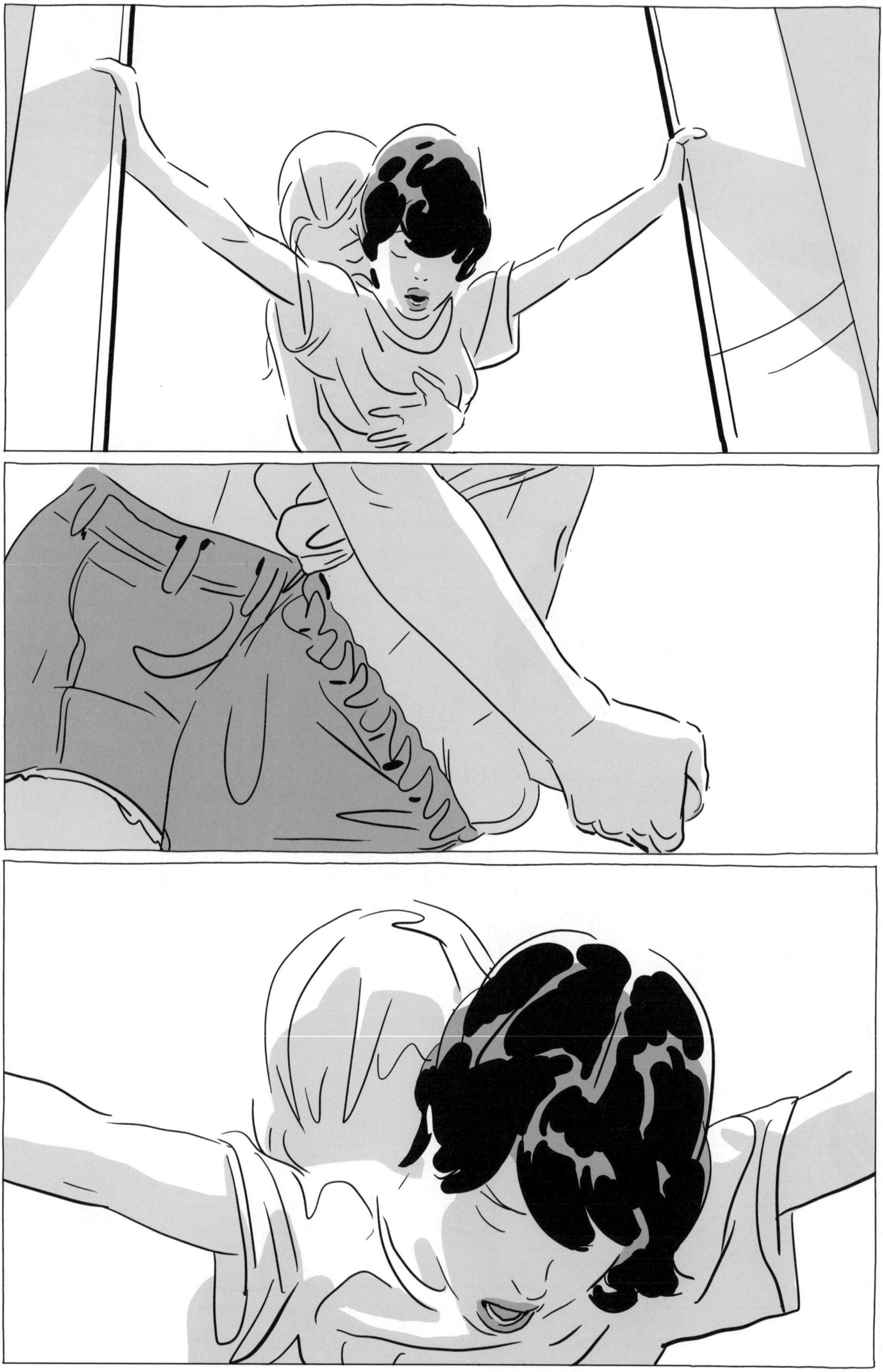

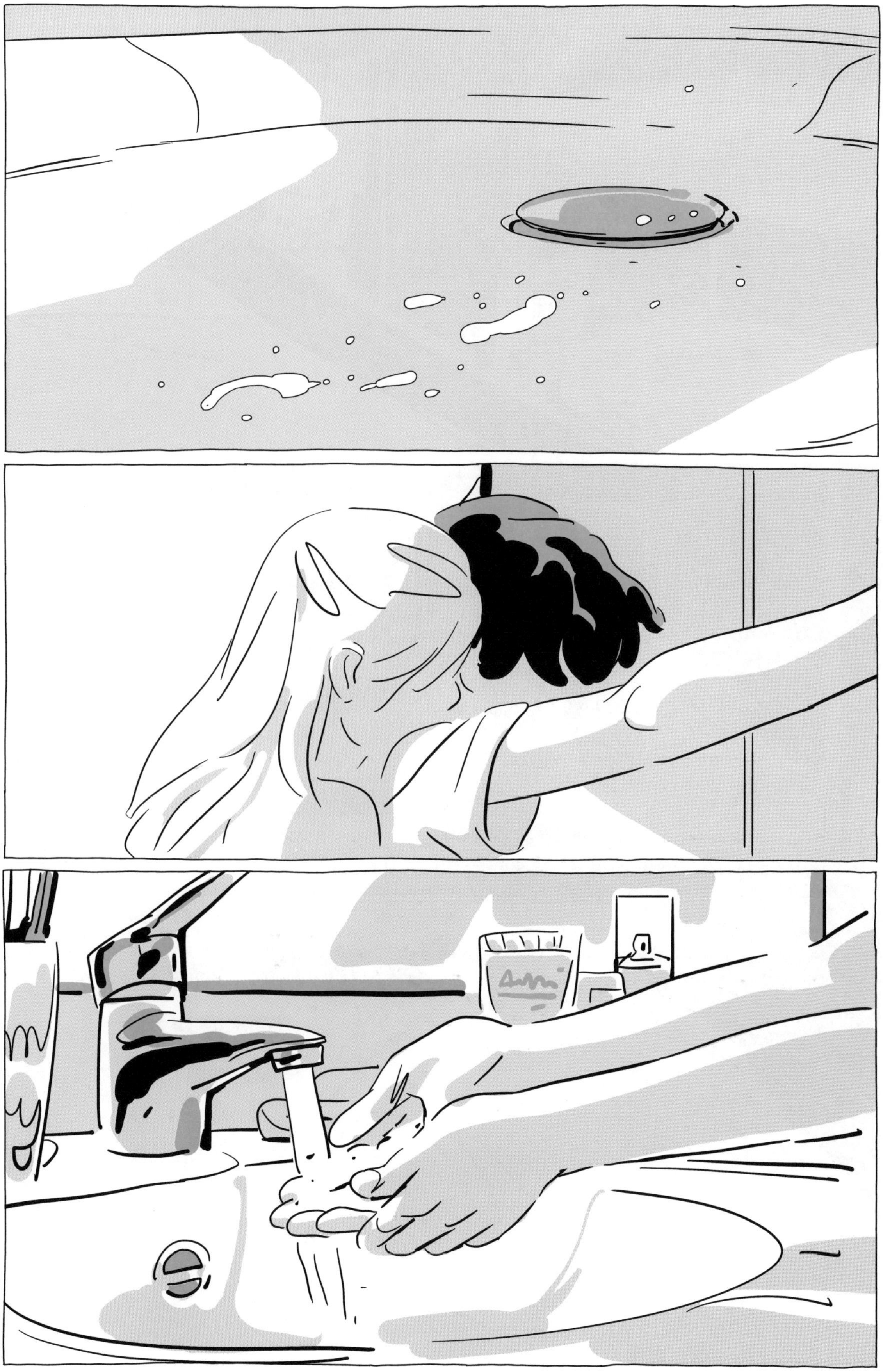

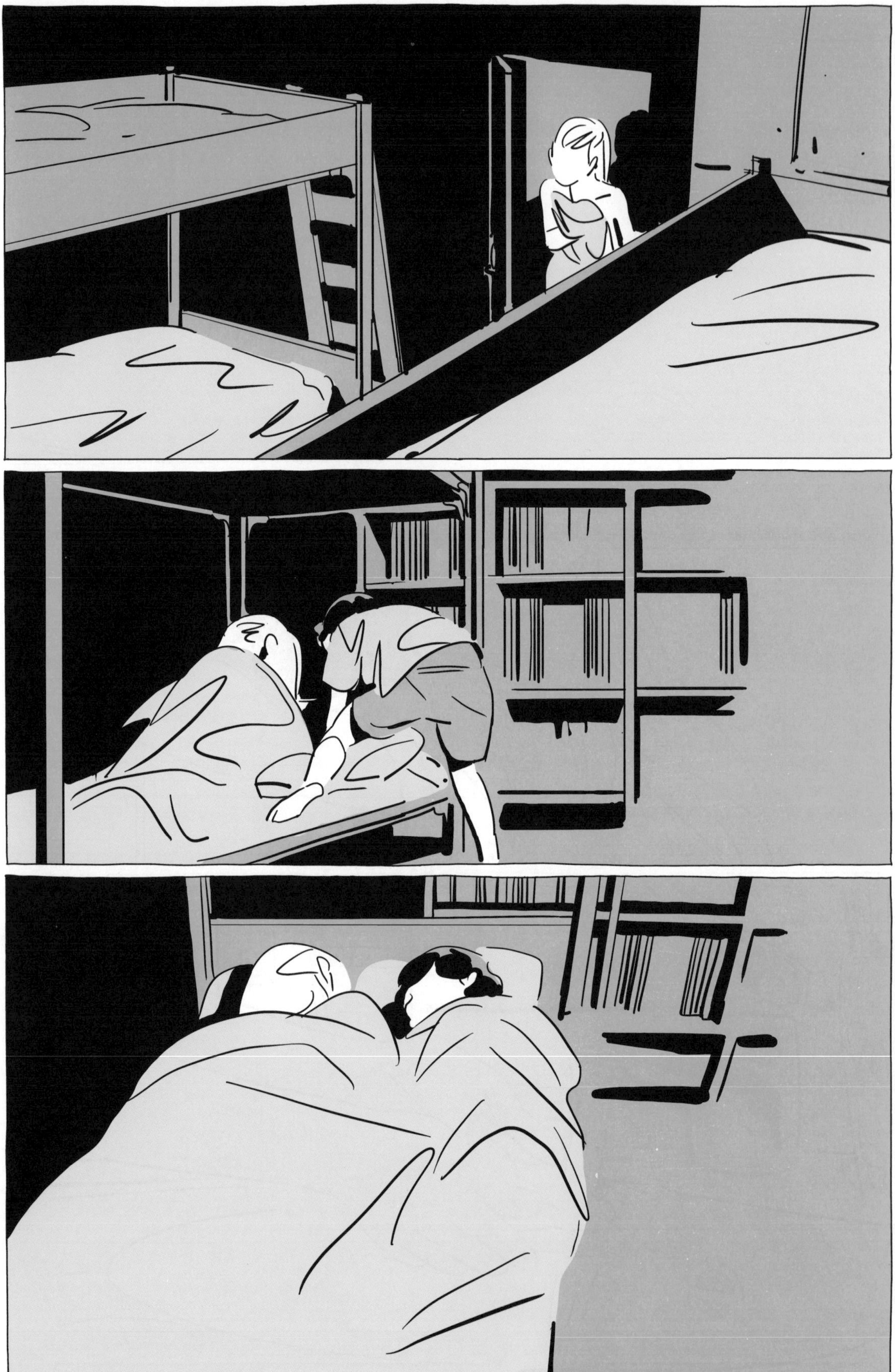

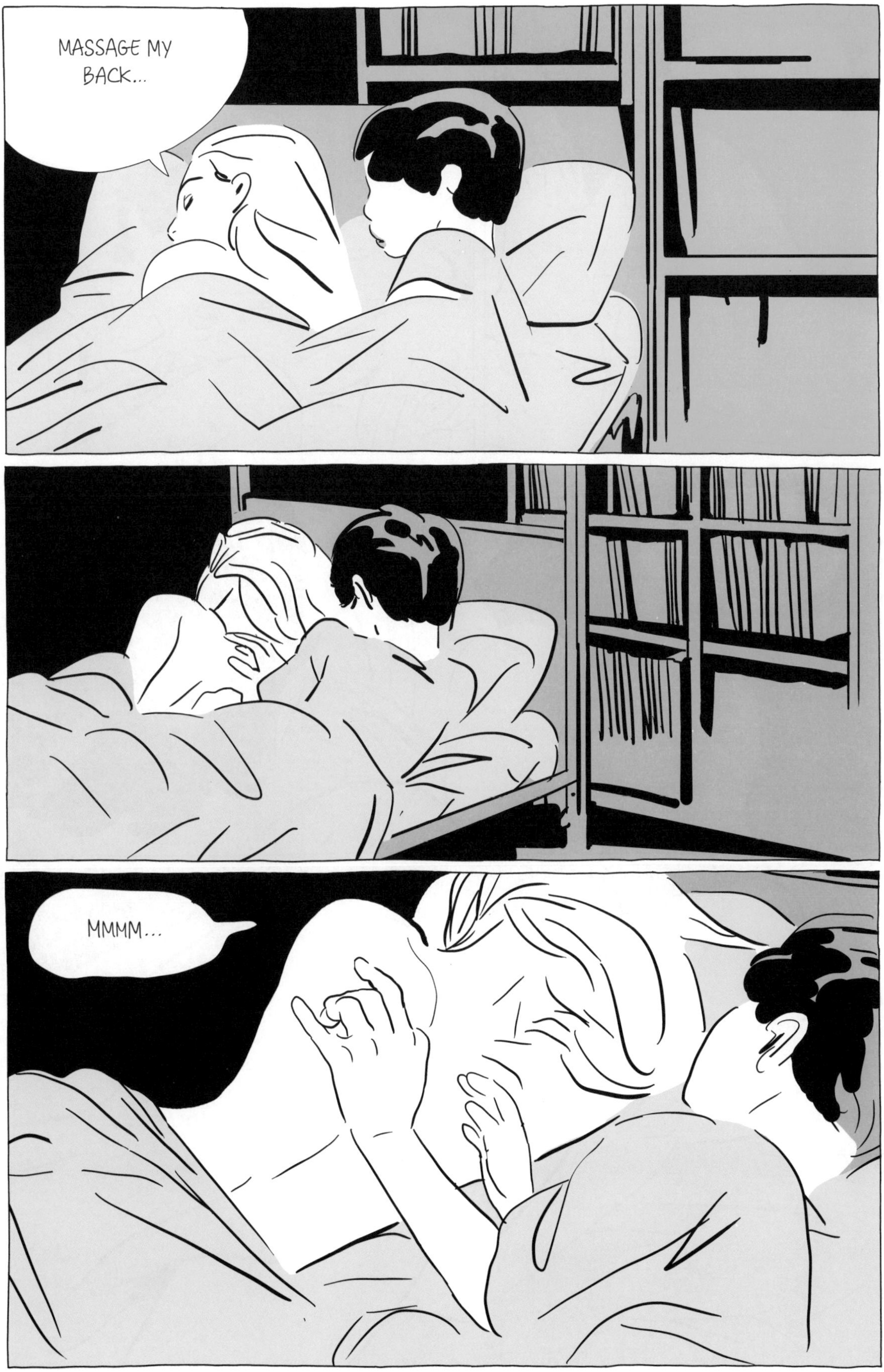
MASSAGE MY BACK...
MMMM...

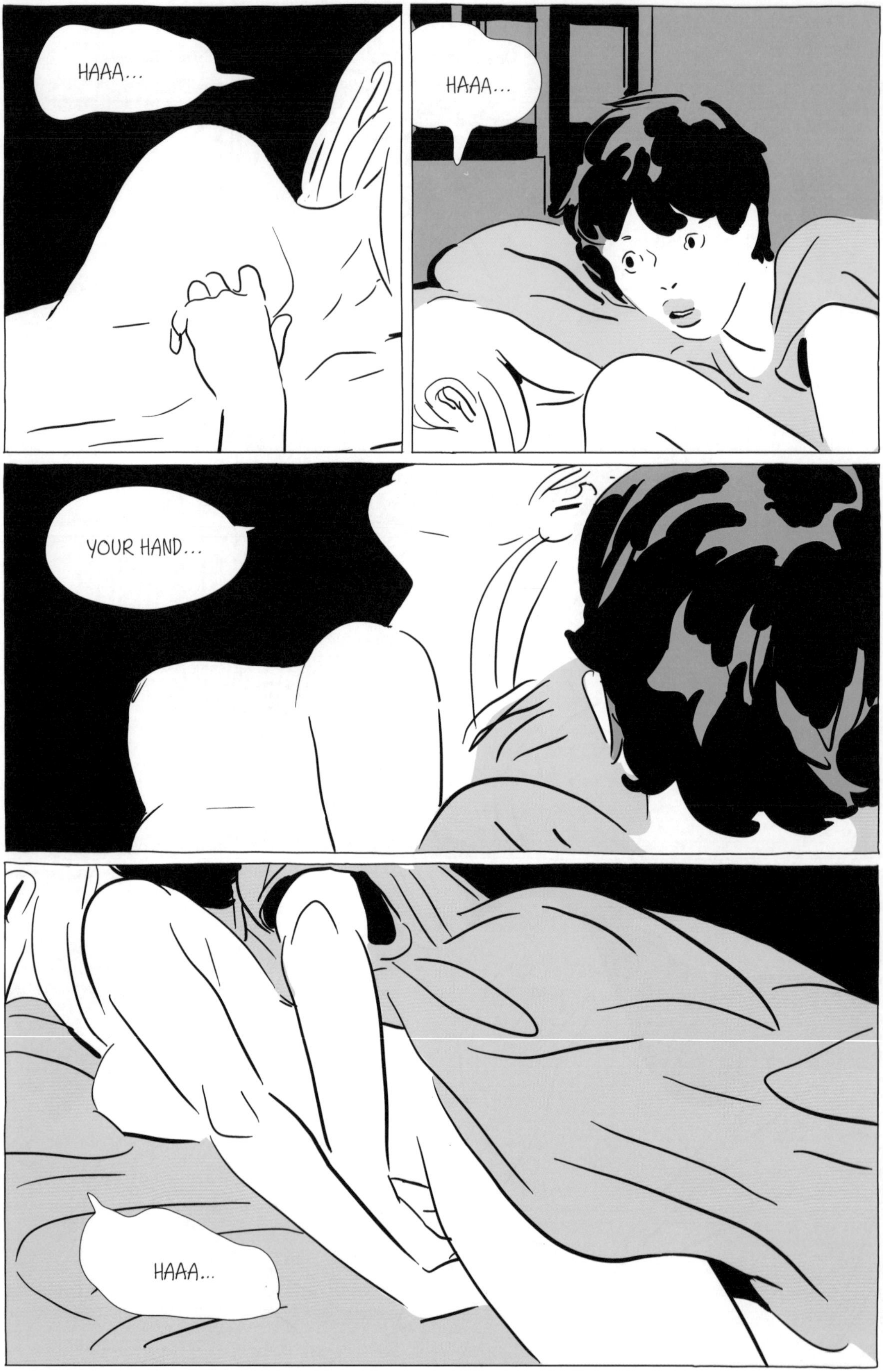
HAAA...
HAAA...
YOUR HAND...
HAAA...

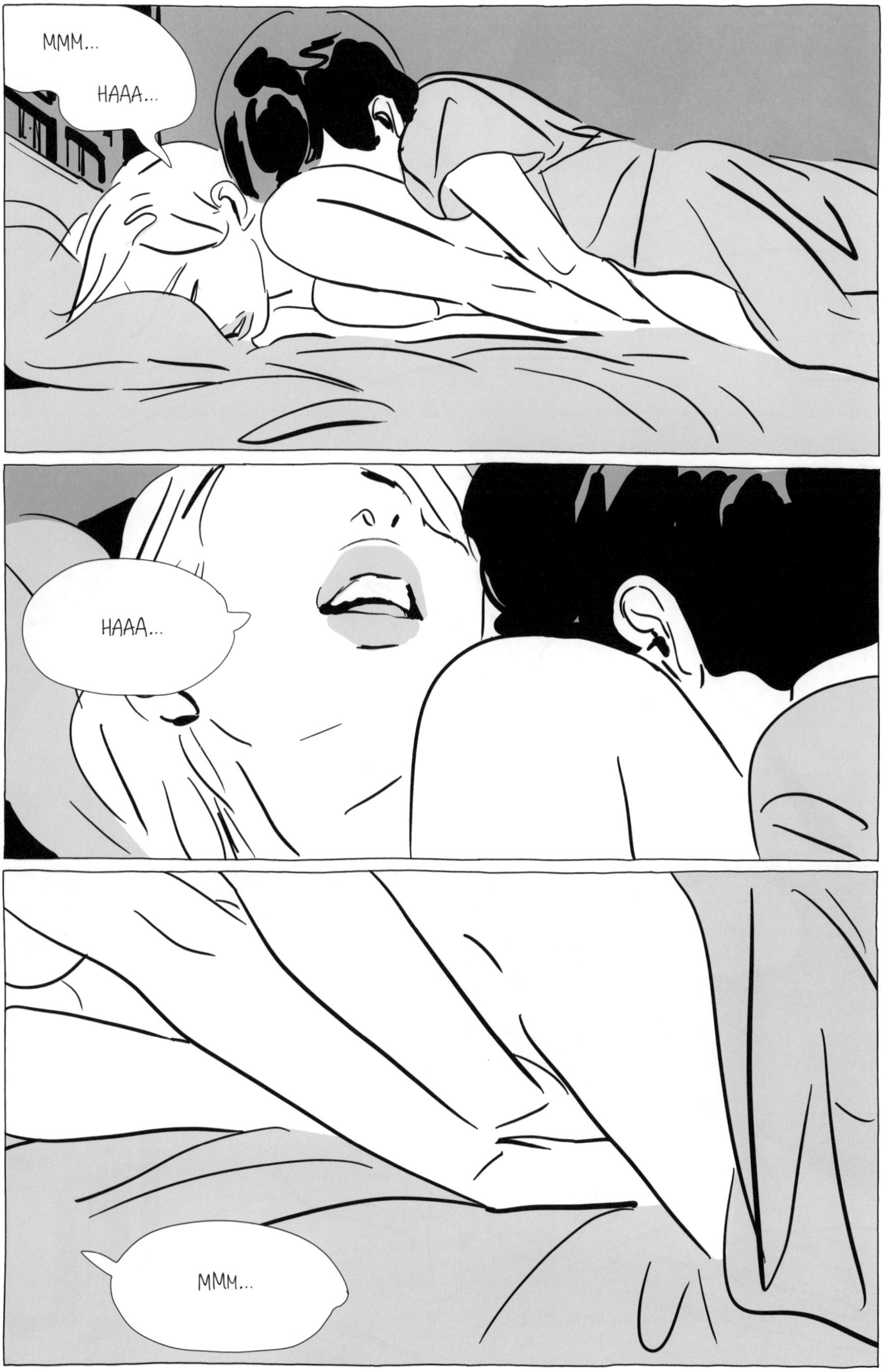
MMM...
HAAA...
HAAA...
MMM...

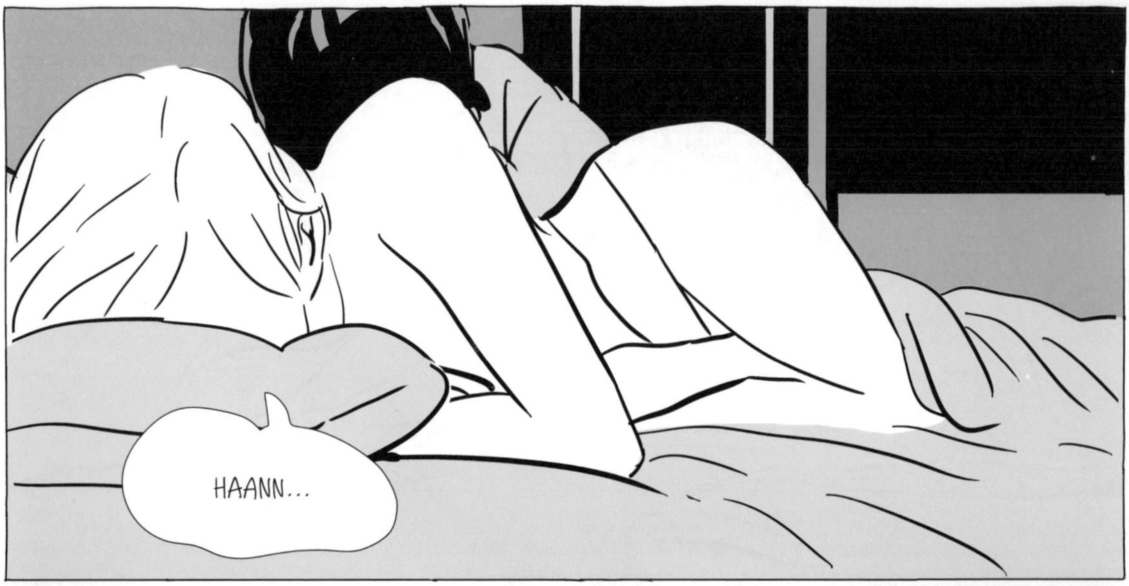
HAANN...

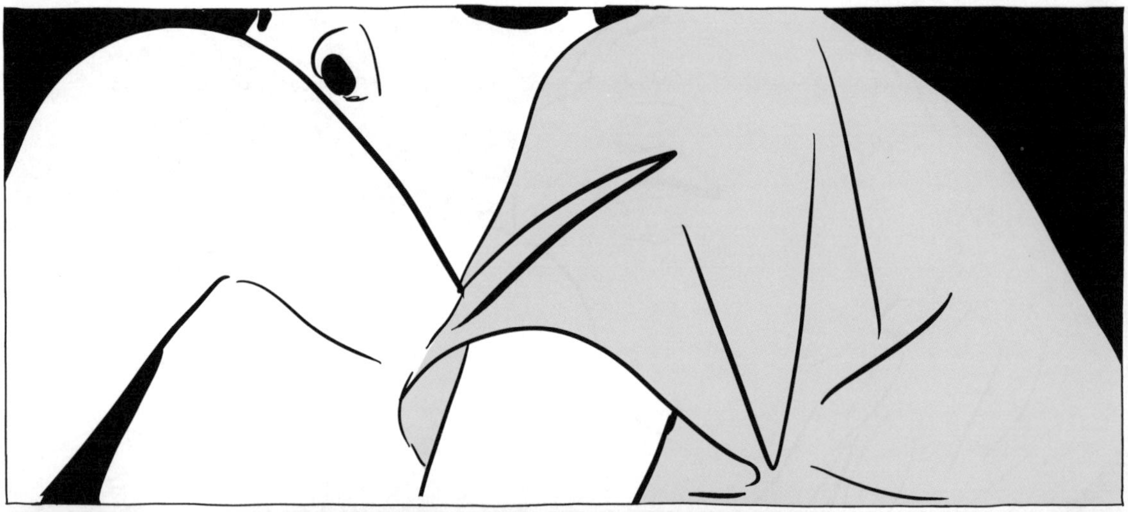

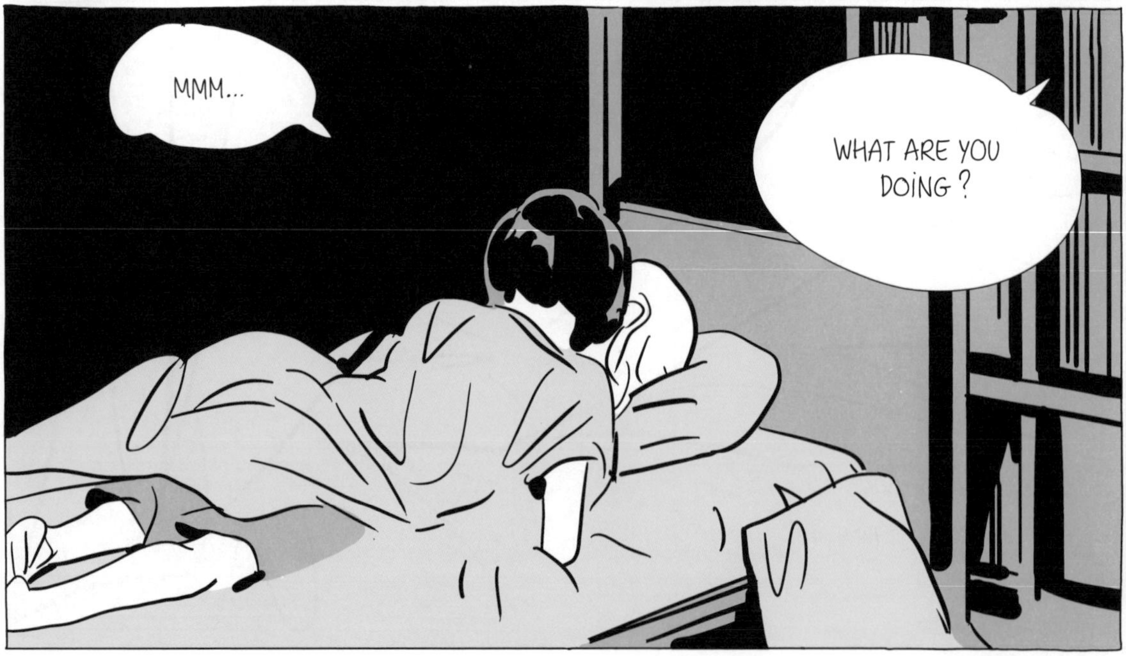
MMM...
WHAT ARE YOU DOING?

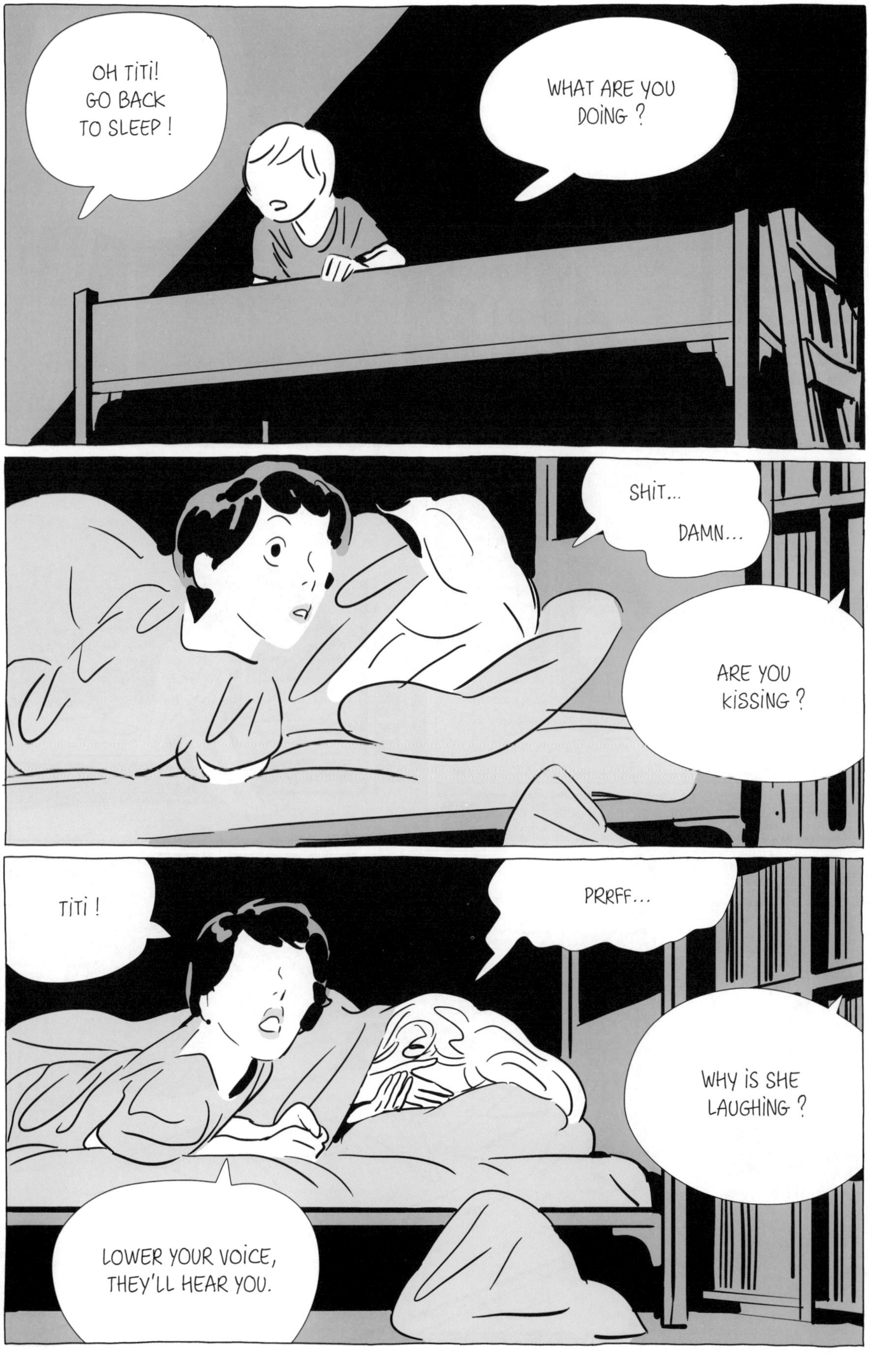
OH TiTi! GO BACK TO SLEEP !
WHAT ARE YOU DOiNG ?
SHiT...
DAMN...
ARE YOU KiSSiNG ?
TiTi !
PRRFF...
WHY iS SHE LAUGHiNG ?
LOWER YOUR VOiCE, THEY'LL HEAR YOU.

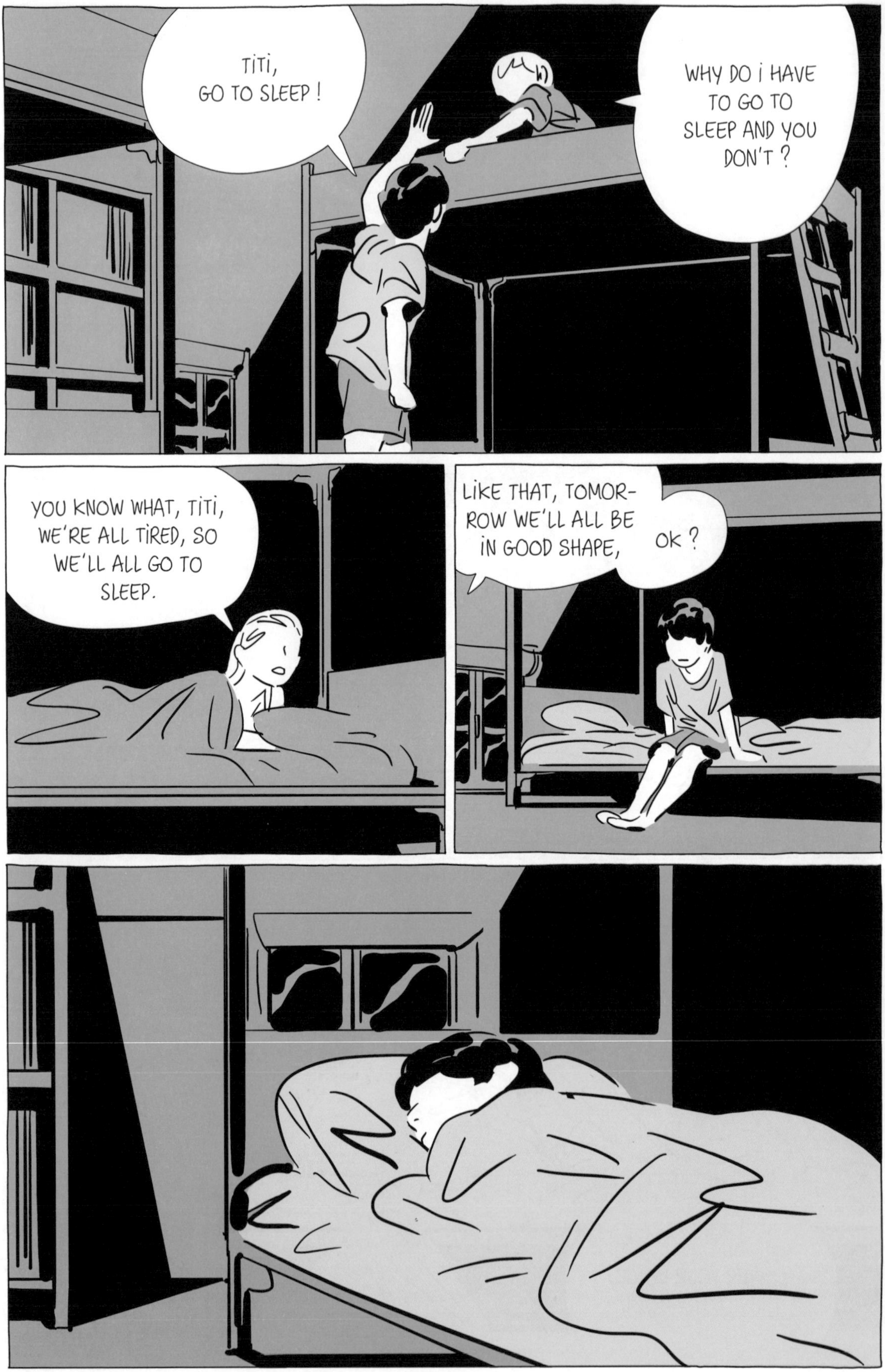
TiTi,
GO TO SLEEP !
WHY DO i HAVE TO GO TO SLEEP AND YOU DON'T ?
YOU KNOW WHAT, TiTi, WE'RE ALL TiRED, SO WE'LL ALL GO TO SLEEP.
LiKE THAT, TOMOR-ROW WE'LL ALL BE iN GOOD SHAPE,
OK ?

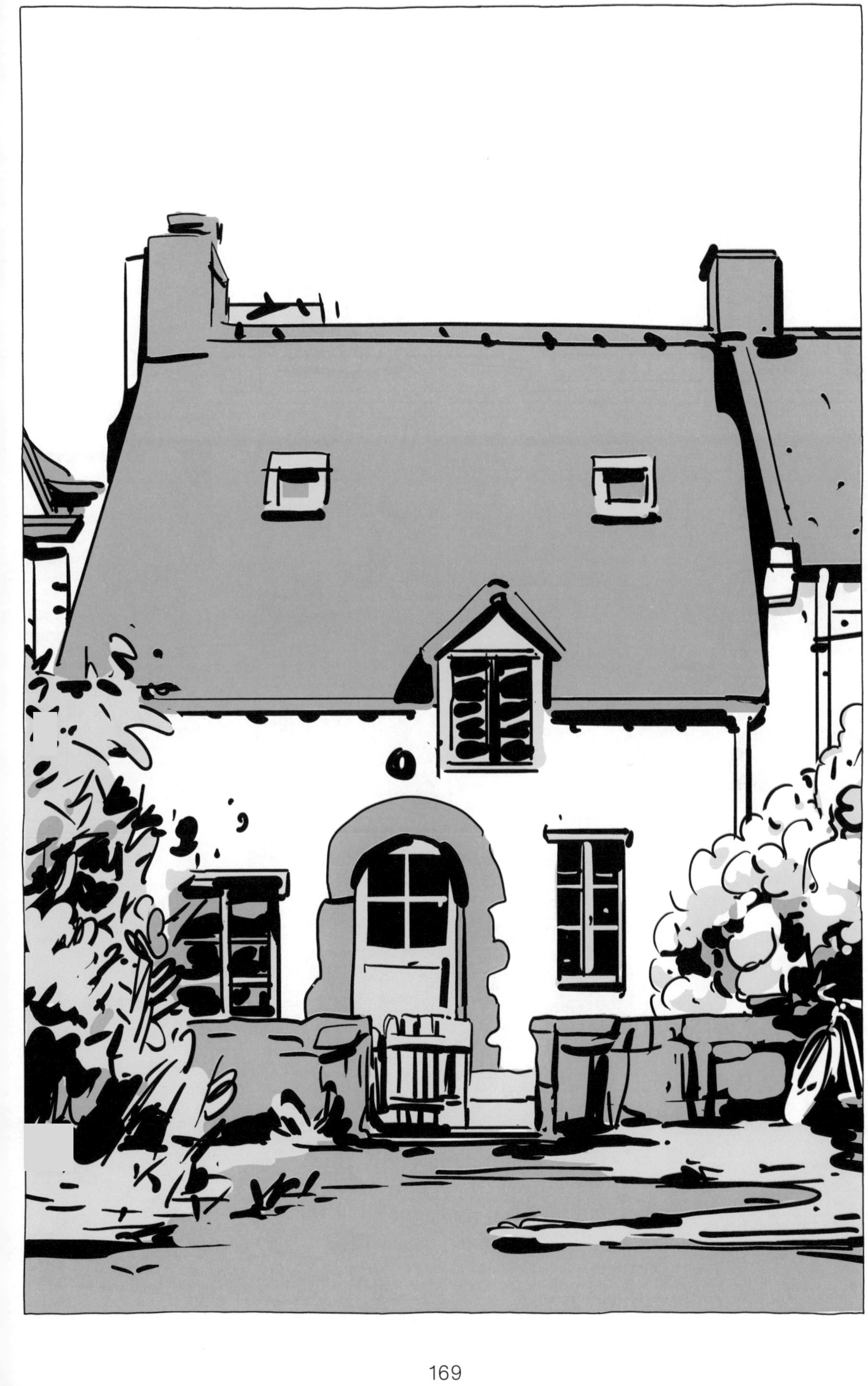

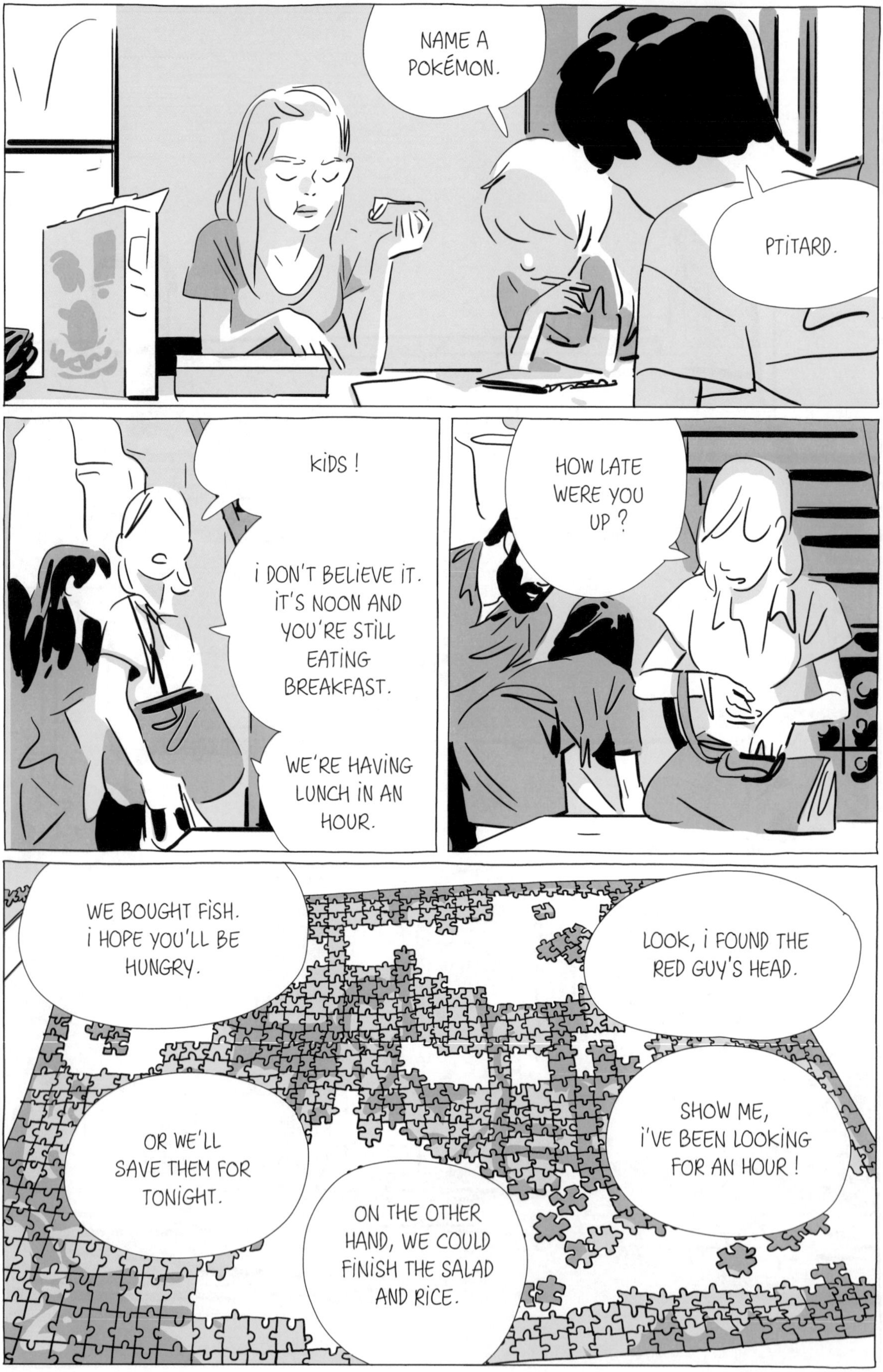
NAME A POKÉMON.
PTITARD.
KIDS !
I DON'T BELIEVE IT. IT'S NOON AND YOU'RE STILL EATING BREAKFAST.
WE'RE HAVING LUNCH IN AN HOUR.
HOW LATE WERE YOU UP ?
WE BOUGHT FISH. I HOPE YOU'LL BE HUNGRY.
LOOK, I FOUND THE RED GUY'S HEAD.
OR WE'LL SAVE THEM FOR TONIGHT.
SHOW ME, I'VE BEEN LOOKING FOR AN HOUR !
ON THE OTHER HAND, WE COULD FINISH THE SALAD AND RICE.

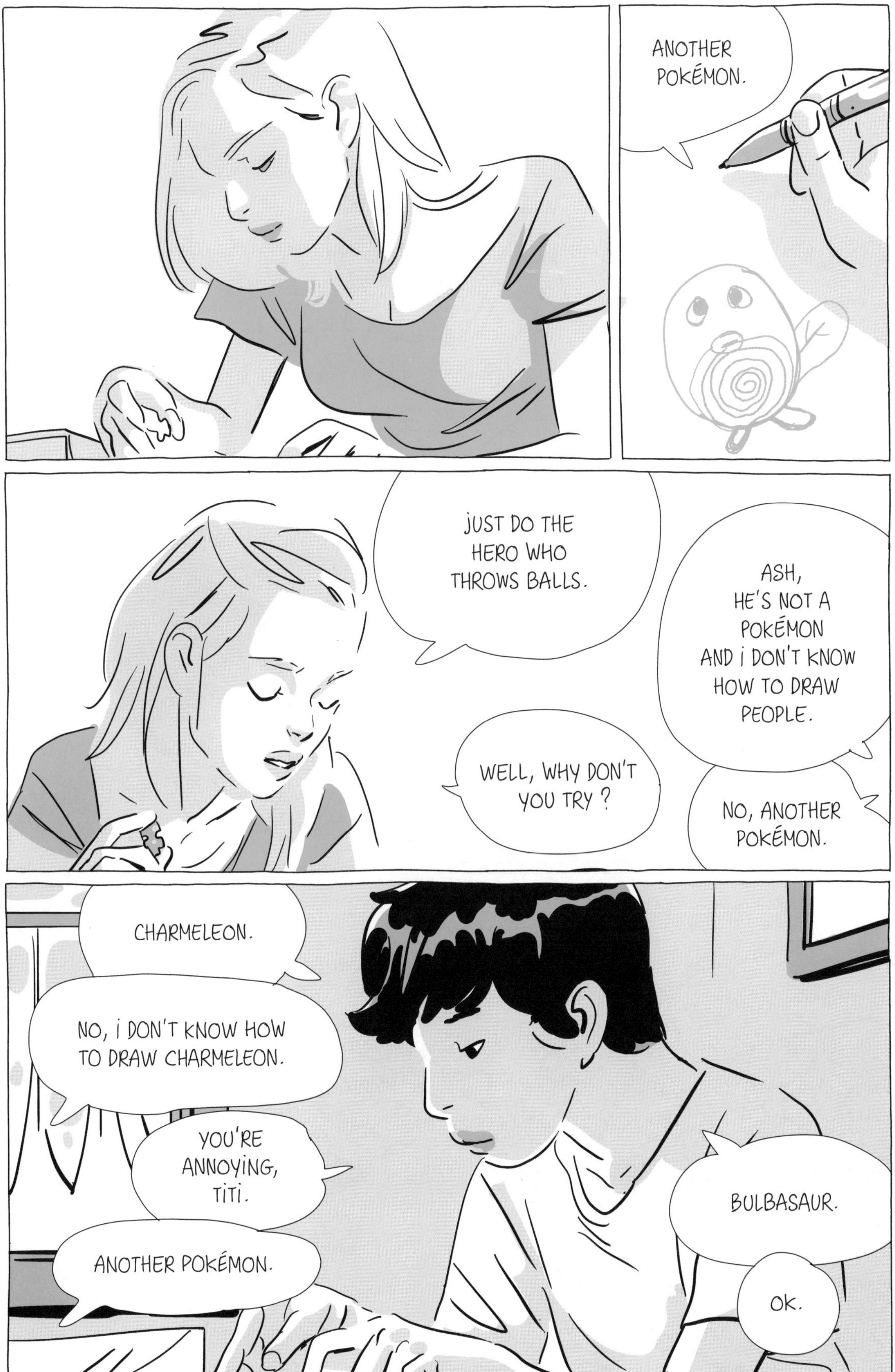
ANOTHER POKÉMON.
JUST DO THE HERO WHO THROWS BALLS.
ASH, HE'S NOT A POKÉMON AND i DON'T KNOW HOW TO DRAW PEOPLE.
WELL, WHY DON'T YOU TRY ?
NO, ANOTHER POKÉMON.
CHARMELEON.
NO, i DON'T KNOW HOW TO DRAW CHARMELEON.
YOU'RE ANNOYiNG, TiTi.
ANOTHER POKÉMON.
BULBASAUR.
OK.

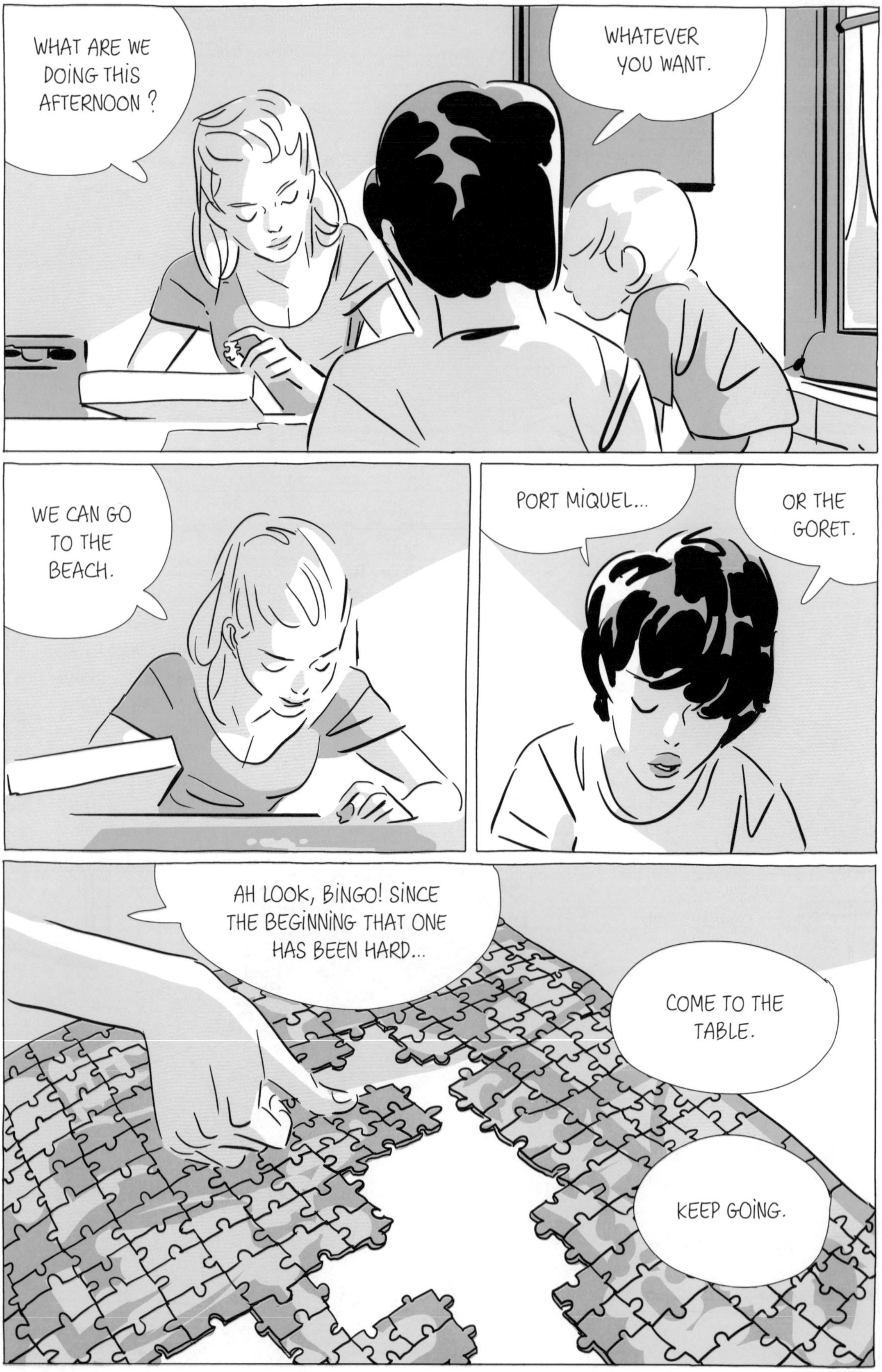
WHAT ARE WE DOING THIS AFTERNOON ?
WHATEVER YOU WANT.
WE CAN GO TO THE BEACH.
PORT MIQUEL...
OR THE GORET.
AH LOOK, BINGO! SINCE THE BEGINNING THAT ONE HAS BEEN HARD...
COME TO THE TABLE.
KEEP GOING.

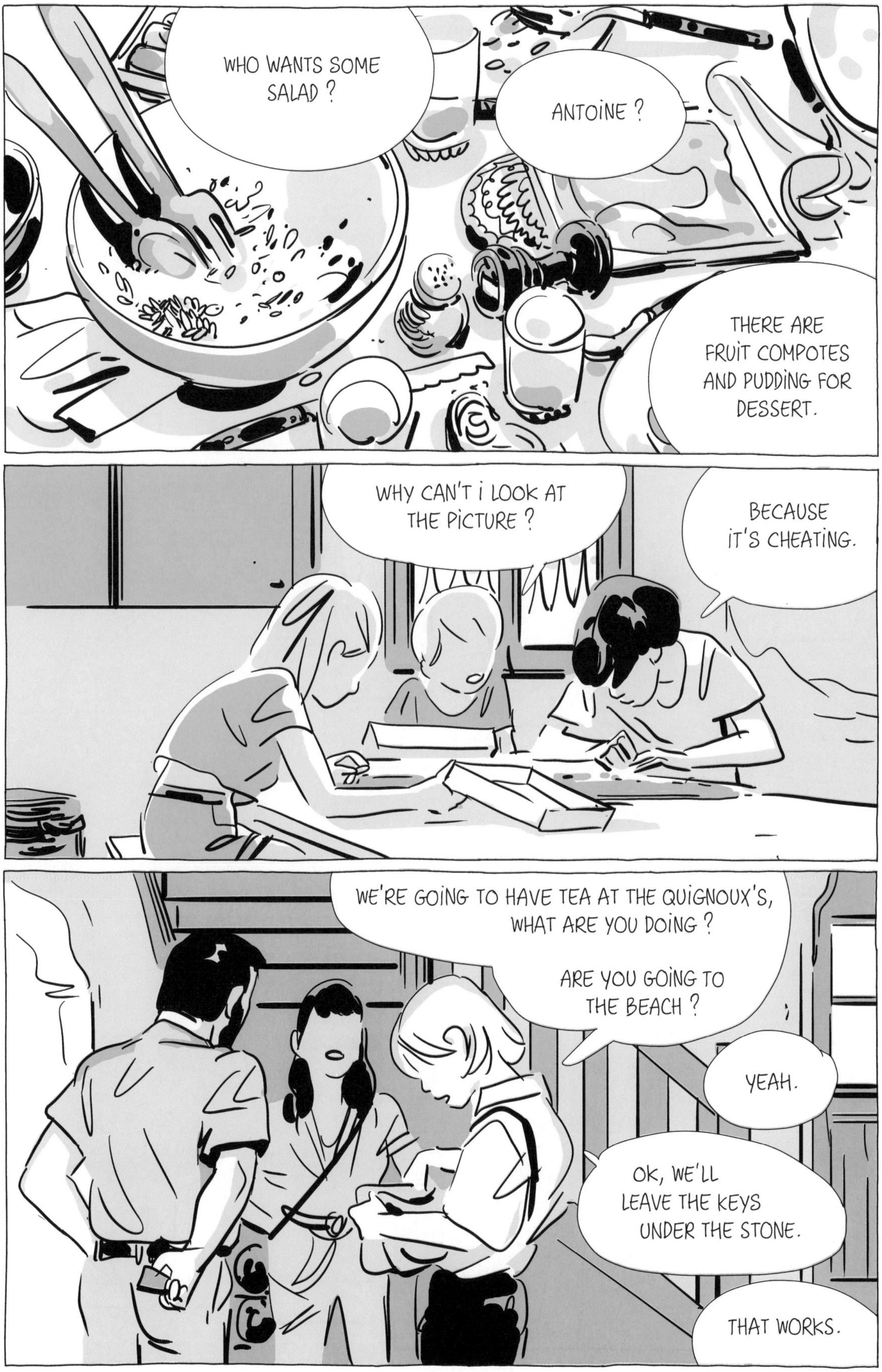
WHO WANTS SOME SALAD ?
ANTOINE ?
THERE ARE FRUIT COMPOTES AND PUDDING FOR DESSERT.
WHY CAN'T I LOOK AT THE PICTURE ?
BECAUSE IT'S CHEATING.
WE'RE GOING TO HAVE TEA AT THE QUIGNOUX'S, WHAT ARE YOU DOING ?
ARE YOU GOING TO THE BEACH ?
YEAH.
OK, WE'LL LEAVE THE KEYS UNDER THE STONE.
THAT WORKS.

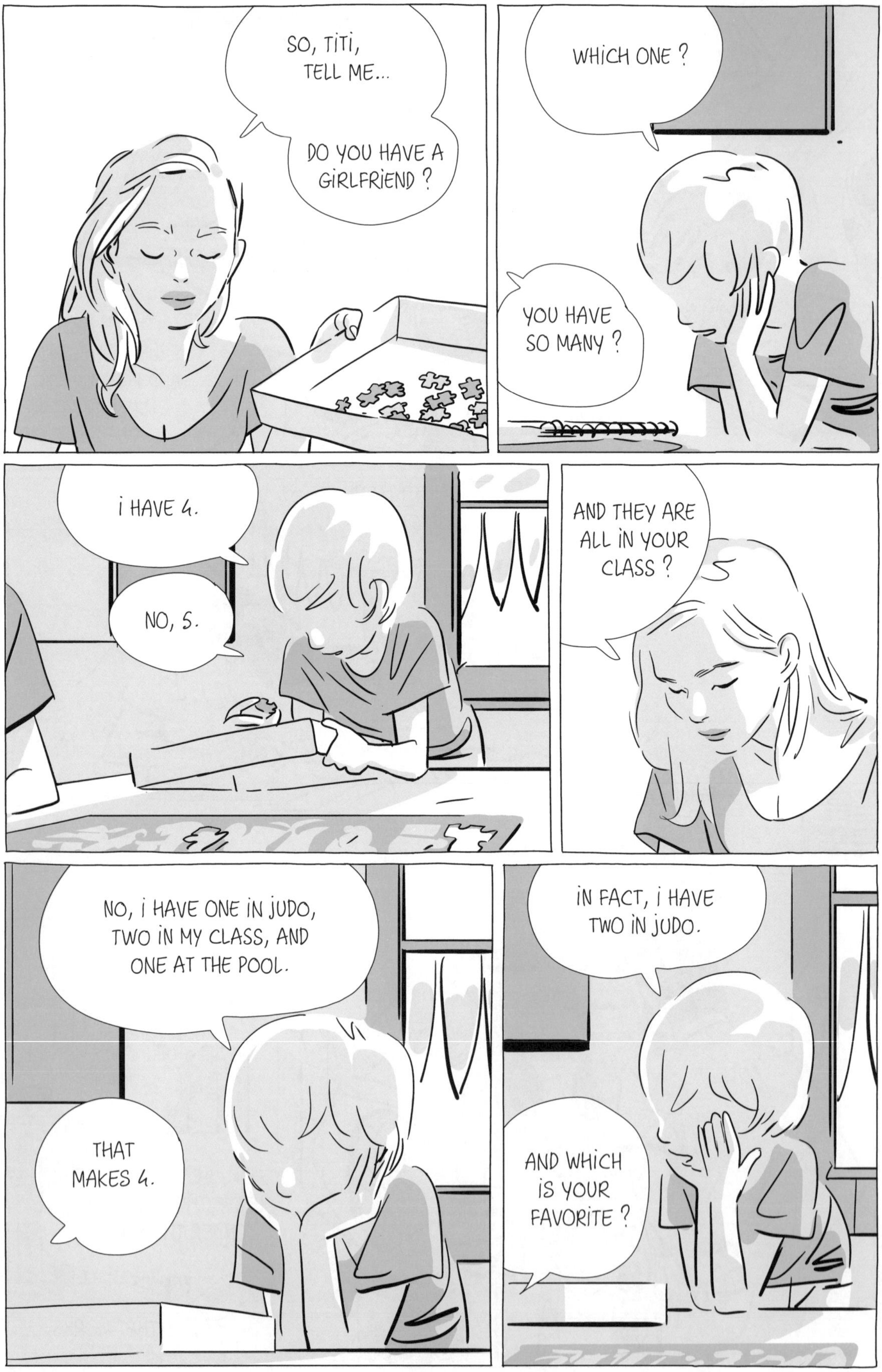
SO, TITI, TELL ME...
DO YOU HAVE A GIRLFRIEND ?
WHICH ONE ?
YOU HAVE SO MANY ?
I HAVE 4.
NO, 5.
AND THEY ARE ALL IN YOUR CLASS ?
NO, I HAVE ONE IN JUDO, TWO IN MY CLASS, AND ONE AT THE POOL.
THAT MAKES 4.
IN FACT, I HAVE TWO IN JUDO.
AND WHICH IS YOUR FAVORITE ?

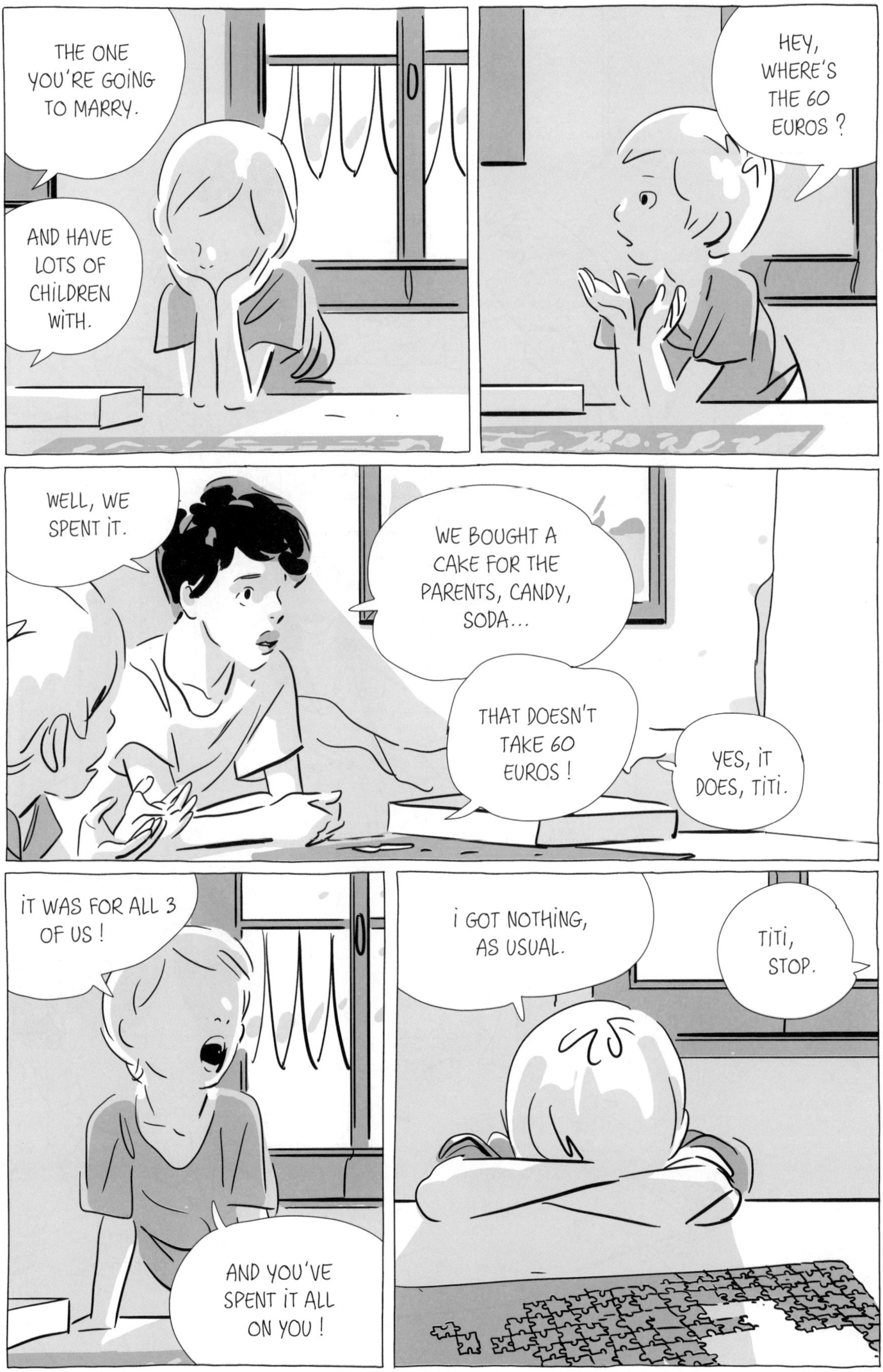
THE ONE YOU'RE GOING TO MARRY.
AND HAVE LOTS OF CHILDREN WITH.
HEY, WHERE'S THE 60 EUROS ?
WELL, WE SPENT IT.
WE BOUGHT A CAKE FOR THE PARENTS, CANDY, SODA...
THAT DOESN'T TAKE 60 EUROS !
YES, IT DOES, TITI.
IT WAS FOR ALL 3 OF US !
AND YOU'VE SPENT IT ALL ON YOU !
I GOT NOTHING, AS USUAL.
TITI, STOP.

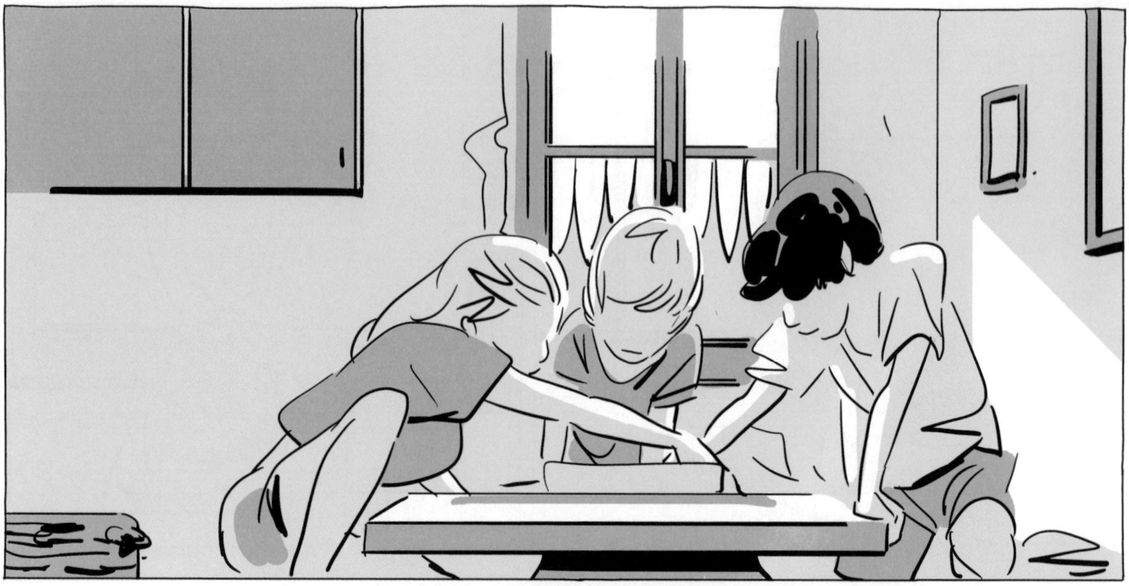

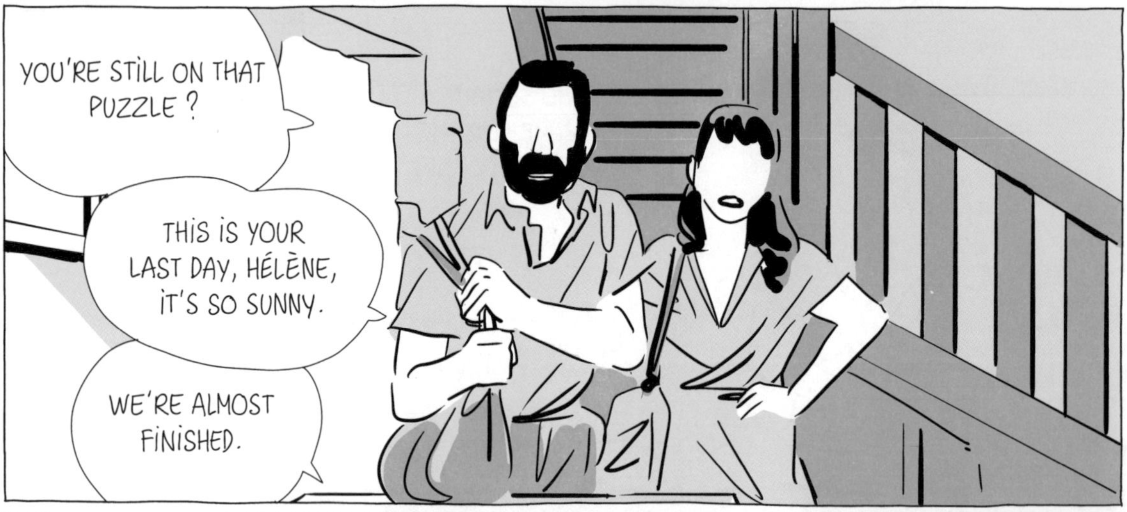
YOU'RE STILL ON THAT PUZZLE ?
THIS IS YOUR LAST DAY, HÉLÈNE, IT'S SO SUNNY.
WE'RE ALMOST FINISHED.

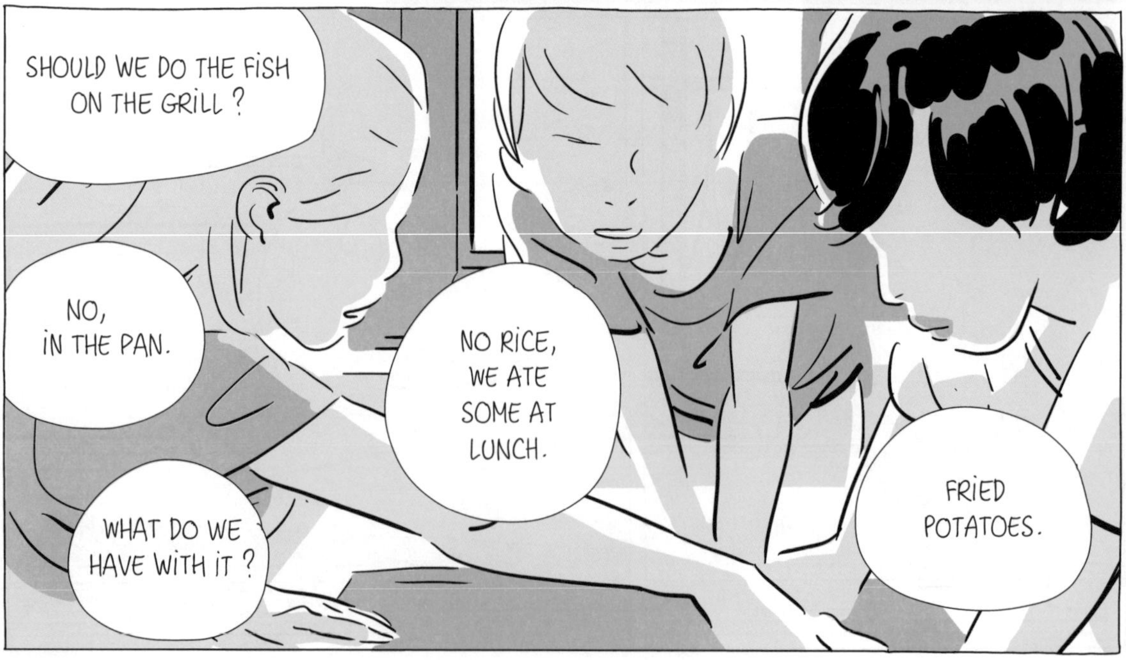
SHOULD WE DO THE FISH ON THE GRILL ?
NO, IN THE PAN.
WHAT DO WE HAVE WITH IT ?
NO RICE, WE ATE SOME AT LUNCH.
FRIED POTATOES.

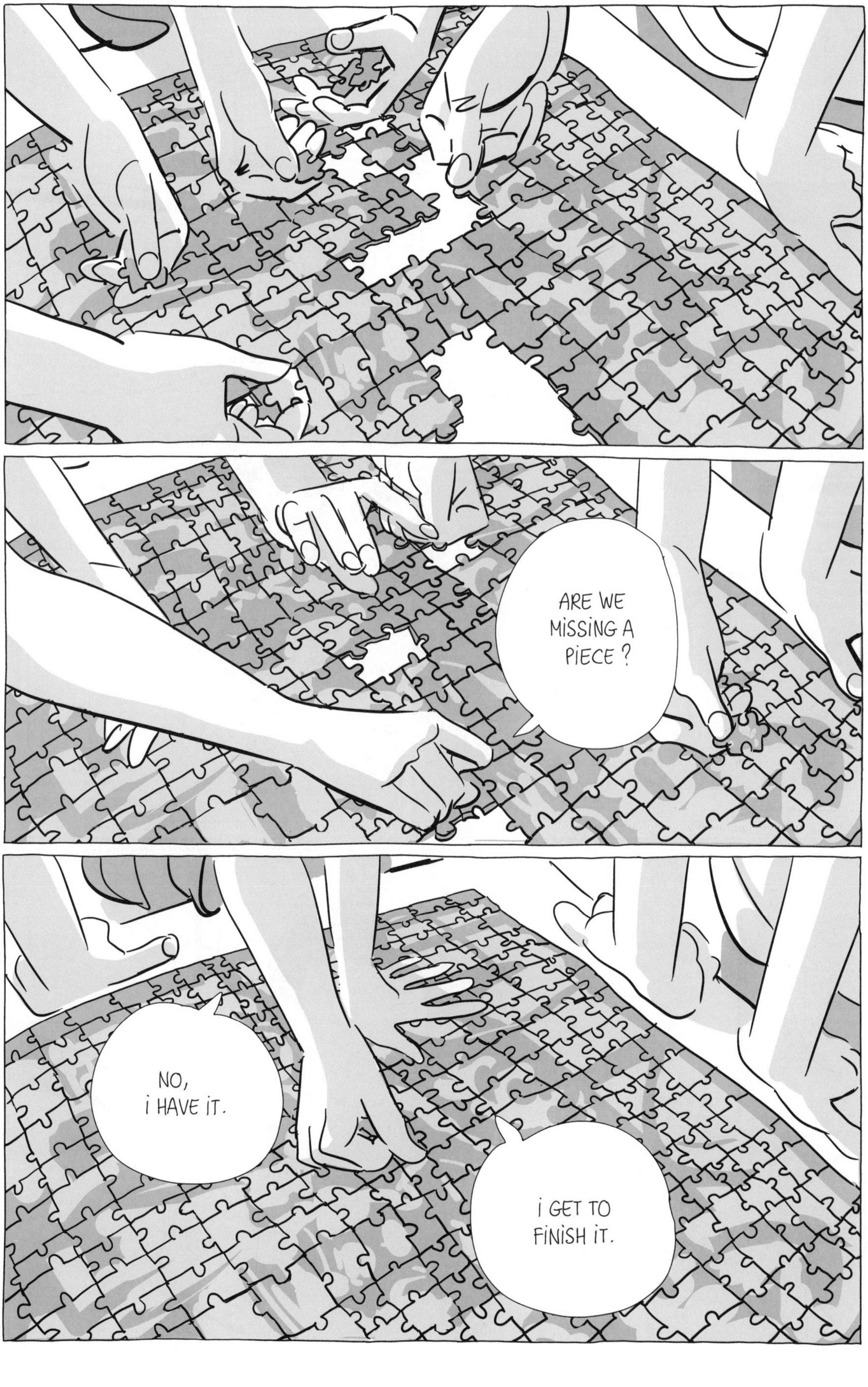
ARE WE MISSING A PIECE?
NO, I HAVE IT.
I GET TO FINISH IT.

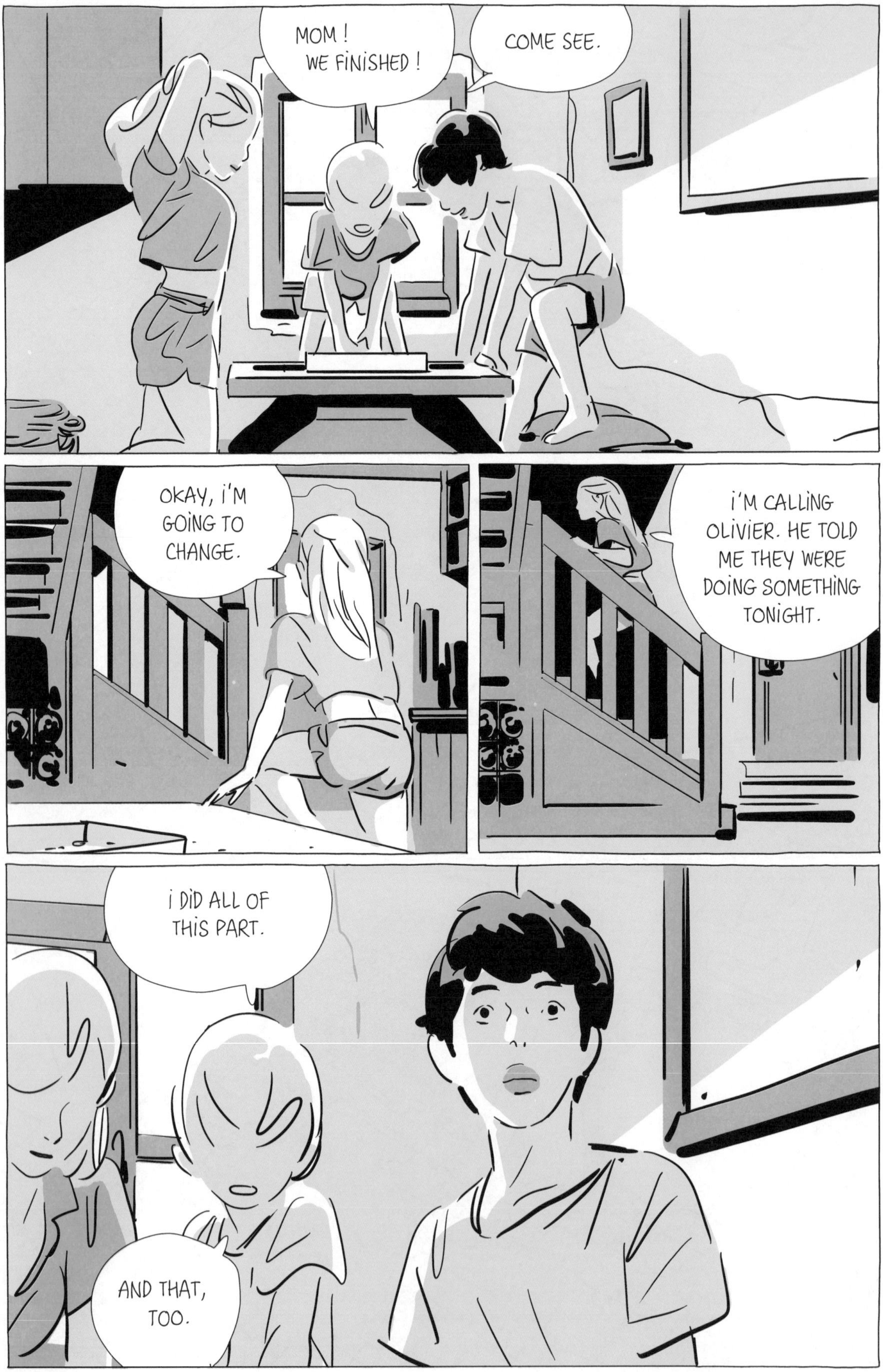
MOM ! WE FINISHED !
COME SEE.
OKAY, I'M GOING TO CHANGE.
I'M CALLING OLIVIER. HE TOLD ME THEY WERE DOING SOMETHING TONIGHT.
I DID ALL OF THIS PART.
AND THAT, TOO.

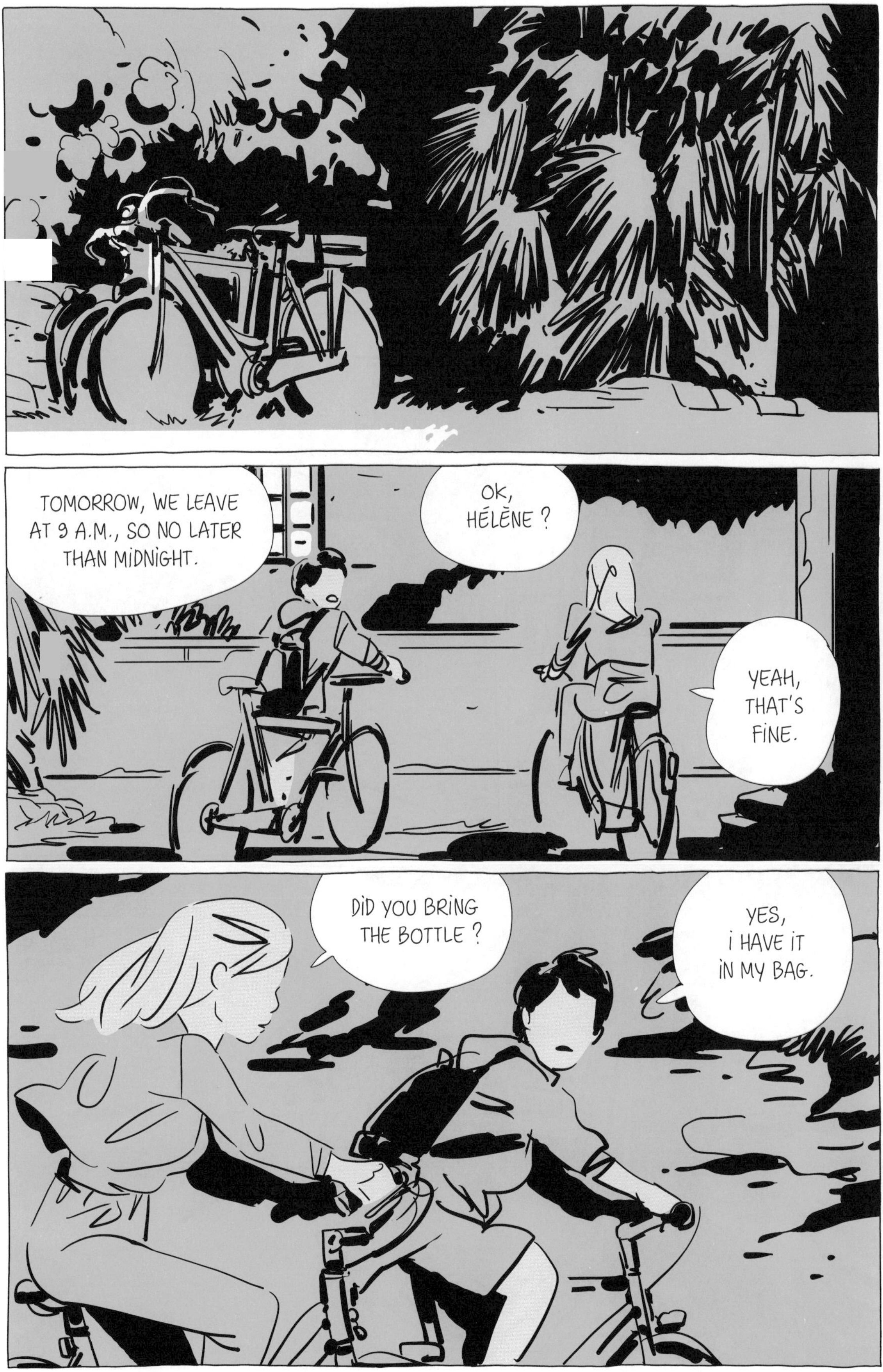
TOMORROW, WE LEAVE AT 9 A.M., SO NO LATER THAN MIDNIGHT.
OK, HÉLÈNE ?
YEAH, THAT'S FINE.
DID YOU BRING THE BOTTLE ?
YES, I HAVE IT IN MY BAG.

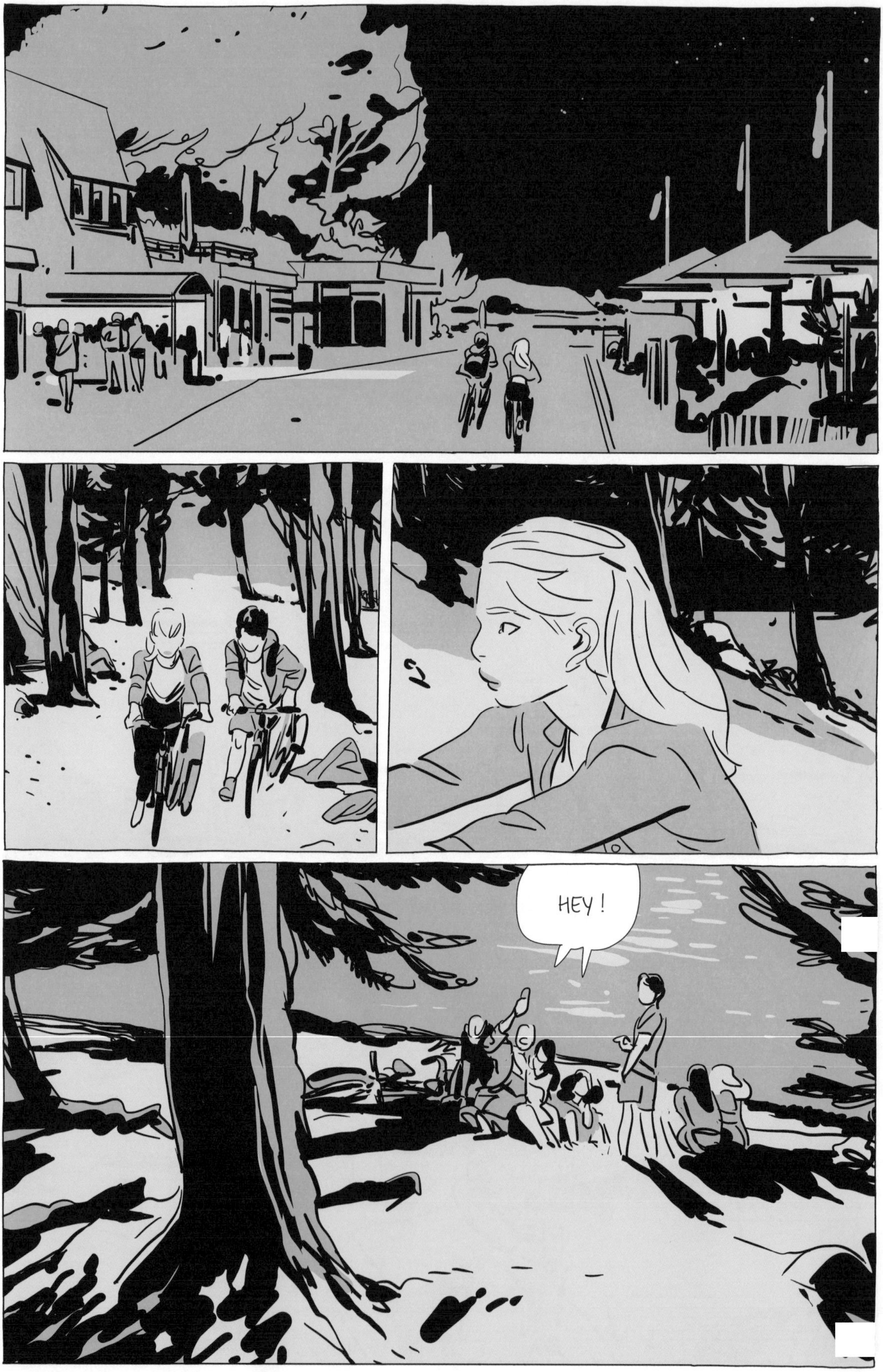
HEY !

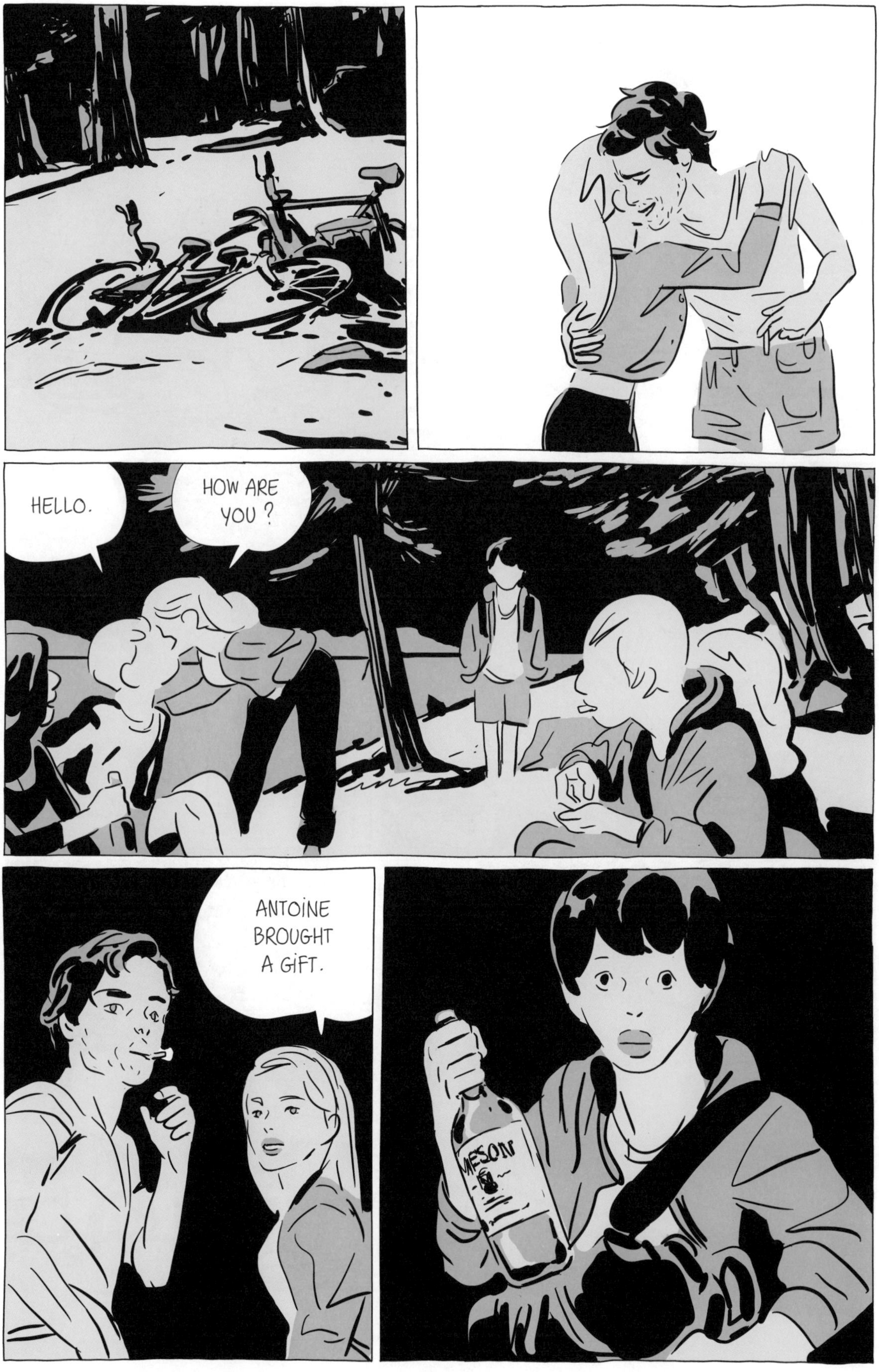
HELLO.
HOW ARE YOU ?
ANTOINE BROUGHT A GIFT.

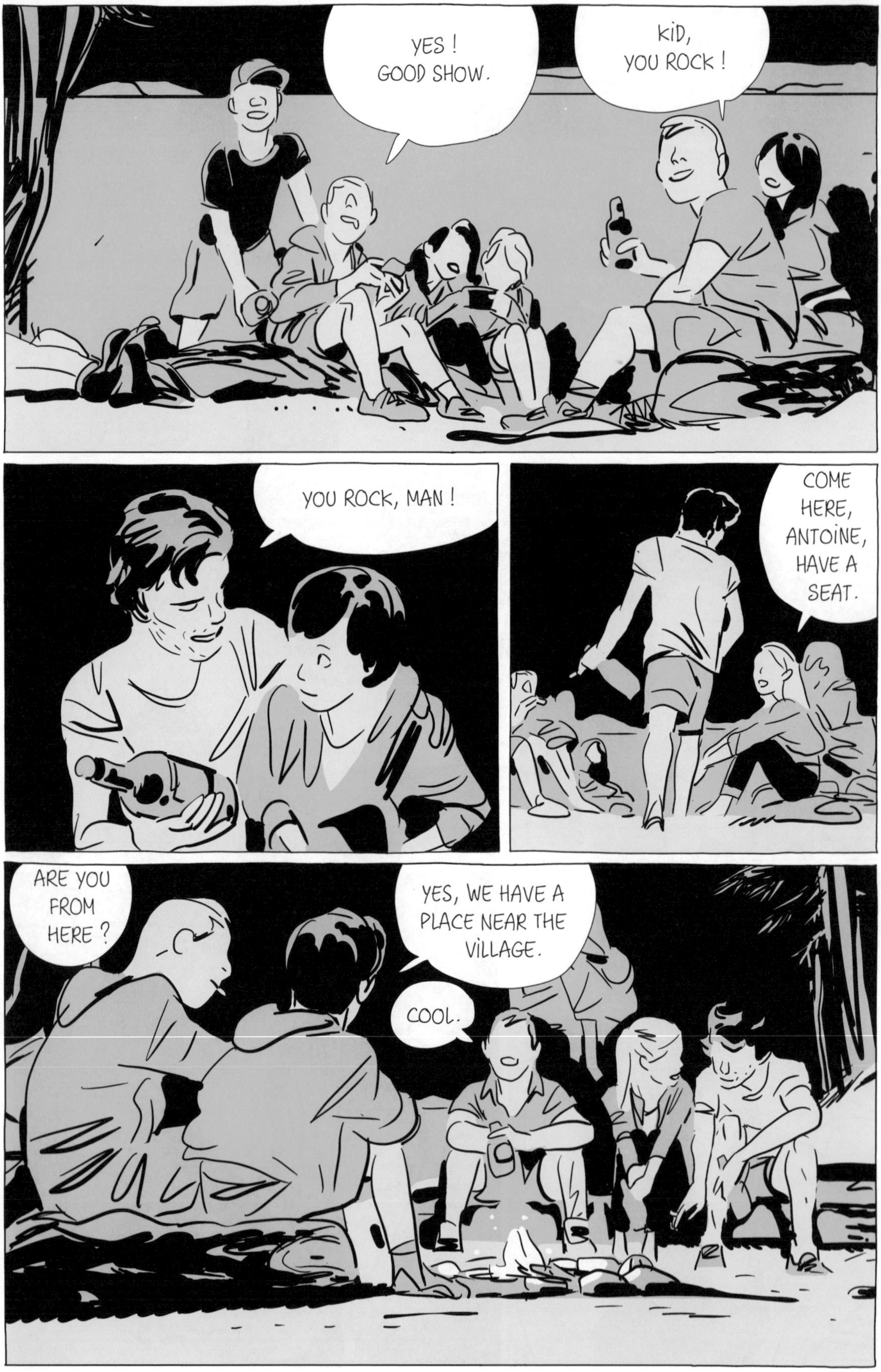
YES ! GOOD SHOW.
KiD, YOU ROCK !
YOU ROCK, MAN !
COME HERE, ANTOiNE, HAVE A SEAT.
ARE YOU FROM HERE ?
YES, WE HAVE A PLACE NEAR THE ViLLAGE.
COOL.

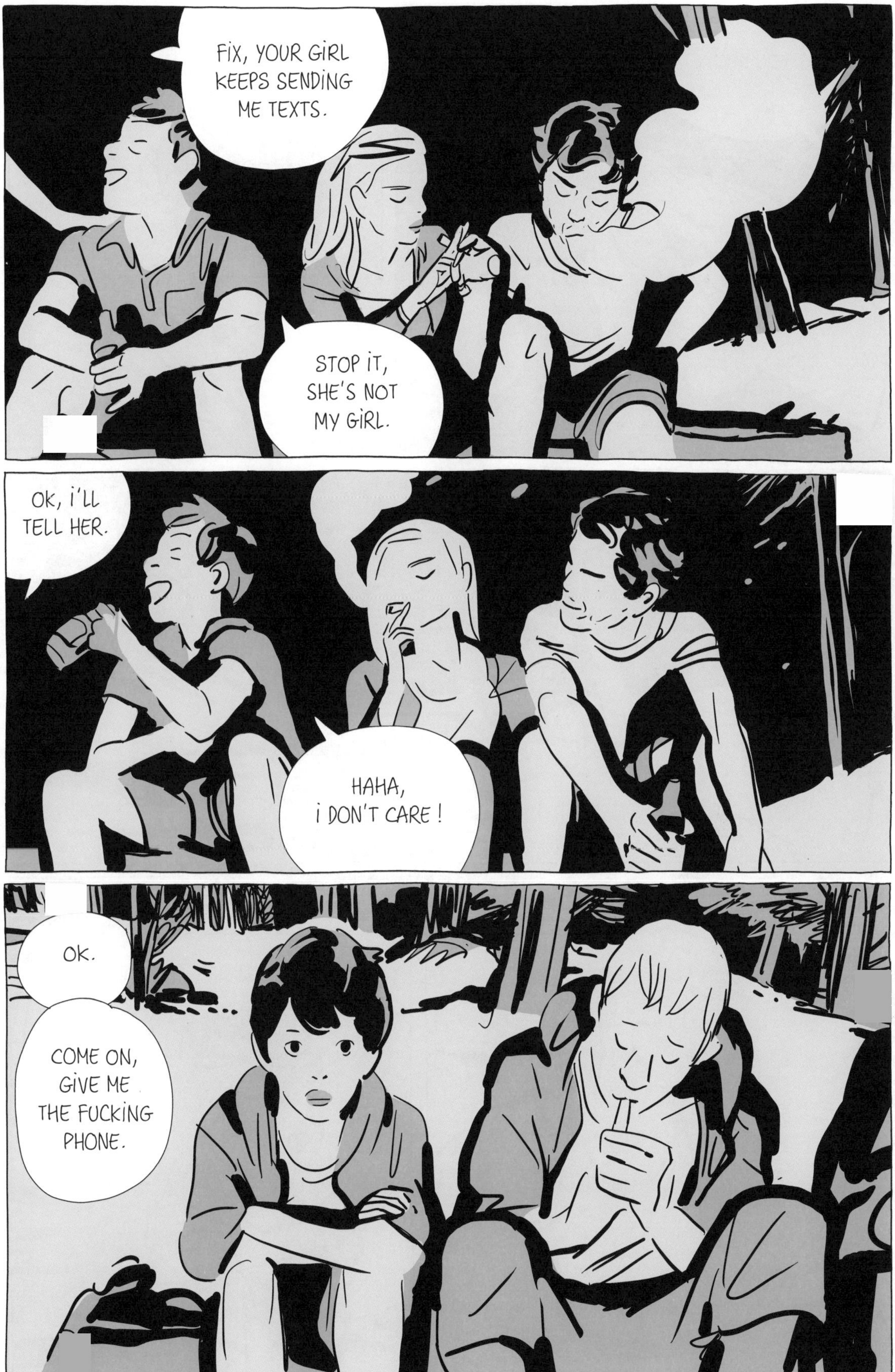
FiX, YOUR GiRL KEEPS SENDiNG ME TEXTS.
STOP iT, SHE'S NOT MY GiRL.
OK, i'LL TELL HER.
HAHA, i DON'T CARE!
OK.
COME ON, GiVE ME THE FUCKiNG PHONE.

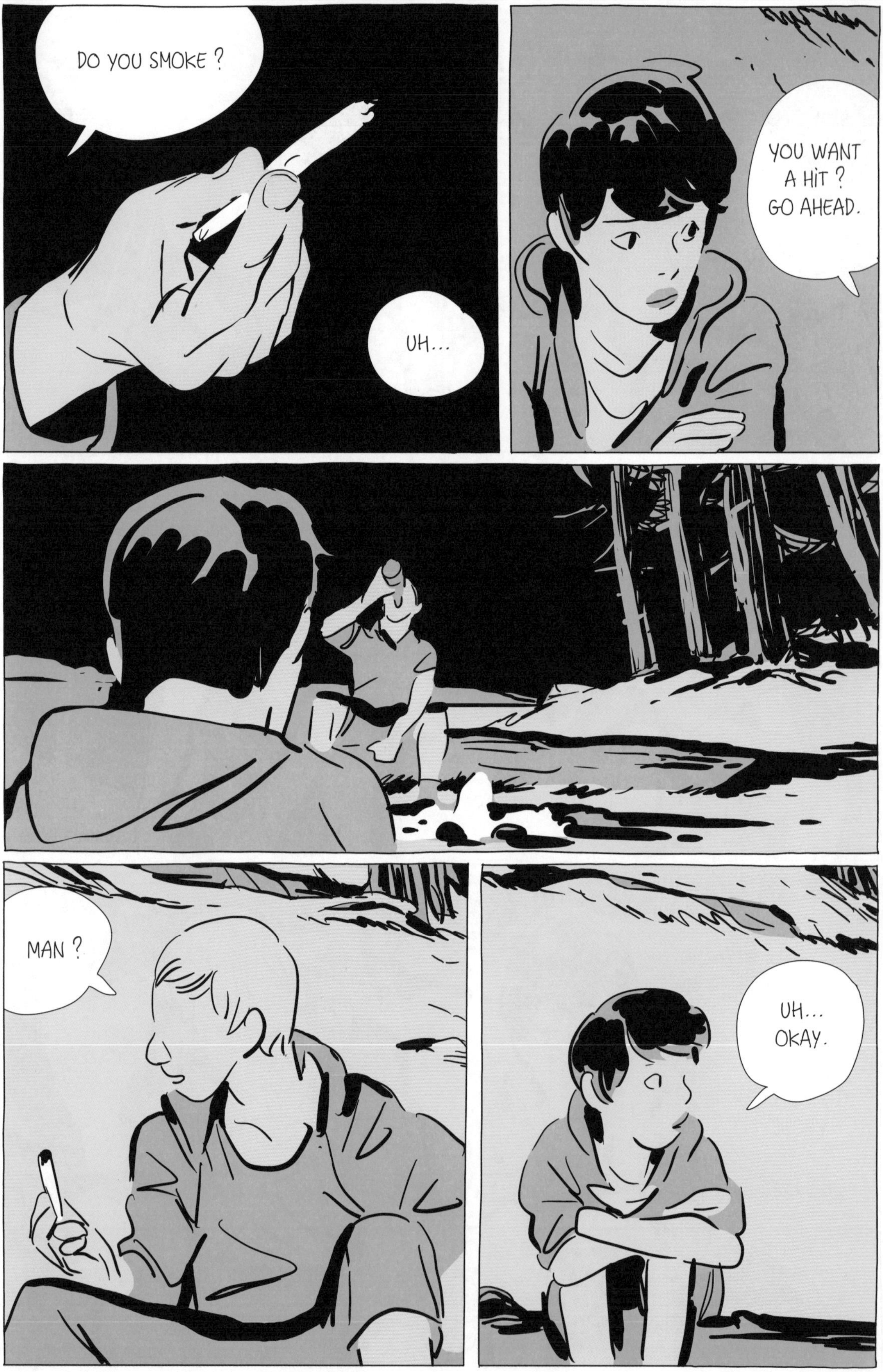
DO YOU SMOKE ?
UH...
YOU WANT A HIT ? GO AHEAD.
MAN ?
UH... OKAY.

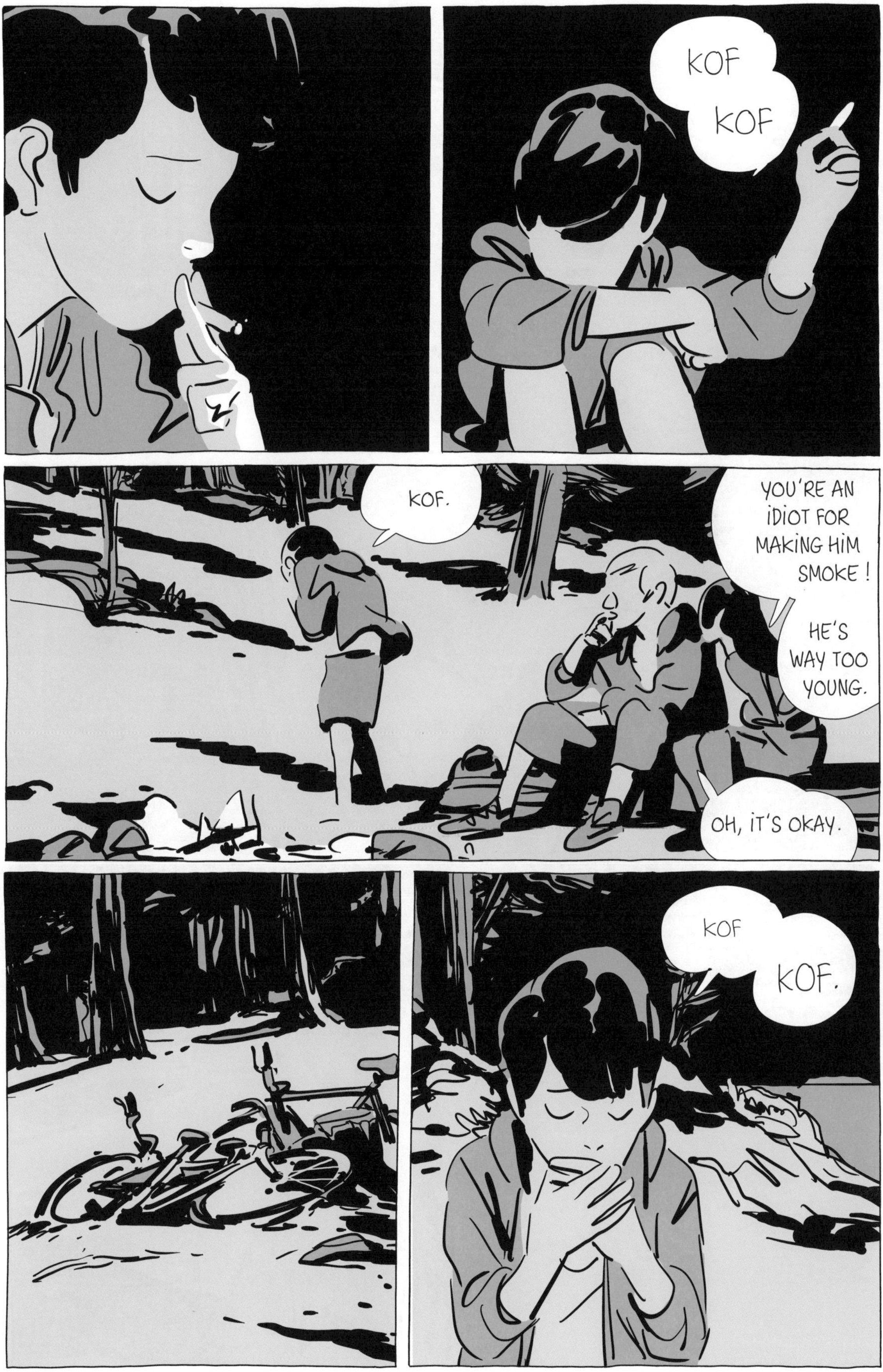
KOF
KOF
KOF.
YOU'RE AN IDIOT FOR MAKING HIM SMOKE!
HE'S WAY TOO YOUNG.
OH, IT'S OKAY.
KOF
KOF.

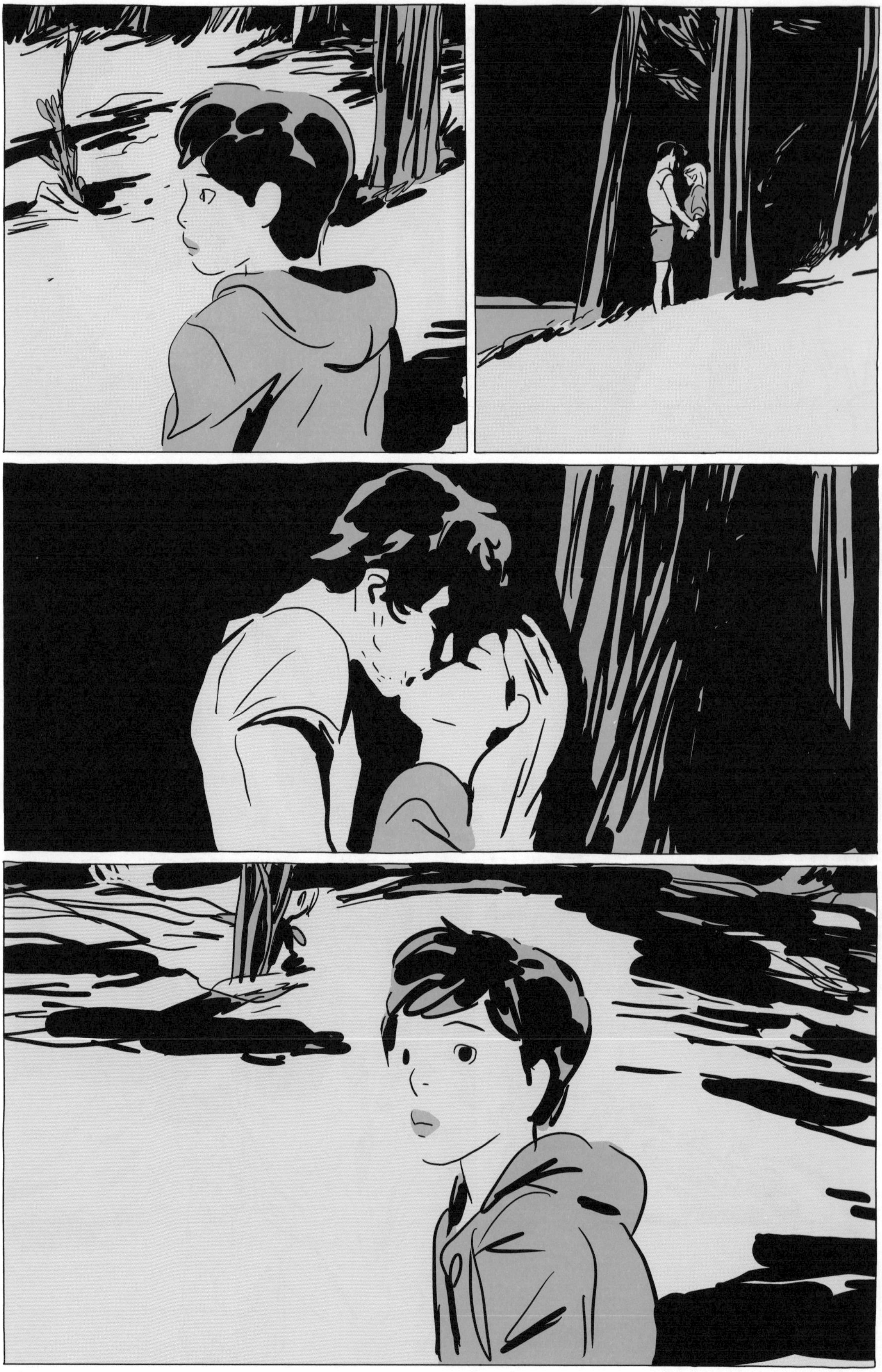

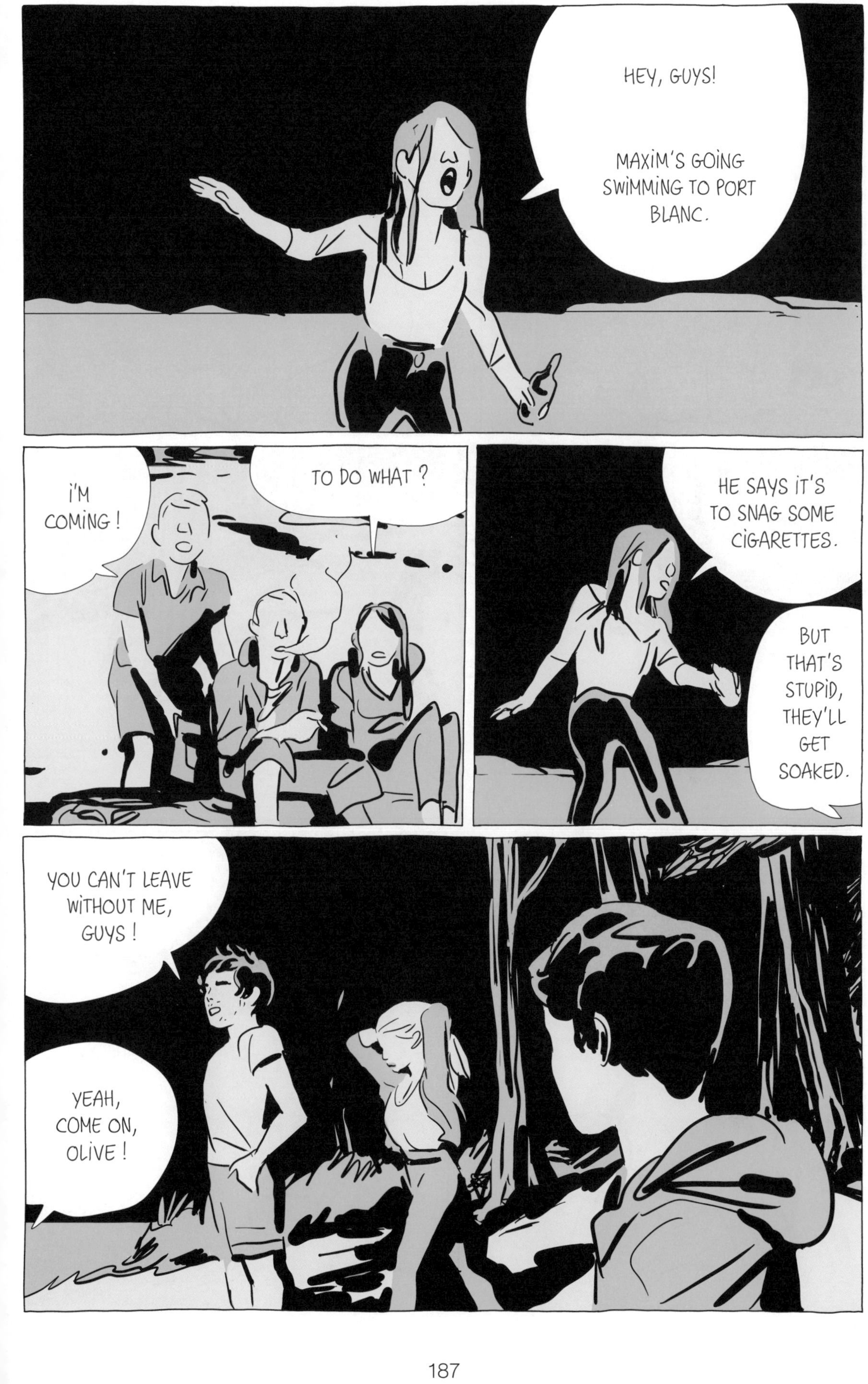
HEY, GUYS!
MAXIM'S GOING SWIMMING TO PORT BLANC.
I'M COMING!
TO DO WHAT?
HE SAYS IT'S TO SNAG SOME CIGARETTES.
BUT THAT'S STUPID, THEY'LL GET SOAKED.
YOU CAN'T LEAVE WITHOUT ME, GUYS!
YEAH, COME ON, OLIVE!

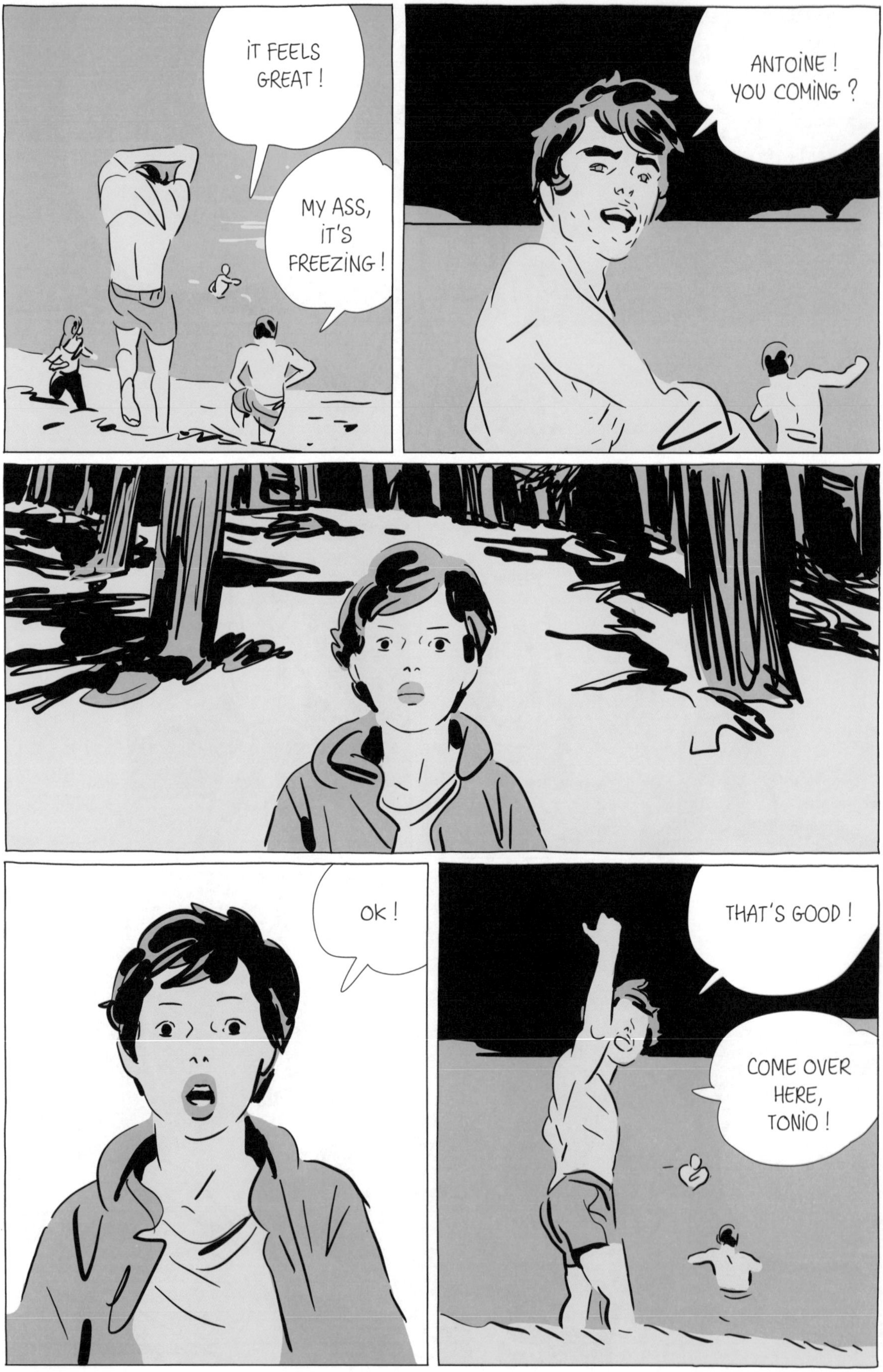
IT FEELS GREAT !
MY ASS, IT'S FREEZING !
ANTOINE ! YOU COMING ?
OK !
THAT'S GOOD !
COME OVER HERE, TONIO !

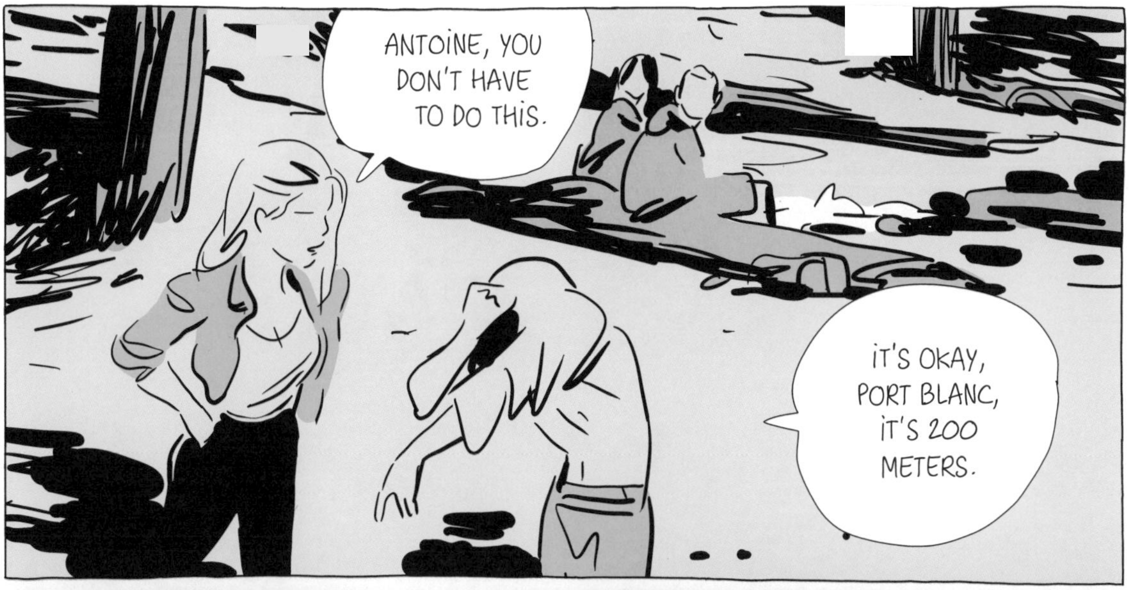
ANTOINE, YOU DON'T HAVE TO DO THIS.
IT'S OKAY, PORT BLANC, IT'S 200 METERS.

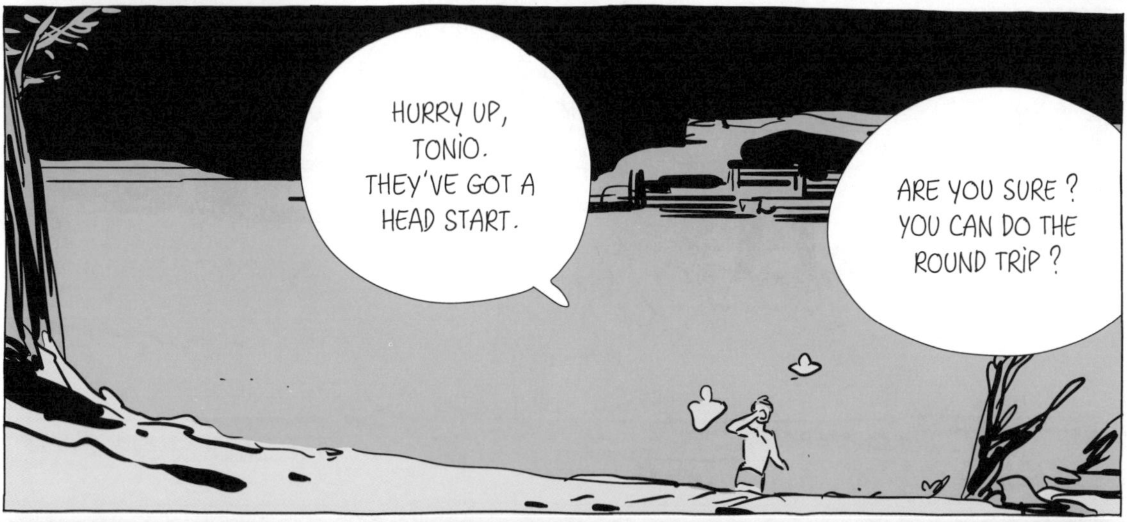
HURRY UP, TONIO. THEY'VE GOT A HEAD START.
ARE YOU SURE ? YOU CAN DO THE ROUND TRIP ?

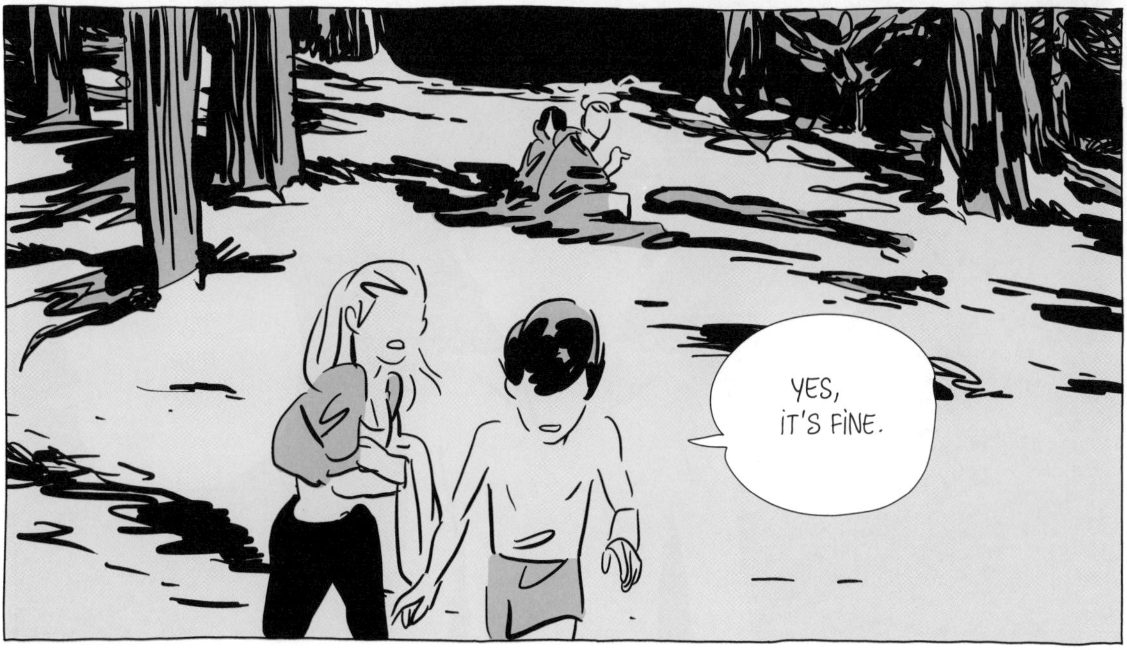
YES, IT'S FINE.

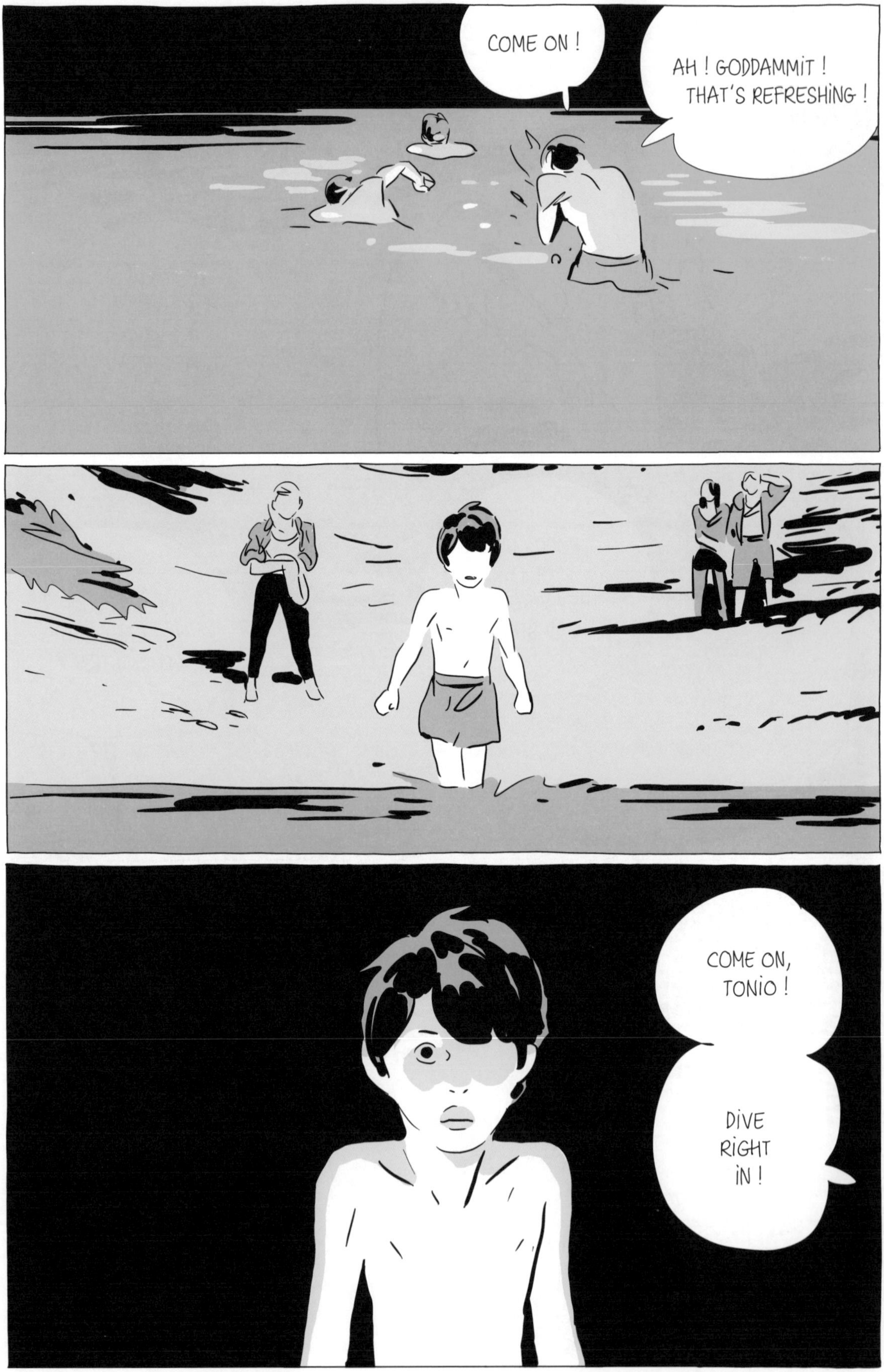
COME ON !
AH ! GODDAMMIT ! THAT'S REFRESHING !
COME ON, TONIO !
DIVE RIGHT IN !

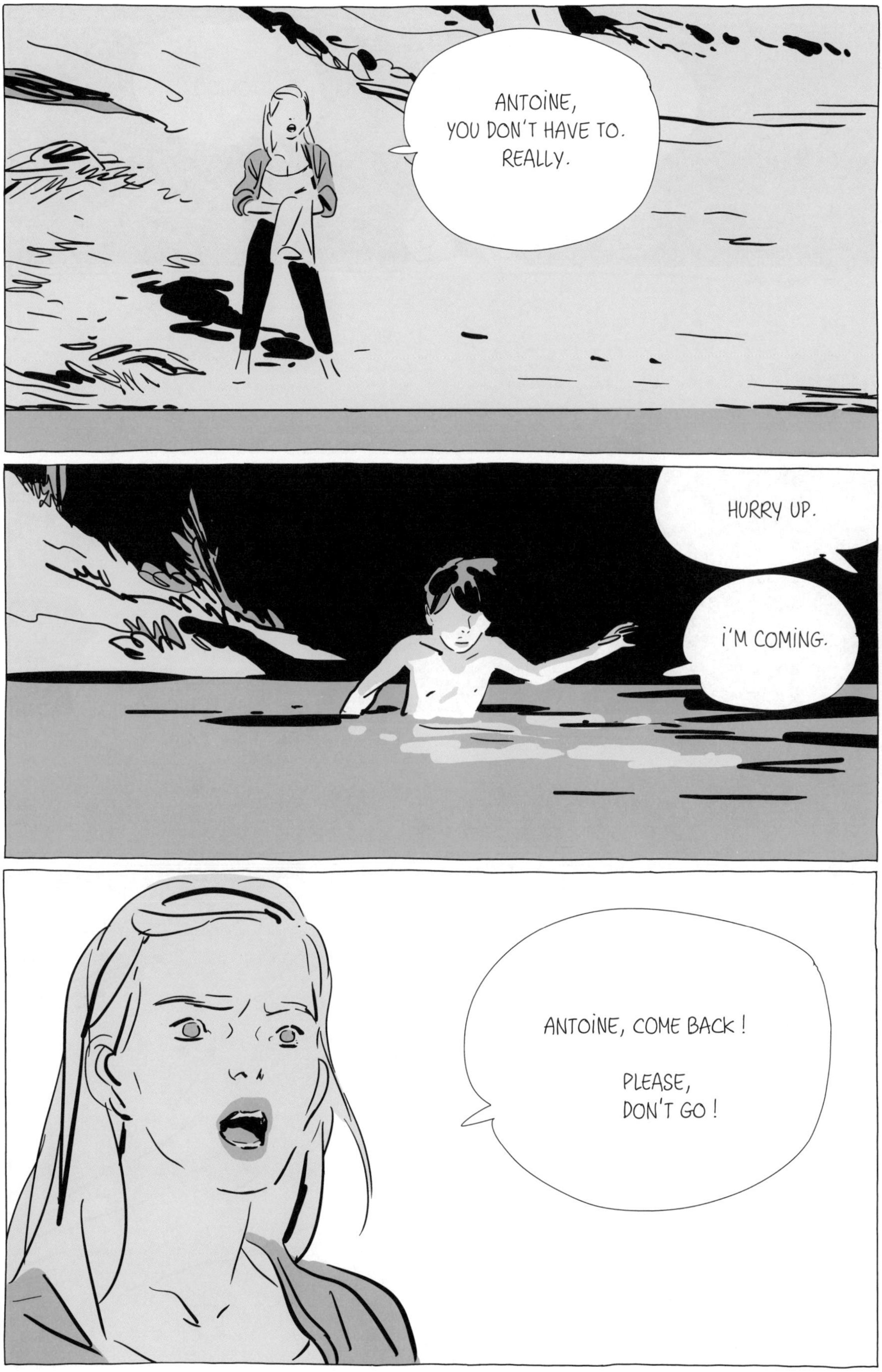
ANTOINE, YOU DON'T HAVE TO. REALLY.
HURRY UP.
I'M COMING.
ANTOINE, COME BACK !
PLEASE, DON'T GO !

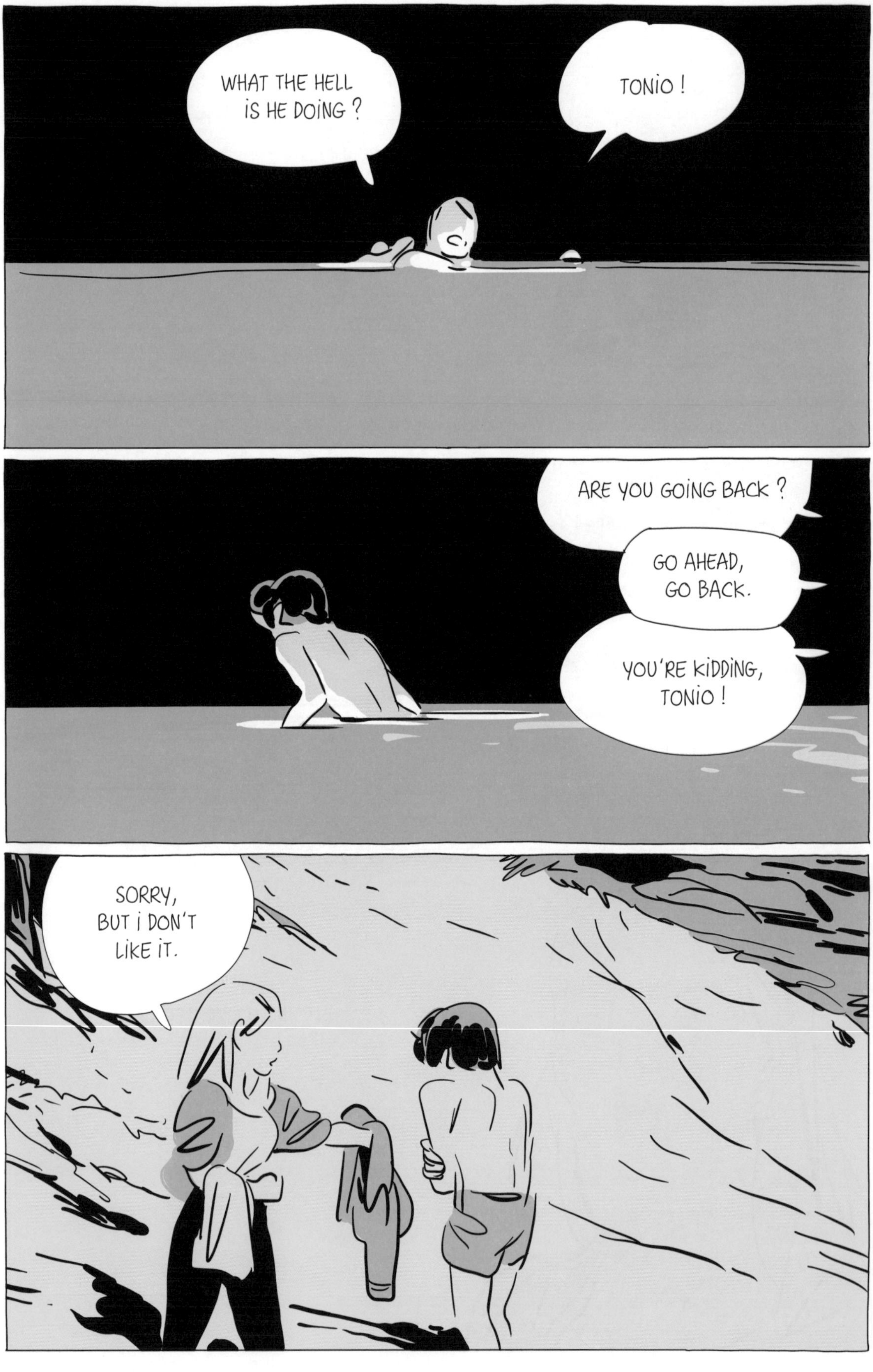
WHAT THE HELL IS HE DOING ?
TONIO !
ARE YOU GOING BACK ?
GO AHEAD, GO BACK.
YOU'RE KIDDING, TONIO !
SORRY, BUT I DON'T LIKE IT.

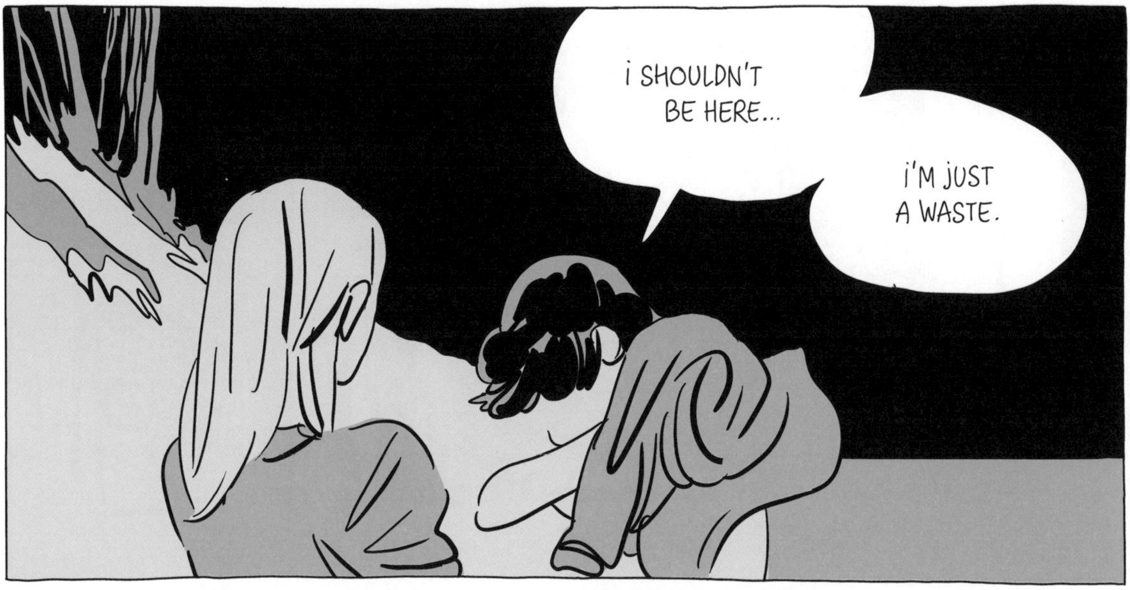
i SHOULDN'T BE HERE...
i'M JUST A WASTE.
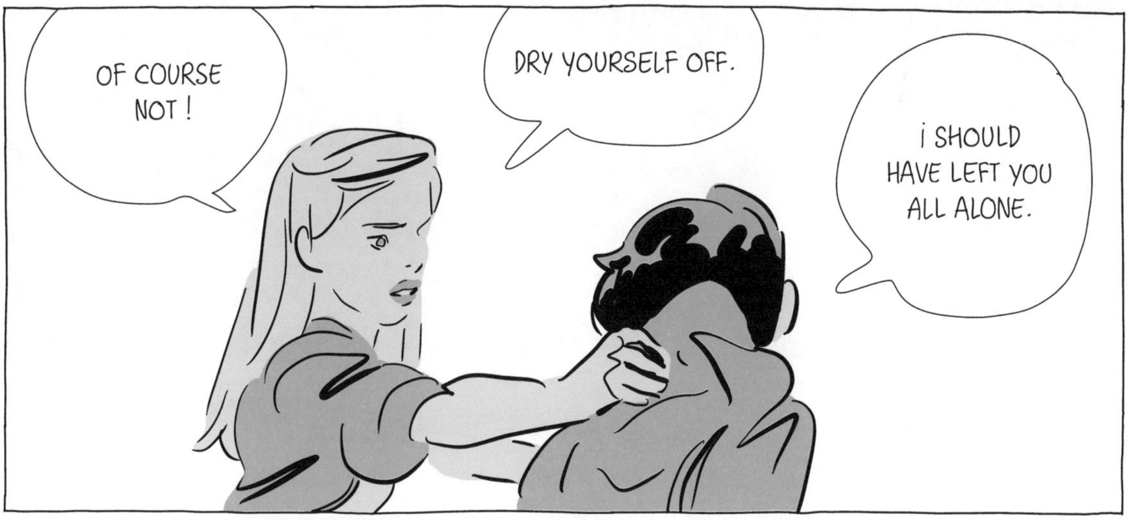
OF COURSE NOT !
DRY YOURSELF OFF.
i SHOULD HAVE LEFT YOU ALL ALONE.
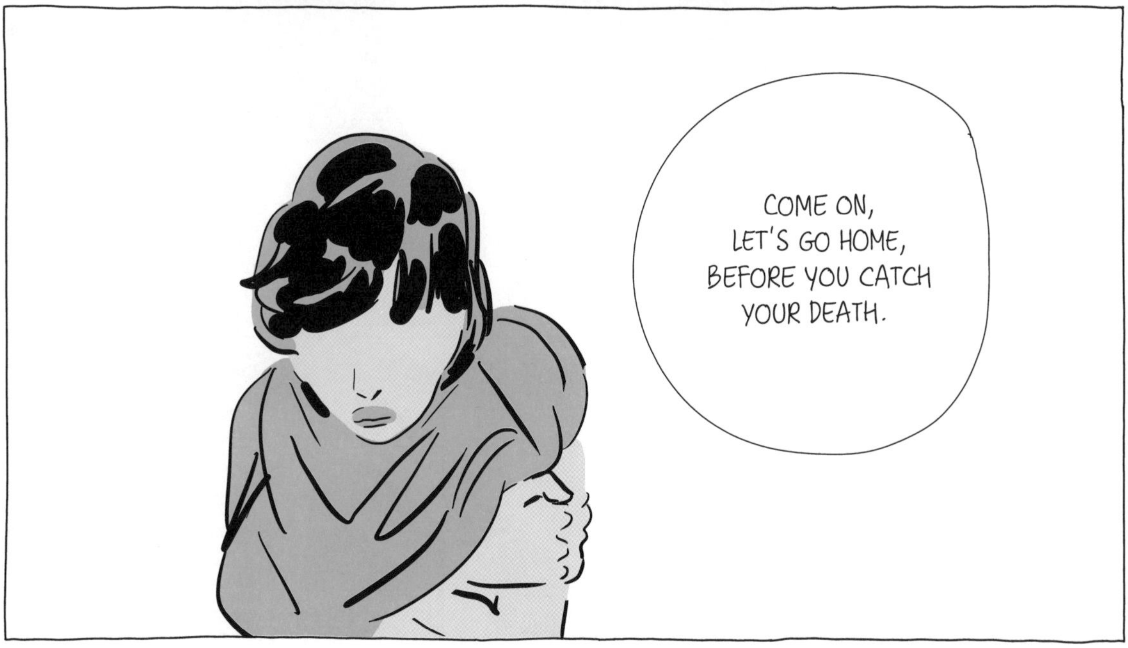
COME ON, LET'S GO HOME, BEFORE YOU CATCH YOUR DEATH.

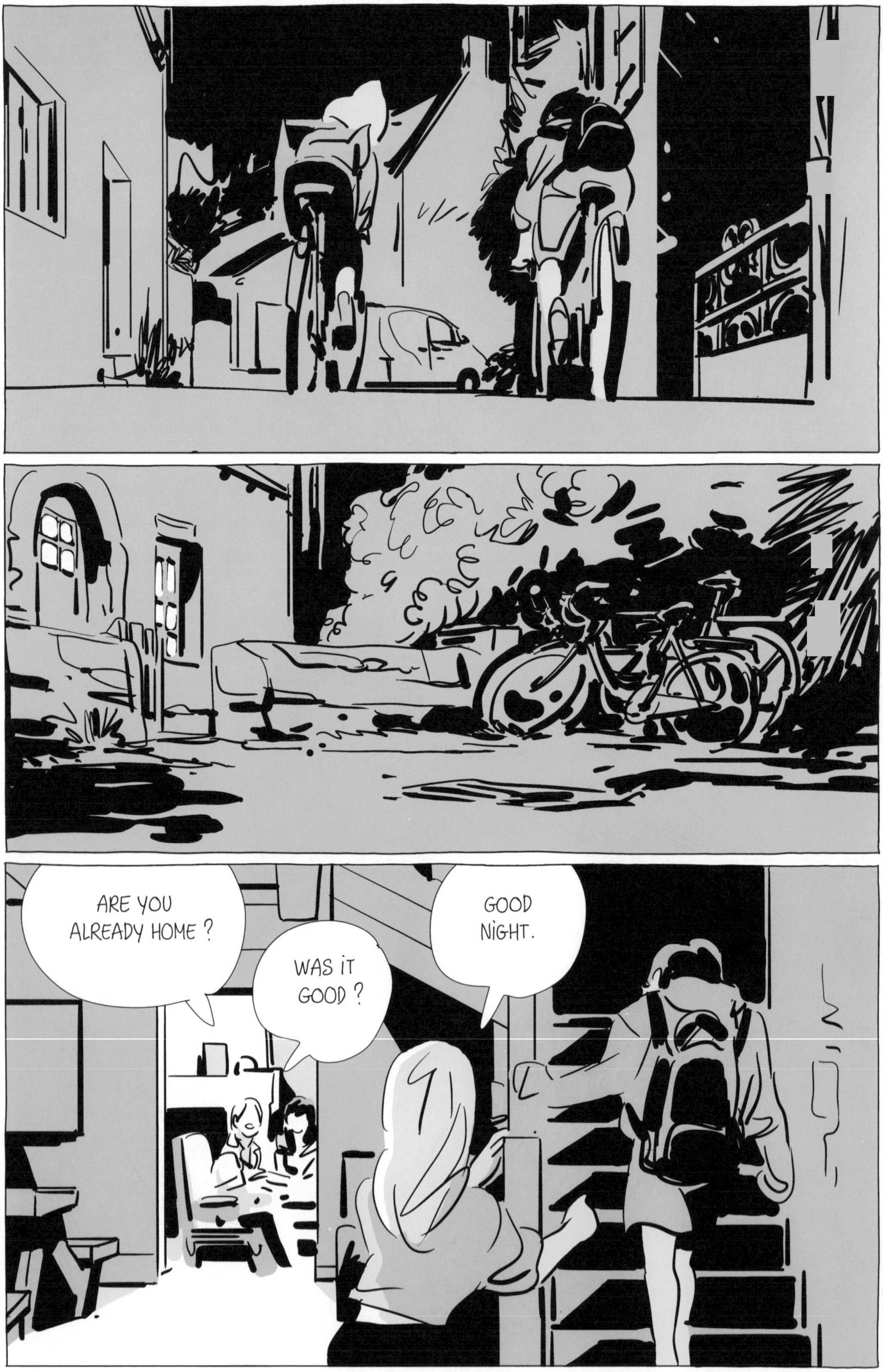
ARE YOU ALREADY HOME ?
WAS IT GOOD ?
GOOD NIGHT.

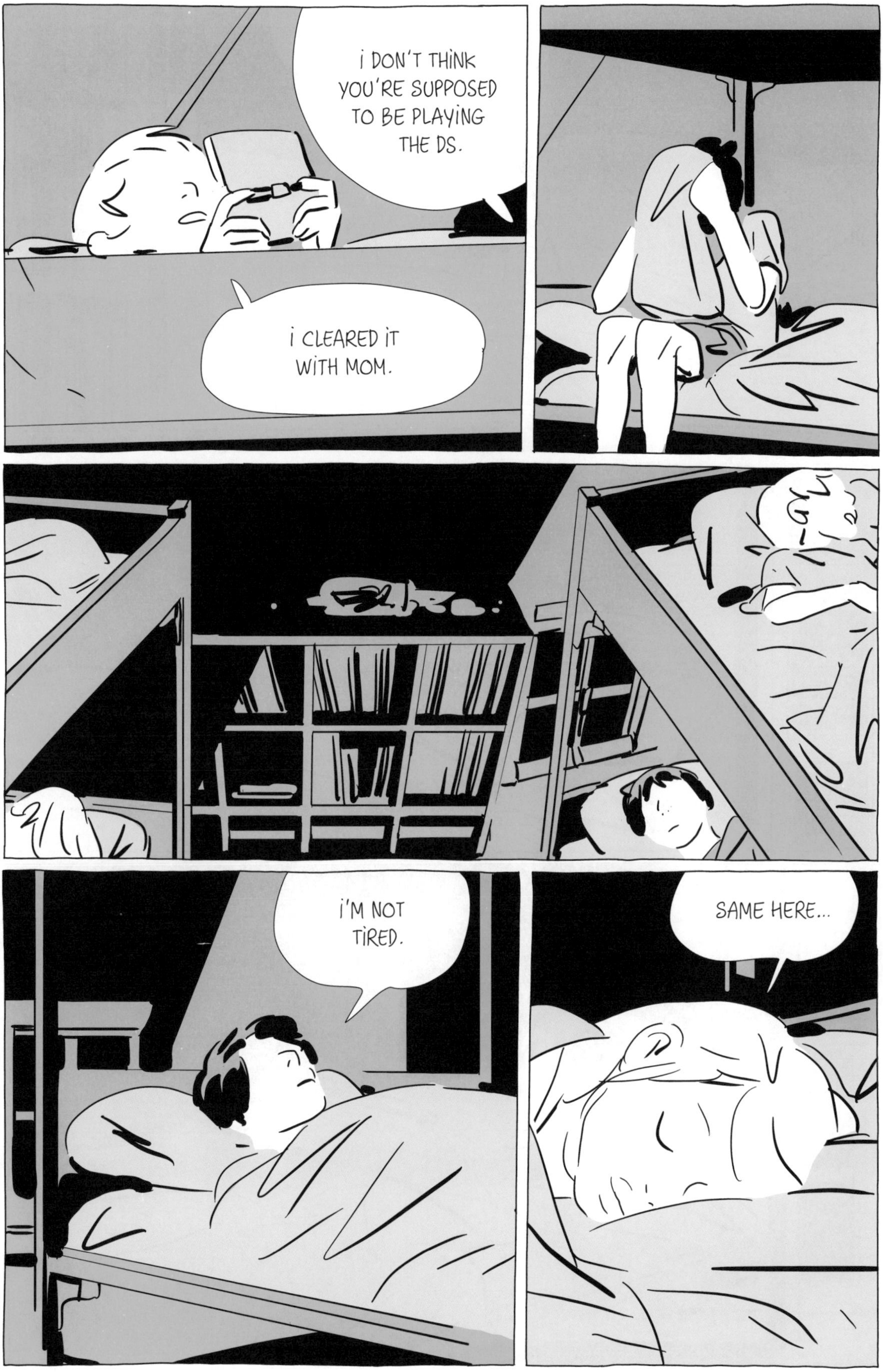
I DON'T THINK YOU'RE SUPPOSED TO BE PLAYING THE DS.
I CLEARED IT WITH MOM.
I'M NOT TIRED.
SAME HERE...

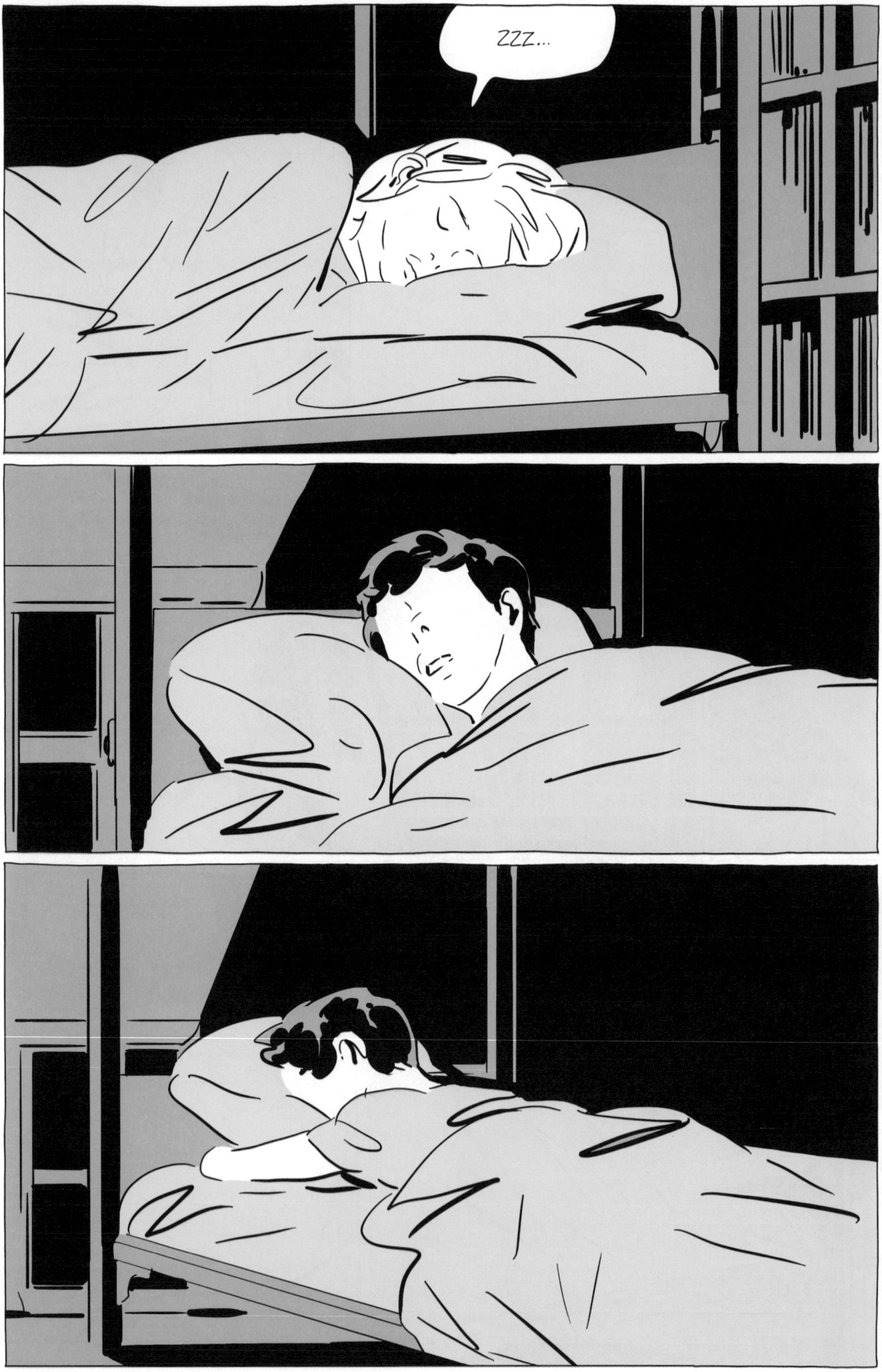
ZZZ...

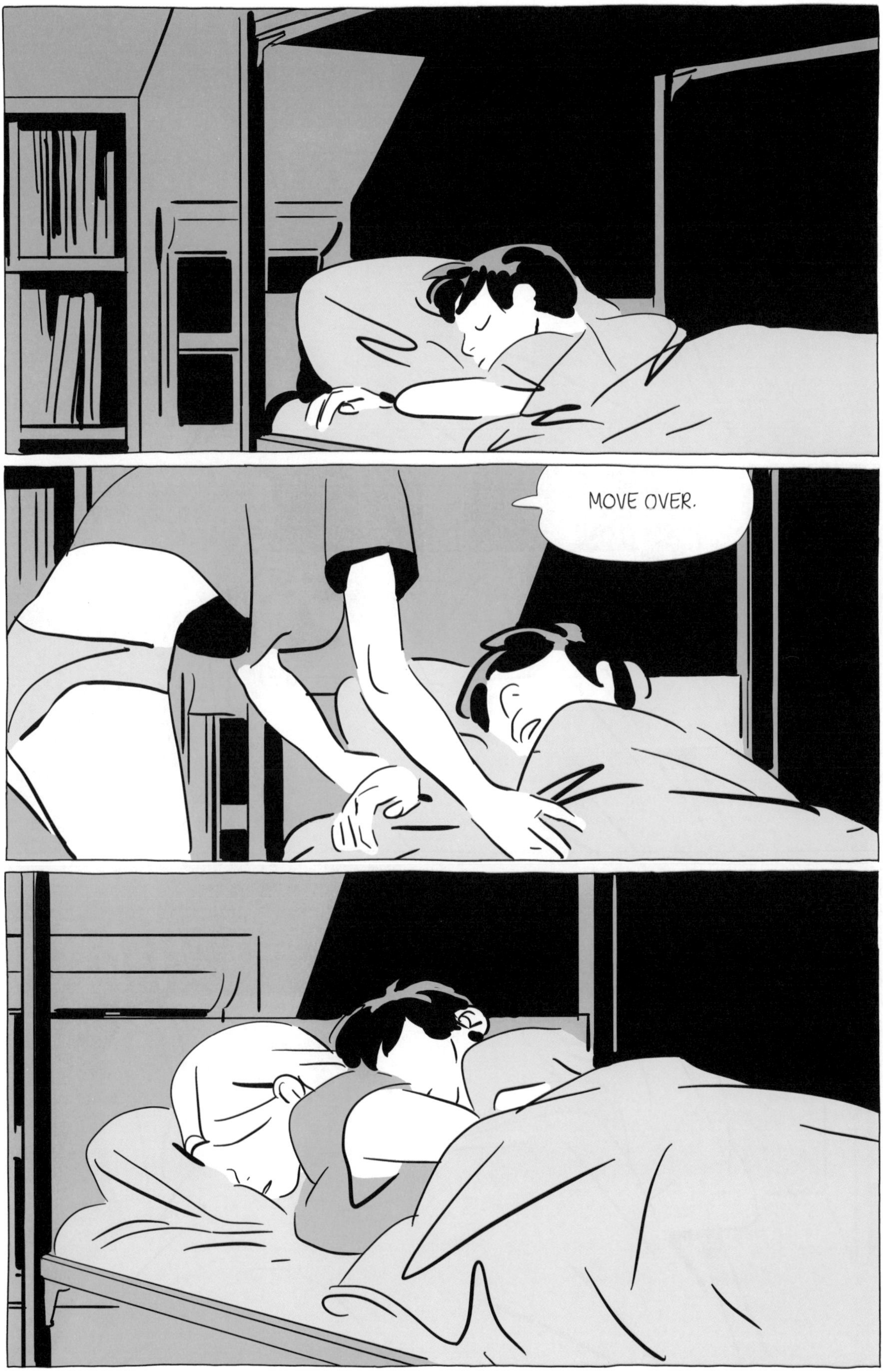
MOVE OVER.

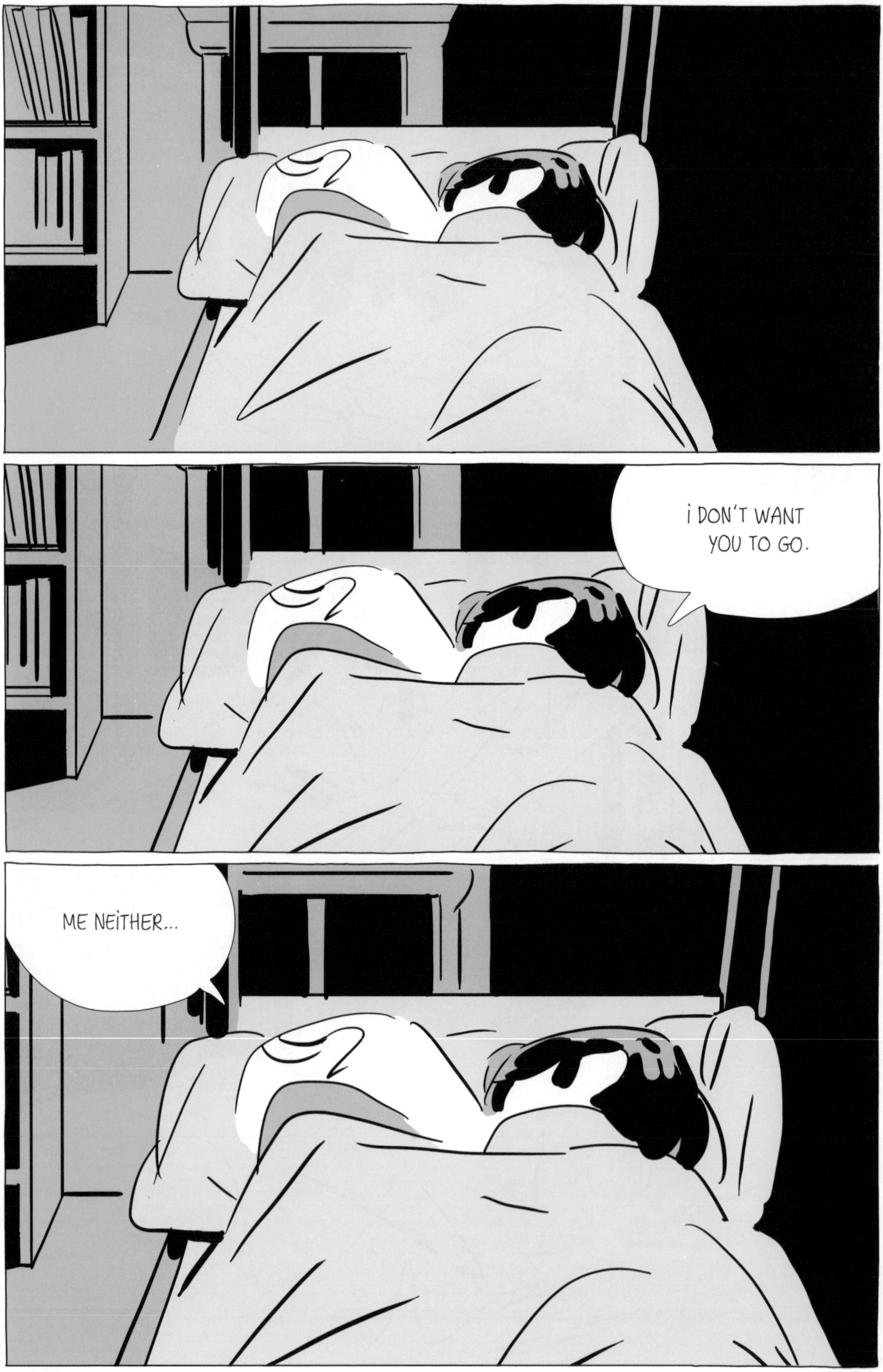
I DON'T WANT
YOU TO GO.
ME NEITHER...

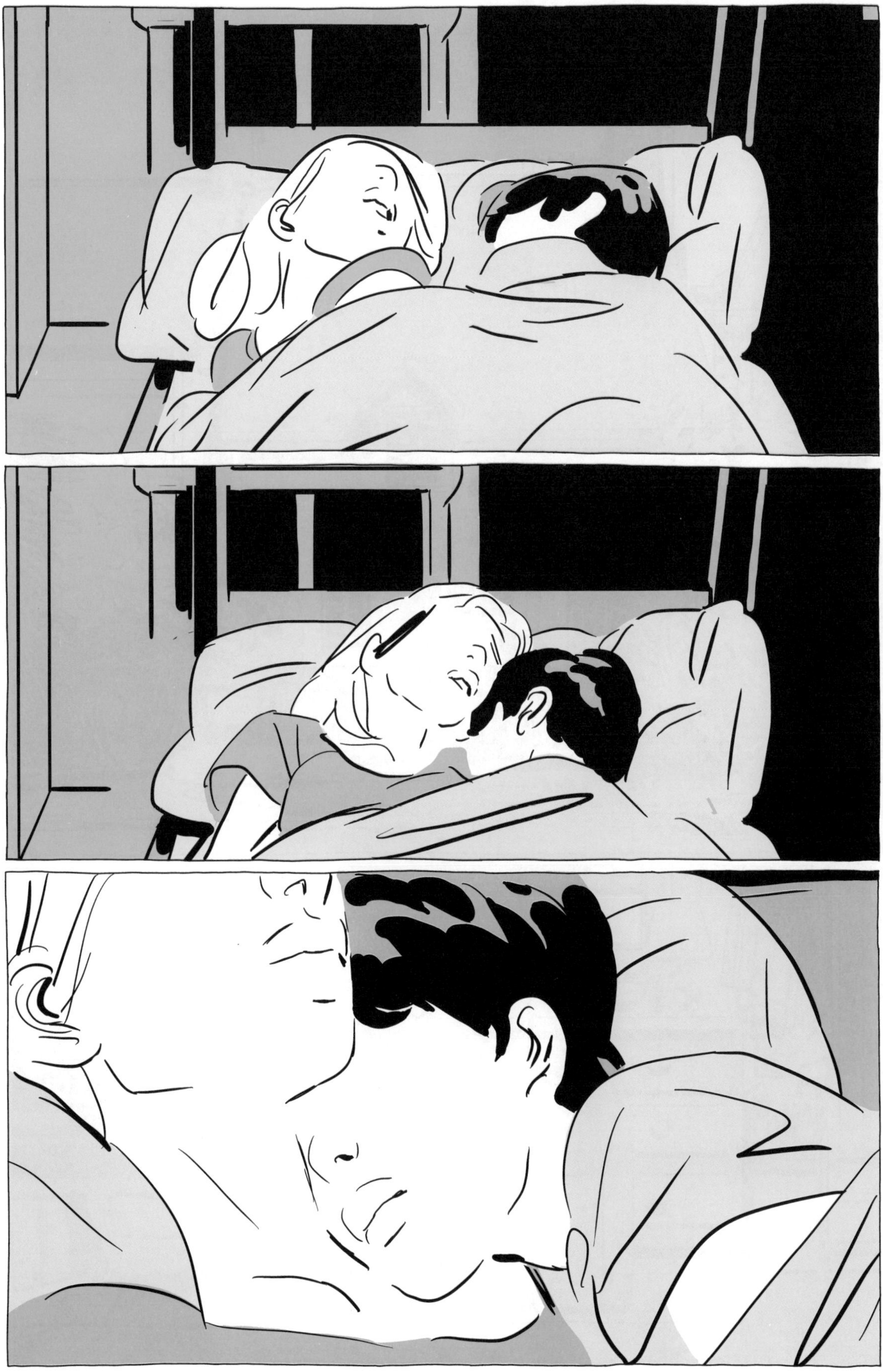

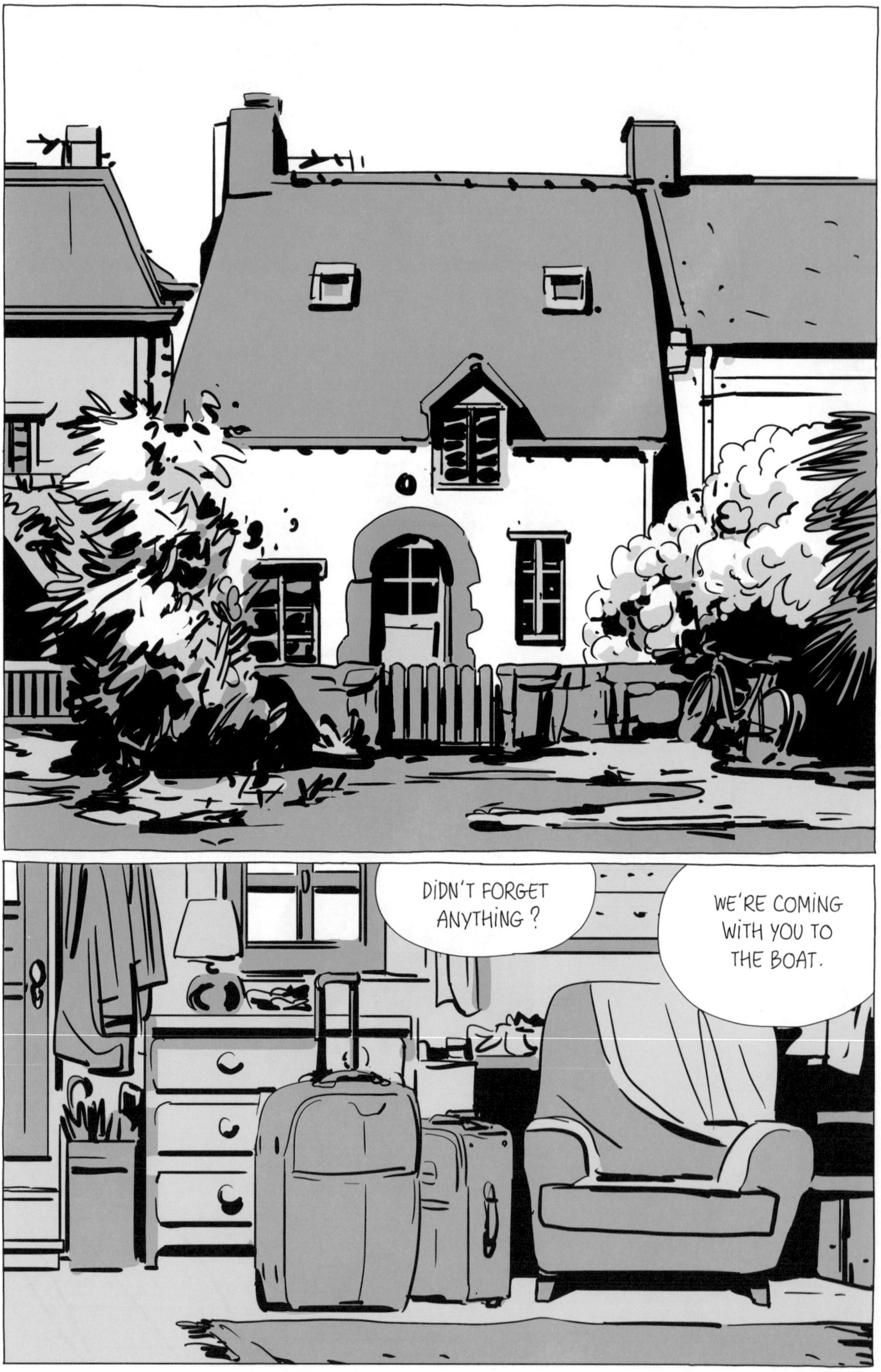
DIDN'T FORGET ANYTHING?
WE'RE COMING WITH YOU TO THE BOAT.

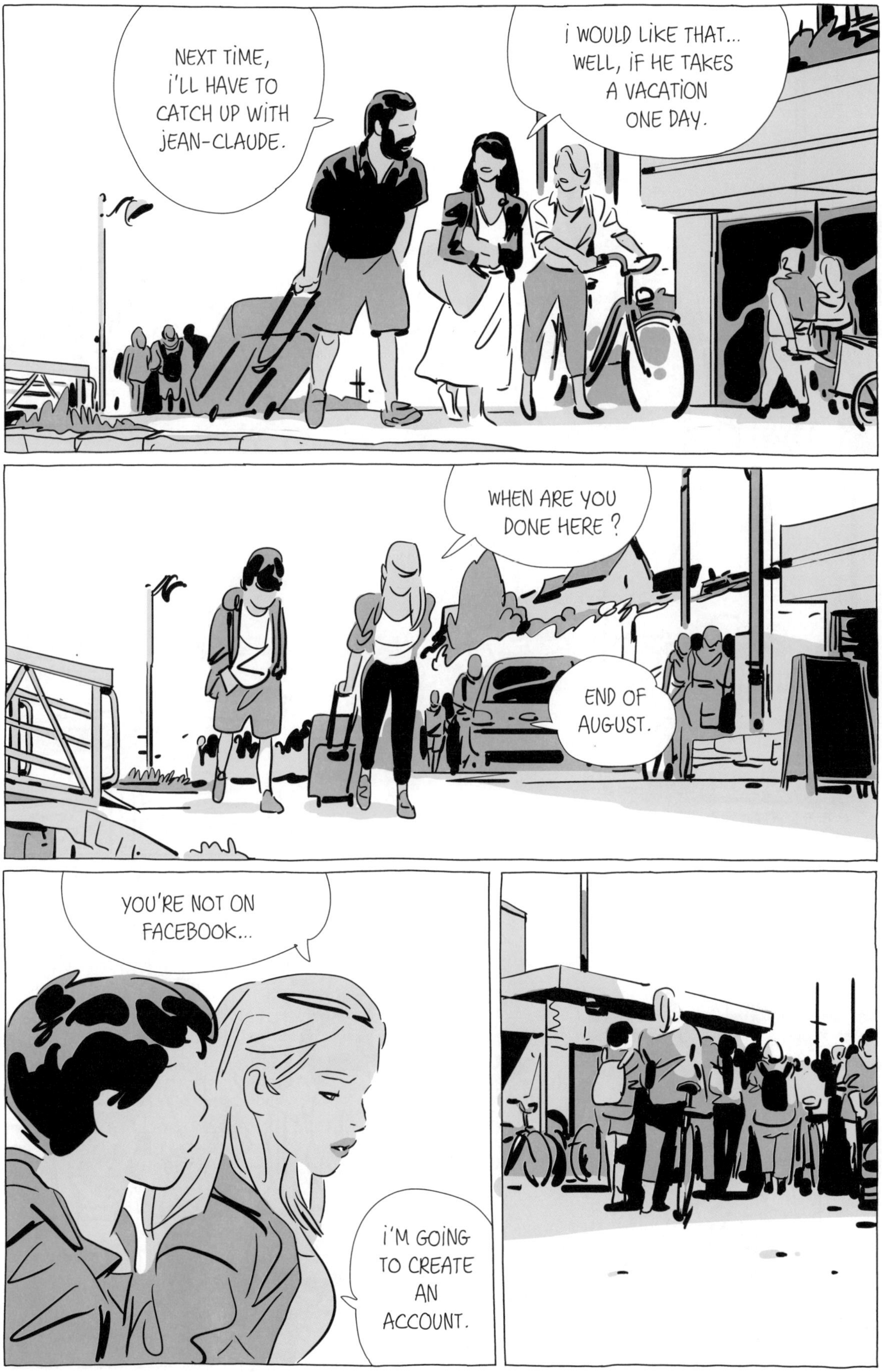
NEXT TIME, I'LL HAVE TO CATCH UP WITH JEAN-CLAUDE.
I WOULD LIKE THAT... WELL, IF HE TAKES A VACATION ONE DAY.
WHEN ARE YOU DONE HERE?
END OF AUGUST.
YOU'RE NOT ON FACEBOOK...
I'M GOING TO CREATE AN ACCOUNT.

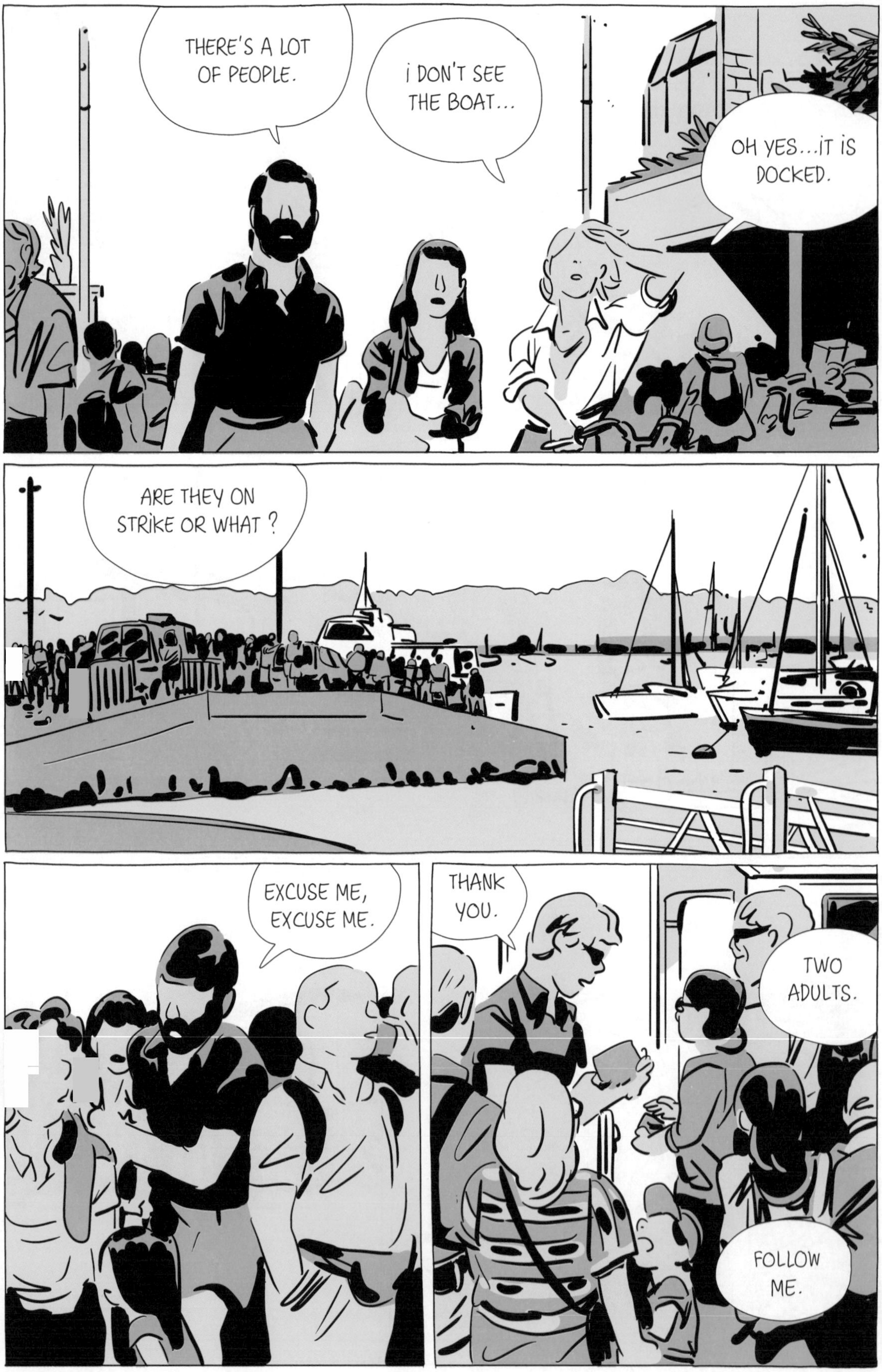
THERE'S A LOT OF PEOPLE.
i DON'T SEE THE BOAT...
OH YES...iT iS DOCKED.
ARE THEY ON STRiKE OR WHAT ?
EXCUSE ME, EXCUSE ME.
THANK YOU.
TWO ADULTS.
FOLLOW ME.

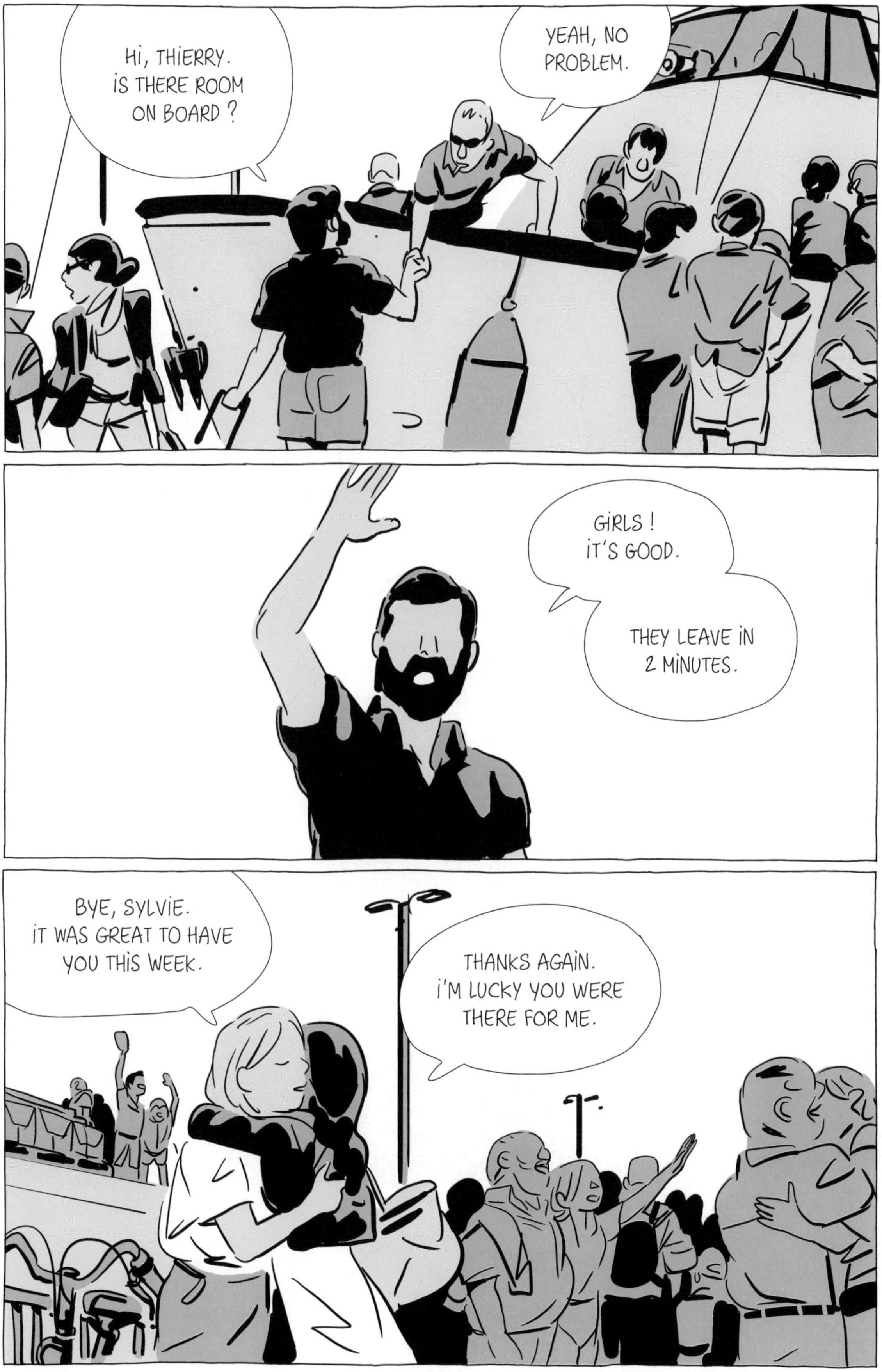
HI, THIERRY. IS THERE ROOM ON BOARD ?
YEAH, NO PROBLEM.
GIRLS ! IT'S GOOD.
THEY LEAVE IN 2 MINUTES.
BYE, SYLVIE. IT WAS GREAT TO HAVE YOU THIS WEEK.
THANKS AGAIN. I'M LUCKY YOU WERE THERE FOR ME.

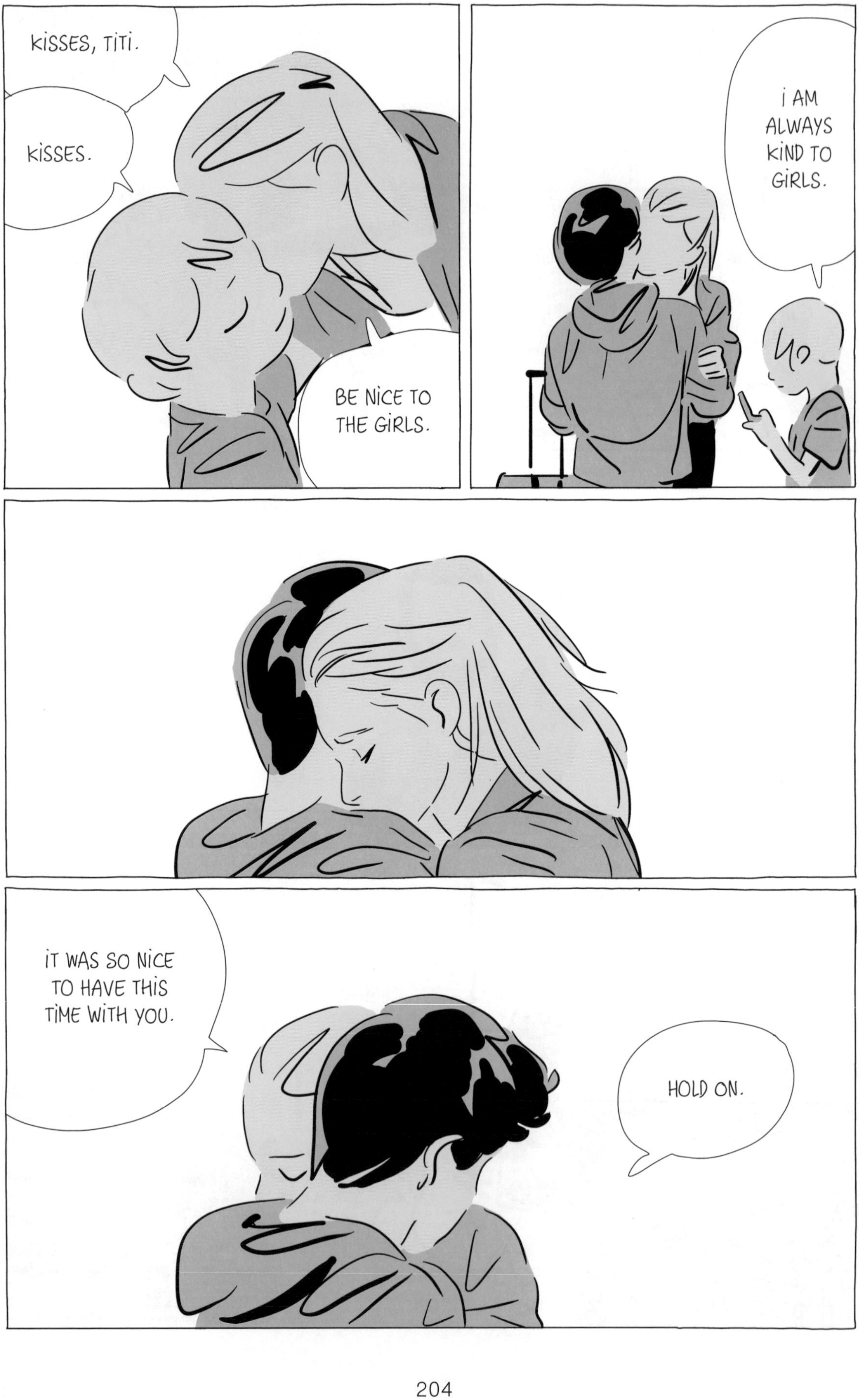
KISSES, TITI.
KISSES.
BE NICE TO THE GIRLS.
I AM ALWAYS KIND TO GIRLS.
IT WAS SO NICE TO HAVE THIS TIME WITH YOU.
HOLD ON.

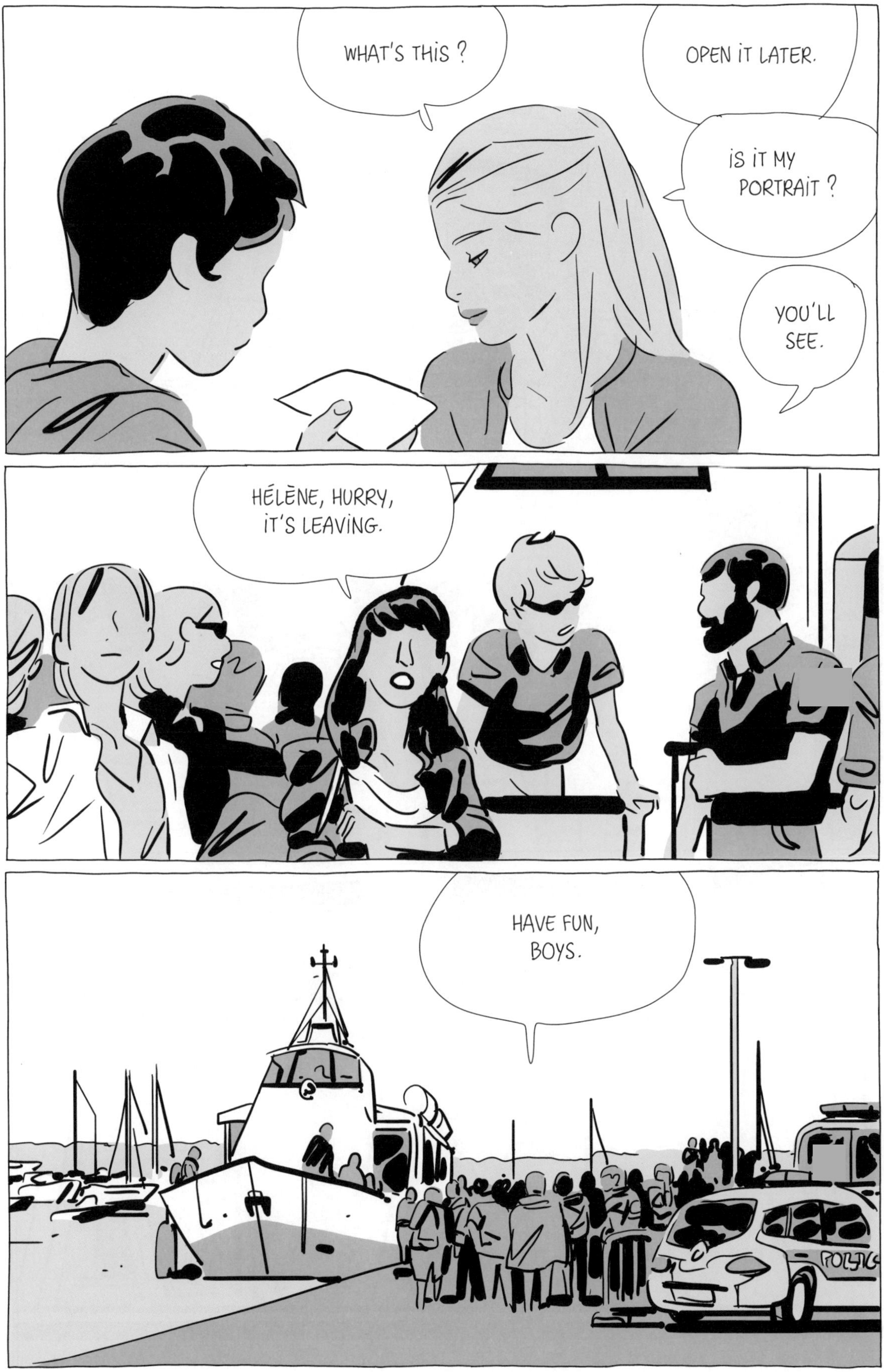
WHAT'S THIS ?
OPEN IT LATER.
IS IT MY PORTRAIT ?
YOU'LL SEE.
HÉLÈNE, HURRY, IT'S LEAVING.
HAVE FUN, BOYS.

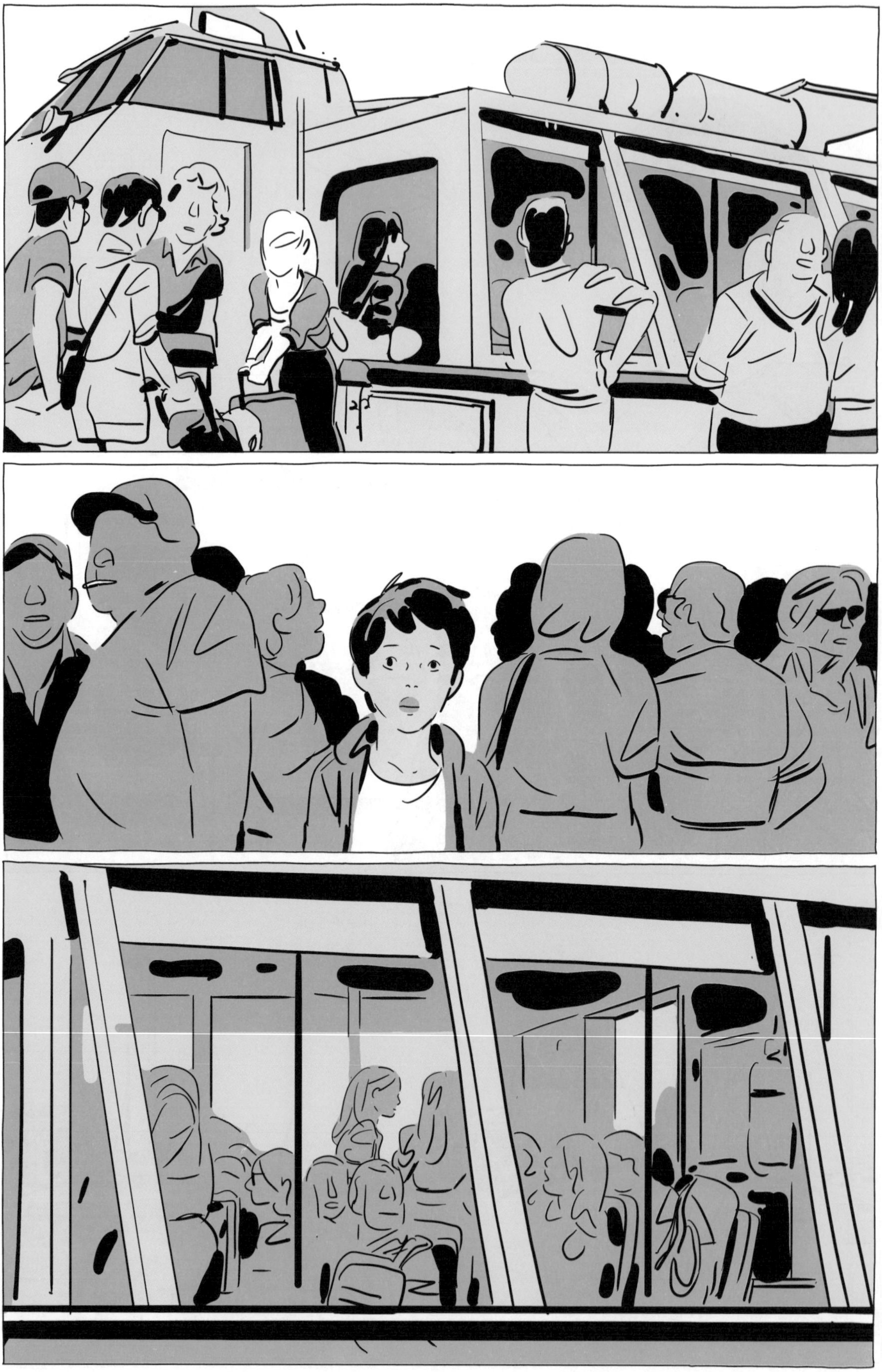

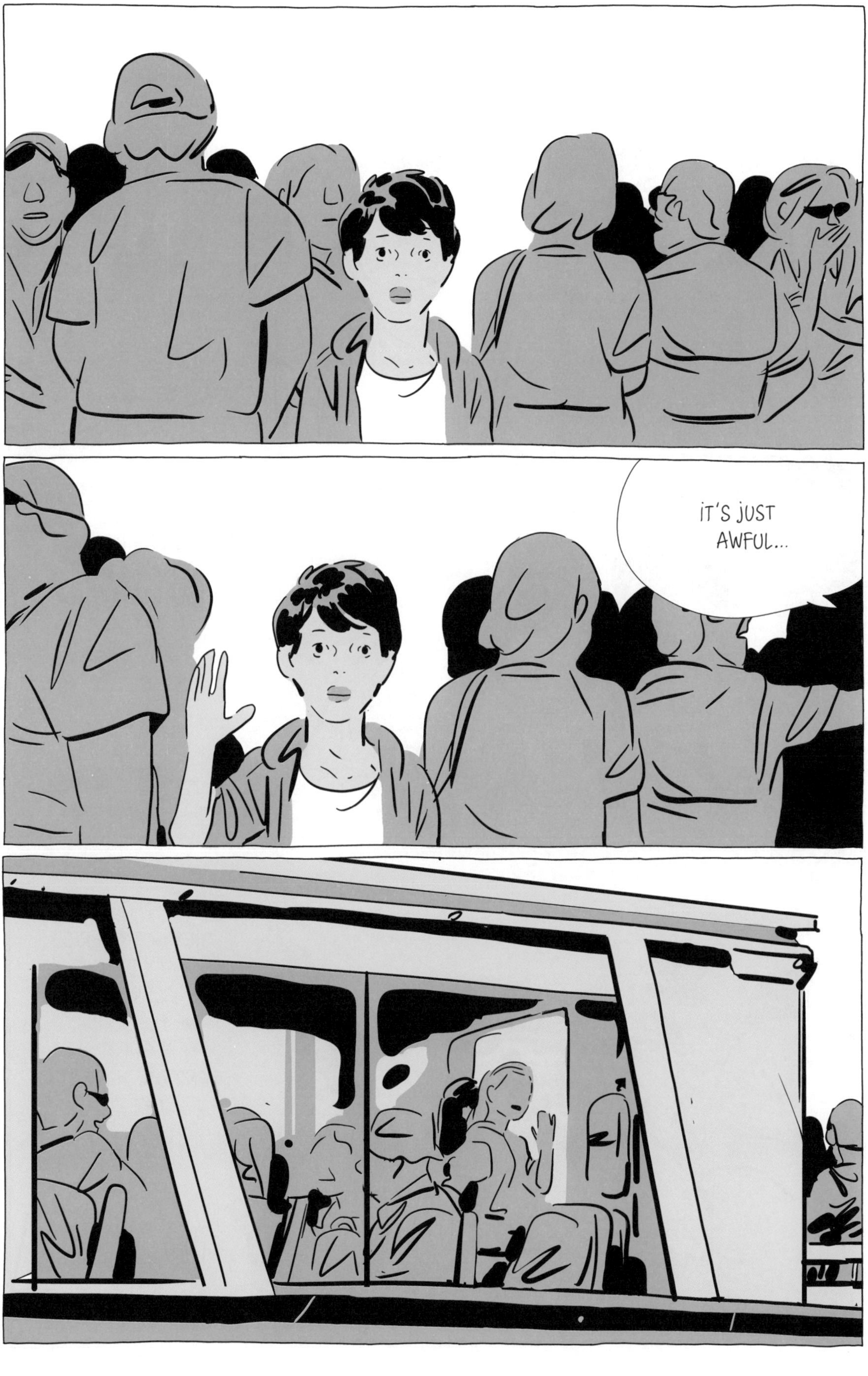
IT'S JUST AWFUL...

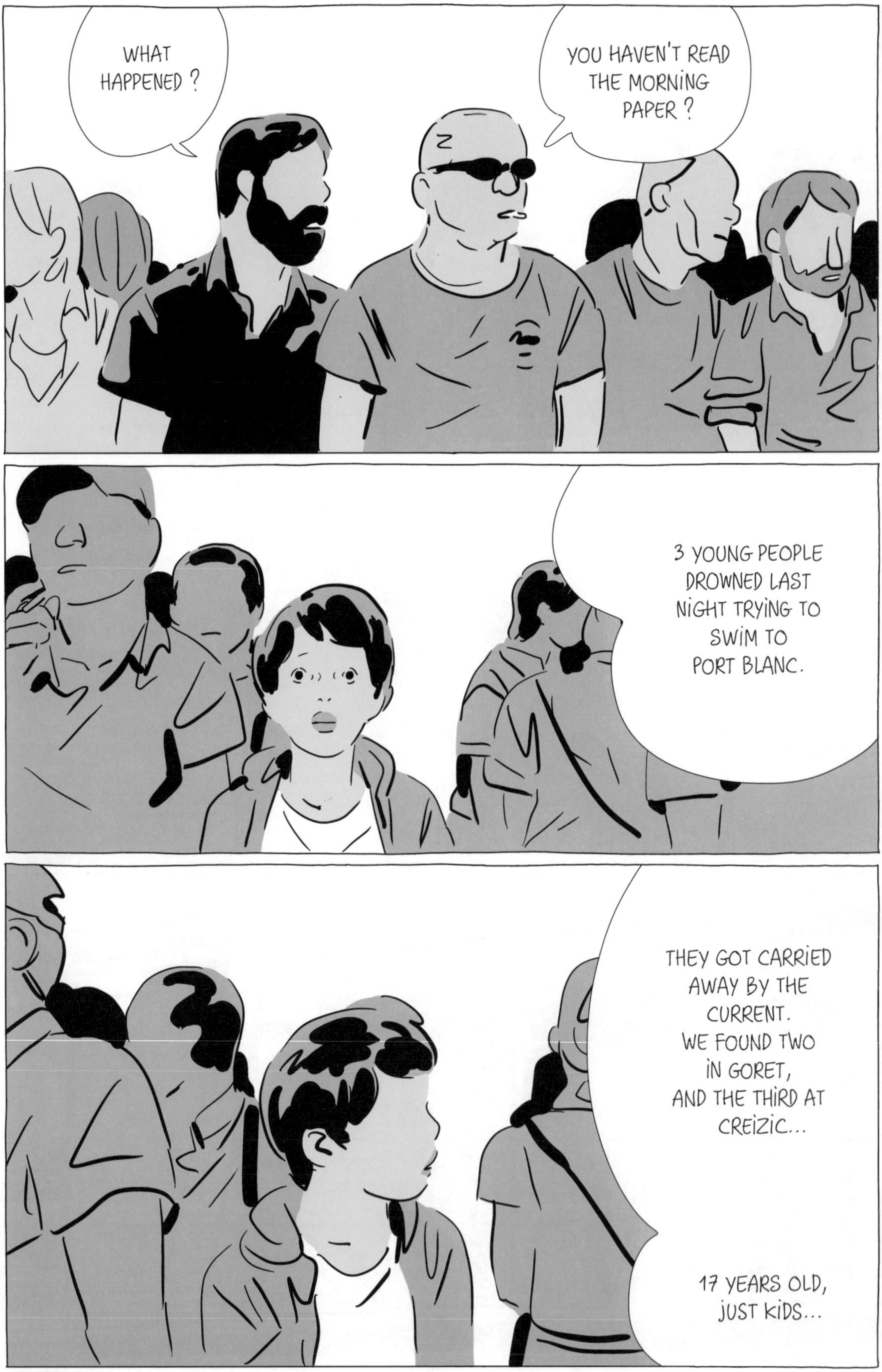
WHAT HAPPENED ?
YOU HAVEN'T READ THE MORNING PAPER ?
3 YOUNG PEOPLE DROWNED LAST NIGHT TRYING TO SWIM TO PORT BLANC.
THEY GOT CARRIED AWAY BY THE CURRENT. WE FOUND TWO IN GORET, AND THE THIRD AT CREIZIC...
17 YEARS OLD, JUST KIDS...

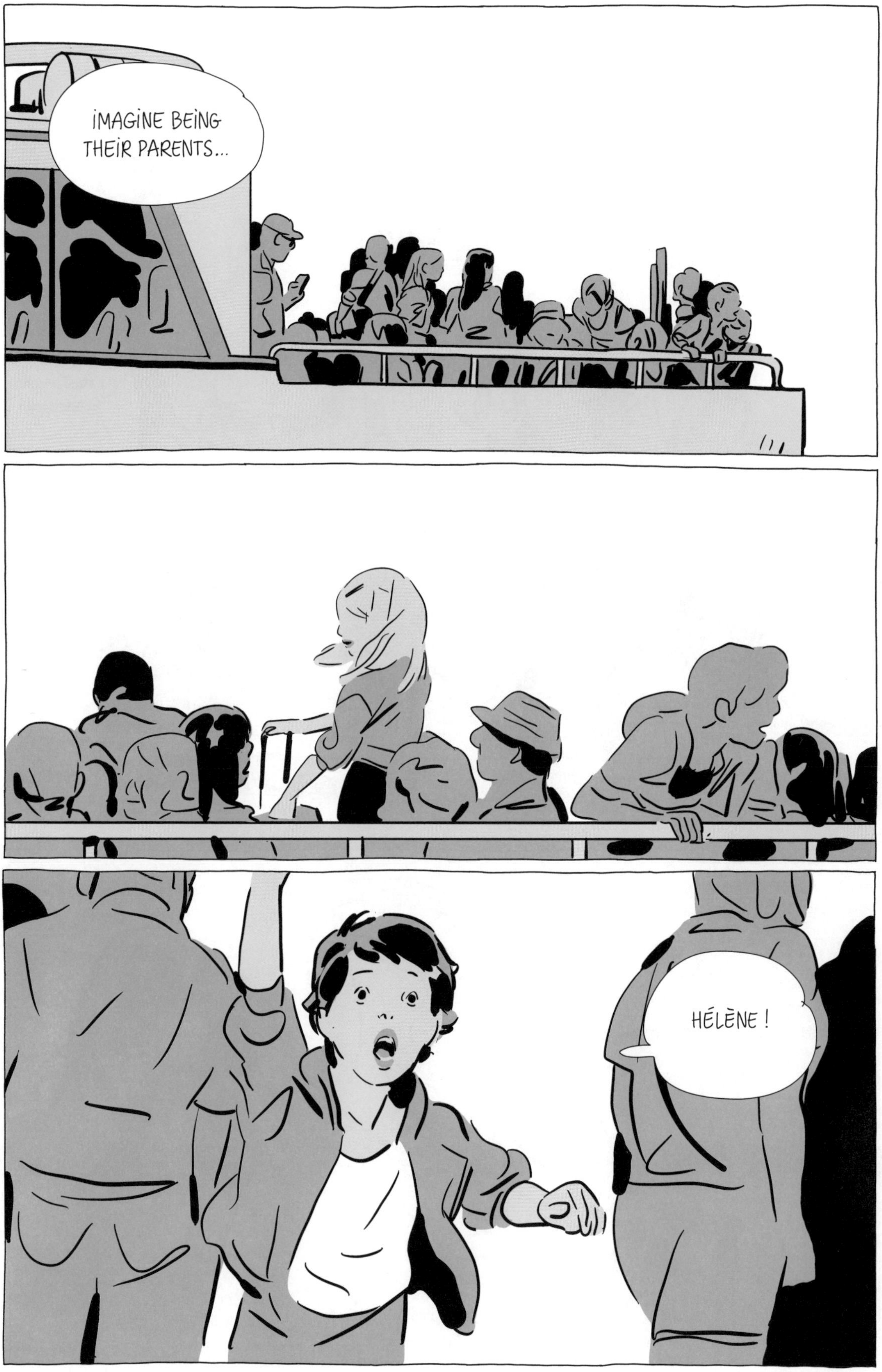
IMAGINE BEING THEIR PARENTS...
HÉLÈNE !

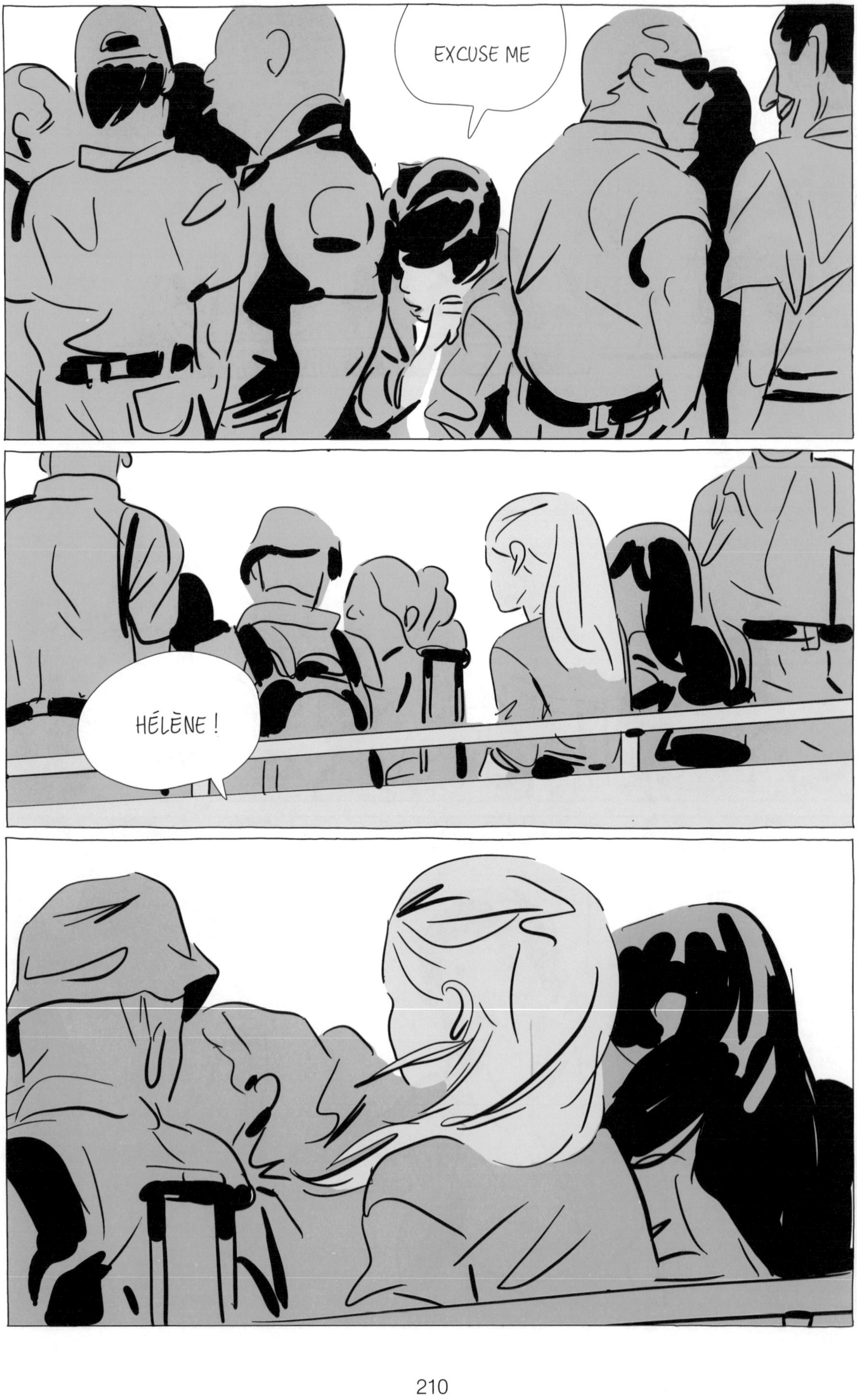
EXCUSE ME
HÉLÈNE !

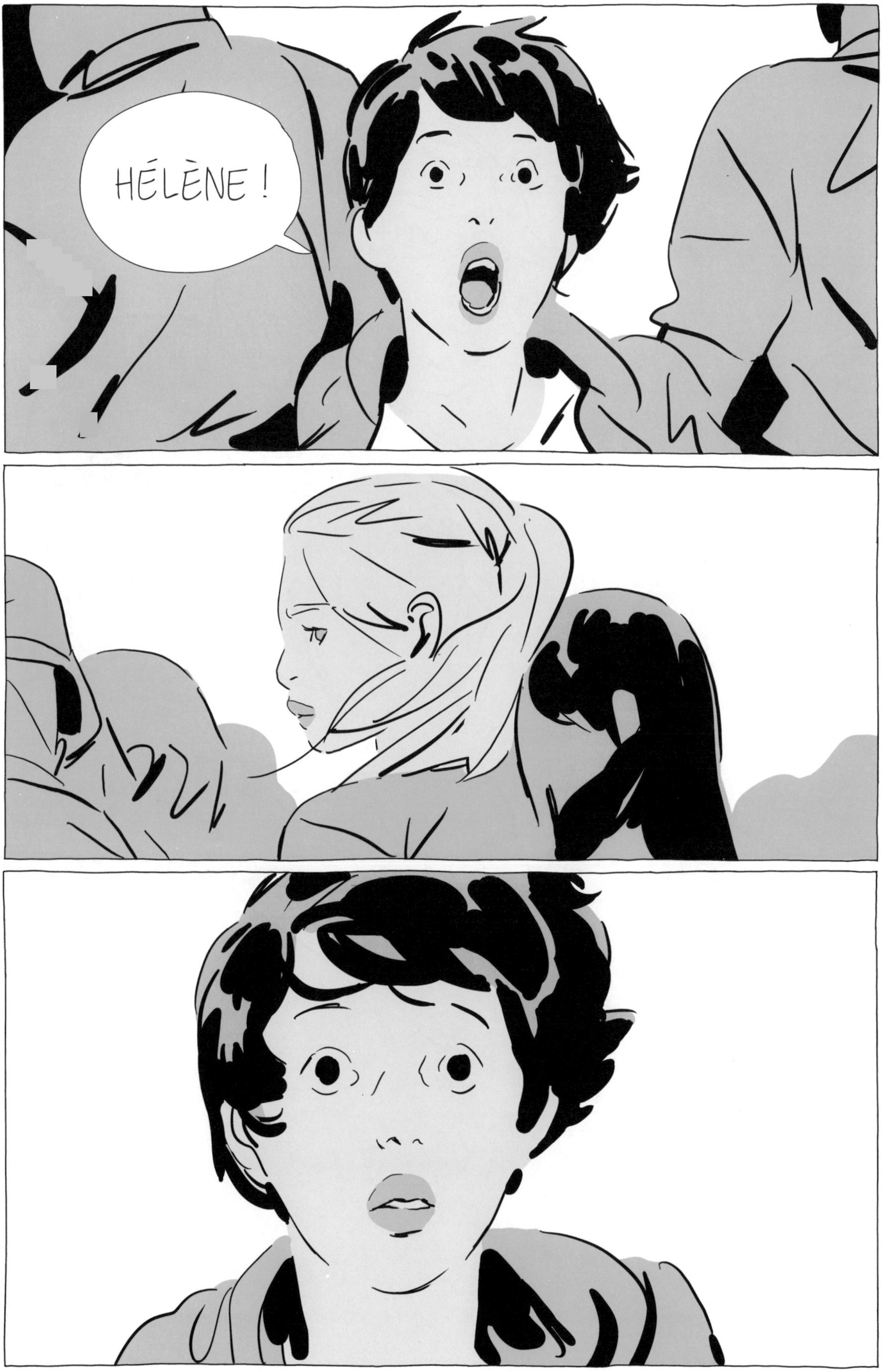
HÉLÈNE !

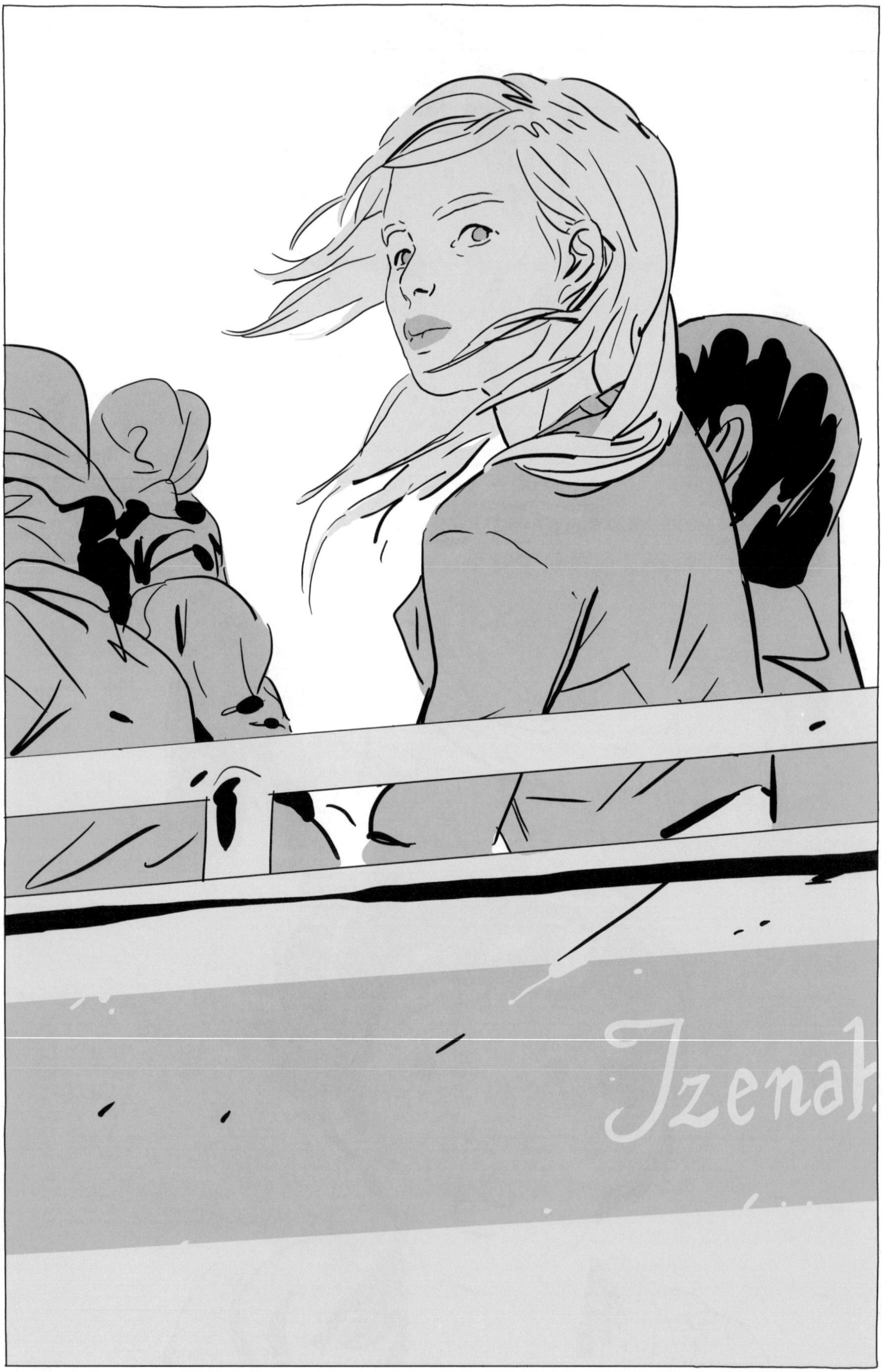
Izenah

DEDICATION
To my brother.

SPECIAL THANKS
Thank you to the whole
"San Francisco" team from
I'lle aux Moines. Thanks to
Didier Borg for his advice
and support.